TURN
COAT

Mauri ora!

[signature]

Lawrence & Gibson Publishing Collective
www.lawrenceandgibson.co.nz

Turncoat
First edition published in Aotearoa/New Zealand by
Lawrence & Gibson.
Copyright © Tīhema Baker, 2023

Printed and bound at Rebel Press, Trades Hall, Te Aro, Wellington

Turncoat / Tīhema Baker
ISBN 978-1-7385903-0-8

Cover image: Judith Carnaby
Cover and page design: Lawrence & Gibson
Design consultant: Judith Carnaby
Copy editor: Johanna Knox

Published with the assistance of a grant from Ngāti Toa Rangatira

Printed on ECO100 post-consumer recycled paper
Bound with Technomelt 3635

Lawrence & Gibson is a not-for-profit publishing collective based
out of Rebel Press in the Trades Hall, Te Aro, Te Whanganui a Tara.
See www.lawrenceandgibson.co.nz for more on the process of how
we work together to print, guillotine and bind these books.

TĪHEMA BAKER

TURN
COAT

LAWRENCE & GIBSON

Live, Laugh, Love
ancient Human proverb

Rank I

Recorded: Cycle 2, Revolution 9-4025·

I - I

I was 21 revolutions old when I decided I was going to change the world. That was appropriate. Not because I had just ascended to Rank 1, but because – for Humans – existing long enough to revolve around our sun 21 times represents full maturity. I was ready to make my mark, as the ancestors would say.

My training regime in Kappeetar had lasted the standard three-revolutions, and in that time, it had been easy to forget just how much poorer it was down on the surface. But now I was standing again within the cracked and crumbling walls of Wellington's grimy terminus. Derogatory symbols and phrases had been projected onto their surfaces, and the air was filled with the stench of urine. In one corner of the grotty floor, two Humans fought over a premium sleeping spot.

By contrast, the terminus I had departed from in Kappeetar was, like the rest of the planet's prime city, stunningly clean. The white walls gleamed, the air was thick with the pleasant smell of cleaning agents, and everyone went about their business, seemingly happy.

---

* Subject notation: I once tried to calculate what this date period would be in the ancestors' form of calendar. It was something like the year 2,507 AD. Don't ask me what the AD stands for.

Or, at least, the Alien equivalent of happy. Hard to tell, most of the time. Aliens had attempted to eliminate the needless capacity for emotion from their collective genome long before they arrived here. But, with almost universally high wealth and life-expectancy, I'm sure they are as happy as any Human wishes to be.

The other, glaring comparison with Kappeetar was the transport availability. Never again would I complain about the circuit runner delays there: a late transport was better than none, which was the situation I found on arriving in Wellington.

Still, no matter. Mother and Father would be busy: Mother at parliament, Father serving at the Allowance Exchange. They wouldn't be at their dwelling yet. So, I convinced myself this was a convenient excuse to take the time to walk the channels of my home district and see what had changed in my absence.

I'd just activated my travel pack to set off across the terminus when I heard a new commotion rising above the one for the sleeping spot. Another Human – a young male, like me – was gesticulating and shouting at a permit vendor. The vendor was shielded behind his transfer field and general indifference.

'Apologies, but our edict is clear,' said the vendor. He was a crusty-looking Alien – even from my few paces away I could see his ruddy coat of fur was flecked with dead skin cells, and the pair of tendrils protruding from his forehead were withered and drooping like dying flower stalks. 'You must have valid identification to purchase a permit.'

'I have identification,' the Human protested.

The Alien's vertical pupils and surrounding irises went blank for a moment and the tiny device grafted to his temple flashed once. 'I cannot see it in your tree. In fact, your tree does not appear to be registered in the Core.'

'Because I can't connect to the Core – my root is faulty.' The Human tapped the device at his own temple.

'Then you should have it repaired.'

'Can't afford to – don't have the Rank.'

The vendor pursed his mandibles and his eyes glazed over again, his root flashing in three short bursts. I suspected he was calling on a Keeper in case the situation escalated.

'Supplication,' the Human pleaded, probably assuming the same. 'I have a balance hearing to attend. I need to be on the next shuttle.'

'Apologies,' the vendor repeated as his eye colour returned. His tone didn't sound apologetic at all. 'I cannot provide you with a permit.'

The Human's shoulders slumped. He turned as if to leave but, instead, slammed his fist into the wall beside the vendor's transfer field.

The vendor gave a small jump, his shrivelled old tendrils flaring defensively. 'A K-Keeper is inbound.' He ran a trembling hand down his encrusted goatee and straightened the band at his neck. 'I suggest you leave immediately unless you wish to be detained.'

The Human muttered something under his breath and backed away from the transfer field. That's when I recognised him.

'Hayden?' I asked.

'Daniel?'

He was a shell of the Hayden I remembered, my closest friend from when we were juveniles. Thin, for a start, but not in the surgically modified way that the wealthiest Aliens are. His tunic hung off his shoulders and his leg wraps had slipped to his ankles. He, unlike me, was one of the Humans lucky enough to have inherited the bare skin of the ancestors, but it was taut across his face and limbs. Pale, too, and his eyes explained why. His pupils were contracted to dots – the tell-tale sign of someone who had cut too much.

Sure enough, his hand was already in his pocket, fiddling with what I assumed to be a cutter. The way he staggered towards me suggested he was probably cut at that very moment. I went to salute him but, before I could, he threw his arms around me. I returned his embrace, noting his stale odour and feeling the slightness of his frame.

Pulling back, he searched me with those contracted pupils. 'Haven't seen you in …' For a moment I thought he might tip over. Then he seemed to catch himself. 'Whatever. It's good to see you again.'

'And you, Hayden.' It had been three revs – not since I ascended to Toor Academy. 'Everything well?' I motioned at the vendor.

Hayden snorted. 'Yeah, stupid Alien just wouldn't sell me a permit.'

I considered pretending I hadn't heard their exchange, but I couldn't help myself. 'Did you say you had a balance hearing? If so, we need to get you one.'

He caught me by the arm. 'No, it's fine, Daniel. Just leave it.'

'But you'll miss your hearing –'

'Wouldn't be the first time.'

I could barely believe he was the same friend I remembered. The Hayden I knew was like me: a high achiever, a faithful son, a competent athlete. Well, *he* was a competent athlete. But still.

Realising that I was entirely unfamiliar with the balance system, I asked, 'What happens when you miss it?'

'The Magistrate will probably give me a Rank penalty.' He grinned. 'Which doesn't really mean anything when you're Rank 0. Got no Rank to take away!'

I couldn't stop staring at this stranger in the haggard body of my friend.

'That's probably when you get detained by the Keepers, Hayden.'

The tendrils at his forehead waved dismissively. 'Not for a Rank penalty. Keepers got more important things to worry about down here on the surface.'

That was when I noticed the Keeper that the vendor had called, gliding into the terminus and locking their augmented eyes on us.

'Things like intimidating permit vendors?' I asked.

'Pretty much. Let's get out of here.'

With my travel pack hovering in tow, I followed Hayden out onto the Wellington channels. I was struck by the darkness. It was mid-rotation but everything was dimmer than it should have been. The skyways were to blame, of course. From up in Kappeetar, the glittering latticework of transit is beautiful to behold, an endless network of vehicles filling the sky, connecting every major centre on the planet.

I'd never appreciated how, down here on the surface, it was like a net, keeping us all trapped inside it.

'Want a cut?' Hayden set off onto the nearest channel-bridge without waiting for my answer. I thought he was cut enough as it was, but I didn't have anywhere else to be and I figured that as long as I was with Hayden, he wouldn't get into any more trouble.

We headed for the Clan Lounge, which I could hear before we even got close. Patrons were proudly bellowing out a Human classic about an ancient vehicle component known as a **wagon wheel**[*] – even the stagnant water filling the channels seemed to ripple with the sound. When we arrived, a second rendition was well underway. Many of the stumbling patrons recognised me and slurred welcoming greetings, followed by well-meaning inquiries about my time at Academy, which they probably wouldn't recall the answers to later. By the time we weaved through them and made it to the vendor, they had all started on that other Human anthem: the **Rhapsody of Bohemia**.

I didn't know whether Hayden had enough Rank to afford another cut, so I offered to purchase one for him. He sheepishly withdrew the battered old cutter he'd been fiddling with in his pocket, which the vendor loaded with the cheapest amusement-infused charge on offer. I bought a cutter with a nostalgia-infused charge for myself and we found a lounger in the corner.

The moment I pressed the cutter to my root and delivered the charge, I truly felt like I was home. I thought about all the times I had, at Father's request, come here to retrieve Mother from **sing-alongs** just like this one, which, often, she was leading. Hayden and I would sneak into the back to steal cutting charges and, once, we accidentally administered a horror-infused charge that kept us awake for several rotations. Although everyone in the Lounge was either out of service or absconding from it, and would likely never leave Wellington or aspire to anything greater than being the best singer of **Mr Brightside** in the room, these were my people.

---

[*] As most dialogue in this account was transferred in Noor, wherever Common Transfer was actually used – or as in the case of this Human masterpiece, it is appropriate to maintain the Common name – I have distinguished it by transcribing it in an ancient script highly favoured by pre-assimilation Humans.

'Welcome home, Daniel,' said Hayden, as if he knew what I was thinking. Soon, it was like nothing had changed between us. He was still the funniest person I knew, with that infectious laugh of his, regaling me with all the controversies and rumours currently gripping Wellington: who had produced offspring with who, who had been exiled, and so on. I asked him what he had been up to these past three revs. Not a lot, was the short answer.

'I tried the whole Academy thing,' he told me, hand lifting the cutter to his root as if programmed to do so. 'In Tarmakee. Felt like I didn't really belong. Then Father took ill with his neoplasm and there was no one else to really tend to him.' (Hayden's mother had, as is unfortunately typical of Human mothers, abandoned him and his Father shortly after he was born).

He took another quick cut. 'What about you? Ascended in the top percentile, no doubt?'

Top two percent to be precise. But I wasn't going to admit that.

I told him all about Toor Academy, and the more I spoke about it the more embarrassed I was by it. The truth was I had thrived there. It had been my gateway to a higher society. There, I was surrounded by intellectual equals; I could converse on topics that interested me, that affected the entire planet – galaxy, even – not just little old Wellington. Unlike Hayden, at Academy I felt I *did* fit in; for once I looked like everyone else and wasn't the most coated person in the room, like I was here in the Clan Lounge. If I hadn't desired to make my mark on the world, I could have easily stayed at Academy to continue training.

'So, Rank 1 … what now?' Hayden asked.

'I don't know yet. But I've thought about serving the Hierarch.'

Hayden flexed his tendrils at me. 'What?'

'The Hierarch – you know, they govern the planet –'

'I know what the Hierarch is, Daniel. I mean: what on Earth would make you want to do that?'

It was the first time anyone had reacted like that to the suggestion. Everyone at Academy had assured me that I would make an excellent

---

* **Earth** is of course the Common name for Teerin' Ho.

servant to the Hierarch. 'Well, I'm Human and one of my primaries is in Human Studies. I thought the Hierarch might find that useful.'

'The Hierarch doesn't care about Humans. It's just a bunch of Aliens in their swanky robes running around pretending they know what's best for everyone else.'

'There are some Humans who serve it.'

'Yeah. **Turncoats**.'

I didn't know what to say to that. I knew the Hierarch was mostly "just a bunch of Aliens" – it is the governing institution borne out of the Alien empire that assimilated us, after all. But I wasn't convinced that the few Humans who served it were **turncoats**. Surely, they were just like me?

'I like to think I could make a difference,' I said. 'Make things better for Humans.'

Hayden laughed. 'Look around.' He swept his hand across the room, gesturing at the two females by the gateway, one passing a package to the other, then at the elderly male unconscious on the floor. 'What's your fancy Academy training going to do for all of us? How are you going to get us all off the cutter so we don't keep wasting our Allowance on it? How are you going to get us our own healing centre so my father can get the treatment he needs? How are you going to make it so I can buy a **fucking** permit so I can get to my **fucking** balance hearing?' He wasn't laughing anymore.

The nostalgic haze that had settled on me was gone. 'Apologies, Hayden. I didn't mean –'

He raised his hand. 'No, my apologies, Daniel. I don't know where that came from.'

We sat for a while, pretending the whole experience wasn't awkward. Things couldn't get much worse, so I asked the question that had nagged at me ever since we left the terminus: 'Do you want to discuss your balance hearing?'

'Not really.' He took another cut and closed his eyes, relishing the amusement-infused scrambling of his root connection. 'Just … made a mistake.'

I didn't press further. 'If you need anything, Hayden, let me know.'

He laughed – genuinely, this time. 'Another cut will do.'

I obliged and returned to the vendor for another charge each. While I waited, I looked back at Hayden and the rest of the Clan Lounge patrons, now brought into sharp focus without the artificial nostalgia coursing through me. This was my home, these were my beings, but we weren't the same. I was an anomaly, an exception to the rules that bound all of them.

I asked myself why, and came up with the following:

1. My upbringing was one of moderate wealth compared to, well, just about anyone else in Wellington.
2. My Academy training made me not only more knowledgeable about Human custom and language than the average Human but also well-equipped and educated to function in an Alien-dominated society.
3. Despite my Human genetics, my physical appearance was completely Alien.

These things already set me apart from my Human relatives in Wellington. But there was something else, an ancient inheritance from the ancestors that gave me a crucial edge:

4. [Requires unlocking *Perk 1* and *Passive Ability: Being Human Male*] The confidence to assume I was capable of anything.

I wondered: why *couldn't* I take all of that privilege – my clan's wealth, my Academy training, my Alien coat of fur – and use it to make a difference? More importantly, why *shouldn't* I? Was that not my basic responsibility as a decent Human: to use my privilege to lift up my fellow Humans with me, just like the ancestors did?

That's when I decided. Then and there. I *would* get these patrons off the cutter and into service. I *would* get Hayden's father the same access to healing as any Alien. I'd go one better than making sure Hayden got to his balance hearing – I'd make sure he never again needed one. And I wouldn't stop there. I'd prevent Keeper brutality against Humans, lower the Human exile population, become the first Human Supreme Rank if I had to.

When I returned to our corner, someone had found a rukoo (because what sort of Human **sing-along** would it be without one spontaneously appearing) and begun tapping out a tune. It must have been ancient because the lyrics were in a transfer I didn't recognise. Clearly, I wasn't the only one who thought so, as someone yelled, 'Play something we all know!' With an irritated tendril-flick, the rukoo-player switched to a beloved Human classic that had the entire Lounge on their feet. I handed Hayden back his cutter, and the timeless words rolling over us said everything I wanted to in that moment:

Never gonna give you up, never gonna let you down ...

1-2

I arrived at my parents' dwelling much later than I had intended, and more cut than I should have been. Riding high on a fresh wave of artificial nostalgia and organic inspiration, I barely made it through the gateway with my travel pack when I was greeted by a flurry of parliamentary documents, beneath which was Mother. She had always been determined to conduct parliamentary business 'the old way' – through an absurd amount of physical documentation rather than the virtual transferral of important constructs through the Core like the rest of the galaxy.

'Welcome home, Daniel!' She shed another layer of pages to kiss my cheek as if I was a juvenile.

'Greetings Mother,' I said between pecks, knowing it was futile to resist her intensely Human, maternal affection and waiting for her to release me from it. When she did, I was finally able to greet Father, who had found his way through the precarious columns of correspondence to salute me.

'It is a pleasure to have you home,' he said, which was about as affectionate as he got, being Alien.

I returned his salute and Mother took me by the arm. 'Come and sit – your father has preserved your darkmeal for you.'

She led me to the consumption mat where we knelt and waited for Father to bring the tray laden with his manually constructed hoo'mart, sweet roasted rekka tubers and crisp wukka leaves.

'So, you are now Rank 1,' he opened as I tucked into the meal.

'Yes,' Mother said, leaning forward. 'What's next for Kytoonoo 1 Daniel?'

I was still getting used to that – the 1 in my title instead of the 0. But I wasn't even sure I should bother: if I was going to change the world, I had to ascend much further than Rank 1.

'I have a plan,' I told them, before detailing my encounter with Hayden, his circumstances, and my observations of everyone at the Clan Lounge.

'Poor Hayden.' Mother shook her head. 'He had such potential, that **boy**. I wonder what trouble he's got himself into now.'

'His Allowance was terminated approximately a cycle ago,' Father reported. As our district's lone Allowance Officer, Father was familiar with much of Wellington's lowest Ranks – which was most of Wellington. 'I recall seeing his profile among a list of local citizens in breach of Allowance edict. I attempted to challenge the case for further investigation, but my appeal was declined.'

'Do you know what he did to breach Allowance edict?'

'He failed a spontaneous memory-trowel by the Gardeners. They discovered mental records of him purchasing illicit cutting charges.'

Mother snorted. 'Disgraceful that they can do that. Just invade our privacy on a whim.'

'I suppose there is an argument that it is necessary,' Father responded, drawing a scowl from Mother. 'Hayden breached the conditions of his entitlement to a Rank Allowance, not only by using it on resources for which it is not intended but for illicit activity at that. There is evidence that if the Gardeners did not conduct spontaneous memory-trowels, then they would not detect this behaviour and Hierarch-distributed Rank would be abused at much higher rates.'

Being substantially more Alien than I liked to admit, I knew Father was not necessarily advocating for the Gardeners' frightening power to randomly search the memories of any individual connected to the Core, but rather making a logical point, as Aliens tended to do on just about any topic. Mother, however, was less Alien than me and, therefore, far less objective.

'But at least a young Human wouldn't have to worry about where his next darkmeal will come from,' she said. 'I'd much rather see the Gardeners trowelling the memories of all the Aliens at Ranks 7 and up who are avoiding their tithe obligations. If the Hierarch wants to crack down on Rank fraud, then they need look no further than tithe evasion.'

It was the moment to make my announcement. I was certain that Mother and Father would support me. 'That brings me back to my plan. After seeing Hayden, I just felt like I needed to help him. And not just give him some Rank, or take him to his balance hearing. I mean *really* help him, and every Human like him. I want to make a difference. For *all* of Humanity.'

Mother's scowl vanished, replaced by a glowing smile. Despite her staunch Human nature and suspicion of just about anything Alien, she was incredibly easy to impress. I had just ascended to Rank 1, something many Humans would only ever dream of, but all you really had to do to earn her respect was display interest or affinity for things Human. That was probably why she fell for the first Alien she met who showed curiosity about Human culture.

'The question,' I concluded, 'is "how?".'

Father stroked the end of a tendril. 'An admirable calling, Daniel. I consider there are many ways you could help Hayden, and other Humans in a similar situation. You could provide education about the detrimental effects of cutting and other illicit substances, or provide greater health services to treat those suffering from addiction. You could improve Allowance edict to remove the barriers that disproportionately affect Humans as the majority of Allowance receivers. All of those options would, however, require service for the Hierarch —'

My ears perked up, but Mother brought them down again: 'The Hierarch is the reason Humanity is in the state it is.'

'Would it not make sense then for Daniel to focus his efforts there?' Father ventured.

'Frankly, no. There is no single factor that has resulted in poorer statistical conclusions for Humans. It is an entire system, imposed by the Hierarch when it assimilated this planet, that is weighted against us. Even if Daniel were to succeed in any of those avenues that you have so clearly suggested – which I am certain he would – it would not change the system at large. It will not change the fact that the Hierarch failed – and continues to fail – to uphold the Covenant of Wellington.'

Father conceded the point with a conciliatory sweep of his tendrils. My own shrank a little as Mother turned to me.

'Your people need you here, Daniel. Not up in the clouds in Kappeetar. Here. Setting an example for them, leading them.'

'Well, how do I do that?' I asked.

That's how I ended up sitting beside Mother on the front bench at parliament the following rotation. I imagine that she had anticipated this moment – seeing her only offspring become a legitimate Member of Parliament like her – ever since my birth. But it didn't feel right.

I'd tried to argue with her that in the ancestors' times these seats had to be earned, reserved as they were for the most senior of our leaders. I couldn't sit in one just because she said so.

'I'm the Leader of New Zealand, son,' she'd said with a chuckle, as we took our places for the debate. 'I can put whoever I choose in these seats.'

Then, with a firm grip on my shoulder, she'd asked, 'And how else are you going to learn? There aren't many of us who can sit here anymore.'

This was true. That room of worn, decrepit seats, rotting wood and faded carpet had once been filled with New Zealand's greatest chosen leaders. Now there was but a handful of aging volunteers, outnumbered by the emptiness. How grand it must have been, those esteemed leaders in all their wisdom, gathered here – in this very chamber – engaging in intelligent and respectable discussion about the issues confronting our people. The abandoned galleries above would have been packed with civilians to watch the enlightening exchanges. I imagine the entire nation would have hung on their every word.

I tried to do just that – follow the debate that was soon taking place before me, the subject of which was a proposal brought by Mother for a much-needed installation of new light emitters in the debating chamber itself. But, while Mother's rearing had given me a base knowledge of our traditional language, and my Academy Training in Human Studies had improved that base to a level well beyond the average Human, it was still rudimentary compared to the eloquent, articulate speech of the parliamentarians.

As dictated by parliamentary protocol, they addressed the gathering entirely in Common Transfer. Theirs was a level of proficiency that seemed unattainable to me, speech embellished with words I didn't understand. Like **economy**, which was repeated multiple times in what must have been an obscure oratory technique that made the speaker sound more knowledgeable and trustworthy than their adversary.

I also couldn't comprehend the role of the **Opposition**, which seemed to be only to reject anything and everything brought by Mother and our side. The lighting even cut out halfway through the **Opposition** Leader's rebuttal of Mother's proposal, plunging the chamber into darkness, yet he didn't miss a beat, continuing his argument with such vigour, I almost found myself agreeing with him. I figured there must have been some deeper purpose to their relentless questioning, a higher principle guiding their passionate objections, that I was simply too young and ignorant of our cryptic customs to understand.

Sitting among them, despite what Mother said, I felt inadequate. Unworthy. Who was I compared to Mother, and the precious few of her generation who were capable of holding a conversation in Common Transfer? Being Rank 1 didn't mean anything in that chamber. Something greater, indefinable, made a Human a leader. I didn't even look the part. I was surely the most coated Human who had ever sat in one of these seats. It was only out of desperation, a hopeless clinging to our custom, that I was permitted to be here at all.

Recess finally gave me a chance to escape. After fumbling my way out through the dark with Mother, I told her I needed a walk and set off through the halls of parliament. Nothing seemed to have changed. I recognised all the same stains on the carpet that Hayden and I used to race each other up and down, as well as the dent in the far wall that we had put there after a particularly close finish. The battered, musty corridors led me to my favourite place in the entire complex: the portrait-laden wall of honour.

As always, my direct ancestor was my first stop. He was located among those who I understand to be the last 'fully genetic' Humans, before we began reproducing exclusively by splicing. The image itself was so old and finely grained that it was difficult to make out his features, but I could see enough to know that I looked nothing like him. He had that smooth, fair skin typical of the ancestors, with fur only covering his crown and jaw. A narrow nose, round ears, irises a shade of blue that simply didn't exist anymore. I tried to find something, some insignificant aspect of his noble Human visage that I had inherited. All I got was the vague impression that, if he were to encounter me, with my ashen coat and amber eyes, he would surely have regarded me as just another Alien.

I walked on, soon reaching what I had privately dubbed 'the point' – a stark line from which the portraits began to show the physical features we had inherited from Aliens, or Noor, I should say, as is their proper name. 'Alien' is, of course, the term we use to differentiate the Noor who are citizens of Earth from those who are still citizens of their home-world, Owteer.

I watched as I walked and saw how our identifying traits faded over generations of genetic splicing. Pairs of tendrils sprang from smooth foreheads and bare skin sprouted into coats of fur. The rigid suits and dresses that were our tradition were replaced by refined robes and bands, and the tiny roots grafted to our temples at birth to connect to the Core became permanent fixtures.

Mother's image, as the incumbent leader of New Zealand, was where I finished. She was nearly as coated as I was, albeit with a rich taupe fur, and she had inherited almost no obvious Human features, either. No round ears or narrow nose. But there was still something undeniably Human about her. It was her pride, I think. The way she carried herself. Not like Aliens, who walk around like they know they're better than us. Mother's pride in her humanity didn't come at the expense of anyone else.

I wondered if that was what she was gazing at in her picture, with her head held high, bearing a dignified smile: the culture she had fought so hard to protect in the face of assimilation by the Hierarch.

I wondered if that was what also set me apart. Why I didn't feel as if I belonged in the debating chamber, or on that wall. It was the same feeling I'd had with Hayden in the Clan Lounge. I just was not like them. I had an Academy training in Human Studies, but that hadn't taught me what couldn't be taught, that which had been ingrained in leaders like my mother by living and breathing our values and customs every rotation of her existence. I didn't know the intricate rules of parliamentary procedure, or what the supreme significance of **economy** was. Maybe I just wasn't as Human as they were. And if that was the case, then how could I ever be a leader of Humans like them?

On the other hand, as the ancestors would say, I had inherited half of Mother's genetic traits. I dared myself to hope that perhaps I could be at least half the leader she was.

A notification in my mental tree told me that recess was over. I couldn't bring myself to go back. I figured no one except for Mother would miss me and, if the light emitters still weren't working, then she probably wouldn't even notice I was gone.

I continued my private tour of parliament buildings, coming across all the places Hayden and I had either played in, been chased from, or damaged in some way. Eventually, this wistful journey took me out of the hallways and into the Hierarch-commissioned museum that had been constructed on top of parliament. It was there, in the well-lit, clean-floored, heavily-insured exhibition hall that I came across our world's founding document – the Covenant of Wellington. (Well, really, that honour belongs to the Proclamation of Power of the United Nations of Teerin' Ho, but the Hierarch doesn't like to be reminded that it exists.)

The Covenant is always smaller than I remember. I've seen it countless times, but whenever I look upon that tiny chip, lying on a simple plinth protected by a coherence field, I'm amazed by it. I imagine the Hierarch's servants, all the way back in Rev 9-3680, trying to convert the construct into Common Transfer so the ancestors could understand it, and then store it on a device compatible with the ancestors' processing machines. It must have been an incredible event, with leaders of nations from all over **Earth**, and their delegations, gathered on parliament grounds, under the armada of Weaver ships anchored in the sky, all to validate the infamous agreement between our two worlds. It always struck me as odd that Wellington, of all the world, was chosen as the place to validate the most significant document in Human history. But according to the ancestors, when the time came for the Human leaders to vote on the best location, the weather in Wellington was so amazing that they unanimously agreed it just couldn't be beaten.

If the Covenant had been transferred to me at the time of its validation, I would have received a clear construct with the following components: a contextual introduction stating the reasons for the agreement, the three Promises, and the ratifying statement, which includes the signatures of all the leaders who validated it. Instead, what I got when I connected my mental tree to the plinth was a garbled distortion. Parts of it I could identify as the Common or Noor conversions of the construct, but with so much data corrupted by its age (plus water damage and nibbled circuitry resulting from its poor treatment by Hierarch servants), it was largely unintelligible.

Fortunately, due to the various surviving copies of it, I knew the entire text **off by heart**, as the ancestors would say.* Now, I was no expert in Common Transfer, but I understood it well enough to know that the Common version – having been converted by Noor who did not have precise understanding of our transfer in the first place – made next to no sense, and certainly wouldn't have meant much to the ancestors.

Parsing the fragmented data, thinking about those Human leaders who had validated it, I wondered if they had any suspicion about what was about to befall them. When he gave his electronic signature to this agreement, could my tendril-less, bare-skinned ancestor on the wall of honour have possibly imagined that it would be broken and we would be reduced to destroying our brains with Alien drugs or fighting over how to install light emitters?

'Not likely,' said a voice which, for a moment, made me wonder if the ectoplasmic entities that inhabited parliament had now migrated to the museum. But it was only a Chronicler, watching me from the shadows, his posture hunched under the weight of the root amplifier

---

* I have transcribed a copy for your convenience at Appendix 1. Not that you'll read it.

adorning his cranium. Shuffling towards me, he added, 'Sequential evidence suggests that the Human Leaders who validated the Covenant expected to retain control over themselves and their affairs and the Hierarch would govern its own citizens here on Teerin' Ho.'

No shit, as the ancestors would say.

When he continued, I realised that his tree was also connected to the Covenant, which explained why my thoughts had transferred to him. 'But the fascinating thing about the Covenant is that the two constructs are not precise conversions of one another. There is a key difference –'

I already knew this, of course. And despite my attempts to demonstrate that to the Chronicler through a not-so-subtle transferring of information to his tree, he was obviously too far into his recital to notice. (There's actually a Common term for this phenomenon: **Aliensplaining**).

'– that Commitment 1 of the Noor version clearly states that the Human leaders give their Rank to the Hierarch absolutely and forever. The Human version ceded Rank to the Hierarch but they did not understand the meaning of the term –'

'It's not that they didn't understand it,' I said, finally succeeding in cutting him off. 'The term meant a different thing. The problem was that the Aliens tried to use a Human term to define an Alien concept. We didn't have the same system of Rank that Aliens did. We had our own power structures that Rank didn't adequately describe.

'Expressed here, in Common,' I said, gesturing to Promise 1 of our version of the Covenant, 'the Human leaders believed they had given the Hierarch what *they* understood Rank to mean: leadership over *their own* citizens on Teerin' Ho. Effectively, they recognised the Hierarch's Rank over the Noor here, but that did not give the Hierarch any Rank over Humans. The concept of giving away the power to rule ourselves would have been, frankly, ridiculous.'

The Chronicler blinked, tendrils twitching. It was probably the first time he had been on the receiving end of a lecture.

I went in for the kill. 'Which makes perfect sense given, only ten revs prior, we had made our own Proclamation of Power.' Why would

---

* I have also, probably pointlessly, transcribed a copy of this at Appendix 2.

we proclaim our power as an independent world in the galaxy only to relinquish it to the Hierarch a few revs later?'

By then the Chronicler must have concluded what I had known the moment he started conversing with me: he had nothing to teach me.

'Impressive. Are you a Chronicler yourself?'

I gave a negative flick. 'My ancestor validated the Covenant.' I scrolled down the list of signatures until I found his. I had seen it so many times that I could trace the looping symbols with my finger perfectly. 'I feel obligated to understand what he believed he was agreeing to.'

I sensed the Chronicler studying me. 'I often wonder how different our existence would be. If what your ancestor agreed to had been honoured.'

'Me too.'

That was when I figured it out. That to change the world, it was not enough to just improve the services provided by the Hierarch to Humans.

I had to make it the one my ancestor had envisioned. A world where the three Promises of the Covenant were honoured:

1. Humans gave the Hierarch Rank over Aliens on **Earth**;
2. Humans retained control over all their territories, resources, and valuables; and
3. Humans were granted the same status and opportunities as Aliens.

Mother was right. Everything went back to the Covenant. The plight of Humans, the privilege of Aliens – it all derived from that vision, those Promises, never being realised. My mission was clear:

I was going to make the Hierarch honour the Covenant of Wellington.

By the following rotation I had it all planned out. I would infiltrate the Hierarch, ascend its Ranks, and establish myself as one of its highest Rankholders. From there, my standing would be substantial enough to influence the way it operated and, eventually, change the entire system of Alien government to one that was a true realisation of what the Covenant of Wellington was meant to establish.

I told myself I was the perfect candidate. I knew how to walk in both the Human and Alien environs. Someone like Mother could never do that; her Human pride would be found too abrasive and emotionally charged for the strict logic of an Alien institution like the Hierarch. I, if I wanted, could be as apathetic as an Alien or as hysterical as a Human. The ability to adapt to my environment, sort of like a shift of code, would be my greatest asset. Once inside the Hierarch I would need to educate every Alien servant I could by appealing not to their hearts but to their ruthlessly rational minds, just like I did with the Chronicler. I may not have been like my Human relatives in Wellington, but it was what set me apart from them that equipped me to do what they could not.

The first step was finding the best place to infiltrate the Hierarch, by applying for service. This was challenging, not for lack of service available within the many Houses of the Hierarch, but because of how often Mother insisted on me joining her for parliamentary work.

As Leader of New Zealand, Mother virtually never stopped working. She was often poring over documents when I woke and deep in conversation with colleagues via the Core when I retired to my sleep capsule. I would be practically working with her from lightbreak to darkfall, helping her craft her arguments for a debate or preparing her answers for **Question Time**. And it wasn't as if I could ask her for an interval or to help me with my mission. She had made her position on me serving the Hierarch perfectly clear.

I used any brief break that I could find – usually whenever the light emitters failed in the debating chamber and no one could see me activating my root – to scour the Core for roles within the Hierarch. I considered the Houses of Knowledge, Healing, Exile, and even Juvenile Wellbeing (which had just been exposed by the propagation for uplifting human infants from their mothers). Despite my wide search, I decided that Houses as notorious as these for negative Human statistics would put me at an immediate disadvantage.

Eventually, my searches brought me to an Operator position at the Chamber of Covenant Resolutions, which sat within the House of Balance. I was somewhat familiar with Covenant Resolutions, the packages of reparations provided by the Hierarch to Human nations in recognition of its past breaches of the Covenant of Wellington. What better way to make the Hierarch honour the Covenant, I figured, than to start in the House that addresses breaches of the Covenant in the first place?

During parliament's ongoing light outages, I constructed a bid for service and submitted it. There was little else to do after that except wait for the response, but I wanted to be prepared. If my bid was received favourably and I was granted an interactive analysis, I would need to be presentable. My next challenge then, which would be far more difficult to hide from Mother, was to purchase appropriate service attire.

Thankfully, a message from Hayden to my tree provided a convenient excuse to take leave from parliament:

Greetings, Daniel. Are you free this rotation? I wondered if you wanted to socialise – maybe get some sustenance and watch entertainments on the Core?

I shared the message with Mother, whose compassion for Hayden could never let her deny such a request.

'Don't worry about applying for leave,' she said. 'I'll tell the **Speaker** the situation.'

'Gratitude, Mother!' I said, kissing her on the cheek and hurrying from our dwelling. I sent Hayden a quick reply arranging to meet him at noon, which provided me with the entire morning to find a robe and band. I had never needed to contemplate purchasing either garment and Wellington wasn't exactly known for its formal attire, so I didn't even know if any local retailer sold them. A quick search in the Core revealed that there was one: the only formal male garb retailer in Wellington's market district.

At first, I thought there was some sort of error. According to the Core, the retailer's name was **The Big Cock**. When I finally arrived in the market suburb, though, and saw the projection on the retailer's front façade depicting an anthropomorphic rooster wearing a robe and band, I figured I was in the right place.

Inside **The Big Cock**, I was greeted cheerfully by the Alien vendor, who must have assumed I was also Alien because, entirely unprompted, he proceeded to **Aliensplain** to me that particularly proud and fashionable Human males were sometimes compared to the domestic fowl known as a **cock**, and that he considered himself to be a bit of a **cock** too, hence the name of his store. He directed me to a booth where the store's private database was made accessible to my tree. Browsing the collection of robes, I had to discard most of them for their Rank cost. Many of the garments could have set Mother back an entire Rank. In the end, I selected the most inexpensive robe – a charcoal-coloured piece that, with flaring tails and a low cut, seemed more appropriate for socialising than service. A reflect field in my booth flickered to life, generating a visual representation of how the robe would appear on me.

Being so inexpensive, it wasn't a perfect fit – the sleeves were a bit long, and I didn't have the Rank to modify it – but it definitely improved my form. It was amazing how a simple robe could instantly elevate one's respectability.

Next, I needed a band. Again, I opted for the inexpensive option – a thin collar of dull Yuna metal – and it was enough to complete the outfit. A perfect template of a servant to the Hierarch stared back at me from the reflect field. I was unrecognisable.

But I liked it. I felt sophisticated and important. I could see myself walking through the front gate of the Chamber of Covenant Resolutions and taking my place among its servants, where I would fit right in.

Where I would fit right in.

It was only then, looking upon this inexplicably more impressive, more appealing, more **cocky** version of myself, that I doubted for the first time whether I really wanted to go ahead with my plan. Was I really ready to serve the institution that had assimilated our people, stolen our airspace, almost eradicated our language and customs? If I couldn't even recognise myself as a servant to the Hierarch, then how could Mother, or Hayden? I wasn't even wearing the garb yet and I could already feel its weight.

This is what it would take, I told myself. This is what I was setting out to do. For Mother and Hayden. For my ancestor, and every Human on **Earth**. I was doing this for them.

I tried to hold onto that thought as I transferred the Rank required for the purchase. Buying my first robe and band – something that finally made me feel like I was really Rank 1 – should have been pleasurable and exciting. Instead, I left **The Big Cock** feeling nothing but shame and self-loathing.

At home, I stashed my new garments under my sleep capsule, then picked up some prime entertainment-viewing sustenance from a local vendor, and set off for Hayden's father's dwelling down in **Oriental Bay**. He'd dwelled there since Hayden and I were juveniles, and it had always been a rundown neighbourhood but, as I found when I got there, it had become almost a slum in my absence. The structural integrity of many of the small dwellings seemed dangerously compromised, with only raw materials being used to prop up roofs and walls. Mobs of juveniles – who I assumed should have been in education – roamed the channels, throwing objects into the foul water because they had nothing else to do.

A female, with a red patch stained onto the skin of her shoulder, watched me from the porch of her ramshackle dwelling – a member of the Mutt Pack, who had never had a presence in Wellington, as far as I knew. I quickened my pace and resisted the urge to vault the flimsy barrier outside Hayden's father's dwelling and beg for sanctuary at its entrance. Instead, I notified my arrival at the gateway and waited to be granted entry.

Hayden's father greeted me and, if I had been stunned by Hayden's appearance, words can't describe my reaction to his father's. He was even more gaunt than his son, bones showing through papery skin, limbs so thin I wondered how they supported his meagre weight. Then I spotted the tangle of cords and wires plugged into his body, trailing up to the ceiling along loosely organised runners. They were probably the only thing keeping him upright.

'Daniel!' His sunken face broke into a toothless smile, a shade of what I remembered. 'It is so good to see you again. Come in.'

I followed him through the cramped, musty hallway, not knowing what to say to him and ashamed because of it.

'Bit of a shock, eh,' he said quietly, gesturing at all the wires.

Finally finding some spine and my voice along with it, I said, 'Sincerest sympathies, Harry. I –'

He laughed my pity away and rattled some of the cords. 'Damned things make it look worse than it is. No need to worry about me. Got my next scan in the following cycle and I have a good feeling about it.'

I felt like he said that more to reassure me than himself. 'If there's anything I or my clan can do –'

He stopped me at the gateway to the next room with a hand on my shoulder. 'It's just good to have you back, Daniel. For Hayden – he needs you more than I do.'

Before I could process what he meant, he shuffled into the room and announced my arrival to Hayden, who was kneeling at a ragged consumption mat, sorting through what appeared to be vials of liquid.

'Perfect timing!' he said, scooping up several of the vials and rising to greet us. 'I'll just put Father in his sleep capsule and administer his medication. Find us something to view, would you? I moved the loungers to a spot with good Core connectivity.'

Hayden's father gave me a parting salute, which I returned, before Hayden took him by the arm and led him down the hallway.

By the time Hayden returned, I had everything set up: a feast of sustenance laid out across the base of our two loungers and one of our favourite comedic series from when we were juveniles primed to view on the Core as soon as Hayden linked his tree to mine.

'Just like old times,' he said, flopping onto the lounger beside me and sticking three fried dough sticks in his mouth.

And it really was. Just the two of us, stuffing our faces with as much sucrose and fat-infused sustenance as Humanly possible and laughing until our diaphragms ached. It had been too long since I had socialised like this. There just hadn't been time for it at Academy. I wondered how long it had been for Hayden.

By the time darkfall neared, we had eaten and laughed ourselves into a bloated stupor. Physically uncomfortable though I was, I could have happily stayed there for the rest of the rotation. And I might have, if it weren't for the notification that pinged in my tree halfway through the next episode. Absently I opened it, expecting it to be yet another document to review from Mother. It wasn't.

Greetings, Kytoonoo | Daniel. I am Porrog 4 Took'itti, a Selector at the House of Balance. I have received your bid for ascension and wish to conduct an interactive analysis of you for service as an Operator, Rank 2.

I didn't even bother downloading the rest. All I needed to know was that I had been granted an analysis. I knew some recent ascendants who were still making bids a whole revolution after reaching Rank 1. This was my first ever bid for service and it had been met positively. I could hardly believe it.

'You bid for Hierarch service?'

Nearly in a sustenance-induced coma, I had forgotten that Hayden's tree was still connected to mine. I rocked myself out of my self-congratulatory reverie and into an upright position to find him looking at me like *I* was the unrecognisable one.

'Why?' he asked simply.

I decided there was no point lying. 'Because it's the best way I can make a difference.'

31

He blinked at me. 'How?'

I told him my plan. Explained my epiphany about the Covenant, how everything wrong with Teerin' Ho went back to the Hierarch's failure to uphold it and, therefore, why my mission was to make the Hierarch honour the Covenant, transforming it from within. But every time I felt I had answered his question, he again asked: 'How?'

I kept trying to explain, not sure how I could be any clearer: I was going to make the Hierarch honour the Covenant of Wellington.

'Daniel, Daniel,' he said at last. 'How are you – as a servant of the Hierarch – going to make the rest of the Hierarch do *anything*? You would need to be part of the ruling clans to make any sort of change.'

Now I understood Hayden's confusion.

'Here,' I said as I sketched a diagram in my tree. 'I'll show you why my other ascension primary is in Memetics.'

Hayden screwed up his nose. 'What's Memetics?'

'Mostly transferring expositional information. Like this.'

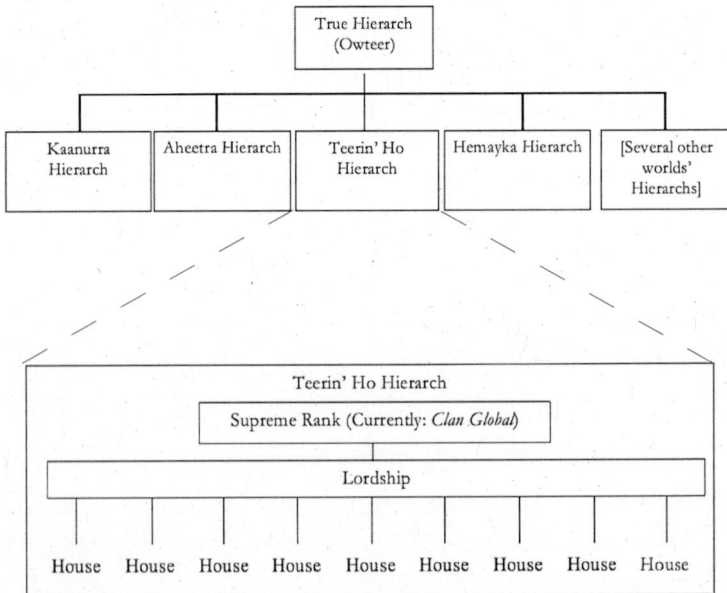

Highlighting the topmost box, I said, 'Everything starts with the True Hierarch all the way in Owteer, right? When it assimilated worlds across the galaxy, like ours, it established lesser Hierarchs on each of those worlds to rule on its behalf. But this is the thing about a Hierarch: it's not people, it's a system – a power structure operated by whoever has the most Rank.'

'Which is Clan Global,' Hayden pointed out.

I highlighted their name next. 'That's right. Clan Global currently has the most Rank in all of Teerin' Ho, which means they're our Supreme Rank. They appoint the Lordship, who are responsible for the Houses.'

'Like the one you bid for service at, the House of Balance?'

'Exactly. The Supreme Rank *decides*, the Lordship *commands*, the Houses *do*.'

Hayden frowned. 'That still sounds like you need to be Supreme Rank if you want to change anything.'

'Let's say the population got fed up with tithing their Rank to Clan Global and gave it instead to someone else – like the Alliance Clans.' I substituted them for Clan Global in the diagram. 'They would become the new Supreme Rank, and they would appoint a new Lordship. But the rest of the system would mostly stay the same.'

'Why wouldn't a new Lord also just appoint new servants in their House?'

'Because they rely on servants in the Houses to run the system for them.' I was getting excited, growing more inspired the closer I came to the crux of my plan. 'And the servants do that by something called edict – kind of like a set of rules for how the Hierarch operates. No matter who the Supreme Rank is, any decision they make has to be in accordance with Hierarch edict. Servants are the ones who create and enforce edict. They make the system work.'

I watched Hayden process this, just about ready to explode if, after all of that Academy-trained exposition, he still didn't understand what I was setting out to do.

'So,' he said slowly, 'if you become a high-Ranking servant, you could make edict so that the Hierarch honours the Covenant, no matter who the Supreme Rank is?'

Bingo, as the ancestors would say.

Popping another sucro-ball into my mouth, I settled back into my lounger and declared, 'Change the system; change the world.'

Hayden fell deep into thought, and I was happy to wait for his verdict. It was a lot to take in. But now, having heard myself articulate it all verbally, I was surer than ever that it was going to work.

Until Hayden said, 'Seems like the best way to change the world is to just get rid of the system altogether.'

I almost choked.

'Maybe the Aliens can have their Hierarch, and we can go back to… whatever it is we had before they **fucked** us over.' He nodded, as if approving of his own idea, then finished, 'But that's just me. What would I know, right?'

Even if I wasn't temporarily gagged by the globule of half-dissolved sucrose, where would I even begin my response? By saying that whether we wanted it or not, the Hierarch was here, and had been for centuries? That it was irreversibly woven into the fabric of our existence? That we couldn't just 'get rid of it' without a complete upheaval of our entire planet's societal structure? That, therefore, the only realistic way to make change was from *within* the system, not outside it?

Maybe it was because I had decided to do this for him that his answer irritated me so much. It was just the way he dismissed me, throwing out this utterly simplistic alternative, as if it was that easy.

In the end, I figured it was better to say nothing at all. It didn't matter. He wouldn't understand.

'So I guess that means,' he said eventually, 'if your bid is successful, you'll have to go back to Kappeetar.'

'Probably,' I replied. 'That's where the Hierarch is.'

When I replay this memory, that line always comes out harsher than I intended. Fortunately, Hayden didn't seem to notice. He just said, 'We going to finish this episode or what?' Then, even if only for a little while, it was just like old times again.

The message from the Selector at the House of Balance requested my presence for the analysis five rotations after I received it. So, I spent what precious time I could find over those five rotes preparing for the analysis by scouring my memory records for accounts I could use to demonstrate my suitability for service. In all that excitement, though, I had failed to ask myself the question I should have when I first submitted the bid: how would I get to Kappeetar for it unnoticed?

I didn't want to ask for more leave from parliament so soon after the last, and there was also the challenge of getting to the shuttle terminus while dressed in my robe and band. I would **stick out like a sore thumb,** as the ancestors would say.

It was the ancestors themselves who gave me the solution. During Academy training, I had come across an ancient practice of theirs that, if the purpose hadn't been to deceive her, I'm sure Mother would have been quite proud of me for utilising. They called it **pulling a sickie.**

It worked perfectly – on Mother. On the rotation of the analysis, after I had executed the deceptive technique, she insisted that I remain at home, kissed me on the forehead, then left for parliament none the wiser. Father, however, was immune to such Human trickery.

'According to your vitals, you appear to be in good health,' he said when he confronted me in my room, apparently checking my profile through the Core. 'Aside from a spike in heart rate at just this moment. Why did you lie to your mother?'

He wasn't so much reprimanding me as asking with genuine curiosity. I knew that he, unlike Mother who was blinded by Human maternal affection, would see right through my deception, so I came clean. I told him about my decision to serve the Hierarch and why I made it, and that I needed to get to Kappeetar – and back – without Mother noticing, or anyone else in Wellington who would recognise me and inform her.

When I finished, he said, 'You do not consider she will approve of your decision?'

'You heard her the other rotation. She told me my place is here, not serving the Hierarch.'

'But if you told her what you just told me, and she understood how important that is to you, she would support you.'

There was that Alien logic again. Of course, it made rational sense. But the idea of Mother being rational just didn't add up for me.

'For a species who conceptualised the notion of **faith**,' he said, 'you seem to have very little of it in each other. Come, then. I will take you to Kappeetar.'

'What about your service?'

'I may be Alien but you are not the only one who has learned some things from your ancestors,' he said with a grin. 'Now, put on your robe and band. I need to contact the Allowance Exchange.'

With a newfound respect for my father, I did as he asked and, once he had **pulled a sickie** too (and shown me how to manipulate my profile's vital readings to further improve the technique's likelihood of success) we clambered into the kawwa, input the coordinates for Kappeetar, and set off for the skyways.

'Gratitude, Father,' I said, watching Wellington fall away beneath us.

'You are welcome. But you must promise me something in return.'

I should have known. Everything has a cost when it comes to Aliens.

'Of course, Father.'

'If you are successful in acquiring service, you must tell your mother. I will not involve myself in any further **sickies** to keep that from her.'

It was a fair compromise, I supposed. And if I hadn't thought as far ahead as to how I was going to hide my analysis from Mother, then I definitely hadn't planned what I was going to do if I was successful in acquiring service.

'I promise,' I told him, and he gave an appreciative tendril flick.

Before long Kappeetar appeared on the horizon, the centre of that monstrous web created by the skyways that encircled the planet. Cloud City, some of the ancestors had called it, apparently inspired by an ancient opera long since lost to time. It was easy to see why they had been captivated by it. Pre-assimilation Humans had barely come to terms with the concept of airspace control when the Noor established this gargantuan airborne fortress. I wondered what they would think of it now, no longer a cobbled-together settlement established to house the Hierarch on Teerin' Ho but a sprawling metropolis of gleaming chrome spires, spanning almost the entirety of the airspace above the Extremely Large Water Expanse (real name: Pacific Ocean). Even though I had attended Toor Academy there for the last three revs, being a simple surface boy, its sheer size never failed to impress me.

The closer we got, the denser the air-traffic became. Soon we joined the ant-like lines of vehicles crawling through Kappeetar's wind barriers. I had never been to the House District before, which occupied the elevated centre of Kappeetar's terraced, concentric design. The colossal, blunt structures that I knew were the Hierarch's Houses jutted into the sky, and in their centre, overshadowing them all, was the black spike of the Apex – the seat of the Hierarch's Lords and Supreme Rank. Towering over the rest of the city, and the world, it was visible from every district. Flying through the House District, in its shadow, its presence was dominating.

'I will occupy myself in the Commerce District,' Father informed me when the kawwa swung in to a stop outside our destination. 'Inform me when you are finished and I will retrieve you.'

I heard him but was too busy staring at the gaping maw that was the House of Balance's gateway to respond. Robed and banded servants streamed into it and, importantly, out of it, which was somewhat reassuring. Simply dressing like a servant of the Hierarch wasn't enough to make me feel like I belonged. Parliament and the Clan Lounge seemed much more welcoming.

'I am certain you will perform adequately,' said Father. 'Remember why you are doing this. That will incentivise you.'

As irritating as cold Alien logic could be, this was hard to argue against.

'Gratitude, Father.'

Keeping my mission at the forefront of my mind, I stepped out of the kawwa and into the jaws of the Hierarch.

I found myself in an immense tunnel, surrounded by a bustle of servants entering and exiting the shifters that lined the tunnel's walls. Despite their number, the servants merged into efficient, fast-moving queues, resulting in smooth, orderly traffic. The surety of movement showed how Alien the organisation was: if these beings had been Human there would have been an endless scrum. I inserted myself into a queue and let it take me up to the sentry station.

There, I stepped out of my lane, and approached the sentry. I informed her that I had an interactive analysis with Porrog 4 Took'itti, within the Chamber of Covenant Resolutions. She pointed at a designated area on the other side of the room: a small collection of uncomfortable-looking perches. There I waited, cycling through the 'Analysis' branch I had created in my tree for one last round of preparation, until another female entered the reception.

She was strikingly well-groomed. Her coat shone with fresh wax and engorgers filled her mandibles attractively. She noticed me, and I was about to stand and greet her when her root blinked to signal she was consulting her tree. I paused, guessing at what she was checking, while I waited for her attention to return. When it did, she scanned the reception one last time before addressing me uncertainly: 'Denial?'

Smiling back the swell of humiliation, I stood and raised a hand to give her the best inferior-to-superior salute I had ever given.

'Yes, uh, Daniel,' I corrected her, once she'd accepted my gesture with a flick of her own wrist and tendrils. 'V-Very pleased to meet you.'

'Oh, *Dan-yell*.' Her fattened jaw peeled apart in a wide smile. 'Did I pronounce that correctly?'

If I was a female, perhaps. But close enough. 'Y-Yes.'

'Oh, excellent. I must confess I was rather confused when I saw you. Based on your name and profile I was expecting – well, something else!'

Something uncoated, I presumed. As familiar as the inference was, I didn't have a response, so, as usual, I laughed and hoped it sufficed. Apparently, it did. She formally introduced herself as Took'itti and led me into the House of Balance proper.

We walked over a bridge that crossed a large grazing below, from which rose a cacophony of conversation and the pleasant, sweet aroma of freshly brewed pennoo. Ahead was a sheer glass wall, through which I could see countless floors of servants conversing or linked directly with the Core at the many rows of terminals that populated each level. I tried to identify any Human servants but they all looked as coated as I did.

A glass wall opened ahead of us and Took'itti led me through a labyrinth of cubicles to a room where two people were waiting: a female younger than her, though a few revs older than me and a similar-aged male. I acknowledged them appropriately, but was surprised when the younger female offered her hand to me.

The movement was stiff in that way that only Aliens can achieve when they attempt a **handshake**, but I appreciated the understanding of our traditional greeting nonetheless. I gave the male a thankful nod as he offered a similarly rigid **handshake**, then moved to the space where Took'itti indicated I should sit.

After carrying out the standard ritual of linking our collective trees to the Core, she took her own seat and began, 'Gratitude for attending this interactive analysis, Dan-yell. We are encouraged by your bid and eagerly anticipate our assessment of you.

'This is Norr'n 3 Armiddia.' The younger female inclined her head. 'And Paree 3 Heppat.' The male did the same. 'They are both Knight Operators here at ChamCov.'

That impressed me: Rank 3 and so young. I decided then and there that I would be where they were by the time I was their age.

'I will begin by briefly explaining the operations of the Chamber of Covenant Resolutions – otherwise known as ChamCov,' said Took'itti. 'As I am certain you are aware, we mediate the resolution of imbalances caused by the Hierarch's failures to honour the Covenant of Wellington. Through resolutions, the Hierarch makes amends for those imbalances by formally acknowledging and apologising for the acts that caused them, and by providing reparations, which are typically composed of Rank and permissions for airspace administration. So far, the Hierarch has reached over 60 resolutions with Human nations, meaning we are essentially halfway to resolving all imbalances. We expect all nations will be resolved by Revolution 9-4034 – and, if you are deemed worthy, you will be helping us do that. It is an exciting time to be working at ChamCov indeed.'

I assumed, by the quality of this **Aliensplanation**, that she must also have had a Primary in Memetics.

She looked to the other two and they hummed in agreement. I felt a rush of exhilaration. Took'itti may have glossed over a few details but she was correct about the time: Covenant resolutions wouldn't be around forever. Being able to say that I helped resolve the grievances of our people was a side-effect of my main mission that I would be honoured to have.

The interactive analysis then began, with Took'itti inquiring about my experience and profile. I had rehearsed this so many times that it came out flawlessly.

'I've just completed my ascension at Toor Academy. My primaries are Human Studies and Memetics, so I have a strong background in Human culture and I can speak, craft, and even **write** to a Third Stage in Common Transfer. I also have a strong understanding of the Covenant and its Promises. Through my Memetics Primary I have developed strong thoughtcraft ability, which I consider will be very valuable in an Operator position.'

Armiddia's and Heppat's roots flickered incessantly as I spoke. Took'itti was smiling. I had, as the ancestors would say, **nailed it**.

'Excellent. Gratitude, Dan-yell. Now I will defer to these two for the proficiency inquiries.'

The Knights alternately inquired about the following proficiencies: Mediation, Edict, Unravelling, Thoughtcraft and Synchrony. I was able to produce an account for each, with none of my narration questioned. Even my response to the Edict inquiry – an account of a dissertation

I once crafted about the effects of the skyways on New Zealand's air quality – passed without any request for clarification. I was particularly proud of my response on Synchrony – demonstrating my recent leadership of Mother's selected committee to review the Accord between New Zealand and the Pacific Territory Congress. Throughout the entire account their tendrils remained flexed, their roots flashing so quickly that the tiny light on their surfaces appeared to be constant. When I finished, the panel took a few moments to record their thoughts before re-focusing on the analysis.

'Those are all the inquiries we have for you, Dan-yell,' Took'itti concluded. 'Much gratitude – you've given us very good accounts.' A few tendril-flicks of agreement from the Knights. 'Now, before we finish, are there any inquiries you have for us?'

I took each of them in. I hadn't anticipated being so impressed. I expected a bunch of Alien bureaucrats but they seemed practical, intelligent and understanding. Having cleared the analysis, my anxiety was slipping away.

'Yes, there is one inquiry I have. What does the Covenant of Wellington mean to you?'

Took'itti stiffened. The other two were impassive.

'Well,' said Took'itti, emitting a nervous, forced chuckle, 'as you know, I am only a Selector so I do not really hold an opinion on that.' She manufactured another fattened smile at me and laughed in Armiddia's direction. 'I will defer to these two to respond to that inquiry.'

A flash of disdain crossed Armiddia's face before her enhancers wiped it.

'Obviously the Covenant is at the heart of what we do,' she said, so quickly it felt as rehearsed as some of my answers. 'But at ChamCov we are really focused on the present and what we can provide through resolutions that have good conclusions for Humans right now. It is important to keep the Covenant in mind, but if you dwell on it too much, things can get quite, what is the concept... **heavy.**'

I wasn't sure how to respond. I was impressed she knew the double meaning of that term, but I wondered if she truly understood what it expressed when she could seemingly divest herself of that weight on a whim.

'Yes, you know, we do not prefer to take things too seriously around here,' Heppat added. 'We like to keep things light and have a bit of **fun.**'

It was my first real taste of what I was signing up for. That's all it was to them, resolving the imbalances of the past: just a bit of **fun.**

'But *great* query,' said Took'itti with a slow, approving flick. 'Anything else?'

'No, gratitude.' I worried that the Covenant question had been too much, that they would think I was *too* Human now.

Thankfully, the analysis terminated and Took'itti informed me that they would leave me alone in the room to complete the mandatory crafting assessment. I was much more confident about this, and thoughtcraft was a strength I was eager to flex. I bade farewell to her and the Operators – perhaps a bit too hastily in my excitement to complete the assessment and make up for asking that question – and I activated my tree to receive Took'itti's message.

It barely registered in my system before I opened it, devouring the missive in seconds. The task was simple: review a sample communication from a member of the public to the Lord for Covenant of Wellington Resolutions, then edit the proposed response. I was surprised by the tone of the message and wondered if it was representative of correspondence the Lord received. It declared that Humans should be grateful for the benefits of assimilation, questioned the amount of public tithe spent on resolutions, and accused a supposed 'Human elite' of hoarding Rank for themselves and spending it on expensive airships. The proposed response was a set of generic lines about the importance of resolutions – nothing that directly addressed the points raised by the hypothetical correspondent.

I resisted the impulse to re-shape the response entirely and held to the allocated instruction, addressing the message's structural imperfections. It took only minutes to skim the message, add a date signature, change 'covenant' from common noun to title, and make other simple revisions. Once finished, I reviewed. Everything seemed in order. The message was clean, simple, polished.

But it lacked substance. I was still tempted to add a direct response to the points raised. I could mention that only 2% of the Hierarch's total Rank distribution was spent on resolutions, or maybe give examples of imbalance committed by the Hierarch – the Invasion of Tokyo was my usual go-to.

I let the thought pass. This reply was supposed to be the voice of the Lord. Which reminded me – I applied a tone change to the message and decided it was complete. I told myself, again, not to overdo it. I didn't want to be *too* Human.

If I ever became a Lord myself, I thought, as I submitted the completed assessment to Took'itti's tree, I could craft whatever I wanted.

Took'itti soon returned to escort me back across the bridge. I looked down on the beings at the grazing below, imagining myself as one of them, picking up a pitcher of pennoo … I already knew I would become unhealthily dependent on it for the sensory relaxation it provided after so much time connected to the Core. I was excited, confident in my analysis and hopeful that I would be accepted.

'Gratitude again, Denial – Dan-*yell*,' Took'itti incorrectly corrected herself when we arrived at the gate. 'I will divulge that you performed very well. Your Human background and knowledge is *very* desirable. You can expect to be informed of an outcome in the following rotations.'

'Gratitude, Took'itti.' I saluted her. 'Much appreciation for the opportunity.'

Stepping out of the House of Balance, I felt empowered – **on top of the world**, as the ancestors would say. I stared up at the Apex and it didn't seem so frightening anymore. For a moment I imagined myself sitting at its peak, the first ever Human of Supreme Rank. Surely that was what it meant to be **on top of the world**.

But that wasn't my mission. I didn't need to be Supreme Rank if I succeeded in making the Hierarch honour the Covenant. Because then it wouldn't just be me at the **top of the world**. It would be all of Humanity.

I was trying to **write** when Took'itti's communication came through. It was a fascinating device, the ancient thing sitting on my lap. Almost like a brain removed from a head and given a screen. To communicate with this brain, I had to punch in codes using the spread of individual buttons on the device's base, which were each marked with a symbol. Combinations of these symbols represented ideas. This was how Humans traditionally visualised communication, well before Aliens introduced direct thought transfer. It's an almost lost form, preserved only in sacred pockets, like the halls of parliament and the under-funded, inequivalent-to-Academy **universities**.

Mother gifted the device to me on the anniversary of my 21st rev around Aar. She had used the same device, at the same age, to teach herself the artform, then bequeathed it to me so that I would do the same.

At times, when I became frustrated with the slowness of punching in individual symbols, rather than crafting the thought needed to transfer an idea with my tree, I questioned the efficacy of **writing** as a form of transfer. It seemed restrictive, limiting. Direct thought transfer was precise, absolute. Ideas were received exactly as they were transferred. **Writing**, by contrast, transferred an incomplete idea, only a representation of the transferor's true intent. And yet, there was something profound about this. It meant every idea transferred by **writing** was received in a way unique to the receiver's own understanding or expression of it. It was uncertain, chaotic and, in those ways, deeply Human.

I was a barely capable **writer** myself, however. I looked down at the two lines I had **written** one painstaking symbol at a time:

I went to the shop
to buy a drink

I felt like I had tapped into something special, a birthright. The fact that this writing would never be understood by most Aliens sanctified it, made it a treasure. Its worth would only ever be known to those of us who did understand it.

Putting the device down, I steeled myself for the incoming conversation.

'Greetings, Denial.'

'Greetings, Took'itti. Are you well?'

'I am indeed. I suspect you already know I am contacting you about your analysis previous rotation.'

I adopted a naïve tone that suggested I had somehow forgotten. 'Oh, yes?'

'I am delighted to inform you that we assessed you very highly, and have deemed you of sufficient Rank for service at ChamCov.'

I allowed myself a moment of silent celebration. Aside from the excitement that the next phase of my plan had been successful, ascending to Rank 2 was no small matter. I had always known that, eventually, I would reach it, but it had seemed a far-off life event, like producing offspring or dying. I had never anticipated how its achievement would feel.

'Gratitude, Took'itti, much gratitude. I am honoured to be recognised as such.'

Took'itti recited the general terms of service, which included the provision of the necessary Rank to reach Rank 2 and an upgrade to my root. The upgrade would allow me to pass through the House of Balance's gates and access the Hierarch's exclusive division of the Core. I mentally accepted the offer.

'Gratitude, Denial. We anticipate you beginning service with ChamCov at the commencement of next cycle.'

After Took'itti's tree retreated from mine, I sat in the quiet of my room processing. I was not wavering from the course. I was determined to carry out my mission. But my promise to Father resounded in my head. I had to tell the Leader of New Zealand that her own son was to serve the Hierarch.

I had prepared a script in my head after Father and I returned from Kappeetar. It can't have been very good because I couldn't now recall it. Mother's leadership was characterised by her resistance to Hierarch edict, championing New Zealand's control over its own affairs in the face of assimilation. Would she understand what I was setting out to do?

My eyes fell to the device still open on my sleeping capsule, and I had an idea. I returned it to my lap, opened a fresh construct and began punching.

I finished well into the dark. Bathed in the device's white glare, I **read** what I had **written**. It wouldn't go down in history as the greatest **letter** ever, but I was certain Mother would understand its significance. Somehow, delivering the message in **writing** felt like the right thing to do.

I rose to my feet, bringing the device with me. Every step amplified my anxiety, so by the time I reached the gateway, I could hardly breathe. But there was no turning back now. **Time to face the music**, as the ancestors would say.

Mother and Father were connected to the Core, Father probably viewing his entertainments, Mother undoubtedly working – her lap was filled with old documents again.

'Mother, Father,' I announced, more loudly than I intended. 'I have something to show you.'

Father locked eyes with me, a look of approval. Mother gathered the fragile documents and placed them on the floor before setting a curious stare on me.

'Father,' I said, holding up the device, 'I'll explain what this is transferring later. As you know, Humans used to **write** the things they considered important. It was our way of validating them.'

My throat tightened – which, though uncomfortable, reminded me how Human I was – and Father gave a tendril-flick of acceptance. I handed the device to Mother.

As she took it, her eyes remained fixed on me, like I was something she needed to **read** first. When she had seemingly gleaned what she needed to, her gaze fell to the device's screen. Her brow furrowed, her jaw clenched. Her eyes lifted to mine again, narrowed, then returned to the device. I braced myself.

'"**I went to the shop to buy a drink**,"' she read aloud. She looked at me again. 'Apologies, Daniel, I don't –'

'What?' I scrambled over to her and ripped the device out of her hands. My earlier construct was still open on its screen. All the tension in my body seemed to release itself in the breath that escaped me. 'The other one, Mother.'

I didn't have anything left to feel. As she read the correct construct, I couldn't conjure any more energy to prepare for her reaction. Whatever it was, I wanted it to be done.

It took me a while to notice that there wasn't a reaction. Mother's eyes were back on me.

'You know I would have preferred you here, in Wellington,' she said, her voice low. 'But if this is what you believe in, then I support you.'

It took me multiple memory replays, and a message from Father that read '**Told you so**', to be sure that was what she'd said.

'Really?'

'Of course!' She rose and swept me into a hug. 'If any of us can make a difference in there, it's you, Daniel.'

If a positive reaction from Mother had seemed possible, I would have anticipated what would follow: her insistence on celebrating with a cut. From her private store she retrieved her prized, vintage cutter – ten revs old but with plenty of joy-infused charges left.

'Daniel,' she announced, handing the cutter to me, 'you have always made us proud. Your achievements in education and your ascension at Academy are testaments to your intelligence and motivation. But this … is something else. An opportunity to do so much for your people.'

She paused then, dabbing at an eye. Father and I exchanged a look – typical Mother.

'I know you will only continue to make us proud.'

'Congratulations, Daniel,' Father added.

My throat was tight again, and I felt if I tried to say anything, whatever was lodged in it would break out. So, I took a hit from the cutter and passed it on.

In a haze of simulated delight, we discussed the service I would be operating. Like many Humans, Mother knew of ChamCov but was largely unaware of what exactly it did, confusing many of its functions with those of the Wellington Commission. When I explained that the Commission inquired into Covenant imbalances and made recommendations on how to amend them, and that ChamCov mediated the actual amending of those imbalances, she laughed triumphantly: 'So, when the time comes to mediate New Zealand's resolution, you'll have all the inside intelligence.'

It wasn't exactly the reason for my world-changing plan but I supposed, if nothing else, she was right. 'Anyway,' I continued, 'as I said in my **letter**, I begin service next cycle.'

'Excellent,' said Mother, eyes glazing over as she accessed her tree. 'I'll set a reminder to see you off at the terminus.'

Panic pierced my synthetic elation. I should have known there would be a catch to Mother's positive response. Too good to be true. 'Are you not ... coming with me?'

'No, why?'

'It's my first period of service. There'll be an ascension ritual – it's standard practice for one's clan to –'

'It might be standard for Aliens, but it certainly isn't for Humans.'

I caught a reactive insult before it escaped my lips. Father came to my aid.

'Michelle, this will be an important occasion for Daniel, and for our clan. The Hierarch has ascended him; it is only appropriate that we reciprocate –'

Mother began one of her lectures. 'Do you think, in the ancestors' times, you would have ever brought your **family** to your first day of service? Never.'

Service didn't exist in the ancestors' times so the point was irrelevant, but saying that wouldn't help. As calmly as I could, I said, 'We're not in the ancestors' times. This is how things are done today.'

'It's not how *we* do things.' Mother's tone was cold, unyielding. 'You secured that service on your own merits, Daniel. Not ours, not your **family's.** You don't need us to hand you over to them like a child. You are Kytoonoo 1 Daniel – no, 2 Daniel now. You make your own **destiny.'**

I should have expected it. Mother was, after all, the proudest Human I knew. But the thought of arriving at the House of Balance next cycle, with no clan to reciprocate the Hierarch's ascension of me, filled me with dread. 'Please, Mother. Please come.'

'I will come with you,' Father offered.

Mother stood. 'No, you will not.'

Father sighed. 'Michelle, this is just how it works. They do not know your ways.'

'Then it's time they learn.'

That was the end of it. There would be no convincing her, and Father knew better than to challenge her on something like this.

As if she realised how she appeared, standing over us both, Mother resumed her seat and said, 'This is who we are, Daniel. You are about to enter an institution that is completely foreign to us. Not only that, but one that has always oppressed and continues to oppress us. You must hold on to your humanity.'

Did she think I didn't know that? It wasn't about letting go of my Humanity. It was about integrating into the system. My success depended on fitting in, establishing myself as one of the 'good ones'.

I retired to my sleep capsule quietly furious, and woke the following rotation even more so. Mother had sabotaged my mission before it had even begun.

I sought out Hayden. I didn't think he would understand, but I needed to vent my frustration and, anyway, I had to tell him my bid had been successful. I asked him to meet me on Wellington's water-front, for no reason other than that it was where we spent the most time when we were juvenile.

I hadn't been back since my return to Wellington, and the harbour seemed smaller than I remembered. Once you've seen the Extremely Large Water Expanse from Kappeetar, no other body of water compares. Still, the harbour was enchanting, in its own tiny way – flat as glass, sparkling in spite of the roving shadows cast by the skyways above, and lapping softly at the edge of the walkway. It dawned on me that I didn't know when I would see it again like this: once I began commuting to Kappeetar, I would only ever be in Wellington during the dark, and eventually I would need to secure my own dwelling in Kappeetar anyway.

'You got the service, didn't you?' Hayden said, appearing at my side. 'Yes.'

His mouth smiled but his eyes didn't. 'Congratulations, I guess. When do you start?'

'Next cycle. I've got until then to figure out how to conduct an ascension ritual on my own.'

He looked confused and I explained: in exchange for ascending me to Rank 2, my clan was obligated to reciprocate by transferring some of our collective Rank back to the Hierarch as a token of gratitude. The entire exchange would also need to be recorded in the Core.

'But you could do that easy, couldn't you?' said Hayden. 'You know your way around all this Alien **hocus pocus**.'

'That's not the point,' I replied. 'If I show up alone it's like … not even my own clan thinks I'm worthy of being ascended. That's what the Hierarch will see. That's what Mother is doing to me.'

Hayden was staring at me with the same expression he'd had the other rotation, at his father's dwelling. Like he was looking at a stranger.

'What?' I demanded.

'Isn't there an old saying,' he said, rubbing his chin. **'A mother is always right?'**

'It's something mothers say so they can get away with saying whatever they want.'

Hayden shrugged. 'I wouldn't know. Never knew mine. But I'm saying maybe you should listen to her.'

I flicked negatively. 'She doesn't understand –'

'Maybe it's *you* who doesn't understand.' Hayden was suddenly almost angry. 'You only just got made Rank 1, and already you're ascending again. Just like you said you would. You can do whatever you want, Daniel. Nothing ever holds you back. If there was ever anyone who was going to break out of this **shithole**, it's you.'

He looked out over the water. I followed his gaze, feeling well and truly put in my place.

'So, if you're going to do this – serve the Hierarch, make them edicts or whatever it's called – then you better do it for all of us. Be a Human in the Hierarch that we need. Not just another **turncoat**.'

I saved these words in a secure file in my tree. 'I will,' I said, holding out my hand. 'I promise.'

Hayden made to grab it, then swiped his own hand out of reach.

'You're a servant of the Hierarch now,' he said, grinning. 'Last time the Hierarch made promises, it didn't work out so well for me.'

I grinned back. 'That's about to change.'

Rank 2

Recorded: Cycles 3 through 4, Revolution 9-4025·

2-1

I was back at the House of Balance, standing outside its massive gateway, alone amidst the lines of Hierarch servants coming and going. I watched them glide past, trying to imagine greeting any of them with 'Hello' or 'Hi there' or 'How are you?' I simulated a dozen introductions of myself, each met with some variation of:

- 'Denial?'
- 'Dan-yell?'
- 'Can we just call you D or something?'

There was no scenario in which I could bring myself to honour my promise to Hayden. Not one where I could imagine saying, 'Actually,

---

* Subject notation: The ancestors had names for individual cycles, which they called **seasons**. They didn't, however, use them as a standard measurement of revolutionary time like we do. Instead, their revolutionary calendar was divided into twelve segments of slightly differing lengths. Despite this seemingly arbitrary approach to time measurement, I assume there was a logic behind it.

no, it's Daniel' or, 'Can I call you **moron** instead? Why not? Because that's not your name? But I thought we were just giving each other new names because we couldn't be bothered putting in the minimal effort required to pronounce each other's properly?'

It was fortunate that I had arrived in Kappeetar a full hour before I was expected, because I had been standing outside torturing myself with this exercise for the past half of that hour. I forced myself to breathe, to draw on the wisdom of the ancestors and suppress my anxiety until I could pretend it didn't exist anymore. It partially worked. I managed to move – but not in the direction of the House of Balance. Instead, I set off down the channel in the opposite direction.

According to the Core, I had twenty minutes before I was due for the ascension ritual. Maybe a nice, hot cup of pennoo would calm my nerves. In the House District – where the Rank that Hierarch servants collectively spent on the beverage must be enough to purchase a small moon – there were at least three pennoo outlets on every walkway. I was spoiled for choice, but it was the morning, so each one I passed was at capacity.

Crossing a narrow walkway between the House of Transportation and the Chamber of Planetary Transit, I spotted a tiny outlet crammed between them, with only a few patrons. I headed towards it, and just when I thought my anxiety couldn't get more crippling, I saw her.

She was one of the patrons waiting for a pennoo. I didn't need to see her face. The flowing dark mane, shining in Aar's light, was unmistakeable. It was Trezza 1 Neekor. Actually, 2 Neekor, I found upon checking her profile in the Core. She had been one of my closest friends during my first rev of training at Toor Academy, and we'd dwelled at the same habitation centre. As was common, our ascension paths took us in separate directions, and I hadn't seen her since.

'Daniel?'

In the time it took for me to look her up, she had received her pennoo and seen me standing there, immobilised. Before I could make myself respond, she scanned me head to toe, then her hazel eyes lost colouring as she looked up my profile. 'I am pleased to see you.'

'As am I,' I managed. 'To see *you*, I mean.'

She hadn't changed since Academy. Her nose still made that little wrinkle when she was amused.

'I see you've ascended too,' she said. 'Are you serving?'

'Yes, at the Chamber of Covenant Resolutions. I actually commence service this rotation.'

A momentary lapse in focus: she didn't know what ChamCov was and was checking the Core for it.

'Excellent,' she said upon returning. 'Congratulations, Daniel.'

'What about you? You must be serving at a House?'

'Yes – the House of Transportation.' She gestured to one of the square behemoths towering over us. 'I am an Operator assigned to Rank auditing.'

That made sense – her path of ascension at Academy had been Rank Calculation.

'I'm pleased for you.'

The conversation stalled. Neekor gave me a friendly smile, which I realised too late probably meant she expected me to say something more. I took the easy option instead.

'Well, anyway, Neekor, I should let you return to service.'

'Yes, I should probably return,' she said with a positive flick. 'It was a pleasure to see you. Perhaps we could socialise again in more depth. I would be interested in hearing how the rest of your training went.'

'Yes,' I said, possibly too quickly. 'I'd like that.'

There it was again – the little nose wrinkle.

'Farewell, Daniel.'

I watched her walk away until she disappeared inside the House of Transportation. The whole engagement had raced by in a blur. It was something that had happened *to* me, not something in which I was an active or willing participant. It left me feeling somewhat weightless, untethered from the walkway I stood on.

It was that feeling that made me turn and head back to the House of Balance, no pennoo needed. Everything suddenly seemed lighter, a new realm of possibility brought within reach. I strode through the gateway, announced my arrival to the sentry and waited, inexplicably ready for anything. I dared someone to pronounce my name incorrectly now.

'Hello, you must be Daniel!'

For a second, I thought I must have been still running simulations in my head, and they had taken on the form of fantasy. But no – a female stood opposite me, and she really had greeted me in Common and pronounced my name perfectly. She was Human, with uncoated, glowing white skin, although she had accentuated her face with an array of enhancements – engorgers, extendrils, eye-bloom, the works. I wondered why she would want to make herself look more Alien. I would have given anything to look as Human as she did.

'Yes, I'm Daniel.' I stood to greet her. 'Nice to meet you.'

'You too! I'm Morgan.' She grabbed my hand and shook it before I could offer it. 'From where do you hail?'

'New Zealand.'

'Ooh, a Kiwi boy! I have family there, you know.'

I couldn't help smiling. 'And you?'

'Russia,' she said, proudly rolling the 'r'. 'Welcome to ChamCov! Apologies for my lateness. When we learned you had come alone, we considered we needed to arrange something for you –'

'No, my apologies,' I said. 'I didn't want to create any trouble. My clan was going to come but –'

Morgan waved her hand. 'Don't be silly! It's no trouble at all. In fact, we should be doing this more often.'

I didn't know what she meant by 'this' but allowed her to guide me, with a friendly hand on my back, through the gate and onto the bridge that ran over the grazing. The great glass wall parted to allow us entry, then the floor opened to reveal a shifter, and Morgan gestured for me to step onto it. A second later, the pool of light had brought us to an identical space several levels higher. The bridge was now distantly below us.

'This way.' Morgan led me into the adjacent area, where I was welcomed by a series of transparent pods, each housing Human artefacts

– a set of golden **medals** in one, an ornate **pistol** in another. She indicated a room nearby and gave me a gentle nudge. 'Go on.'

I took a breath. I had never conducted the other side of an ascension ritual before, but I'd spent the entire trip to Kappeetar replaying my account of the one Father had led for my ascension at Toor Academy. My tree was primed to transfer our clan's collective profile to the Hierarch and I also had my paltry Rank offering ready. Forcing a confident expression, I stepped into the small room.

A single consumption mat lay in its centre, with some containers of sweets and two pitchers of pennoo. Eleven individuals surrounded the mat, two of whom were obviously Human. One of the two, dressed immaculately in a robe of plum hue and a gleaming platinum band around his neck, opened his arms.

'**Attention, everyone**,' he said in perfect Common, even though most of those gathered clearly didn't understand the transfer. '**Thank you. Today we have Daniel Kytoonoo starting with us. I hear he is a Kiwi boy, so we know we've got a good sort on our hands.**'

The other obviously-Human laughed, as did Morgan and I. I wasn't aware New Zealanders had such a reputation among Humans, but I was happy to take it.

The speaker looked at me directly and continued, '**I wanted to take this opportunity to welcome you, Daniel – to properly welcome you. We're really happy to have you here, and we know you'll be a great addition to ChamCov. We hope you appreciate this little morning tea we've managed to put together for you.**'

'**Hear, hear,**' said the other Human.

The welcomer turned to his colleagues and repeated his greeting in Noor. Then he explained to them, 'In the ancestors' time, it was common practice to hold what was called a '**tea**' – either in the morning or afternoon – for welcoming or bidding farewell to a colleague. We share sustenance as a means of acknowledging that colleague. On this occasion, where we are welcoming the individual, it also provides an opportunity for introductory dialogue, which we would call **small-talk** or **chit-chat**. Daniel, would you like to say anything?'

I cleared my throat. 'Yes, certainly. **Thank you very much for the warm welcome. I was not expecting anything like this, so it is a pleasant surprise.**'

It was about as much Common as I was willing to speak without prior preparation. But something about the welcomer made me want to do more. To impress him like he and Morgan had impressed me. I could think of nothing more Human than talking about myself, so I continued, '**A little bit about me: as has already been said, I come from New Zealand. I have just completed training at Toor Academy, with primaries in Human Studies and Memetics. In my leisure time I enjoy thoughtcraft.**'

I repeated my message in Noor and impressed murmurs filled the room. I noticed the welcomer almost imperceptibly raise one of his tendrils – and I imagined I had proven myself in some way to him.

'Gratitude, Daniel, and welcome once again,' he finished. 'Can I interest you in something to consume?'

The formalities closed and I allowed him to pour me some pennoo, which he passed to me before shaking my hand. His grip was firm, natural.

'I am Lincoln,' he introduced himself. 'Lincoln Samuels. It's nice to finally meet you.'

It was the second time he had used the Common name convention, rather than Alien. The lack of emphasis on Rank was utterly refreshing.

'And you,' I returned. 'I am ready for the ascension ritual.'

'Taken care of. We thought this was more appropriate.'

I tried not to let my relief show. 'Apologies, I didn't mean to make a fuss with all this.'

'Not at all. It's the least we can do.' Glancing at the others in the room, he leaned towards me and whispered, 'We may serve the Hierarch, but here we look after our own.'

My remaining anxiety vanished. I was clearly not alone in my desire to change the Hierarch from within. I wondered how many more of us there were.

'So, a Kytoonoo,' he went on. 'Am I correct in assuming you're one of the Wellington Kytoonoo?'

'Yes! My mother is Michelle. Do you know her?'

'I know *of* her. She has quite the reputation. A proud woman.'

That was putting it lightly, I thought. I asked him where he was from.

'The great United States of America,' he proclaimed wryly. The reason being, I later learned, was that the massive, unwieldy nation of America had been unable to even begin mediation due to leadership disputes and some of its states desiring their own, separate resolutions – and this made Lincoln's service at ChamCov awkward, to say the least. 'But anyway, Daniel, I must return to service now. Again, it was a pleasure to meet you. Please ensure you take it easy today. We have a great task ahead of us so you must take your time to settle in.'

He clapped me on the shoulder and I said, 'Yes, I will. Gratitude, Lincoln.'

As soon as he departed, Morgan swooped in so I was not left alone.

'He's **awesome**, isn't he?' she said, watching him exit the room. 'You're lucky you get to have him as your first Commander.'

My coat stood on end. 'Commander? You mean he's Rank 5?' I couldn't believe I had neglected to appropriately salute someone three Ranks higher than me.

Morgan gave a dismissive wave. 'Relax. Lincoln doesn't care for that Alien **shit**.'

I asked her what her own role was.

'I'm Lincoln's attendant. So, if you ever need access to him – and I encourage you to make use of that – just let me know. I'll make it happen.' She gave me a smile then flicked her tendrils at the others in the room. 'Let's meet your squad.'

She escorted me to the group. The first, a large male with a perpetual grin, turned as we arrived. He had a short coat, which made me wonder if he was Human. I made sure to give him the appropriate salutation, which he returned before offering me his hand.

'Greetings,' he boomed, in a voice I suspected was always louder than it needed to be. 'I am Partookoo 4 Teemot.'

I shook his hand, which had that tell-tale limpness of unfamiliarity with the custom.

'Teemot will be your Captain,' said Morgan, to which he chuckled.

'I am unsure what to tell you, young one,' he joked, 'but I do not know how that happened either.' Morgan and the other Human laughed, and I got the impression this happened often.

Teemot's speech had an accent, quite distinct from Teerin' Ho Noor or even Owteer Noor. I thought maybe he was Human after all, perhaps from some obscure nation I hadn't encountered, like Antarctica.

Morgan then introduced me to the other nine Operators in the squad. Only one was Rank 2 like me – the rest were Rank 3. Eight were Alien, and the one Human Operator reminded me of the uncles you might find at the Clan Lounge: he had excess body mass, with pupils permanently contracted from a history of cutting, but he received me warmly, with a vigorous handshake.

'**Welcome, welcome**,' he said, beaming widely. 'I am Kerra 3 Phil. From Australia.'

'**Nice to meet you**,' I returned, releasing his hand. 'I have **family** in Australia.'

'So do I!' Unlike with Teemot's joke, no one in the room laughed except Phil himself. I got the impression that also happened often.

'Anyway,' Morgan said with a barely concealed eyeroll, 'I might leave you to settle in with your new squad. Remember –' she stabbed a finger at my nostrils '– if you ever need Lincoln – or me, for that matter – don't hesitate. We'll look after you.'

Too intimidated to say anything, I simply gave a positive flick, which seemed to suffice. She turned her finger on Teemot, which said all it needed to, and he responded with an equally fearful flick.

'You are fortunate,' he breathed once Morgan had departed. 'She is quite the ally.'

'I can tell,' I said, which elicited a hearty laugh from Teemot. I would normally have been wary of such an imposing Captain of Rank 4 but, just as Lincoln and Morgan did, Teemot made me lower my guard. A part of me still wondered if I was unconsciously running simulations,

59

or even **dreaming** (fantastical visions the ancestors claimed they would experience in their sleep, before the universal installation of roots).

'Come,' said Teemot, leading me from the room. 'Allow me to show you ChamCov.'

The rest of my squad departed, leaving Teemot and myself by the capsules of Human valuables. He saw me eyeing them and informed me that they were gifts from nations who had reached resolution of their imbalances.

'Gifts? Why?'

I didn't dare say: 'So the Hierarch took our autonomy and airspace, gave us back 1% of it, and we gave them gifts for the privilege?'

Teemot shrugged his ears. 'Humans are gracious?'

Too much so, I thought. I wondered if the nations that gave those gifts would have so readily done it if they knew ChamCov would display them like trophies. I made a mental note to ensure Mother gave no such gift if she was still in power when New Zealand reached resolution.

Teemot navigated us through the level, pointing out each squad and its specific function in the mediation process, none of which I remembered. Physically, it was identical to the level I'd had my analysis on: a labyrinth of pens and terminals full of activity, with Operators hurrying back and forth. I spotted the Knights who had analysed me, Armiddia and Heppat, who gave a friendly salute. Most other servants were equally friendly, and I received many smiles and salutes, except from a final squad of aged servants who didn't even look up from their terminals as we passed.

'They are the Elite Operators who advise ChamCov's 5th and 6th Ranks. Do not take offence, they are incredibly busy,' Teemot said as we walked on. 'And not the most stimulating conversationalists anyway.'

Finally, we arrived outside a sealed room – the only one we had come across so far.

'This,' said Teemot, 'is the private terminal of the General of ChamCov, Laffee 6 Neweek.'

At that moment, the room's gateway expanded, and a female strode out. If Lincoln was well dressed and groomed, the General put him to shame. Her silver coat grew at her neck into a luxuriously long mane, her robe was deep black, and both were accentuated by the shining golden band at her throat. She passed us as if we were invisible, her distant eyes indicating she was in communication via the Core. I watched her billowing black robe disappear into the maze of ChamCov. I had never been in the presence of a Rank 6 before.

'As I'm certain you can appreciate, she is also very busy,' Teemot said. 'And an even less stimulating conversationalist than the Elites.'

We both laughed and Teemot began leading the way back to our own squad's pen. I asked him what part of mediation we were responsible for.

'We are Authorisers, assigned to the region of Europe.' In his unusual accent, he pronounced it 'Yoorupp'. But I had decided I liked Teemot, so it no longer bothered me. 'We have a unique role because we engage with nations who are not yet Authorised to mediate with ChamCov.'

'Authorised?' I hadn't come across the term during Academy training.

Teemot flicked positively. 'The Hierarch will not mediate with a nation who is not Authorised. If a nation wishes to mediate, the Hierarch requires its leadership to seek Authorisation from its citizens to do so on their behalf.'

I was confused. Most nations had some form of authorised leadership already – just like Mother. I decided not to ask for clarification. It was all going well and I didn't want to squander my progress by appearing as if I didn't already know everything about ChamCov.

We arrived at our pen – a cluster of terminals occupied by the squad I met earlier. Teemot directed me to the one available terminal: a lounger-like chair attached to a tangle of cords and wires protruding from the floor.

'This is your station,' he said. 'Everything you require is here; hydration and sustenance is replenished every rotation, and connecting to your terminal's secure link will give you access to the Hierarch's division of the Core. For this rotation, please feel free to explore that division as much you please.'

In the terminal beside me, Phil leaned over. 'The *Manual That is Blue in Colour* would be a good place to start. Has everything you need to know about the mediation process.'

'*The Manual That is Blue in Colour?*' I clarified.

'Yes – or **Curing the Past, Constructing the Future** if you want to call it by its real name. But no one does.'

'Why not?'

'Too hard to remember.'

'Excellent assistance, Phil,' said Teemot, to a proud puffing of the chest from Phil. 'If you require anything else from me, Daniel, please do not hesitate to contact me.'

'Gratitude.'

I appreciated their warm welcome, but I was also eager to explore the division of the Core that had become newly accessible to me. There was an implication to that privileged access, though. When connected through the terminal, which was the only way to access that division, anything I viewed could be seen by the rest of the squad and all of ChamCov. It allowed multiple people to view the same content while their trees were connected, but it was also a form of controlling what content was accessed. You would think twice about what you looked at if others could see. Of course, I had no intention of viewing anything I shouldn't, so I dived right in.

I was overwhelmed by the magnitude of information on ChamCov's private sector in the Core's Hierarch division. It took a few moments – which, while connected to the Core, felt like a lifetime – for me to process what I found: endless databases on nations, screeds of data on the resolutions that had been or were still being mediated, and the *Manual That is Blue in Colour*, which I downloaded to my personal tree for observing later.

I was still curious about something. So far, I had met three Humans: Lincoln, Morgan and Phil. Potentially Teemot, too. I wanted to know how many others served at ChamCov – potential allies in my mission to change the Hierarch.

I searched through ChamCov's service statistics until I located the current revolution, then executed a search of 'quantity/servers/Human', which returned a proportion of 14%. This was slightly less than the general proportion of Humans on Teerin' Ho, which I supposed was not entirely unexpected. Next, I requested an organisational chart, with a filter to identify which of those belonged to the 14% of Humans within ChamCov. A pyramid of roles was constructed, with those who identified as Human highlighted in grey. I noticed a significant concentration of red at the base of the pyramid.

I zoomed in to view only Tiers 4 and above:

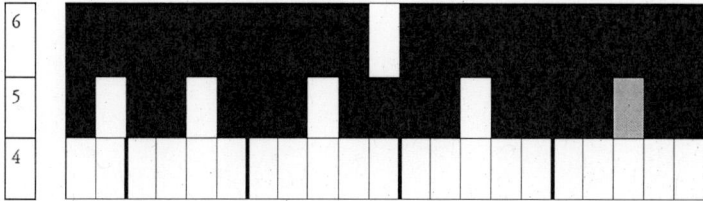

Of twenty-seven roles, one was held by a Human. I contemplated that lone grey role, the highest-Ranking Human in ChamCov. Morgan was right. I was lucky to have Lincoln as my first Commander.

My first few rotes at ChamCov were a bombardment of new experiences. The amount of information I attempted to process through my root was so enormous it left me with a migraine by the end of the week.

The first thing made known to me was the utter size of the Hierarch. ChamCov was just one of several chambers within the House of Balance, which itself was only one of the scores of Hierarch Houses. There must have been millions of servants to the Hierarch, the vast majority based in Kappeetar. That explained why the city was so sprawling: it had to be to accommodate the Hierarch's immense workforce.

The Hierarch's size became even more astounding when I thought about how Teerin' Ho's Hierarch was still subordinate to the True Hierarch, seated on the other side of the galaxy in the Noor home-world, Owteer. There were hundreds, if not thousands, of sub-Hierarchs across the galaxy, all tithing their Rank to a ruling clan that wouldn't have the first inkling nor concern about what went on in their worlds. Bizarre as the concept was, it was hard not to recognise the genius of a system that had guaranteed the True Hierarch's Rank indefinitely. For the first time I began to understand the scale of the task before me.

The servants of ChamCov seemed pleasant and sociable. Many appeared to have no understanding of Human values or of Common. I must have been called 'Denial' more times in that week than in my entire existence. But a significant number of Aliens also seemed genuinely committed to the cause of resolutions and were open and respectful about Human culture. It wasn't unusual, for example, to hear Common greetings by these servants. Not even at Toor Academy, which was, at the time, in the process of renaming itself **Victorious University** to demonstrate how progressive it believed it was, had I encountered such friendly Aliens.

A few of these Aliens were, thankfully, in my squad. Pa'zan, the only other Rank 2, assigned to the nation of Switzerland, was one; he only commenced service a cycle before I did, so he became my guide in ChamCov, teaching me everything there was to know about serving there.

Another was Moolas, assigned to the Nordic nations of Sweden, Norway and Finland; he was a former Decree-crafter, and surprised me on my second rote by engaging me in a discussion about the similarities he saw between Alien Decree and the Human system of **law.** It was incredible, really, that he had even the slightest understanding of **law.** It was a system so sacred and complex – even more so because it was so different between Human nations – that the ancestors had financed special experts to interpret it for them. These highly esteemed practitioners were known as **lawyers** or, in some dialects, **liars.**

There was also Vuneen, responsible for the squad's priority Authorisation of Italy. She was the longest-serving and most experienced member of the squad. This had afforded her the same understanding that I was already developing of the Authorisation process our squad administered: that it was a complete undermining of independent Human control.

'In the eyes of the Hierarch, Authority has to be proven,' she explained to me over a pitcher of pennoo one morning. 'It is not enough for a nation's leaders to already be in control of their nations: if it is not recorded in the Core by the Hierarch, it is invalid. The Hierarch designed a process that forces a nations' leaders to prove they have the Authority to represent their nations. It is only once this process is complete, and the result validated in the Core, that the Hierarch will mediate with them.'

'Shouldn't a leader's authority be proven by virtue of them being a leader at all?' I asked, thinking of Mother. 'Just because it's not in the Core doesn't mean it isn't valid.'

'Correct. Although, one could argue that it is a safeguard as a resolution is a significant event. Not only for the reparations but because of the way it eliminates imbalances. Once a resolution is reached, all the imbalances committed by the Hierarch against that nation are wiped from the Core. Balance is restored, and that nation can never again accuse the Hierarch of inflicting past suffering – even if it occurred but was not recorded. So, with what is at stake, the Hierarch requires certainty that whoever claims to represent their nation has sufficient Rank to do so.' She sipped her pennoo, then concluded, 'One *could* argue that. I certainly would not.'

I pondered this until we both finished our pennoo, then I asked, 'Why do you serve the Hierarch, Vuneen?'

She paused, swilling the dregs in her pitcher. 'Why do you?'

Touché, as the ancestors would say.

It was fortunate that my commencement at ChamCov coincided with an actual resolution. I arrived on my third rote to Operators rushing about even more frantically than normal and ChamCov's Core usage at its highest since I arrived. Pa'zan told me this excitement was standard when a resolution was about to be reached.

'After all,' he pointed out, 'it is a significant achievement for ChamCov.'

I liked Pa'zan so I resisted the urge to ask, 'Don't you think it's a greater achievement for the nation reaching resolution?'

That nation was Peru, so while everyone around me was caught up in infectious anticipation, I dug out the Resolution Pact that would soon be validated by the Lord for Covenant of Wellington Resolutions. It was an immense construct – far too large for me to process in such a short space of time – but I skimmed as much as I could. I was impressed by the opening component, the Sequencing, which formally recorded in the Core the suffering the Hierarch inflicted upon the people of Peru. It was quite affecting, particularly the account of the Acre Affray in which, I learned, a delegation of Peruvian leaders was attacked by Noor who had settled in Brazil. Following the conflict, during which the husband of the Peruvian Prime Minister had been disintegrated, the Hierarch detained the Peruvian President without cause and exiled him to Asia for four revs. The Hierarch then pressured the remaining Peruvian government to yield swathes of airspace in exchange for the

President's return – airspace which the resolution with Peru was not going to give back.

As I read on, I found many of the reparations to be provided to Peru seemed of insufficient value to correct the imbalances caused by the Hierarch's actions. I was well aware of the general narrative that the value of what was lost wasn't equal to what was returned, but seeing actual examples of this was striking. I was particularly stunned by the reparations involving Machu Picchu. What was once a heritage site of immense cultural and historical value was to remain what it had since become: a Hierarch-controlled Conservatory. A donation, the Pact called it, from the people of Peru to all of Teerin' Ho.

Yes, the Hierarch literally gave Machu Picchu back to Peru on the condition that Peru then give it back to the Hierarch.

I concluded that dwelling on the grave injustice Peru's resolution was about to commit would only undermine the authority of the Peruvian government, who had agreed to the resolution on behalf of their people. What choice did they have, really? It was that or nothing.

Later that rote, I joined Pa'zan in observing the projection of the Lord for Covenant of Wellington Resolutions validating Peru's resolution. Before commencing service, I knew very little about him, but, from my new colleagues, I had learned a great deal. He was the most successful Lord for Covenant of Wellington Resolutions there had ever been, with more resolutions reached under his Rank than any other. He also had the highest Rank tithing from Humans of any Lord in the Teerin' Ho Hierarch, which meant he was the most popular Lord among Humans. And, of the Lordship duties assigned to him, Covenant of Wellington Resolutions was apparently his favourite.

'Such a great being,' insisted Phil, who was particularly fond of the Lord, although he had never met him. 'He freely admits he was entirely ignorant of Human ways before being assigned this duty. But it has taught him a lot about us and our culture.'

This was evidently true: during the Peru projection the Lord expressed the same idea. I found it interesting given what else I had learned about him in my research through the Core: he was a devout member of the

Empiric Observatory which, during assimilation, was responsible for the conversion of entire Human populations to Empiricy and the consequent elimination of many basic Human philosophies.

Mother wasn't fond of him, although not necessarily for his association with Empiricy.

'He visited us once, you know,' she told me, when I recounted my first service period at ChamCov to her over darkmeal. 'Back when he was Lord of Transportation. He came to talk to us about the Pacific Air Channel when it was first proposed.'

'What did you think of him?'

'I thought he was a disrespectful little **muppet**,' was the swift response. 'It was clear the conversation with us was only a **tick-box exercise**.'

I tried to convince Mother that he must have changed, based on what everyone at ChamCov had told me. I even sent her his Peru projection as evidence.

'Maybe he has,' she conceded. 'Regardless, I'll never trust him. I'll never trust the Hierarch.'

With the issue of Mother's absence from my commencement at ChamCov long behind us, I relished the opportunity to tell her everything I had learned. She keenly absorbed it all, inquiring about the most mundane of minutiae, such as how ChamCov opened and closed gatherings or how many in total served there. She was particularly relieved about the way Lincoln and Morgan had cared for me and even asked me to pass on her personal gratitude to them. But her sudden declaration of mistrust caught me off-guard. The conversation continued but my thoughts were dominated by the question I couldn't ask: did she trust me?

Thankfully, Father was far more encouraging. Conversations with Mother had consumed what little energy I had at the end of each rote, so my service interval gave me ample time to catch up with him – once my overload migraine had subsided.

'Do you know yet which nation you will be assigned to?' he asked.

'Not yet, but Britain is currently unassigned. Their previous Operator was demoted.'

'Demoted!' Father gasped. Although not technically a Hierarch servant, even Father knew of the tremendous shame that was demotion. Servants are only ever meant to ascend – a practice I initially found unusual given the Hierarch is a tiered organisation in which every tier has more Rank than the one below it. But, as I had come to learn, that structure relies on some servants going down instead of up. I'll let you guess which species those servants typically belong to. 'Whatever for?' asked Father.

'No one seems willing to tell me.'

'Well, if nothing else, it presents an opportunity for you.'

'How so?'

'To achieve what the previous Operator could not.'

'I'm not sure, Father. Everyone talks about Britain being the most complex Authorisation the squad has. From what I've gathered, it is a priority resolution. That makes me anxious enough, without the added challenge of having to succeed where the last Operator failed.'

'This is how you climb Rank, Daniel. By proving yourself worthy of it.'

The idea appealed to my ambitious side. I could see it: the young, fresh-faced Operator, assigned the most complex Authorisation ChamCov had ever had, winning the favour of the British and ensuring their Authority at an unprecedented degree of certainty. I would be instantly promoted to Rank 3 as a result and it would be the perfect way to continue my journey upwards.

But then I imagined the inverse: a new, inexperienced Operator, assigned the most complex Authorisation ChamCov had ever had, losing the favour of the British and compromising their Authority in a new breach of the Covenant of Wellington.

That was the next implication of my grand scheme that I had failed to foresee. Although ChamCov's purpose was to resolve imbalances caused by the Hierarch's past breaches of the Covenant, the Hierarch was still found by the Wellington Commission to breach the Covenant on a regular basis. At times, even the resolution process itself was found to breach the Covenant, causing imbalances that then, in turn, had to be resolved at a future time.

So, I began my second week of service by following Morgan's suggestion to speak with Lincoln. She made me an appointment, and the next rote, I met Lincoln at the grazing inside the House of Balance.

After he insisted on purchasing my pennoo for me, which I made sure to pretend I didn't want, even though I did, as is the Human custom, we found a mat to sit on and he asked about my first service period at ChamCov.

'Honestly, it's been incredible,' I said. 'There's so much to process – I had a migraine from overload at the end of last service period.'

Lincoln chuckled. 'You get used to that. And your squad?'

'They're brilliant. Pa'zan's been showing me around and Vuneen has been teaching me a lot.'

'Pleased to hear it. They are a great squad. Others in ChamCov may not appreciate it, but what your squad does is incredibly important. It is crucial that a mediation is built upon a strong foundation, which is why your squad's role is essential. You would be amazed at how many mediations encounter significant setbacks due to a weak Authorisation.'

'Actually, Lincoln, that's one thing I wanted to talk to you about.' I tried to calm my nerves with a sip of pennoo. 'Have you ever done something in service to the Hierarch that breached the Covenant?'

Lincoln took a sip of his own. 'I see you're coming to terms with what it means for a Human to serve the Hierarch.'

'Well, I know that a lot of Hierarch edicts completely contradict Human values. I was prepared for that when I began here –'

'Were you?'

I paused, mouth half-open.

'It's okay if you weren't – I'd be surprised if you were. Many Humans serving the Hierarch think they're prepared for that and find, quickly, that they're not.'

'I thought I was, but maybe …'

'May I ask you something? You don't have to answer if you don't feel comfortable.' I nodded, and Lincoln leaned forward. 'Why *do* you want to serve the Hierarch?'

I shrank back. In front of him, my mission to change the world seemed like a juvenile's fantasy. I knew I could trust Lincoln, but I couldn't bring myself to answer him.

'I can tell you why I wanted to serve the Hierarch. Why I still do,' he offered. 'I wanted to make a difference. I don't know if you've ever been to Los Angeles, where I grew up, but it's one of the poorest places on Teerin' Ho. No local healing services, only a handful of educational facilities. When I was a juvenile, it had the highest self-termination rate in the world. I spent my adolescence hating the Hierarch, hating Aliens, for this. In time, I realised hate would not change anything. I could stay in Los Angeles, angry at a system deliberately designed to make existence hard for us, or I could get off my ass and make a difference. Make the Hierarch be what I wanted it to be. Make it keep the Promises I wanted it to keep. I have a feeling you want the same thing.'

As uncomfortable as it was under his gaze, I couldn't look away. I wished I could describe my wants with his same conviction. Instead, I just gave a slow, positive flick of the tendril.

'If so, there are some things you need to understand,' Lincoln continued. 'The Hierarch doesn't change easily. To even contemplate it is to suggest the dismantling of a galaxy-spanning, millennia-old empire built on the assimilation of other worlds. But that is not to say change is impossible. Look at Covenant resolutions: though far from perfect, they are the result of gradual, hard-fought change by countless Humans with the same vision as you and me. I'm not telling you this to deter you, Daniel, but to ensure you understand exactly what you are setting out to do. It may take you revolutions to see the type of change you want. It may not even occur in your lifetime.'

'How, then? How do you do it?'

'First, by understanding how the Hierarch operates.' Lincoln sat back, staring up at the glass walls. 'Think of the Hierarch as a massive machine. Every component – right down to individual servants like you and me – serves a specific purpose, and together they serve one higher purpose: self-preservation of the Hierarch itself. To even begin to consider how to alter that machinery, you must understand how it works. How every one of those components fits together.'

I thought of the diagram I had transferred to Hayden – rudimentary compared to what Lincoln was describing.

'You will be challenged. Every time you enter this House, you are walking into an Alien environment which, by nature, is hostile to us. You will be forced into positions where you must put aside your Humanity in favour of serving that great machine for now, so that you can change it in the long run. Trust me when I say you cannot understand the weight of that conflict until you have to carry it. So, let me ask you again: are you prepared?'

I thought of everyone I was there for, and my promise to Hayden.

'I am,' I said. Proud, certain.

Lincoln smiled and held his pitcher out to mine, an ancient gesture. I clinked my pitcher against his, and in that collusion felt that nothing – not even the machinery of the Hierarch – could take our Humanity away from us.

With my resolve bolstered, I threw myself back into service. I still hadn't been allocated a nation for Authorisation, although Pa'zan assured me it would happen once Teemot felt confident I was ready. Instead, I was fast establishing myself in the squad as a thoughtcrafter. It turned out that many Humans saw the flaws in the Hierarch's approach to Covenant resolutions: the Lord was constantly receiving complaints and, where they concerned the Authorisation process, it fell to my squad to answer on the Lord's behalf.

The first communication I was asked to respond to was from an individual member of Portugal, who claimed he alone had the Rank to represent the nation in mediation. He was so desperate to assert whatever Rank he believed he had that he was attempting to discredit the entity who clearly did have this Rank – the Portuguese Government.

'He's making some serious allegations,' I said to Phil, who was assigned to Portugal's Authorisation. 'Rank-fraud, exploitation – even that the High Rank of Portugal abuses his own mate. Why would he do this?'

Phil shrugged. 'It's most likely he just wants to resolve his own imbalance and not have it resolved by someone else.'

That was the reality of Covenant resolutions, I supposed. Any Human could make an appeal for imbalance suffered by the ancestors, but the Hierarch didn't resolve imbalances on an individual basis. When it mediated with a nation, every individual imbalance suffered by members of that nation were collectively resolved – whether those members wanted it or not.

Before crafting the response, I dived into the Core for some research. Phil was right: the communicator had an imbalance registered in his name. His grandmother had owned airspace in Lisbon, which the Hierarch had confiscated once it introduced the tithe system, and she had refused to pay. I looked up the communicator's profile. He was elderly, lived alone, had little more to his name than the imbalance he wanted to resolve on his grandmother's behalf.

After confirming with Phil that, as far as ChamCov could ascertain, none of the allegations were founded, I set to work on the Lord's response. I started by simply acknowledging the communicator and his appeal – that felt appropriate. I then clarified that there was no evidence to suggest that the Portuguese Government had committed any of the imbalances the communicator was accusing them of. Finally, I encouraged him to discuss with the Portuguese Government how they might work together to ensure his appeal was resolved in a way that was suitable to him and that honoured his grandmother.

When I showed the message to Phil for his review he laughed in his hearty, Uncle-at-the-Clan-Lounge way and said, 'If only it was that simple.'

I didn't see why it couldn't be that simple. All the Portuguese Government had to do was convince the communicator that they would honour his grandmother's imbalance.

Teemot had a similar reaction to Phil – his booming laughter rang out across the level – but he didn't reject my work. 'This is great, Daniel. I like the tone you bring to this. You have given it something … Human.'

From that point on, Teemot allocated me every message for the Lord that our squad was tasked with crafting, and even a few for other squads. It was an excellent way to build an understanding of the world of Covenant resolutions. In only a few weeks, I was familiar with the progress of every Authorisation the squad was working on and the key players from each of them.

I also learned that Aliens had a lot to say about Covenant resolutions.

'How about this one,' I said to Pa'zan one rote, pulling up a new communication I'd been tasked with responding to. '"This grievance industry has to cease. Why should I continue to tithe my hard-earned Rank so that these part-Humans can be paid out for dubious claims about matters that occurred in sequences long since past?"'

Pa'zan had one better. 'In my first-ever period of service I saw one that tried to claim a clan of Noor actually existed on Teerin' Ho before Humans.'

'Or this one,' I went on. '"The Covenant is clear: Humans gave their Rank to the Hierarch. Any argument to the contrary is just more revisionist fiction pushed by the separatist agenda."' I stared at Pa'zan in disbelief. 'This is factually incorrect. Does this person just deny the existence of the Common version of the Covenant, which literally did not give away Humans' Rank to the Hierarch?'

'They tend to do that,' said Pa'zan. 'Try not to let it bother you, Daniel.'

But the more of these communications I read, the more it did bother me. I knew Alien supremacy existed in Teerin' Ho but the sheer volume of it being expressed to the Lord was overwhelming. It became harder to craft responses that were aligned with Hierarch edict, that respectfully acknowledged the correspondent's opinion, that didn't say what I really wanted to say.

It finally became too much when I received a message that said: 'We should delete the Covenant. It was declared by Magistrate Gaa'prin in Rev 9-3754 to be invalid because it was agreed to by 'primitive imbeciles' who had no concept of what a Covenant even was, which we all know is true.'

I left ChamCov to get some oxygen. As had become habit since that chance encounter with Neekor on my first rote of service, I headed for the outlet next to the House of Transportation. I needed my daily pitcher of pennoo, but it was also a shameless attempt to see Neekor again. I hadn't been successful yet, so I didn't expect this latest trip would be any different. But as I passed by the House of Transportation, I spotted her – dark, shiny mane bouncing on her shoulders, powerful legs striding with intent – exiting its gateway.

I steeled myself and saluted her.

'Greetings, Daniel,' she said, returning my salute hurriedly, but not unkindly. I noticed she had applied a few subtle enhancers – her cheeks were slightly engorged and a touch of eye-bloom made the hazel of her irises glow.

'Are you getting some pennoo?' I asked her.

'No, actually. I am travelling to the Accountancy for a gathering.'

So that was the reason for her hurry, and her enhancements.

'But it would be my pleasure to share darkmeal with you tonight, if you are available?' she said it so quickly I wasn't sure I had heard it correctly.

'Yes, of course!' I knew I was grinning like an idiot but I couldn't help it. 'I would like that very much.'

Neekor smiled and brushed past me. 'I will contact you when I am finished service. Until then.'

I spent the rest of the rote in the same weightless state I had experienced when I last saw her. I must have been floating around the pen; at one point, Pa'zan put a hand on my arm, asking if I was okay. I told him I was fine and happily resumed my thoughtcraft. Nothing could ruin my mood – not even the most offensive of Alien correspondence. Nothing, at least, until I arrived at the House of Transportation later just in time to see Neekor dismiss another male with a courting salute.

I could feel myself deflating, stuck in place as this well-groomed male strolled past me with a contented smile, a waft of musk trailing in his wake.

I should have anticipated that Neekor would be courting potential mates. Aside from her obvious physical attributes, she had always possessed several attractive qualities, such as ambition, empathy, and mathematical competency. No doubt that toothy, pungent suitor wasn't the only one she was courting.

I did my best to hide any reaction, made a mental note to purchase my own musk, and forced my legs to move.

Neekor and I had enjoyed a strong companionship back at the habitation centre, but it hadn't lasted. We had barely remained in contact since, so it wasn't as if she had any obligation to me, nor I to her. I could have been courted too. Not that had I been, but that was beside the point. I reminded myself that I had no right to feel anything about who she was courting, and I saluted her as naturally as I could.

'Are you well, Daniel? You appear ill.'

I cobbled together an answer. 'Yes, I'm fine. How was the rest of your service?'

'Unstimulating and repetitive,' she replied. Then she smiled. 'You must be familiar with the experience by now!'

I was grateful for the laugh – I needed it to help me relax. As we set off towards the grazing she recommended, we informed each other about what had happened since we went our separate ways. Our accounts were strangely similar: being the educational achievers we were, neither of us had much to report other than that we had both completed our respective trainings then immediately pursued service. She'd had a couple of cycles' head start on me in achieving Rank 2, but that was no surprise, given her desirable qualities. She was still attentive, inquisitorial, and eager to understand things. Like why I had bid for service at ChamCov, of all places.

'From recollection, you intended to become an educator,' she said. 'That was the very reason you were learning Common Transfer, was it not? So you could teach it to juveniles.'

I was impressed she remembered this, and even more impressed that she didn't look down on me for it. Despite the invaluable service they provide, educators aren't afforded the same Rank as Hierarch servants, nor held in the same regard.

'That *was* my intention,' I said. 'But the more I learned, the more I came to realise that there was still so much left to learn. I didn't think it was appropriate to educate juveniles on the transfer when I was by no means an expert on it.'

Neekor eyed me in that quizzical Alien way that told me a challenge to my answer was incoming.

'But you are a proficient transferor of Common, are you not? You can speak it?'

'Of course I can speak it,' I said, with a little more fire than I intended. 'But when you learn another form of transfer, you realise there's more to it than just being able to hold a conversation. Consider it: you're a native transferor of Noor. You don't even have to think about what you transfer – it just happens. That's because you've transferred Noor all your life. That, and you are surrounded by it in every possible way. The same can't be said for Common.'

She processed this then shrugged her ears. 'I can understand your point.'

'What about you? What led you to bid for service at Transportation?'

She shrugged again. 'They were recruiting and I needed service. Quite simple, really.'

So it is, for most Hierarch servants, I imagined. I wished it could have been as simple for me.

'I remember you wanted to serve at the Accountancy,' I said. 'You had some strong opinions about how the Hierarch manages its Rank.'

'Oh, I still do,' said Neekor, with a self-amused smile. 'But only the best servants are accepted there. It will take me some time to prove myself.'

The grazing Neekor had suggested served Happanee cuisine, which was something of an extravagance to me. There were no Happanee grazings in Wellington. As our conversation moved from interrogation into anecdotes about the past three revs, I relished the plates of sustenance that were delivered to our mat. Rolled ryhee, bundles of reemoo, and – to my surprise, and Neekor's glee – a pitcher of boiled lubag. I had never tried the infamous beverage, but had always wondered if it was true that it could sever the brain's capacity to connect with its root, like a more intense version of cutting.

At the very least, the rancid concoction lowered my defences.

'You never answered my earlier inquiry,' said Neekor. 'About why you bid for service at ChamCov. In fact, I am surprised someone like you would apply for service with the Hierarch at all.'

'Someone like me? You mean someone Human?'

'Well,' she said, processing how to answer that. In the end, she gave up with an embarrassed laugh. 'Yes, actually.'

I was still hesitant to tell her my plan, but the lubag had made me hopeful. 'You have to promise not to ridicule me.'

Neekor gave a formal salute. 'I promise.'

'I applied for service with the Hierarch because I believe it's the best way I can make a difference.'

The laughter I'd braced myself for did not come. 'In what way?'

'You know why ChamCov does what it does, don't you?'

'Because the Hierarch committed many imbalances against Humans in past sequences?'

'And you know that Humans are still suffering from those imbalances today?'

'Somewhat, yes.'

'Well, Covenant resolutions are only a start to fixing that. The Hierarch still operates the way it always has – the Alien way – and that way doesn't benefit Humans. It will only change if it learns to understand Humans. To keep the Promises it made in the Covenant. I want to make it do that. From within.'

Neekor still didn't mock me, but her reaction was worse: her face was impassive, inscrutable. She lapped once at her lubag then straightened in her seat.

'I am not criticising your intent, Daniel. Only questioning it. The Hierarch is an enormous institution. What difference can one Human make?'

The question hurt more than I wanted to admit. I wished that I could answer like Lincoln, with something profound or articulate, worthy of Neekor's scrutiny. What came out was, 'I don't care how long it takes. I don't care how hard it is. Maybe I won't succeed. But I have to try.'

Neekor studied me. I sat there, awaiting her judgment.

'Is that a Human thing?' she finally asked. 'Knowing something is nearly certain to fail and attempting it anyway?'

I thought about this. 'Yes,' I declared, downing the last of my drink. 'Yes, it is.'

By the time we left the grazing, the rumours about lubag had been proven true. We could barely stand. I had no idea how I was going to make my shuttle journey home to Wellington. Relying on each other for stabilisation, we staggered to the nearest sub-street terminus, so Neekor could catch a transport to her dwelling.

'Educate me in Common,' she blurted, drawing stares from others standing much more stably at the terminus. 'I want to see what Educator Daniel would have been like.'

I felt as if my entire Common vocabulary had dissolved. 'How about: **Hello**?'

Neekor flicked her tendrils dismissively. 'Everyone knows that. Teach me something that most Aliens would not know. Something just for me.'

You'd think it would have been easy to teach her something most Aliens wouldn't know, what with the sheer volume to choose from. But that made it hard to pick something. I said the first coherent thought my mind produced.

I missed you.'

'Ai maissed yew,' she tried. 'What does it mean?'

For some reason, I hadn't anticipated that. There was no Noor concept for '**missing**' someone or something.

'It means I enjoy your presence.' It sounded much more banal than it did in my head. 'And in a recent period when I was not in your presence, I would have preferred to be.'

A nose wrinkle. Then, 'How do I say: I enjoy your presence as well and, in a recent period when I was not in your presence, I would also have preferred to be?'

The transport arrived. We had to part but it didn't matter. Nor did it matter when my stomach expelled its contents on the floor of the shuttle back to Wellington and I had to pay a Rank penalty. It was worth it just to hear her say: 'Ai maissed yew tew.'

The following rotation, I woke to intense nausea and the unsettling sensation of my own heart pulse pounding in my head. A quick search in the Core – which only intensified the throbbing in my skull – established that lubag was the cause. Why anyone would willingly ingest such a substance, knowing its vile consequences would far outweigh the brief euphoria it provided, escaped me.

'The ancestors had a similar beverage, you know,' Mother said as I struggled to keep down my lightmeal. 'We were way ahead of Aliens when it came to ingesting intoxicating substances.'

'I don't know if that's something to be proud of, Mother.'

'Like it or not, it was part of who we were.'

That was always her response to criticism about Humanity. Humans were animal slavers? It's just who we were. Humans paid greater respect to the dead than the living? It was just our way. Humans had caused irreversible damage to the planet's eco-system? We didn't know any better!

She was right, of course. As always. But perhaps holding on to what made us Human sometimes came at the expense of asking ourselves what parts were worth keeping. Assimilation had taken so much from us that we were desperate to hold onto anything we could.

'So,' Father asked across the consumption mat, in a searching tone I was not in the mood to deal with. 'What kept you out so late?'

'Socialising.'

'With?'

'An acquaintance.'

'A potential mate?'

I shot him the most vicious glare I could muster. In the state I was, it probably looked more like I was about to vomit again.

Father lifted his hands in feigned surrender. 'I am only curious, Daniel. You are at courting age, you know.'

'Oh, really? Am I? I hadn't realised.'

'Daniel,' Mother scolded. 'Don't be sarcastic with your father. You know he rarely understands it.'

'You don't say?'

Mother gave me the death stare I had tried to give Father and it was infinitely more effective.

'Apologies, Father.'

'Good,' said Mother with a satisfied nod. 'Now tell me: is it a Human you're seeking to court?'

That was when I really did vomit again, all over the consumption mat and Mother's and Father's lightmeals.

I didn't want to make my first ever application for leave so soon after commencing service, but there was clearly nothing else for it. Father dutifully cleaned up the vomit-soaked mat for me, and Mother assisted me back into my sleep capsule, which she programmed to deliver a powerful dosage of vitamins and carbohydrates normally reserved for poisoning treatment.

'Should I be worried about you, Daniel?' she asked, as the capsule's concoction entered my bloodstream.

'No, I don't think my stomach has anything left.'

'I meant regarding your service.'

I could feel the capsule's sedation beginning to take effect, but I fought it. 'Why would you be worried?'

'You're only a few weeks into service, and I've never seen you do anything like this.' Her eyes ran the length of my body, almost sadly, which triggered an unsettling feeling that I was like a corpse lying in a traditional coffin. 'The ancestors didn't only ingest intoxicating substances for enjoyment, you know. They often used it as a means of self-medication.'

'That's not what I was doing, Mother.' The thought of her comparing me to someone like Hayden made me angry. 'I just didn't know what the stuff did.'

'Everything is okay at ChamCov? Serving the Hierarch isn't troubling you?'

I got the vague impression she knew something I didn't. I tried seeing into her mind in the same way she was reading mine. Unfortunately, as well as always being right, telepathy must be a skill that only Human mothers possess, because I couldn't figure her out.

'I'm fine, Mother,' I said, giving up. 'Service is great. It feels like I'm where I need to be.'

I truly did believe this, which might be why Mother seemed to relax. Whatever she was reading in my eyes matched what had come out of my mouth. Satisfied, she kissed me on the forehead and rose to her feet.

'You know there's always a seat for you in parliament,' she said, with a cheeky smile.

'Maybe one day I'll earn it,' I yawned, before my sedation took full effect.

When I woke again, the headache and nausea were gone, and in their place was a tremendous hunger alongside a steadily growing shame as visions of the previous rotation came back. It took several replays of my darkmeal conversation with Neekor and the impromptu Common Transfer lesson to be satisfied that I hadn't humiliated myself as much as I could have. Relieved, I decided it was courteous to construct a short message to Neekor thanking her for the experience. Once I had finished drafting it, an hour or so later, I sent:

> Greetings, Neekor. I trust you returned safely to your dwelling. I just wanted to express gratitude for a very pleasurable experience previous rotation.

And, within minutes, I received:

> Greetings, Daniel. Gratitude – I, too, had a pleasurable experience, and it would please me even more if we were to socialise again in the near future.

I was glad no one could see me giddily grinning within the sleeping capsule. It could only mean that Neekor really was interested in me as a potential mate. I assumed it was something to do with the fact that I was Rank 2 and – based on our conversation the previous rote – perhaps she was confident that I would ascend further.

My elation grew beyond my capacity to contain it. Leaping out of my sleep capsule, I sent a communication request to Hayden.

'Daniel? What are you –'

'Are you busy?'

'Uh –'

'I desperately need some sustenance. Would you like to come over and share some?'

There was a pause that immediately struck me as unusual. All it should have taken was the mention of sustenance for Hayden to be halfway out the gate.

'Aren't you at service?'

'I took leave,' I said impatiently. 'So, are you keen?'

'I can't. I mean, I can have sustenance. I just can't … come to you. I've got to be home. For … Father.'

I didn't exactly feel like making the trip across suburbs to Hayden's, and I was, after all, supposed to be on service leave in need of healing. But I did need sustenance and was desperate to tell him about Neekor in person.

'That's fine,' I told him. 'I'm on my way.'

A short while later, I was hauling a bundle of sustenance up the hill towards Hayden's father's dwelling in **Oriental Bay**. I noticed that same Mutt sitting on the porch of her own dwelling, watching me, her eyes lingering on my bundle. I sped up, reaching Hayden's father's place only to find the gate covered from the inside by a sheet of construction material.

I sent Hayden a confused message, then heard a commotion on the other side of the sheet. There were a couple of whirs before Hayden poked his head out from the side he had loosened.

'Come on in,' he said, peeling back that side of the sheet so I could squeeze my way inside it. After I had wriggled my ankle through,

Hayden picked up a magnetiser and reattached the sheet to the inside of the gateway.

'What happened?' I asked.

'Keepers.' He tossed the magnetiser onto the floor and headed through to the main room. I followed.

'Keepers were here? But I thought you said the Keepers had other things –'

'Well, I was wrong, wasn't I?' Hayden slumped into one of the loungers. 'You know that balance hearing I missed? Magistrate issued a summons, so they came to detain me. Broke the gateway open because Father didn't answer it when they alerted their arrival. He was in his sleep capsule.'

I looked back over my shoulder at the covered gate. The floating sensation that had carried me all the way there had become a sinking one.

'Is he okay?'

'He's fine. Not really talking to me though. Probably glad he's got his scan today for the excuse to get away from me.'

I remembered Hayden's father mentioning the scan, and how positive he felt about it. I was struck by the strangest convergence of conflicting feelings: that I should leave Hayden alone, but also that I didn't want him to be left alone.

'Where were you?' I asked. 'When it happened?'

'Out.'

I took the hint that he wasn't going to elaborate and sat on the lounger next to him. 'Did the Keepers find you?'

'They were waiting for me when I got home. Detained me and took me to another balance hearing.'

'And?' I wasn't sure I wanted to know what the Magistrate's verdict was.

'Confinement, for a whole cycle. If I leave this dwelling, then the Gardeners will know about it, and the Keepers will be back. That's why I couldn't come over.'

I didn't know much about the balance system, nor what crimes justified which penalties. But I had the sense that confinement was among the first of a range of more serious punishments. I wanted to know what Hayden had done, but I didn't want him to have to tell me.

'Can we appeal it? Surely the Keepers can't just force their way into your dwelling like they did. And if missing your hearing was a factor, I can tell them it was my fault. I persuaded you to come have a cut with me –'

'You really don't get how this works, do you? The Keepers can do whatever they want. They could have atomised Father in his sleep and no one would care. And even if your story was true, the Magistrate wouldn't care about that, either. I missed my hearing and that's all that matters to them.'

I was overcome by the feeling that Hayden and I were worlds apart. I didn't understand Keepers and balance hearings as much as he didn't understand Covenant resolutions and Hierarch edict.

Hayden cleared his throat. 'So, any time you want to come through on that promise and change the world, go ahead.'

Despite his tone, the corner of his mouth curled, so I said, 'I'm working on it.'

A full smile came across his face that felt like a small victory. Leaning over to take a pack of fried doughsticks from the pile of sustenance I'd brought, he said, 'Apologies, Daniel, for bringing you down with me. Tell me how your service is going.'

It didn't feel right to tell him how much I was enjoying it, and even if I did, I wasn't sure he would understand why. I simply said, 'It's good.'

'That's it?' he said through a puff of doughstick flakes. '"It's good?" You're not exactly selling it. Is that why you're on service leave today? You don't like it?'

'No, that's not why,' I said with a laugh. 'Service really is good – I'm enjoying it.'

He flexed a tendril in my direction. 'Then why are you on service leave?'

Grateful for the excuse to finally tell him, I launched into the story about Neekor, including how I had met her and befriended her during Academy training, and our encounter with each other in Kappeetar, culminating in the lubag incident. (At its mention, Hayden said, 'What's this stuff called?' and, after I repeated it, I'm certain he took a mental note for future reference.) Soon Hayden's infectious laughter had me giggling like a juvenile too.

'She sounds **cool**,' he said once I had finished. 'For an Alien.'

A laugh caught, halfway out my mouth. 'What do you mean "for an Alien"?'

'Nothing. Personally, I'd just prefer a Human mate, but who you court is your business.'

'No, hold on.' A defence mechanism I didn't know I had seemed to have activated. 'What's wrong with courting an Alien?'

'Nothing's wrong with it. They're just a bit, well, boring.'

'Boring?'

'Yeah, boring. They don't court beings they feel physically attracted to, or even like the company of. They just enter partnerships for material gain, mutual benefit and all that.'

'I don't think that's totally true,' I said, ignoring the question of whether Neekor felt any physical attraction towards me, or even liked my company. 'I mean, that was how Noor society operated when they assimilated Teerin' Ho but things have relaxed since then. Aliens enter partnerships with people they like or are attracted to all the time – look at my father.'

'Yeah, but he's lived here so long he's more Human than most actual Humans,' Hayden countered. 'You can't deny that most Aliens just don't do relationships like we do.'

'What do you mean?'

'Have you ever, you know, done it with an Alien?'

'Done what?'

'Exactly. That's what you get when you eliminate the need for organic reproduction from your species – and every other species you assimilate into yours. Boring.'

My defence mechanism armed itself.

'Hayden, the many benefits of reproduction by splicing, compared to organic reproduction, are well-established; population control, eradication of venereal disease, significant harm reduction –'

'I'm just saying,' Hayden finished, with what seemed like a conceding shrug, 'I'd find the lack of emotion a bit weird. Seems like courting an Alien would just be business for them. That's all.'

'Aliens feel emotion, Hayden. They just think existence is easier without it.'

'Well, they're proving their point then, aren't they? Because it's pretty **fucking** hard for the rest of us.'

It was like we had swapped places. Now I was the one who couldn't look at him.

'Anyway,' he broke the silence as he always did, which I was always grateful for, 'apologies to do this, Daniel, but Father just let me know he's on his way back from his scan. I don't want him to know you were here. He'll be embarrassed by ...' He jerked his head in the direction of the broken gate.

'Oh, of course.'

It was hard not to feel like he was throwing me out, even though I believed his reason for ending the visit was genuine. I couldn't figure out why this kept happening. Why every interaction between us seemed to end in what bordered dangerously on a full-blown argument. We had never argued about anything when we were adolescent.

Maybe it isn't only Human mothers who have that ability to read minds, because, after de-magnetising the construction sheet from the gateway, Hayden turned to me and said, 'About that Alien you want to court –'

'I didn't explicitly say that I definitely wanted to actually court her in particular, but –'

'You should, if you want to.' He laughed at my puzzled stare. 'Forget what I said before – don't let me bring you down.'

I took him in, studied the mask that was his smile. I was supposed to be pulling him up with me. It was the whole reason I had set out on this mission. But all I had done was remind him how far below me he was. I couldn't let that stand.

'Here,' I said, transferring his tree a hefty portion of Rank. 'To repair the gate.'

Hayden paused, checked his tree, then blanched when he realised the amount.

'Daniel.' He shook his head at me. 'I can't accept this.'

Invoking the ancient **law** of the ancestors, I declared, 'No givesies-backsies.'

'How will I explain it to Father?'

'Tell him the Hierarch paid for it.'

I spent the rest of the rotation in my sleep capsule, finishing the sustenance I brought home from Hayden's dwelling, and pondering his comments about courting Aliens. Even though he had politely retracted them, they would not stop bouncing around in my head. It was true, after all: Aliens are more emotionally restrained than Humans.

Or perhaps it's that Humans are more emotionally unhinged than Aliens. Mother weeps at just about any emotion she experiences; joy, anger, disappointment – once I found her sobbing in her lounger and when I asked her why, she transferred me a visual recording she had found in the Core of a now-extinct infant elephant and wailed, 'It's just so cute!'. I could see why Aliens had willingly begun to diminish their emotional capacity through splicing back in the 7th Age. Everything worked better when you took the emotional influence out of it, including a galaxy-wide assimilation machine, I supposed.

Even this thought process would have been more straightforward without my Human traits complicating it for me. If my genome was 100% Alien, it would have been simple:

1. Neekor wishes to court you
2. You wish to be courted by her
3. You should ask her to court you

Instead, it looked more like:

1. Neekor wishes to court you
    But does she?
    How can I know for certain?

Why would she want to court me anyway?
Is it only because I have a high likelihood of
achieving a decent Rank?
Not because she finds me physically attractive and/or enjoys my
company?

2. **You wish to be courted by her**
    I feel slightly more confident about this one

3. **You should ask her to court you**
    What if she says no?
    What if she says yes but really does only want to court me for
    business?
    And then our courtship becomes a partnership!
    By which point I've invested too much time and Rank in it.
    If we produce offspring that kind of locks me in anyway ...
    Then before I know it I'm elderly ...
    And it's far too late to realise that ...
    Aliens really are kind of boring

This was the problem with that line of thinking: I didn't feel the way
I did about Neekor about any Human – or any other being, for that
matter. I never had. Granted, I was too Alien to understand exactly
what the feeling was, but I knew it was something. And that something
produced an alternative thought process, one that was paradoxically
more rational and more emotionally inspired than the above:

1. Neekor wishes to court you
2. You wish to be courted by her
3. You should ask her to court you
4. And maybe, just maybe, everything will be fine

It was on this basis that I mustered up the courage to invite Neekor on
what the ancestors would have called a **date**. On the face of it, a **date**

was merely a form of organised socialising between two individuals. In reality, it was a complex ritual of social interaction. There were certain things that could not be said in such a context, and actions that could not be taken unless under specific circumstances, the exact details of which weren't necessarily universal.

I doubted Neekor, being Alien, would find much use in such an exercise. If she wanted to know more about my personal traits, capabilities, and clan, she would simply ask, instead of deducing them by observation through a series of manufactured social engagements. But I reasoned that she didn't even need to know that what I had asked her for was a traditional **date**. Technically, the lubag incident was a **date** and she would never have known. So, while I would use this **date** to help me decide whether I really did want her to court me, she only needed to see it as a basic social interaction, which even Aliens require now and again.

I chose Anor as the location. I had wanted to go back to the lunar body ever since a visit when I was juvenile, on an excursion coordinated by the Wellington education facility.

It turned out to be the perfect choice.

'I have always desired to visit the conservatory there,' Neekor exclaimed when I suggested it. 'It would bring me great pleasure to see a real rat in the wild.'

'Excellent.' I said. 'Me too!'

This was a lie; I never really understood the status of our native rat as the **cute** mascot of Teerin' Ho. I appreciated the intensive effort to conserve their population on Anor, away from the predators that Aliens introduced. But my understanding was that real rats were anything but **cute** and had no such status among Humans pre-assimilation. Personally, I would have preferred to see a real **dog** or **cat**, at least something that the ancestors had a close relationship with. But all we have left is what isn't extinct, which I suppose is better than nothing.

After coordinating our service intervals to fall on the same rotations, we were on our way to Anor, riding the inter-celestial ferry up through the layers of atmosphere and the rings of space-traffic into the emptiness of the void. As it was only the second time I'd made the journey,

I spent most of it with my face pressed against our cubicle's insulation field, marvelling at Teerin' Ho's glaring curvature dropping away while Anor's shining white face rose up to meet us. This time, that face was smothered in construction; even more conservation domes, tinged green by the flora fostered within them, had been planted across the craterous surface since my last visit, and each dome was connected by a network of tetherings, the floating structures that served as docks for the steady band of cruise barges orbiting the satellite. As our own vessel came in to land at a tethering, I couldn't help thinking the whole lunar body looked like a titanic virus molecule.

Once we had docked, we were directed to our tethering's detection field, to confirm that we were bringing no invasive species before being granted entry. Our tube-like tethering was filled with noise: hordes of education-facility juveniles and regular announcements in multiple transfers – though none in Common – of ferry and cruise barge arrivals and departures. I was drawn, again, to an insulation field, where I looked down at the dusty, pock-marked rock and imagined finding the legendary footprint of the first **astronaut** to land there.

'Come, Daniel,' Neekor urged, appearing at my side. 'Our tour unit is assembling.'

She gestured towards a sentry who was herding a group of assorted beings together. I guessed Neekor and I were the only citizens of Teerin' Ho. Most appeared Noor but I could tell from their accents that they were from all over the galaxy: Wuka'korta, or Kaanurra maybe, and some I didn't recognise. Neekor led the way, introducing herself and me to the others with an ease I couldn't replicate. I found myself concentrating so hard on clearly enunciating my name that I didn't remember any of theirs. Except for one that remains burned into my memory.

'Powra,' the tall, grinning male said. I didn't need to hear his accent to know he was Alien. It was evident in the way he recoiled from my own name and said, 'What?'

'Daniel,' I repeated. 'It's my name.'

The process that followed was familiar – Powra's eyes roved over me before he made a noise that was something like a laugh, then said with a dismissive flick of his tendrils, 'I am not going to remember how to pronounce that.'

I was about to put as much distance as I could between me and him when his female companion saluted me and said, 'Daniel – am I saying that correctly?'

She was far from Alien herself and was coated in feathers, which probably meant she was from one of the outer systems of Eeporoo.

'Yes, actually.' I wasn't used to saying this. I felt obligated to add, 'Gratitude.'

The corners of her huge eyes creased in a friendly smile. 'I am Threah. Powra is my partner.' She motioned towards Neekor. 'Are you partners also?'

'No,' Neekor and I said together.

I looked at her, she looked at me, and she added, 'We are simply socialising.' Then, before it could get any more awkward, Neekor skilfully changed the subject. 'What brings you to Anor?'

'It is my first time visiting Powra's homeworld,' Threah replied, 'and I hear it would not be a visit to Teerin' Ho without a tour of Anor!'

Neekor turned to Powra. 'Oh, so you originate from here?'

'Yes, I was reared on Teerin' Ho,' he said, 'but I have not dwelled here for revolutions. Once I had sufficient Rank to leave the system, I never wanted to return!'

I wondered why he was even here, if he had been so compelled to leave.

'If you haven't already,' I said to Threah, 'you should spend some time down on the surface.'

Her eyes widened to massive, enthusiastic proportions as she swivelled to Powra. He replied, 'There is not much of note down there, though, correct? And some parts are quite dangerous, are they not?'

I was just about done with this conversation. Whether Neekor sensed this was unclear, but she saved me from having to answer. 'Some parts, but not all. Every journey I have had to the surface has been extremely pleasant.'

While I tried to guess which parts of the surface she had been to,

Threah chirped and ruffled her feathers at Powra. 'We will have to fit something into our schedule.'

Powra gave a non-committal flick, then we extricated ourselves with vague sentiments about seeing them again on the tour.

'They were quite a pleasant partnering, were they not?' Neekor remarked, once they were out of earshot.

'Threah seemed nice,' I conceded. It bothered me that Neekor didn't seem to have noticed Powra's comments about my name or the safety of Teerin' Ho's surface. I tried to put it out of my mind, eager to enjoy both the time with Neekor and my long-awaited return to Anor. As long as I didn't encounter Powra again, I thought, I would have nothing to worry about.

As it turned out, I had plenty to worry about. It was as if Powra wouldn't leave us alone. Throughout the first portion of the tour – a guided walk through one of the larger conservation domes – he often ended up immediately behind us. Almost every time I turned to speak with Neekor, or point out native flora to her, he was there, talking loudly enough to make others assume that he was somehow an authority on the plant life of the planet he hadn't lived on for most of his existence. No matter how hard I tried to lose him, to either the rest of the tour unit or the undergrowth, he had an uncanny knack for popping up at my side, like a weed among natives, sucking up all the air and my patience.

Powra's interruptions continued into the second portion, which was supposed to be the tour's highlight: a journey into the domes on the dark side of Anor, where the rat population thrived. In the dark he was constantly bumping into me, never apologising, and the one time on the tour that the guide hissed, 'There!' and shone her spotlight on what was supposedly a rat, I spun about and saw only the back of Powra's head. As we returned to the Centre for the final portion of the tour – the barge cruise around Anor – I had to endure his endless stream of boasts about the elusive rat only he, aside from the guide, had been lucky enough to see.

'Just beautiful,' he bragged to the rest of the tour unit, including Neekor, who I was beginning to feel I had barely socialised with at all. 'Terrifically fast – so fast, in fact, that I almost did not see it. But it could not escape *my* sight, no. I am so fortunate, am I not? A once-in-a-lifetime experience, really.'

Desperate to escape him, I retreated to the on-board cutting bar, where I ordered a double-charge of an aesthetic-appreciation cutter and watched the globe of **Earth** outside. Not even the cloud of space-junk that encircled the planet could detract from the sudden perfection of its roundness, or the vibrancy of its blue against the infinite void. From that distance, all its awful detail was invisible: the disproportionately high Human mortality rates, the unchecked violence of the Keepers against Humans, the mere existence of Aliens like Powra. I wished I could keep pretending it didn't exist, preserving that satisfying simplicity forever.

But the problems of Teerin' Ho were inescapable. Powra slumped into the perch next to me. 'So, Denial,' he said, pressing his own cutter to his root. 'That is a Human name, is it not?'

'Daniel,' I corrected him. 'And yes, it is.'

'But you are coated,' he pointed out, as if I somehow didn't realise it.

'I am.'

'So, you *are* Human? Even though you have a coat?'

'Yes, even so.'

Like an **angel** from the myths of old, Neekor appeared with Threah in tow. Not in time to save me, though.

'Do you transfer Common?' asked Powra.

'I can transfer Common, yes.'

'Fluently?'

'I wouldn't say I'm fluent, no.'

'Is it useful?'

'Apologies, can you clarify?'

'Well, it is only transferred on Teerin' Ho, correct? And even then, only by a fraction of the population. Are there any benefits to transferring it? Has it assisted you, for example, to find service?'

The benefits of being able to transfer Common went well beyond simply finding service, obviously. But, being Alien, the notion that something could have value even if it wasn't quantifiable in terms of

Rank would have been lost on him.

'Actually, it has,' I replied, taking satisfaction in the surprised flex of his tendrils. 'It was a key factor in my ascension to Rank 2 at the Chamber of Covenant Resolutions where I am in service.'

My triumph was short-lived. That annoying smirk had returned. 'You mediate Covenant resolutions?'

'Yes – well, not me personally. There are mediators –'

'How do you find it?' He leaned towards me, strangely eager.

'I enjoy it. It is a challenging environment, but as a Human I believe it is important for all of Teerin' Ho. I find great meaning in serving there.'

I thought I had taken Powra aback; he seemed thoughtful as he reclined on his perch, watching **Earth** roll lazily by. I couldn't see Neekor's face, but I could almost imagine it, bright with proud, admiring affection.

Then Powra said, 'Regarding Covenant resolutions, I have always taken issue with the greed.'

'Greed? Whose greed?' I was genuinely unsure.

'Humans',' he stated. 'It seems nothing is ever good enough. We give them Rank, we give them airspace, yet they are always asking for more. When will it stop?'

Everybody on the barge, including the cutting vendor, was listening to our conversation. It dawned on me that I was the outlier, the one whose history, experiences, and perspectives were not shared by the rest. Not one of them would have been on my side. My imagined construction of Neekor's face converted itself into one of shame, a silent plead, a desperate request to fall in line. To give up the fight. Assimilate.

If I'd had this conversation with Powra now, it would have gone something like this:

Fuckface: '... When will it stop?'

Me: 'Did you know that, since the first Covenant resolution in Rev 9-3980, the Hierarch's expenditure on resolutions is estimated to be only 2% of its total expenditure in that time period?'

Fuckface:	'No, I did not.'
Me:	'Did you know that the Hierarch has spent more Rank on exiling Humans in the last two revolutions than it has on every Covenant resolution combined?'
Fuckface:	'I did not know this either.'
Me:	'How about that the amount of reparations Humans receive through resolutions is estimated to be less than 1% of what they lost to assimilation by the Hierarch?'
Fuckface:	'...'
Me:	'So I wonder who the greedy ones really are; Humans, for simply trying to reclaim what they once had, or the Aliens who took it all away in the first place.'
Fuckface:	'I would argue we gave Humans more than what they had. When we arrived, Humans were already destroying themselves, through warfare and environmental devastation. When we gave Humans photonics, they almost massacred each other with them. If it was not for all the benefits of assimilation, they would have wiped themselves out.'
Me:	'Actually the array of diseases Aliens brought that we had no immunity against might have done that first. Aliens also enacted decrees preventing us from practising our own forms of healthcare to treat those diseases.'
Fuckface:	'We brought Humans the Core.'
Me:	'Which we weren't eligible for connection to until Rev 9-3734, and even then we had to own airspace, which most Humans had conveniently lost by that point.'
Fuckface:	'Before we arrived Humans had not even invented lightspeed travel. Perhaps they can keep all their airspace and international warfare and animal slavery, and we shall keep all the advanced technology we created.'
Me:	'Did you create any of it? You, personally? Did you personally invent any of your advanced technology? Do you know how a lightspeed engine operates?'
Fuckface:	'Of course I do not.'

Me:	'Then I don't see why you have any greater claim to that technology than Humans do.'
Fuckface:	'What about you? You admitted yourself; you're not even fluent in your own transfer.'
Me:	'Which is exactly why Covenant resolutions are so important. So we can reclaim what was taken. And they'll stop when we get it all back from Aliens like you.'

But I was 21 revs old, and I had never encountered such Alien supremacy directed at me personally before.

'When will it stop?' Powra repeated.

Words swam in my head, too many to speak aloud. I felt every eye on me, every held breath, Neekor's anticipation that seemed like the precipice on which a courtship with her rested. It occurred to me that I was waiting for her, silently begging her to intervene, to say what I couldn't. And, as the urgency for a response seemed to become absolute, I realised that she could never do that. Because she was Alien too.

When I finally mustered the strength to speak, it didn't even sound like my own voice: 'The Hierarch estimates all resolutions will be complete by Rev 9-4034.'

Perhaps Powra expected the fight I simulated in my head. Maybe he thought, being Human, I wouldn't be able to resist the urge to make a fool of myself in public. He frowned, as if I had disappointed him with a legitimate answer to his question, then said, 'Well, not long to go then!'

Of course, the completion of all Covenant resolutions would not be an 'end' in any sense. If anything, they were only the beginning of a renewed relationship between Humans and the Hierarch. One based not on grievance but on partnership.

But I didn't say that.

Instead, I faked a smile and moved to the insulation field, where I pretended to observe something, anything, and found only the conservation domes that dotted the surface of Anor. I wished I had one of my own, a private bubble of safety and security for me and all my kind, where the predators who had driven us to the edge of extinction could never reach us.

I returned to Wellington overwhelmed by the feeling that my attempt at a **date** with Neekor was a failure. I was no more certain about whether I wanted to be courted by her. If anything, I was *less* certain. It had nothing to do with her character – she was not like Powra – but rather a sinking feeling that had only intensified since we parted ways. She had given me a delighted salute and said, 'Gratitude for such an enjoyable outing, Daniel. It would please me to socialise with you again soon.' Not a word about the incident with Powra; no inquiry about how I felt. I watched her catch her transport, envisioning a future in which she would never understand me or what it meant to be Human. Somehow, I found that more depressing than anything Powra could have said.

Mother proved her telepathic ability again by stopping me before I left for service the next rote. 'Is everything well?'

I contemplated telling her. Mother must have navigated the same dilemma with Father, and perhaps that would make her an excellent source of advice. But the idea of telling her about a potential mate was, frankly, mortifying.

'Everything is well,' I replied.

Mother's eyes narrowed. 'Daniel, **a mother always knows**.'

Yet another saying mothers use to justify their unwelcome insertions into their offspring's lives. 'Knows what?'

'Whatever it is that needs knowing.'

'Then I guess you don't need to ask about it.'

I used her brief moment of hesitation to kiss her on the cheek and run for my shuttle.

Returning to service meant I could forget about Neekor for a while and lose myself in all the waiting correspondence. It would probably all be as anti-Human as Powra's comments, but it would be easier to process if it wasn't aimed directly at me.

I arrived at service, however, to find that I was not returning to thoughtcraft. Teemot stood by my terminal, grim.

'Greetings, Teemot,' I said nervously.

'Come with me, Daniel.'

He took me to a room, where Lincoln and two others – Humans – sat. One, a male, had incredibly pale, uncoated skin and a crop of floppy blond hair that fell into his eyes, making them flutter. Stains smattered the belly of his vest. The other was a more dignified female, with a straight back and pursed lip, dressed in a simple but elegant robe.

I already knew where these Humans were from.

'**Here he is**,' Lincoln said as I arrived, gesturing to the perch beside him. '**Just the man for the job.**'

I slid onto the seat while Teemot took the perch on my other side.

Lincoln cleared his throat. '**I now officially open this meeting to discuss the Authorisation of Britain.**'

The confirmation made me feel ill. It was happening: I was being allocated the squad's most complex Authorisation. This, I knew, would define my mission in the Hierarch from here on. **Make or break, sink or swim,** as the ancestors would say.

It is my pleasure to welcome our guests: Edward Moon, Leader of the Britain Deciding Body, and Anita Maccassa, Appeals Coordinator. Before we begin, I will ask that we each introduce ourselves –'

'We can dispel with the formalities,' Edward cut in. Even by Human standards that was rude. 'We've waited long enough for ChamCov to continue progressing our Authorisation. We want to know when that will be.'

Lincoln responded with a smile. 'This rotation, Edward. But if you would indulge me just one introduction, this is Kytoonoo 2 Daniel. I have assigned him to Britain.'

Edward stared at me through his curtain of hair, probably just as incredulous as I was.

'Really? The Authorisation of Great Britain in the hands of this juvenile? **No offence, boy.**'

As is typical of this confusing expression, it did nothing to alleviate offence.

'Daniel may be young,' said Lincoln, apparently unfazed, 'but he has proven himself a skilled Operator. He understands Common, our values –'

'Does he know anything about Britain?'

'Edward.' Lincoln's voice rose ever so slightly. 'I would not have assigned him to you if I did not consider him capable. You know me that well.'

Edward sized me up again. From the blinking of his root, I knew he was inspecting my profile. When he finished, he let out a sound hallway between a snort and a cough.

'So – Daniel, is it? – what *do* you know about Britain?'

Not a lot, was the truth. I did my best. 'Located in the Northern Hemisphere. Famously ruled by a Monarchy, was part of the European Union –'

'We dispute that,' Edward proclaimed. 'Britain was once one of the superpowers of the Human world. Our sovereign was so powerful they ruled over not only Britain, but many nations across **Earth**. That was one of our most substantial losses to assimilation by the Hierarch.' There was something in the way he delivered that line – a pointedness, an underscore of allegation – that struck me. It felt as if he was directly accusing me. '*Great* Britain *and Northern Ireland* was a mighty nation, but we are a shadow of what we once were. We have the European nations to the south reaching resolutions of exorbitant value; we have so-called Ireland seeking mediation separate from us. I hope you know what you are dealing with. I will not tolerate any further setbacks.'

I had never wanted to dislike another Human, but Edward was testing that.

'As I said, Edward,' Lincoln repeated, 'I would not have assigned Daniel if I did not consider him capable.'

Edward leaned back. 'Very well, then. Let us pick up where we left off.'

Anita connected her tree to ours and circulated the most recent set of constructs. 'The last time we engaged with ChamCov, we had just completed our Authorisation process.' She highlighted one of the constructs. 'Our draft Authorisation Record sets out everything our organisation has done to comply with the Hierarch's edict for Authorisation. We have demonstrated we have sufficient Rank to enter mediation on behalf of Britain with an approval rating of 77% by our population. All that is left is to be validated by the Hierarch.'

'Which we cannot do without first addressing the remaining 23% percent that represents Ireland,' said Teemot. 'The Ireland issue needs investigating before mediation can begin.'

'Has it not been investigated enough?' said Edward. 'We had this conversation with the last Operator countless times. Ireland is a part of Britain – always has been, always will be.'

'We need certainty,' said Teemot.

'Typical,' Edward snarled. 'You have a Leader of Britain sitting here, telling the Hierarch what our history is, and still it won't take us at our word.'

'Come now,' Lincoln said. 'It's not us you have to convince, but the Wellington Commission if they ever inquire into your Authorisation, which we both know is extremely probable with the likes of Sophie Winnra leading Ireland's opposition to you. If we deal with this issue now, we prevent it from becoming an even greater barrier to resolution later.'

That made sense to me, and I had no idea what any of them were talking about. Edward whipped his floppy fringe back and forth between Lincoln and Anita a few times before leaning back and folding his arms, apparently acquiescing

'May I make a suggestion?' said Teemot. 'Daniel will familiarise himself with your Authorisation progress and the Ireland issue. We will consider the situation and convene with you again to determine how we should proceed.'

Edward contemplated this, blinking through his fringe at Anita, whose face was inscrutable.

'Fine,' he said, slapping both hands on his knees. 'I want an update in five rotes' time.'

Lincoln subtly signalled I should remain in the room while he escorted Edward and Anita to the exit. As soon as they had left, Teemot let out a breath.

'Intriguing character, is he not?'

'That's one way of describing him,' I said.

Teemot barked with laughter. 'Ever the diplomat, Daniel. Try not to take offence. You get used to this sort of thing.'

A lot of people at ChamCov had said that to me. I wondered how long it was supposed to take.

'May I ask,' I said, eager not to dwell on Edward, 'about the previous Operator? I heard he was demoted. Is that true?'

Teemot sighed. 'Yes, unfortunately. It was this issue with Ireland that was the cause. He associated too closely with them. Refused to continue working on the Authorisation if it included Ireland.'

'Was the previous Operator Human, by any chance?'

Teemot gave a positive flick. Thought so.

'Apologies, Daniel,' Lincoln said on his return. 'I had intended to tell you I was allocating you to Britain, but Edward arrived unannounced. If I'd known –'

'No need for apologies.'

He held up a hand. 'You are gracious. But please, accept them. This is a priority Authorisation that will be extremely challenging – as I'm sure you gathered – and I do not currently have anyone else to assign. I had hoped to ease you into things. In any case, I meant what I said. I have total confidence in you.'

My chest swelled with pride. 'Gratitude, Lincoln.'

'Now,' he said, 'we don't have long to respond to Edward with our proposed next steps. Let's not waste any time.'

So I didn't. With Neekor and everything else pushed to the back of my mind, I returned to my terminal to immerse myself in Britain and its Authorisation process.

Anita, the Appeals Coordinator, had best summed it up: the Britain

Deciding Body had done everything it needed to prove it had the authority to represent Britain. The problem was that the definition of 'Britain' – which had been verified by ChamCov's own Chroniclers – included Ireland, which Ireland had refuted every step of the way.

'We're stuck in the middle,' I concluded to Mother that night, pacing back and forth across the main room. 'We have to decide which nation is telling the truth. No matter which way we go, we're going to be criticised. **Damned if you do, damned if you don't.**'

I didn't realise until I said it out loud that I was sympathising with the Hierarch.

Mother must have felt I was too. 'Well, what does the Hierarch expect? They wipe out most of our recorded histories, then get surprised when we don't know what they are. They created this mess, now they have to deal with it.'

'But that's the problem. They don't have to deal with it. I do. A Human.'

'Then show them how a Human would deal with it.'

I pretended I took something from Mother's undoubtedly wise advice. But, really, I had no idea what it was supposed to mean.

Edward's deadline crept closer, and the pressure of having nothing to show for my research mounted. I was trapped: if the Hierarch took Britain's side, and Authorised their definition as including Ireland, then it would undermine Ireland's independence. Conversely, if the Hierarch requested that Britain remove Ireland from its definition, that would be an undermining of Britain's independence. The terrifying threat of a Wellington Commission inquiry into either option hung over me. Both seemed to lead to an inevitable conclusion – a new breach of the Covenant of Wellington.

In desperation, I began scouring through the extensive evidence in ChamCov's database that had been provided by Ireland to prove its independence, hoping to find some tiny detail everyone had missed. I figured that Britain had the advantage in all this. They were the ones on the cusp of being Authorised, and the issue was less about them proving that that the definition included Ireland than about Ireland proving it didn't. But for every assertion Ireland made, Britain had already made one to counter it. Where Ireland said they were independent from Britain at the time the Noor arrived, Britain claimed Ireland had always been a part of them. Where Ireland claimed to have their own form of transfer separate to Common, Britain claimed to have once had many other forms of transfer besides Common. And where Ireland claimed to have once belonged to the fabled European Union, Britain claimed that they didn't, because Britain itself wasn't part of the European Union, so how could Ireland be?

The only thing that stuck out to me in all this evidence was a name, the same one I had heard Lincoln mention: Winnra 5 Sophie, the High Rank of Ireland. Her name and title were attached to every single piece of evidence that had been provided.

If there was some crucial piece of evidence that would prove Ireland's independence once and for all, she would be the one who could provide it. Contacting her directly seemed like a bold initiative. After all, she was the leader of an entire Human nation. I tried to imagine Mother receiving a communication request from a lowly Rank 2 servant of the Hierarch. This simulation didn't last long.

I contemplated suggesting to either Lincoln and Teemot that they contact her, with a script that I would prepare for them.

'We do not usually arrange communications between High Ranks of opposing nations and Commanders or Captains unless there is a specific message we need delivered,' Pa'zan cautioned me. 'Do you have such a message for the High Rank of Ireland?'

'Not really. I just want to hear what she has to say – for myself, more than anything.'

Pa'zan grimaced, but spoke politely. 'In our experience, opponents of Authorisations are not the most pleasant of conversationalists.'

I decided Sophie couldn't be a less pleasant conversationalist than Edward – if she even agreed to speak with me – and spent the rest of that rotation crafting a message that requested a direct conversation with her. It was my first formal communication as a Human servant of the Hierarch with another Human, so I laboured over it for hours, ensuring I introduced myself appropriately in Common, that my tone was respectful and so on. I hoped being Human would at least give me some advantage.

Within minutes of sending the message, I received a request for connection from the High Rank of Ireland herself. Stepping out of my pen and earshot from the rest of the squad, I took a breath then accepted it.

'Hello, ma'am,' I said, making sure to use the old term of address.

'Hello, Daniel.'

It was nice to not be addressed as 'boy', I thought. She had an impressive voice, reminding me of the commanding tone Mother used when she spoke in the debating chamber. 'You must be ChamCov's latest assignment to Britain's Authorisation.'

'Y-Yes, I am.'

'Then I assume you are familiar with Ireland's concerns in respect of that Authorisation?'

'Yes.'

'Can you tell me how ChamCov intends to address them?'

I hadn't expected control of the conversation to be wrested so efficiently from me. A discord of babbling Hierarch-speak rampaged through my head, a jumbled combination of *consideration–streamline–framework–synergy–moving forward* that almost leaked into the connection. When I realised I had been silent for several seconds, wading through the nonsense trying to string a sentence together, I panicked.

'I don't know.'

'Excuse me?'

Well, there was no point now in denying it. 'To be honest, Ms Winnra, I'm not sure how to address it. I'm still trying to figure that out. That's why I wanted to speak to you.'

There was a pause. I prepared for impact.

'I have a suggestion,' she said instead. 'A simple gathering. Between us, the Britain Deciding Body, and the Hierarch. Let us confront the issue of Britain's Authorisation and resolve it the old way, the right way – through healthy discussion and debate.'

Suddenly, I realised. That was it, the 'Human way' Mother had recommended: a good old-fashioned shouting-match. Part of me was beginning to wonder if Winnra 5 Sophie and Mother were somehow related.

'Do you think you can arrange that, Daniel?'

'I'll see what I can do.'

It was my first deployment for ChamCov, and we were late to the Irish-British gathering.

'Do not fret,' Teemot said cheerfully, while we waited outside the Irish parliament to be let in. 'This happens often.'

If there was one thing I'd learned since commencing service, it was that the Hierarch was obsessed with precedent. It absolved them of ever needing to do better.

I wished Lincoln had accompanied us, instead of travelling to the Italy Forum with Vuneen and Pa'zan. I had nothing against Teemot but, going into such a Human environment, the responsibility for navigating it would naturally fall to me. Something about being asked to wait was odd, like they were setting up for us to make an entrance. I'd understood that we were there to observe, but this suggested they expected more.

I distracted myself by inspecting the parliament's architecture. It was unremarkable compared to the ancient beauty of some parliamentary buildings, or to the sophistication of our own in Wellington. Neither grand nor distinctive, the building was hardly more than a chunk of stone with windows – similar to Noor architecture in that regard. And Ireland's drab climate, with the extra layer of darkness imposed by the skyways, made everything look grey.

But the appearance was irrelevant, I reminded myself. I should have been honoured to visit at all. I wondered if Teemot and I were the first representatives of the Hierarch to set foot on the Irish parliament grounds. If we were, we were about to set a precedent.

At last, the elderly male who had asked us to wait reappeared, gesturing towards the entrance. He led us through what once would have been security gates, now obsolete. The walls were peeling, revealing crumbling wood, and I could see through the holes in the floor. It was hard to believe that, even by Human standards, it would once have been a place of government.

As we walked the dilapidated halls, my sense that something was off grew. I sent a mental message to Teemot:

> They might ask us to give a **presentation**.

He shot me a blank expression so I clarified:

> A traditional form of transferring information.

Panic swept Teemot's face. But he wasn't the one who needed to be worried.

We arrived at an old wooden door and the elderly male opened it. The din inside died as we were ushered into the large room, not dissimilar to the debating chamber back home. The Irish Parliament contained tiered rows of dark wooden benches and seats arranged in a wide semi-circle around a podium. Standing behind it was a well-groomed female – Winnra 5 Sophie, who I recognised from her profile – who was watching us expectantly. Beside her were two empty chairs.

There was no denying it now. They had been setting up for us after all. I would have to give a **presentation**.

As we walked down the aisle that divided the seats, their occupants twisting round to stare at us, it must have dawned on Teemot what was about to happen. He sent a rushed message. I didn't need to open it to know that he was asking me if I could do the **presentation**. I told him I'd do my best, even though I'd never given one before. It was exactly why I would have preferred Lincoln here – I had no doubt he was capable of doing it.

We reached the podium, and the well-groomed female standing behind it gestured to two chairs placed to her side. She was Winnra 5 Sophie – I recognised her from her profile – and easily the most uncoated person I had ever seen. Aside from her short, combed red crown hair, there was not a single strand of fur on her white skin.

We sat and Sophie addressed the gathering by speaking into a black appendage attached to the podium, which amplified her voice. I believed this was called a **mic.**

I didn't listen to her: there wasn't a lot of time before she introduced me. I trawled the Core for relevant information, images I could project to the audience to support my address, and tried to recall what Mother had once told me about the basic structure –

Strong open and close, that's what people remember ... don't go into too much detail, key messages only ... oh and jokes! Don't forget to crack a joke here and there ...

'I would now like to invite the representatives of ChamCov to speak.'

Time had expired. For a moment I was frozen. I didn't have any pictures to show, and I couldn't think of any jokes. I thought of Mother: would she be angry with me? I wasn't even fluent in Common Transfer. But what else could I do? Teemot couldn't give a **presentation.** I didn't have a choice. The honour of the Hierarch was at stake. I could feel it on my shoulders as I rose to my feet and took the stand.

A hundred eyes were on me. They seemed sceptical, judgmental. I knew what they were thinking without needing to link my tree to theirs: who the **hell** is this coated **boy** and why does he think he can stand before us? Well, I decided, I would show them who I was. It would probably be the worst **presentation** they'd ever seen, but at the very least they would know I was Human, that I understood them.

'**Thank you, ma'am,**' I started slowly. First step done. '**And thank you all for having us. We're very pleased to be here.**'

Silence, but a few raised tendrils told me they were surprised at my greeting in Common. I decided I needed to give absolute confirmation of my Humanity sooner rather than later.

'**What's the difference between an Englishman and Irishman?**' I asked, casting a desperate eye across the room for the socially courteous response that would allow me to deliver the punchline. The question lingered painfully in the air and I glanced at Teemot, who was completely oblivious to the meaning of any of it and therefore no help at all. Just when I thought I was never going to be able to show my face in Ireland again, a reluctantly sympathetic voice reached me from the back of the room.

'What?'

I swallowed.

'I don't know, that's what we're here to find out.'

A cough rang out, followed by a snicker or two. I spotted a couple of stern expressions give way to suppressed smiles. I didn't dare look at Winnra 5 Sophie but I was certain I heard an exhalation of air through her nose. The crowd wasn't exactly rolling on the floor with laughter, but I had **broken the ice**, as the ancestors would say.

'My name is Daniel Kytoonoo,' I continued. 'I am an Operator at the Chamber of Covenant Resolutions, and this is my Captain, Teemot Partookoo.' He lifted a hand in an imitation of a wave.

Next was the hard part. I didn't really have the vocabulary to accurately convey why we were there, although the joke had basically summed it up. 'We want to talk to you all about the Authorisation process for the resolution of your Covenant imbalances. We hope this conversation goes well.'

That was it. All I had. I scrambled for more, but my mind had gone blank. Common terms slipped out of my grasp. I decided to finish before I made things any worse.

'Thank you.'

I braced myself. The reaction would be the test of whether my **presentation** was well received or not.

A single clap echoed, and it prompted another. Soon, applause filled the room. I let out the breath I'd been holding; it was barely a **presentation** at all but I must have done enough to earn their respect. I resumed my seat, and Sophie returned to the podium.

While she thanked me for my **presentation** and moved into her own – a beautifully-designed traditional **PowerPoint** complete with transition animations and even an ancient **meme** that elicited a hearty laugh from the audience – Teemot messaged me:

That was amazing, my friend.
Well done.

Gratitude, but it was actually quite poor by
Human standards.

Better than I can do.

I appreciated the sentiment, but he didn't understand the position I had put myself in. I just hoped I'd be able to tell Mother about it in my own words before anything showed up in her newsfeed.

Sophie's **presentation** turned out to be a masterclass. In an informative but succinct manner, she took us on a journey through Ireland's history, with supporting evidence by recognised Chroniclers, and even made several inferences that their inclusion in Britain's definition wasn't the first time Britain had tried to erase Irish identity. I had to admit that I was convinced. She finished with a single quote displayed on the screens: '**YOLO**'. It rightfully received a standing ovation.

'That brings us to our noonbreak,' she said once the audience resumed their seats. She gestured towards the far corner of the room, where a door was opened by the same male who led us there. 'We will resume proceedings in an hour.'

Chatter rose and Sophie gave me an appreciative nod before signalling for us to join the throng of people moving into the next room – a fraction of the larger one's size, and containing only a few mats laid out on the floor with trays of sustenance, and squares of soft, white paper. On the way, Teemot was pulled aside by the British Appeals Coordinator, Anita, leaving me to acquire sustenance alone. I waited for everyone else to fill their trays until a kindly old female handed me one and nudged me towards the mats. I picked a few pieces of parowa bread and a handful of meeko berries, then a male appeared at my side, inspecting my tray. He looked an equivalent age to mine.

'Not into **black pudding**?' He pointed at another tray with several slices of dark material.

'No, gratitude.' I'd heard the delicacy used to be made with animal meat. 'I have quite the Alien stomach.'

'More for me, then.' He took two pieces then jerked his head at me. 'That's a nice robe.'

It was only then that I realised Teemot and I were the only people in the room wearing robes.

I said, 'It's the only one I've got.'

He said, 'One more than me.'

I passed noonbreak sitting by the elderly female who had welcomed me to the consumption mats. She asked me where I was from, and her face lit up when I told her New Zealand. She said she had relatives in New Zealand, and we tried in vain to identify a link between our clans. Before noonbreak ended, she admitted that, while the Authorisation process had been divisive for Ireland, she didn't have a strong opinion on it. She said she was well aware she was elderly, and only wished to see Ireland's imbalances resolved one way or another before she **met her maker**, as her ancestors would say.

I told her the Hierarch would do its best to reach resolution as soon as possible, even though I had no authority to give that promise. It just felt like the right thing to say. I suspected she was aware of the emptiness of my words, but she humoured me with a smile anyway.

Soon we were invited back into the main room. I thanked the old female for her company and found Teemot, who had spent so long talking with Anita that he hadn't eaten, and we were directed back to our seats near the podium.

Sophie resumed the proceedings. 'I now invite the Head of the Britain Deciding Body to talk us through what benefits to Ireland there would be if we were to join their Authorisation.'

Edward waddled up to the podium, eyes fluttering at Sophie through his hair. He moved the **mic** closer to his mouth, and for the next hour he attempted to explain why Ireland should remain included in Britain's Authority, an argument that seemed to hinge on a single point: Ireland was geographically close to Britain. He seemed to lose track of even that argument fairly quickly, then talking about how great the Britain Deciding

Body was under his leadership and why it deserved the Rank to represent Ireland in mediation. He made a lot of promises about what reparations he would seek, none of which seemed specific to Ireland. By the time he was finished, a self-satisfied beam stretching his face, most of the room seemed to be wondering what case he had even made – me included. Even Sophie let her façade drop ever so slightly with a curl of her lip.

Queries were taken from the floor, with Anita joining Edward at the podium. I recognised many of the inquirers' names as people who had signed the same correspondence that Winnra 5 Sophie had. They asked what reparations the Deciding Body would seek for imbalances like the Galway Skirmish and whether they would support the revitalisation of Gaelic Transfer.

'Edward has failed,' Teemot muttered to me. 'This was his opportunity to make the case for Ireland's inclusion, to establish himself as the High Rank who can provide for them. He has not swayed a single one.'

'Maybe we should consider a separate Irish Authorisation,' I said.

'That will not happen, Daniel. Ireland must be included in Britain's Authorisation. The entire purpose of this gathering was to convince Ireland to agree to that.'

I stared at Teemot, wondering if I'd missed something. That wasn't why I'd arranged the gathering for Winnra 5 Sophie at all.

'But it's clear they *were* independent from Britain,' I said. 'And they seem entirely capable of representing themselves. Edward doesn't have the first clue about their imbalances.'

'That's Hierarch edict for you,' Teemot said with a shrug. 'Anyway, some sort of closure needs to occur. We must depart soon for our shuttle.'

I didn't understand what Teemot meant about Hierarch edict, but I would figure it out later. According to my timetracker, our allotment was indeed running out, and the gathering was taking a turn for the worse. Anita was trying to speak over a number of disgruntled voices. Another female, younger even than me, addressed her: 'So what you're really saying is: you only want Ireland included because it increases the value of your reparations?'

'Yes!' Edward snapped, and the effect was like a detonation; noise exploded in the room and the entire meeting seemed to collapse on itself. People leaped to their feet, charged down the aisles, and thrust fingers at Edward, who held up his middle one in response. Time was disappearing, and I wondered how on **Earth** we could leave in the middle of it all. For some reason, the word 'precedent' was repeating in my head.

'Excuse me, everyone,' Teemot called, rising to his feet. The clamour faded as all eyes turned to him. 'I apologise for the interjection. However, I feel obligated to insert myself here.'

In that moment, I felt like Teemot was the bravest person I knew.

'What Edward has said is technically correct. If Ireland is included in Britain's Authorisation, the value of reparations made through the resolution will increase to reflect that.'

Someone let out a low, '**Boo**'. Teemot would have understood the intent, if not the word.

'What I wish to clarify,' he continued, 'is that Ireland's inclusion is not the fault of the Deciding Body. The Deciding Body did not design this process. They are only following the edict declared by the Hierarch. I understand it is divisive. I understand it is disempowering. But let me be clear: it is the Hierarch's process. Therefore, I implore you: do not direct your criticism at the Deciding Body. Direct it at me – direct it at the Hierarch.'

The Irish didn't hesitate. Teemot received a barrage of verbal and likely mental abuse that would have overwhelmed me. The young female who had held the flame to Edward's spark descended from her seat to the centre of the room and unleashed a tirade in Common that brought her to tears. Teemot took it all, waiting for the deluge to end.

'Once again, I apologise profusely,' he said after taking a moment to compose himself, 'and I appreciate the strength of emotion. I must apologise one more time, for Daniel and I now need to depart.'

We were **booed** from the building. How typical, I thought, for the Hierarch to come here, sow dissension, then leave the Humans to pick up after them, while they jet back to Kappeetar on the comfortable shuttle that Ireland's tithes bought them. What a precedent we had set.

As we clambered into our shuttle, my head was still back in that room. I'd thought they would see me differently. That my name and my Common Transfer established that I was on their side. That I was one of them. But their words were meant for me as well as Teemot. To them, I was no different than him. I saw myself in their angry eyes.

I was not Human. I was a servant of the Hierarch.

The return journey to Kappeetar seemed longer for its silence. We were almost back when Teemot finally spoke.

'We are fortunate to have escaped with our lives,' he joked.

I mustered a weak chuckle.

'That young female who was so enraged; I gathered she was insulting us. What did she say?'

I wasn't quite sure how to express it. 'She … well, among other things … she called us probably the most offensive thing a Human could in Common Transfer.'

One of Teemot's tendrils flexed. 'Which is?'

'**Cunts.**' I left out '**fucking**' – he wouldn't have grasped the versatility of the word.

His root flashed as he searched the Core for the term.

Knowing he wouldn't find it, I explained, 'It's a derogatory word meaning … a female's genitals.'

'Oh.' He frowned. 'I am afraid I do not understand the insult. What is offensive about a female's genitals?'

'I … don't know,' I replied. I hadn't thought about it before. I supposed Humans had to be a bit creative with our insults. All Aliens needed to do was point out how much lower in Rank you were than them.

After a period of quiet, Teemot shrugged. 'What else did they call us?'

I repeated as many of the insults as I could remember, noting how many of them were also based on Human genitalia. But I didn't tell him the insult that was meant specifically for me. I didn't want him to know what a **turncoat** is.

I must have stood outside the gateway to Mother's and Father's dwelling for a good ten minutes. I'd had the entire return journey to Wellington to think about what I was going to tell Mother, but nothing had come to mind. I was a better crafter than orator, but I didn't want to relive the experience by crafting an account of it to share with her. I had checked the **net**, too. There weren't many who still used the ancient, pre-assimilation network anymore but you never know. Thankfully, no footage of me seemed to have surfaced on it.

As with the Neekor issue, I contemplated not telling Mother at all. The idea had, as the ancestors would say, **see-sawed** the whole way home, but I knew the answer all along. I couldn't hide this one from her.

I opened the gate and stepped inside. Mother and Father were in their expected positions – Mother working and Father viewing entertainments.

'Welcome home,' said Mother, setting down a handful of documents.

'How was your first deployment?' Father asked.

It was difficult to find the words. 'I need to tell you something.'

Father detected that this was a Human issue, so left Mother and me to it while he prepared darkmeal. I took a seat with Mother and recounted the entire experience to her. She listened intently, without interrupting or asking questions. The only part I left out was being called a **turncoat**. I was never going to admit that to her.

When I finished, she was silent, processing everything. I waited, unable to look her in the eye.

'They should never have put you in that position,' she eventually said. 'Forcing a Rank 2 to address another nation's government? Disgraceful. Do they not send social support or something like it when you are deployed into the field?'

'Normally they do. They didn't think it was necessary for this gathering. We were only meant to observe.'

'They should have known better.' Mother stood, which was never a good sign. 'This Captain – Teemot – why didn't he **present?**'

'He wasn't capable.'

'That's not your concern. This is the problem with these Aliens in the Hierarch. They don't bother to learn our ways. They conscript our people in to perform these tasks, not understanding the compromised position it puts us in, then cast us aside when we're no longer needed.' Hands on hips, she looked down at me. 'I am coming to ChamCov tomorrow with you. They need to know what they've done.'

I rose to my own feet. 'No, Mother –'

'What if you had made an error, or humiliated yourself? If it was uploaded to the **net**, your reputation – and New Zealand's – could be ruined for revolutions, for the rest of your life and beyond. Look at the **Freedom Movement**. I still wonder how we're ever going to live that down …'

'Mother, please,' I insisted. 'You said it yourself: I need to make my own **destiny**. I can handle this.'

She stared at me, one tendril raised. I held her stare until the tendril dropped. 'I'm just worried about you. Promise me you will discuss this with them.'

I had thought about that, too. It was hard enough raising it with Mother, let alone the Hierarch itself. I was doubtful anything would be done about it. But I knew Mother wouldn't let this go until I gave her my word, so I did.

I spent the next rote's commute crafting what I would say about the gathering. I decided I would raise it with Lincoln, who I was confident would understand my feelings. I also wanted to discuss his and Teemot's reasons for agreeing to the gathering at all. Not that I intended to accuse them of anything underhanded, but the more I thought about it, the more it seemed that they hadn't agreed to the gathering because they thought a mutually beneficial outcome might be reached. Rather, that was only what they wanted it to look like. So that, when the Wellington Commission inevitably inquired into the Authorisation, they could point to the gathering and say, 'Well, we tried to make them cooperate and they wouldn't!'

When I arrived at the House of Balance, I went straight to Morgan's terminal and asked if I could speak with Lincoln.

'Apologies, Daniel, he's still in Rome. The Forum was extended.'

'Do you know when he's expected back?'

She flicked her tendrils negatively. 'The reports from Vuneen suggest the Forum could go on at least another rote.' At last, she looked up from her terminal. 'Everything okay?'

'Yes, it's fine,' I lied.

I trudged back to my pen, where Moolas and Phil greeted me cheerfully. I wished Pa'zan, who was with Vuneen and Lincoln at the Italy Forum, was there so I could at least debrief with him. I didn't feel like discussing the meeting with these two, so when they asked about it, I lied again that it had gone as well as it could have. I told them that there was no real outcome, but it was important that the gathering was held. The irony that I had so easily adopted what I assumed was Lincoln's and Teemot's reasoning for the event wasn't lost on me.

'Sometimes that's all we can do,' Phil said in what he probably thought was a sage tone. 'Create the space for Humans to make their own decisions and hope for the best.'

Later that morning, I felt a tap on the shoulder. Teemot stood beside me. 'Can I speak to you? Privately?'

That was odd. Teemot wasn't one for serious conversation. I nevertheless agreed and we found a vacant room.

'Are you well, Daniel?' he asked once we were seated. 'Truthfully?'

There was no point lying to him. 'Was it that obvious?'

'I noticed you looking at images of those extinct animals – **cats**? It seemed unusual.'

I sighed and flicked positively. 'A traditional form of self-therapy.'

'Previous rotation was difficult for you, wasn't it?'

'I know there was nothing you could do, Teemot. It's just … giving a **presentation** like that is a very risky thing for a Human to do. You don't usually make addresses like that unless you are of sufficient standing and you have revolutions of experience at it. And then the way it ended …'

Teemot's tendrils drooped slightly. 'Please allow me to apologise, Daniel. We were ill-prepared, and it was my responsibility.'

'Gratitude, Teemot, but I should have known. I'm Human; I should have anticipated that was likely to happen –'

'I am the Captain, Daniel. I am responsible for your wellbeing while in service to ChamCov. I may not understand the complexities of Human custom but I understand now I put you in a compromised position. It will not happen again – I give you my commitment.'

I'd had esteem for Teemot before, but this earned him my respect. 'Much gratitude, Teemot. That means a lot to me.'

He waved it off and said, 'Now, then. The other thing we need to discuss is our next step following that gathering. Edward and Sophie have both contacted me. Edward has demanded that we seek the Lord's Authorisation of them immediately. Sophie has confirmed that Ireland wants a separate Authorisation and, if the Hierarch validates Britain with Ireland included, they'll seek an urgent inquiry by the Wellington Commission.'

Back to square one, as the ancestors would say. 'We've achieved nothing, Teemot.'

'I expected as much,' he said, exhaling. 'Quite the dilemma we have. I am afraid there is little more we can do other than let the inquiry run its course.'

I wasn't sure I'd heard correctly. 'You're going to proceed with validating Britain's Authority?'

'What else can we do? Neither side is going to give in.'

'We could seek a separate Authorisation for Ireland. If you give me time, I can craft a case for it –'

'It will not work, Daniel,' Teemot said, more softly than he had the rote before. 'The Lord has decreed he will not recognise any nations other than those he already has.'

'Why not?' I couldn't fathom why an Alien Lord would just decide he wouldn't recognise the existence of independent Human nations.

'The Hierarch is on a deadline for resolving all Covenant imbalances, one that is looking increasingly unlikely to be met. The general population is fatigued and it is showing – the Hierarch is losing Rank over it daily. If the Lord was to recognise Ireland separately, it would be another delay. And if Ireland is recognised, how many other small nations will seek separate Authorisation? How much more will the resolution process be prolonged? The Hierarch cannot afford to do it.'

I could feel my passive, compliant Human exterior crumbling. It wasn't that Teemot's explanation didn't make sense – there was always a reason for everything the Hierarch did – but I couldn't accept it.

'It's just wrong,' I said, before I knew it. A slip I never should have made. 'Apologies, Teemot, I –'

'I know it is wrong, Daniel.'

An awkward silence came between us. I wanted to ask: if he knew it was wrong, then what was he going to do about it? An answer came anyway.

'I do not know if this will be of any use to you, but I would like to share with you perhaps the one thing, above all, I have learned serving the Hierarch on Teerin' Ho.' This was not the loud, boisterous Teemot I was familiar with. 'There are no absolutes in this reality. There is no such thing as perfection, and nothing is guaranteed to anybody. The galaxy is complex, inhabited by countless entities with infinitely varying perceptions and beliefs. It is impossible to do good by every single one of them. All one can do is their best for as many of them as one can.'

I wasn't sure I agreed. That may be the view of Aliens, I thought, but it was counter to everything Humans believed was right, just, and fair.

'I serve the Hierarch here, on Teerin' Ho,' Teemot continued, 'because the resolution process is like no other anti-assimilation initiative in the galaxy. Where I am from, in Kaanurra, the Hierarch has reached exactly one resolution with just one nation. One nation out of thousands. This is a world where entire generations of offspring were forcibly removed from their homes and institutionalised in Empiric

Observatories. Entire generations of beings who lost everything: their transfer, culture, and they never saw their parents again. My grandfather was one of them.'

Shame settled on me. So, he wasn't Alien after all.

'I have nothing to give my people back in Kaanurra. I do not speak their transfer, I do not even know who they are. And even if I did, it is too late for them. They will never get back a fraction of what Humans can get back through resolutions – even though that itself is but a fraction of what they lost too.' He paused, then laughed, but not in his usual, booming way. 'I do not mean to imply being assimilated is some sort of competition. Only that, rightly or wrongly, Covenant resolutions can still do a lot of good. You may disagree, but for me, some good is better than none.'

'You would rather Britain be Authorised at Ireland's expense,' I eventually said, 'than neither nation be Authorised at all.'

Teemot gave a long, slow, positive flick. 'If my nation – whoever they are – were in Ireland's position, I would want them to take what they could get.'

He said I could have the room to myself for a while longer. I thought about New Zealand, and if, when the time came, I would be willing for us to settle for whatever we were given. No amount of **cat** images could help me decide.

The rest of the week passed in a haze. Words echoed in my head from Lincoln, Teemot, Mother, Hayden. The word **turncoat** repeated over and over. Less than a revolution into service and I had already done what the Hierarch did best: broken my promise.

To complicate matters, Neekor was eager to socialise again and I couldn't find the motivation to respond. The question of whether I wanted to be courted by her seemed trivial next to everything else.

Reality caught up to me when Lincoln, back from the Italy Forum, pulled me aside.

'Ever heard the expression **"going nuclear?"**' he asked in a hushed tone. I figured it must be an American thing and flicked negatively.

'Edward is escalating matters. He's given us three rotes to Authorise Britain or he's going to the propagation about it.'

It was official: Edward had become the first ever Human I disliked.

'He's threatening us?'

'Essentially, yes. He is calling it an ultimatum,' Lincoln replied. 'Look, Daniel, frankly I don't care if he goes to the propagation over this. As far as I'm concerned, the propagation is breaking this story one way or the other. What I care about is the fact that we need to conduct a mediation to resolve this nation's imbalances. I do not want it to start off this way.'

'Does that mean you want me to craft the Authorisation bid? Even if we haven't resolved the Ireland issue?'

Lincoln gave me what I thought was a sad smile. 'I don't want you to do anything you don't want to do, Daniel.'

I knew what he meant. I had to put my Humanity aside in order to serve the great machine that was the Hierarch.

I trudged back to my terminal. Ireland deserved their own resolution. They were their own nation, with their own interests and grievances. They deserved the right to resolve them on their own terms. I knew this now, but I also knew that the Hierarch doesn't change easily. Teemot had shown me why it would never agree to separate Authorisation for Ireland.

But Mother had said to show them how Humans deal with an issue. It dawned on me that the 'Human way' was not, as I'd thought, to shout at each other until the problem exploded in our faces. Our ancestors were renowned for their ingenuity and creativity, their ability to problem-solve – just like our planet's mascot, the cunning rat. There must be a way, I convinced myself. There must be a way through.

An outright change in Hierarch edict allowing separate Authorisation for Ireland was clearly out of the question. It was the type of change that maybe, one day, I would be able to influence. But I had to accept that, for now, as a lowly Rank 2 Operator, I couldn't. I would have to find something else, something smaller, that could be done for Ireland within the limitations of Hierarch edict. If the Britain Deciding Body was Authorised to represent Ireland, then how could its accountability to Ireland be assured?

Then it hit me. The simplest, most straightforward of Human representation models: **co-governance.**

I turned to Pa'zan. 'Are there examples of Authorisations made with conditions?'

'I do not know of any myself,' he replied, before swivelling in Vuneen's direction and asking her the same question.

'I can recall one,' she said. 'South Africa. I remember their representative entity's Authorisation was conditional on updating their citizen register. But that was before the decree that made updated registers an absolute requirement. I am not aware of any conditional Authorisations since.'

I thanked Vuneen and dived back into the Core, soon locating South Africa's Authority Record. It was indeed old, over ten revs in fact. But it had exactly what I was searching for: a statement clarifying that it would only be considered valid by the Hierarch if it contained an active, accurate register of South Africa's population. An addendum to the Record was added half a rev later – which contained the required register.

I duplicated the statement of conditional Authorisation, substituted the condition with one of my own crafting, and inserted it into my bid. The Britain Deciding Body might get the Authority to represent Ireland, I thought, but not without the involvement of, at the very least, Winnra 5 Sophie.

The bid was complete. I made the final polishes, published the file, downloaded it from the Core to my tree, then hurried across the level to Lincoln's terminal. I wanted to discuss it with him in person.

He looked up, one tendril lifted curiously. 'That was quick.'

'I have the bid,' I said breathlessly. 'But I added something.'

Lincoln's surprised expression became one of concern, making my coat bristle. I pushed on.

'It's to seek a conditional Authorisation – it's been done before, South Africa –'

'Just transfer me the bid.'

I shut my mouth and did as he asked. His eyes glossed over while he processed the construct and I waited anxiously until he recited aloud, '"We seek your validation of the Britain Deciding Body's Authority to mediate the resolution of Britain's Covenant imbalances on the condition that a standing position be held by the High Rank of Ireland, who is to be given the full and equal Rank of existing members of the Britain Deciding Body."' The colour of his eyes returned in a piercing stare. 'Edward will never agree to this condition.'

'The decision isn't Edward's, though. It's the Lord's.'

Lincoln shook his head. 'This would be an abuse of the Hierarch's Rank, Daniel. To deliberately undermine Britain's autonomy.'

'But it's already undermined Ireland's.' I knew I was speaking out of turn, that I was risking demotion speaking to a Commander like this. I pushed on. 'If Hierarch edict dictates what it can't do, then why can't it be utilised for what it *can* do? Hierarch edict decides what representative models are appropriate, and there's nothing preventing it from imposing conditions on an Authorisation. In fact, there's precedent for it. This is the only way we can ensure Ireland gets a say in their resolution without breaching Hierarch edict.'

I forced myself to hold Lincoln's gaze. This was where I would make my stand – in the place where the values of Humanity clashed with the strict rule of the Hierarch's edict. There had to be a world in which both could co-exist, and if there wasn't, then I would create it. A place where both were realised and neither were compromised. Because wasn't that what honouring the Covenant of Wellington really was?

Finally, a smile broke on Lincoln's face. 'You're beginning to understand how the machine works.'

I let out a relieved breath. 'Yeah, I think I am.'

With my bid approved by Lincoln and submitted to the Lord, I finally felt like the time had come. I'd established myself as a capable Operator within ChamCov's Europe Authorisation Squad, and a valuable servant of the Hierarch. I could see the path towards Rank 3 and beyond. I was ready to leave the keep of Clan Kytoonoo of Wellington.

Father was more than willing to help me search for a dwelling of my own. Mother, on the other hand, took a while to come to terms with my impending departure. She kept trying to suggest dwellings in Wellington, the suitability of which she based solely on how close they were to her and Father's dwelling. I had to break it to her that this defeated the purpose of relocating at all, after which she begrudgingly left us to it.

In the end, I was successful in purchasing a tiny but adequate dwelling in Central Residential District 1, the only district I could afford. It was in one of the myriad rod-like structures that characterised the district, each containing countless identical dwelling units stacked on top of one another, so high they almost reached the second tier of Kappeetar. I knew I wouldn't mind the cramped conditions, though, or the commuting distance to the House District – not much shorter than the one from Wellington. The tiny space would be mine, a privilege so many Humans had never been able to claw back from the Aliens who took it from us. It would be that private bubble of sanctuary I had craved since the trip to Anor, even if only a fraction of the size.

I couldn't leave without telling Hayden. Somehow, that obligation intimidated me more than having to tell Mother about the Irish gathering. It was hard not to feel guilty as we had only just reunited. And, of course, there was the fact that his father was terminally ill and he was still under confinement for imbalance.

Or, so I thought. Having amassed another impressive pile of high-fat and -sucrose sustenance and a couple of pure joy-infused cutting charges to soften the blow, I made my way to Hayden's father's dwelling only to find Hayden leaning on its boundary, with the biggest grin I think I had ever seen on his face. At my puzzled expression, he said, 'My cycle is up – confinement finished two rotes ago!'

'Fantastic,' I said, pretending not to be irritated that he hadn't told me earlier, so he could have come to me instead and I wouldn't have had to lug my sustenance-bribe all the way over there.

'And,' he continued, pushing off the boundary, 'Father's scan results came back: his neoplasm has stalled!'

'Stalled?'

'It's stopped growing. He was told that it will probably resume at some point, but for now it seems to be under control. We have a bit more time than we thought!'

He hugged me before I could say anything. Even if I'd had the right words, Hayden's embrace was so tight I wouldn't have been able to say them. So I just returned it, hoping that was enough.

Over Hayden's shoulder, I saw the gate of his dwelling was still covered by the sheet of construction material.

Hayden released me and, able to breathe again, I asked, 'Is he inside? Your father?'

'Yeah, but he's in his sleep capsule. Still has to keep taking his medication, even with the news.'

I glanced at the construction sheet again. Hayden didn't seem to realise that I had noticed it. 'Oh, well, it would be good to see him when he wakes.'

'I've been cooped up inside for the last cycle, Daniel,' Hayden said with a stretch. 'I had somewhere else in mind.'

He jerked his head upward, towards the peak of Tungee'kyor (real name: **Mount Victoria**) that overlooked the neighbourhood.

'Come on.'

I still had a bulging pack of sustenance to carry, and I couldn't take my eyes off the construction sheet that shouldn't have still been there. But that same Mutt with her hungry gaze was watching me from her porch, so I followed. I didn't want to complain anyway, not when he seemed so happy for once, and I knew I had only bad news to lay on him.

I may have previously mentioned that Hayden was a competent athlete in his adolescence. I doubted he still participated in any physical activity beyond what was necessary, but he seemed to have retained the physical capability of his youth despite his slim frame. By the time I made it to the summit of Tungee'kyor, panting hideously, he had already vaulted the flimsy barriers erected by the House of Preservation and begun scaling the ruins that sat atop its very peak.

'Keep up, Daniel!' he called over his shoulder.

Resisting the urge to leave my peace offering of sustenance, I gritted my teeth and pushed on. Even after all these revs, I knew the way, through the tangled overgrowth and the barricades that we had broken on previous trips. At last, after finding the worn steps that the ancestors had carved into the peak, and climbing them until they flattened into a broad, crumbling platform overgrown with weeds, I arrived.

Hayden was waiting at the opposite end of the platform, legs dangling over its jagged edge.

'You made it,' he joked. In reply, I dumped the pack of sustenance next to him. He barely registered it. His gaze was fixed instead on the water in the bay, greyer and rougher than the last time we viewed it from the waterfront. On rotes like these the water did a much poorer job of distracting from the skyways.

I took a seat beside Hayden and followed his view, wondering why the House of Preservation wanted to keep us out of this place so badly when all we wanted to use it for was the same thing the ancestors had.

'You're relocating to Kappeetar, aren't you?' he said abruptly.

I turned to him.

'Had a feeling,' he added, only now reaching into the pack to withdraw a pair of sucro-balls. 'Knew it was coming.'

I was beginning to wonder if, actually, telepathy was a universal Human skill that I somehow hadn't inherited.

'Apologies, Hayden.'

He shrugged. 'What for?'

There was an answer to this. I just didn't know how to give it.

'It's fine,' Hayden said, speaking yet again to save me from having to. 'You're just doing what you have to do.'

I had a flash of memory; the distraught face of that young Irish woman, her screaming voice echoing in my head.

'I'm trying,' I said.

'I know.'

It was quiet for a while, no sound between us but the soft whistle of the wind and the regular rustle of a whole packet of sucro-balls, the steady crunch of two packs of fried dough sticks, the hiss from a canister each of vitamin gel, the fizz of five sour strips, and the odd belch that went echoing down the cliff-face below.

Then Hayden reached into a pack of his own and withdrew what, at first glance, looked like a cutter.

'Well, in commemoration of our final gathering here in Wellington,' he began with some ceremony, 'I've brought us a little something to celebrate.'

He held the cutter out to me, and I was about to take it when I realised it wasn't a cutter at all. The delivery unit was too large, too sharp, and I could see where the panelling had been removed and resealed after whatever modifications had been done to it. I'd never seen a real cleaver before, but had heard enough.

'Where did you get this?'

'Doesn't matter. Just give it a go. Here.'

He dropped it into my hands. It was heavier than any cutter would be. I still couldn't take my eyes off the delivery unit, which looked powerful enough to fry my brain completely. I felt dirty holding it, and angry. Like it was a weapon for a murder in which I was now complicit.

I threw it over the edge of the cliff.

It seemed to take Hayden a few seconds to understand what I'd done. He watched it soar out over the treetops, his eyes gradually widening in realisation, until it tumbled out of sight. Then he scrambled to his feet, as if the extra few feet of height would somehow help him find wherever it had fallen.

'What the **fuck** did you do that for?'

'Those things kill people, Hayden.'

'How the **fuck** would you know?' It was like he had transformed, towering over me, teeth bared, fists clenched. 'Seriously, Daniel – how would you know?'

'Because I've studied it, Hayden. I've seen what that stuff does to people, how many die from it. And do you know who dies the most?'

'Oh, **fuck off** with your Academy **shit**. Sitting up there in the big city with your head in the clouds. You don't know **shit**, Daniel. Do you have any idea how much that cost me?'

'Let me guess: about as much as the Rank I gave you to fix your gate?'

I'll never forget the glare he gave me then. Like he could have thrown me off the cliff too. I almost wish he did. It might have been preferable to what he did next.

He bent down, picked up his empty pack (and a handful of fried dough sticks), then left. Didn't say a word more. I could almost hear it, the word he might have said, burning unspoken in the air between us. But he just left me there, looking down at the rest of Wellington, alone.

And it was the first time in my existence that I did feel truly alone. Not in the Alien sense, which was a simple, physical solitude. It was more than that. I wasn't just an anomaly among my people. There wasn't a place for me among them. Not at the Clan Lounge, not at parliament. Not in **Oriental Bay**, not in all of Wellington. I could see every part of it from where I stood, and there wasn't one where I felt I belonged.

But if not there, then where? I wasn't convinced that there was a place for me in Kappeetar, either. Even when Mother and Father delivered me to my newly purchased dwelling and began unpacking for me, the space didn't feel like I thought it would. It had all my material possessions – my sleep capsule, my attire storage, the **writing** device that Mother carefully placed in the corner that she deemed appropriate for such a treasure. But that was all it was: space, in which I was permitted to exist, and nothing more. There was no one else to share that existence with, nothing connecting me to it beyond the gravity keeping my feet on its floor.

When everything was unpacked, and Mother and Father started to say their farewells, I realised that I didn't want them to go.

'You will be safe here, in this big Alien city?' Mother whispered in my ear. I pondered it for a moment: in Kappeetar I was a minority, I could barely afford anything, and I was as likely to get hit by a circuit runner as I was to get mugged just outside my dwelling door. But that wasn't what she meant.

'I'll be fine, Mother,' I told her. I hoped she was more convinced than I was.

'You can always come home. I know this Hierarch needs you now, but there is always that seat in parliament for you too, remember?'

I didn't **have the heart**, as the ancestors would say, to tell her that I had already decided I could never fill that seat. So, I just nodded, and she stepped aside to let Father salute me.

'Go well, Daniel,' he said. He lifted a hand and, after some hesitation, put it on my shoulder. It was the first time I could recall him attempting an actual display of Human affection, and as awkward as it was, it meant more to me than he would ever know. I patted his hand and that seemed to be all the validation he needed. He retrieved his hand then used it for a rigid Alien salute, as if to make up for the Humanness he had just practised.

Mother could find no more convenient excuses to delay their departure. They left, and in their absence I felt empty, as if they took some vital part of me with them.

I didn't know what to do with myself. Inspecting the features of my new dwelling took only a couple of turns. I tried finding something interesting or entertaining to view in the Core. But even with its infinite choices, nothing could hold my attention. Usually when I felt listless, I fired up the **writing** device and channelled the feeling into it. That didn't work either. I sat staring at a blank screen for what felt like over an hour, then, after accepting that a whole new construct just wasn't going to happen, I began cycling through existing projects, hoping I could at least muster the motivation to continue working on one.

That's when I came across it:

I went to the shop
To buy a drink

It made me think of pennoo, and the tiny outlet Neekor and I fre-
quented. I'd barely thought about Neekor since the disastrous date
on Anor. What was worse, I had ignored her subsequent communications in a deliberate attempt to avoid having to think about it. I knew
that needed rectifying first and foremost but, feeling as intensely
alone as I did, I found myself craving that sensation of weightlessness
I had in her presence, of being unbound from the planet's clutches.
I thought if I could capture that feeling again, it wouldn't matter
that I didn't belong anywhere, that there was nowhere to ground me,
because I would be drifting, floating wherever that feeling would take
me.

'Daniel?' Neekor accepted my request with a tinge of surprise in her
mental voice.

'Neekor, greetings –'

'You did not respond to my communications.' Her tone was icy. 'I
briefly speculated whether some tragedy had befallen you, but according to your profile no such thing has occurred.'

'No, it hasn't, Neekor. Apologies.' I hoped the desperation in my
voice wasn't too obvious. 'The truth is …'

I caught myself. How to explain to her exactly what had been going
on in my head for the past few weeks? I barely understood it all myself
and I was Human.

'Can I see you?' I asked, before I realised what I was doing.

There was a pause that felt too long to be good, then she said, 'See
me? As in, you wish to socialise again? Now?'

'If you are available?'

Another pause that was even more unbearable than the last. Then,
'At which location, and at which time?'

I hadn't actually expected to get this far. 'How about a walk along
the Edge? In half an hour?'

'I shall meet you there.'

One of the few benefits of my new dwelling was its proximity to a sub-street terminus. Unlike the torturous cross-district commute to ChamCov, it was a reasonably short ride to Leisure District 1, with its multitude of parks, recreational facilities, and other entertainment venues. But none of those features outshone my favourite place in all of Kappeetar: the Edge. Aliens never went there, because they didn't understand its appeal. And the timing was perfect: by the time I arrived, Aar was about to set.

Neekor was waiting by the entrance to the huge, flat expanse of concrete. As expected, there were few others around – only a few Humans dotted the Edge's boundary. I hurried over to her, eager not to keep her waiting any longer than I already had. She greeted me with a single lifted tendril – a wordless instruction to explain myself.

'Neekor, sincerest apologies about not contacting you after Anor –'

'Did you not enjoy the socialising?' I was surprised to hear what sounded like a tinge of hurt in her voice.

'I did.' But even I knew it was a flimsy lie. It was becoming instinctive, this ability to lie without thought, an automatic reflex designed to protect me from conflict. I didn't want it anymore. The niggling doubt that Neekor would ever understand me and my Humanity persisted in my gut, but I willed myself to ignore it. 'Actually, Neekor, I didn't enjoy it at all.'

The hurt in her voice appeared on her face then, followed by an angry flaring of her tendrils. I acted quickly.

'It wasn't you, not really – you wouldn't have known otherwise.'

'Known what?'

'That male, Powra. He just said some things that … upset me.'

She let out a sort of knowing sigh. 'Such as Humans being greedy?'

I flicked positively. 'Among others.'

'Apologies, Daniel,' she said quietly. 'I, too, thought that was an inaccurate statement. However, I did not know how to respond.'

'Well, neither did I. It's beings like him that make the Hierarch what it is, who perpetuate everything the Hierarch does to keep Humans at the bottom of the pile. It's beings like him I'm meant to be standing up to, for all of Humanity who can't do it for themselves. All I did was sit there and let him get away with it.' I was aware that my voice was rising, beginning to echo across the vast concrete platform. I couldn't stop it. 'Then I went back to service only to find that the Hierarch wanted me to solve a conflict between two Human nations that *it* created. They put me in front of my own people and made me fight them when I should be fighting Aliens like Powra. I have a friend who I promised that I wouldn't become a **turncoat** and I –'

My voice snagged in my throat. I could still picture him. That look on his face.

'Daniel,' Neekor said, softly. 'You are not well, are you?'

'No.' I tried to turn my quivering tendrils away from her. 'I don't think I am.'

She gestured towards the Edge. 'Let us walk.'

Grateful for the diversion, I followed her, chin tucked against the wind, until we arrived at the Edge's limit, which afforded us the view through the immense gap in the barriers that protected Kappeetar from the worst of the elements. From there we could see right down to the glittering expanse of ocean far below and all the way to its hazy horizon, where Aar – in all its golden glory – had almost finished its descent.

'It means traitor,' I said. Neekor flexed a tendril at me and I clarified, '**Turncoat**. In case you were wondering.'

'I have not heard the term before.'

'It might have had an older meaning pre-assimilation, but during the Sky Wars it was a label for Humans who fought for the Hierarch. Implying that they wanted to be Alien, or in other words, "**turn coated**."'

Neekor frowned at me. 'But those Humans were waging war on other Humans, were they not? Killing, murdering their own kind. That is not what you are doing. You are serving the Hierarch for the good of other Humans.'

'But that's what **turncoats** believed they were doing too. They had their reasons for serving the Hierarch, just like I do.'

She was silent again. I didn't mind. Just being able to say it was enough.

'I do not know what to tell you, Daniel,' Neekor said. 'I am probably not qualified to have an opinion on these things. But, for what it is worth, I do not consider you to be a traitor.'

She smiled at me, and I found it hard to resist smiling in return. Skin burning beneath my coat, I returned my attention to the orange blaze that Aar had cast across the horizon.

'This reminds me of Academy,' Neekor said, copying me. 'All those times you tried to convince me of the pleasure in viewing Aar disappear for the rotation.'

'Are you saying it never worked?'

'It is something that I just cannot understand. Where is the pleasure in it? Which senses does it satisfy?'

We'd had this argument plenty of times. I had never been able to come up with an answer that was suitable to her. Nothing had changed.

'It's just one of those Human things,' I said. 'It can't be explained. It has no reason. **Sunsets** – that's what we call them – are just beautiful, that's all. And this is the only place in the world you can still see them without the skyways or anything else blocking the view.'

I could feel her studying me while I let the last light of the sunset wash over me, melting everything away.

'We did take a lot from Humans, did we not?' Neekor said after a time. 'It is such a simple thing – perceiving the planet's rotation away from Aar, even though the phenomenon will reoccur time and time again and it will be almost visually identical on every occasion. But we took even that away from you.'

In all the time I'd known Neekor, she had been a questioner of Human principles and values. Not so she could criticise them, but because she earnestly sought to understand them, even though she rarely did. It was the first time she seemed to truly grasp what assimilation had meant for us.

'I think you can do it,' she said suddenly.

'Do what?'

'Your mission. To change the Hierarch. I think you can do it.'

This surprised me even more. 'What changed your mind?'

She shrugged. 'You did.'

I saved and triple-backed up this memory. Recorded all the way until Aar vanished beneath the horizon and the dark fell on us. I replayed it that night while I waited for my sleep capsule to sedate me, just so I could keep drinking in Aar's light, listening to Neekor's looping affirmation of me and my mission. Belonging, in that eternal, guiltless **sunset** with her.

Rank 3

Recorded: Cycles 2 through 4
Revolution 9-4028

3-1

It all started with Commander Kookee. Not the actual being himself, but the event celebrating his arrival on **Earth** back in Revolution 8-3538. Then again, Kookee's arrival was the catalyst for the Hierarch's assimilation of **Earth** so, in a way, this really did all start with him.

Neekor and I were on a shuttle to her settlement of origin, Wyakek, for my courtship ritual when she shared a propagation story about the event. The footage showed a monstrous space vessel under construction, the silhouette of which I recognised instantly. Those solar sails belonged to the *Ingunna*, the vessel that brought Commander Kookee and his squad – the first Aliens to set foot on **Earth**.

---

* Subject notation: There is not much to report from the previous three revs, other than that my ascension from Operator to Knight was apparently the quickest in ChamCov's records. I owed it to the Britain Authorisation, really; my use of a conditional Authorisation had become, as the ancestors would say, **all the rage**, being employed across all Authorisation squads. As a result, the rate of Authorisations increased by approximately 20%. More Authorisations meant more mediations, which meant more resolutions, which meant the Hierarch's goal to have completed all resolutions by Rev 9-4034 was that much more realistic. With the Britain Authorisation, I had achieved what cemented me as a true servant of the Hierarch: set a precedent.

'A perfect replica of it,' Neekor explained. 'Apparently it will recreate the original's journey around Teerin' Ho.'

'Why?' was the only thing I could think to say.

'To commemorate the arrival of Aliens on this planet.'

I wanted to point out how grossly offensive it was for one of the greatest symbols of Human assimilation to be flying in our skies again. But with our courtship ritual looming, I couldn't risk starting yet another debate about Humans and Aliens.

'Have you heard the story about Kookee and the exiled **dog**?' I asked, in what I thought was an appropriate tangent. She flicked negatively. 'A squad from Kookee's vessel was attacked by Humans down on the surface, right here in Asia. The rest of Kookee's crew demanded retribution but he recognised that they were intruders in Human territory. So instead of abducting the Humans responsible, he took their pet **dog** and gave it a balance hearing as a substitute for the Humans. He found the **dog** – on behalf of the Humans – guilty of committing imbalance by attacking the crew, and punished it with exile.'

'That is one of the most bizarre stories I think I have ever heard,' said Neekor, frowning. 'The poor **dog**. A shame it met with such a fate due to an act of violence it had no part in.'

'You have to understand: these Humans had never seen Aliens before.'

'So that gave them license to attack?'

In the two revolutions since Neekor and I began formally courting, these types of conversations had become regular. I'd found that hypothetical scenarios serving as allegories were often the only way to progress them.

'Imagine if inter-dimensional beings suddenly appeared in our reality,' I said. 'They look nothing like us, they have forms of transfer we don't comprehend, and their technology and weaponry is unlike anything we've ever seen. Would you not be wary?'

'Yes, but I would not assume they were here with ill intent.'

'What if they were?' I took Neekor's pause to be a sign that she understood my point, and carried on just to make sure. 'There's a

Human expression: **Shoot first, ask questions later**. It means: protect yourself above all else, then seek to understand the situation.'

Neekor frowned again. 'That just sounds like a guaranteed way to make enemies.'

This was a point I hadn't considered before. I wasn't going to let her know it. 'Maybe so, but it also provides the highest guarantee of protection. You can't be betrayed if you don't trust in the first place.'

'Perhaps things would be better for Humans if they were more trusting.'

'Like when we trusted Aliens to honour the Covenant?'

Neekor returned her gaze to the shuttle's observation field and I knew I'd gone too far. Again. When I wanted Neekor to see things from my perspective and she couldn't, it was almost impossible to control myself. The anger that took hold of me in those moments was unbearable, like all the frustration and rage that I had ever felt towards any Alien chose Neekor as their target. I knew it wasn't fair on her, as an Alien who was almost as open and empathetic to the Human condition as Father was. But it had been two revs and here we were again. Even though it was far too early to be thinking about reproduction, it was hard not to with the possibility of a formal partnership hanging over me. I feared for my theoretical offspring, unable to bear the thought of them being as ignorant as Neekor was of my Humanity – of their own Humanity.

The thought of Father reminded me that I had turned out just fine. His Alienness hadn't been a barrier to Mother rearing me in the ways of Humanity. So perhaps there was hope for Neekor yet. I tried to hold onto this thought as our shuttle touched down in Wyakek and we transferred to the circuit runner that would take us to Neekor's clan's commune.

The Commune of Clan Trezza, like every other we passed, radiated Rank like a miniature Kappeetar. Its cluster of chrome towers with wide, disc-like tops climbed out of an immense garden of exotic flora, making them look like a metallic forest. The combined Rank value of the place was probably more than the entirety of Wellington.

Clan Trezza was waiting for me at the commune gateway. I estimated there were fifty or so, mostly elderly members who had probably returned to the commune for an early service retirement after accumulating more Rank than they knew what to do with. In the centre of them all was the unmistakeable matriarch, the only one standing. She was like a future version of Neekor – the same deep, dark coat, the same shrewd stare. Looking at the males kneeling around her, none of whom I could visually identify as Neekor's father, it was easy to see whose genetic traits had been passed on.

As we approached, a coherence field lit up in the space between us. Through the shimmering green miasma, Neekor's mother gestured for me to sit, so I did. Then I felt the virtual contact of her tree against mine, and I accepted her connection to join the clan's network of linked trees and begin the welcoming ritual.

It was fairly standard: Neekor's mother, who introduced herself to me through our connection as Haapetti, greeted us then asked us to declare the purpose of our visit so it could be recorded in the Core. Neekor confirmed what that purpose was on my behalf: to participate in a courtship ritual. Haapetti detailed the terms of my entry to the commune and I formally agreed to them in the Core. Then the coherence field deactivated and I was able to enter the commune without being atomised.

Once Neekor had less formally greeted Haapetti and her father – who turned out to be the slight, greying male who had knelt at Haapetti's right side – I offered the best inferior to superior salute I could and transferred them my Rank contribution in reciprocation of their hospitality. Neekor's father acknowledged it with a respectful salute of his own.

'Denial, is it not?' he said.

'D-Daniel.'

'Duh-dan-yell?'

'Just Daniel.'

'Dan-yell?'

Close enough. 'Yes.'

He beamed at me. 'It is a pleasure to finally make your acquaintance, Dan-yell. I am Kreetop.'

Haapetti didn't say anything. She waited for me to be introduced to every other member of the clan before setting off towards the tallest tower that rose up from the commune's centre. Together we followed her, and as we walked through the jungle-like garden, I wondered how long it would take before the inquiries began (it took exactly six seconds, according to my records).

'So, Dan-yell,' said Kreetop, 'I understand you are in service at the Wellington Commission?'

The mention of it sent a shiver through me. I had been largely successful in ignoring the fact that the Commission still hadn't released its decision on the Britain Authorisation. Although it was not unusual for a decision to take that long, many servants at ChamCov believed that it meant the decision would probably be negative.

'The Chamber of Covenant Resolutions, actually. Many beings confuse the two. My own mother still does, sometimes.'

'Oh, of course,' said Kreetop. 'And how long have you been in service there?'

'Nearing three revs now.'

'It must be fascinating service. Have you interacted with any of the Human nations in this territory?'

'No, my squad interacts exclusively with European nations.' Kreetop's blank face told me he didn't know what they were, so I clarified, 'Basically the Nordic and Mediterranean Territories.'

'I am curious,' another of Haapetti's mates chimed in. 'What exactly are the nations here in Wyakek?'

'Well, there are a few: Japan, Korea – North and South –'

'What is the big one?' said the third of Haapetti's mates. 'Chy... Chynee...'

'Chylee,' Kreetop said, with a look that seemed to be searching for my approval.

'I believe it's pronounced: Chile,' said the second mate.

'I think you mean China,' I said. 'They're a bit to the west –'

'China, yes,' said the third mate. 'That is what I meant.'

'Doing so well, are they not?' said Kreetop.

'The wealthiest country out of all of them, I understand,' said the second mate.

'Yes,' I interjected, 'although they had one of the very first resolutions so they've had the most time to benefit –'

'A great example to the rest of them,' concluded the third mate.

I decided not to respond any further. But I wasn't free from the inquisition.

'What nation are you?' Haapetti addressed me for the first time, over her shoulder.

'I'm from New Zealand. It's a small nation in the Pacific Territory.'

'And are they also quite…' I waited patiently for her to finish, then realised she expected me to do it for her. With what might have been an irritable sigh, she added, 'You know, like China.'

'Wealthy?'

'No, I mean…'

What she meant then hit me. 'Coated?'

'For want of a better term, yes.'

'Mother!' Neekor scolded her.

'You know what I mean,' she said quickly. 'China *are* quite coated by Human standards, are they not? If you saw one you would not assume they are Human. I only thought –'

'Mother,' said Neekor, 'please stop.'

'I meant no offence. You are not offended, are you, Denial?'

'Of course not,' I lied. 'And to answer your question, I would say New Zealand Humans are generally not as coated as the Chinese. My coat is mainly inherited from my father, who is from Aheetra.' This wasn't a completely accurate justification as the indigenous species of Aheetra are scaled, but no one ever thinks of them when they think of Aheetrans. Just like when people think of Teerin' Ho, they don't think of Humans.

'That makes sense,' said Kreetop.

Neekor sent me a private, '**Apologies**' and I dismissed it with a flick. I just wanted to get the courtship ritual over and done with.

When we arrived at the base of the main tower, it opened to reveal a shifter lobby. Neekor activated one of the shifters for me and it took me to the top of the tower, where I found myself in a room that was like something straight out of a *Superior Habitation* construct. It was huge, for a start, bigger than Mother's and Father's entire dwelling. A massive consumption mat dominated the centre of it, and sumptuous loungers lined the walls, which were coloured with lush, floral plant life. One corner featured an enormous containment unit with rows of carefully placed vintage cutters, their labels all facing forwards. Mother would have been in absolute awe of them.

'Welcome, Dan-yell,' said Kreetop, leading me over to the unit. 'Can I interest you in a cut?'

'Yes, gratitude,' I said, inspecting the array before me.

'We have an Aak'remari Maarm, an Orhor from Eesaar – my personal favourite, a Koorteeri Tow –'

'I'll take one of those, please.' I knew Tow was a calm-infused cut and I needed all the calm – synthetic or not – I could get.

'I will have an Airungi Aror,' Haapetti requested, which was an intriguing choice. Was I so dull that she needed artificial interest to converse with me?

Kreetop handed us our cutters and gestured for me to sit at one end of the consumption mat. Neekor gave me a furtive, encouraging salute before sitting next to me and waiting for the rest of the clan to make themselves comfortable around the mat. Haapetti was the last to sit, at the opposite end.

'Let us complete this business sooner rather than later,' she declared, as if she had better things to do. She took her cut.

I took mine too, in preparation for what was to come, then connected my tree to hers again, this time granting full access as per the courtship ritual's requirements.

It was unnerving having my personal tree completely open to her – and through her, the whole clan – to inspect. I felt exposed, with my entire profile and sequencing laid bare to her scrutiny. What would she think of my training? My ascension primaries? My Core search history?

But I was most worried about what she thought of my own clan, which would surely be several cumulative Ranks below hers. There probably wasn't a lot my clan had to offer theirs, and, based on the sheer wealth that surrounded me, I was beginning to doubt how much I could actually offer Neekor except for my **love** – but that would have been like telling them I could offer her a **dragon** or a **god**.

'Your Mother is the High Rank of … your nation,' Haapetti eventually noted, her voice flecked with artificially enhanced interest.

'New Zealand,' I said as pointedly, but also politely, as I could. 'And yes, she is.'

'That must make your clan among the highest Ranking in your nation.'

'I suppose so, yes.'

The search through my tree continued. I took another few cuts. After a while, Haapetti stated, 'Your genome is overwhelmingly Noor.'

I wasn't sure how to respond to that. Somewhere within me, smothered by the artificial calm I had doused myself in, was a part of me (the tiny Human percentage of my genome, I presume) that wanted to tell her that no one talked about genome percentage anymore. It was an outdated expression that only perpetuated the elimination of Human identity. I took another cut and buried that part completely.

Finally, through the higher plane of relaxation I felt I had reached, I sensed Haapetti's tree retreat from mine. I snapped myself back to reality and looked at her, waiting for some sort of judgment. She only gave me a stiff salute of approval and announced, 'Darkmeal is prepared.'

Sustenance appeared before us: bowls of what looked like naturally harvested hoo'mart, blocks of flavoured bean curd, pitchers of juice – all shifted directly to the mat from what I assumed was a cookery somewhere on the lower levels of the tower.

Neekor messaged me privately: '**You can relax. You are approved.**'

I snuck a smile at her that didn't come close to conveying the relief that washed over me. Whatever doubts I'd had, being deemed worthy by Neekor's clan of her courtship was one of the proudest moments of my existence. I felt like dancing around the room in celebration. But

I restrained myself. I had just successfully convinced this entire clan how civilised a Human I was, and I wasn't going to risk sabotaging that impression for anything.

Except, perhaps, to make the most of Clan Trezza's extravagant hospitality. With the ritual behind me, I was ravenous, so I piled my tray high with anything that was within reach. It was, I have to admit, quite an enjoyable meal.

Neekor seemed to have forgotten our earlier squabble. I noticed her watching me a couple of times, wrinkling her nose at me. That meant she was happy, and that made me happy. The questions kept coming but they felt less probing and more genuinely curious. Kreetop was particularly fascinated by the subtle distinction between **fries** and **chips**, and I ended up prompting a commitment from him to make some the next time I visited. I finished the meal in a pleasantly contented haze and a stomach full to bursting.

But I was not to be released without one last interrogation.

'So, Denial,' Haapetti cut across all other conversation from the other end of the mat. 'What does it mean?'

The room fell silent while I tried to work out what she was referring to. 'My name?'

'Yes.'

'I don't think it has a meaning.'

Haapetti blinked at me. 'Surely it has a meaning?'

'Well, it may have, a long time ago. But as far as I know it's just a given name for males.'

Haapetti continued to regard me as if I had said something nonsensical. 'Is that typical of Humans? To have names given for … well, no reason at all?'

'Yes.' The pleasant haze was rapidly dissipating. 'My Mother's name is Michelle. That probably had some meaning in ancient times, but now it's just a name. Human parents choose names they like.'

'I think that is very admirable,' said Kreetop. 'Why not choose a ＿dom oral sound for your offspring's name? How creative.'

＿suppose that is to be expected for a transfer that was not by thought,' Haapetti said. 'With no way of transferring ideas directly, I can understand that their meaning was often lost or corrupted. Especially with no way of recording them.'

'Humans had ways of recording transfer,' I said, doing my best to keep my tone level. 'We transcribed it, either physically or onto the **net** –'

'Not very reliable though, was it? Anyone could just transcribe anything – how would you know it was legitimate?'

It was the barge cruise above Anor all over again. Every Alien eye was on me and the effect was paralysing. I couldn't speak, couldn't even think.

That's when the anger came. The same anger I felt every time the Alien Operators at ChamCov talked about Covenant resolutions like they were just a bit of **fun**. Every time I read those messages to the Lord from the Alien public, or saw the commentary by the propagation weighted against Humans. Every time Neekor didn't see the Human perspective, or notice the blatant Alien supremacy playing out right in front of her. It was becoming wild now, this anger, threatening to break loose.

By some miracle my shaking hand found the Tow-infused cutter beside my tray. I pressed it to my root and batted the writhing beast inside me back into submission, where it stayed for the rest of the rote.

Before Neekor and I clambered into our sleeping capsules that night, she gave me an affectionate salute.

'Much gratitude, Daniel.'

'For what?'

'For coming here and going through with the ritual. And putting up with my clan's relentless questioning.'

I laughed in place of telling her that putting up with it had only been possible with the assistance of the cutter. For the first time in my life, I understood why we were so addicted to it.

The following two rotes were, thankfully, much more pleasant. We spent them down on the surface – Neekor, Haapetti, her mates and I – joining the multitude of mariners on their vessels in the great expanse of flat, calm water once known as the **Sea of Japan**. It was the first time I had been anywhere on the surface that was somewhat free from the dominating presence of the skyways, a fact that puzzled me until I realised what we were there for: to harvest aquatic flora from the Trezza Clan's private orchard. The Hierarch wouldn't dare construct a skyway above an aquaculture site, especially one controlled by a collective of high Rank Alien clans like Trezza. Much easier and cheaper to run it above a low-Rank residential area or a Human heritage site.

Having a direct, unbroken view of the sky from the surface – just like the ancestors would have had – was a private thrill all on its own. But the excursion was made even more enjoyable by the lack of questioning from Haapetti, who largely left me alone. I didn't know if this was a positive or negative sign but I welcomed the reprieve. It allowed me to simply enjoy the time with Neekor – and Kreetop, to a lesser extent, who I was getting along with quite well. He had an impressive knowledge of all the aquatic fauna we encountered, and was able to identify them and explain their unique characteristics to me with ease. At one point I almost felt comfortable enough to tell him that the ancestors would have harvested nearly all of those animals for consumption instead of the **seaweed** we were gathering. I thought better of it.

Despite how much I enjoyed being on the water and feeling closer to Neekor, I was glad for the visit to come to an end. Once I bid farewell to Haapetti, Kreetop, and the rest of the clan, and slumped into my seat on the runner, I felt so exhausted I almost could have slept without my sleep capsule. And maybe I would have, if I hadn't noticed Neekor's tendrils quivering when she sat beside me.

'Apologies,' she said, trying to cover them. 'I always find leaving the commune difficult.'

It took me a little while to register what I was seeing. It was rare enough for Humans to exhibit grief, let alone Aliens. Instinctively, I put my arm around her – a gesture she wouldn't have understood but, for some reason, didn't reject.

'Do you remember that phrase I taught you, after we had lubag that time?' I asked. '**I missed you**? This is what that feels like.'

She didn't say anything, but I felt her relax in my arm, nestle her head into my shoulder. We stayed that way for the entire journey, and I wished it had taken longer.

When it came time to return to service, and we pulled ourselves away from each other, that blissful, weightless sensation returned. I didn't even need to be in Neekor's presence anymore to feel it. The mere thought of her was enough. Every step was a bounce and I rode that feeling all the way to ChamCov, bobbing into my squad's pen and greeting everybody cheerfully.

The few mumbled responses I got brought me back down to **Earth** again. I paused to properly inspect the squad who were eerily quiet, each connected to their terminals. Linking up to my own, I found Pa'zan's tree and asked him what everyone was doing. His only reply was the propagation stream he shared with me, which showed a sophisticated, well-groomed Human male with a banner under his name that read: **Karkoora 7 Darius, Alliance Clans**. It wasn't unusual for contenders like the Alliance Clans to show up in the propagation every now and again with their latest attempt to discredit the reigning Hierarch, but the rapidly rising view counter suggested they were onto something big.

'– and now the Hierarch pulls this,' the male was saying, 'a replica of Commander Kookee's ship, the *Ingunna*, flying around **Earth**.'

My mind went back to the stream Neekor had shown me, with the *Ingunna* under construction. I had assumed it was just another example of the type of casually offensive community event often financed by the highest Ranks of Aliens. Not one financed by the Hierarch itself.

'What I want to know is,' Karkoora 7 Darius continued, 'how far will this replication go? Are they also going to replicate Kookee's first encounter with Humans by killing a few of them? Abducting and probing them on board the *Ingunna* like Kookee did?'

Even connected to the stream, I felt several other members of the squad flinch. I had never seen this member of the Alliance Clans before, but I already thought he was brilliant.

'The Alliance Clans condemn this event,' he declared, 'which is just the latest in a string of failures by this Hierarch, at the expense of Humans. The time for change is now. A Lordship held by us would see the most Human Lords ever appointed in the history of **Earth**. We would put an end to initiatives like this, which only perpetuate the grievances of the past. Our Hierarch will be one that delivers for Humanity. We just need your tithing to do it.'

Pa'zan disconnected from the stream and turned to me.

'Getting serious now that the Alliance Clans are involved, is it not?'

I flexed a tendril at him. 'Involved in what?'

Pa'zan's eyes widened. 'You have not seen what is occurring down on the surface?'

At my confused look he relinked our trees and showed me another propagation stream – a sizeable mass of kawwas suspended over a huge span of water. In their midst was the immediately recognisable hologram of Commander Kookee, which I knew stood in the **Bay of Bengal** – the first place he visited. The hologram flickered in and out of sight. Someone was attempting to deactivate it.

'The High Rank of India is with me now,' said a propagator's voice as the image shifted to a Human male standing by the water's edge, 'to tell us why India is reacting this way.'

'The last time the *Ingunna* flew in this bay,' said the Indian Leader, whose fury was so great he was shaking, 'at least twenty of our people were disintegrated by Kookee's crew. Six juveniles were abducted and taken on board. The Hierarch's celebration of this event is a disgrace. The *Ingunna* is not welcome here.'

Pa'zan raced through several other streams. All over the world, Humans were reacting: demonstrations massed and holographic replicas of Commander Kookee, which had stood in public spaces for countless rotes, were being destroyed.

'It has been going since previous rotation,' said Pa'zan. 'I am surprised you were not aware of it.'

'There was no Core connectivity down on the **Sea of Japan**,' I said, although it was also likely that Haapetti's clan couldn't have cared less about it and didn't think it worth alerting me to.

Disconnecting from Pa'zan's tree, I scoured the Core and found that the situation was even worse than it seemed. The event had a title, one that had been appropriated from Common: **Meet**. The event's official profile defined this word as: 'a first encounter between two species, an introductory exchange of identities, forever bound together by the sharing of experience to become one. A fitting name for this celebration of our two species' first engagements with one another.'

What was more, the event didn't just feature an *Ingunna* replica circumnavigating the planet. It would be accompanied by a fleet of traditional Human space vessels and vessels from other parts of Mornanook – an entourage of all the worlds the Hierarch had assimilated in this region of the galaxy. It was painfully clear that whoever was organising this event knew it would draw criticism from Humans, and, in response, had made a cynical attempt at Humanising it.

I was interrupted by a communication from Morgan, inviting me to a private gathering. I wasn't the only one who received it: Pa'zan lifted his head from his terminal, sharing a puzzled glance with me, as did Vuneen and Moolas. Teemot walked by the pen, indicating with a subtle flick of his tendrils that we were to follow him. I waited to see if Phil or any of the others in the squad had also received such a message, but they remained fixated on their terminals, and Teemot hurried the four of us with a gesture. We slipped out of the pen and into one of ChamCov's gathering rooms, where Lincoln and Morgan waited.

'Perfect,' Lincoln said, once the gate closed behind us. 'Everyone is here. I am sure by now you are all aware of what has been happening for the past rote or so. The news of this event, **Meet**, has had a far more negative effect than the Hierarch anticipated. Already, the Accountancy is reporting a minor decline in the Hierarch's Rank.'

'Surely not as a result of this?' said Teemot.

'The decline is inconsequential,' Lincoln said, 'but forecasters are suggesting it could be the beginning of a trend.'

A tremor of murmurs ran through us all. It was rare for anything to really threaten the Hierarch's Rank.

'This event shows that the Hierarch does not understand what is important to Humans,' Lincoln continued. 'The Alliance Clans are leveraging this situation in what could become an ascension attempt and they are showing some signs of success. If the Hierarch doesn't address this promptly and effectively, we may well see it change from Clan Global. For this reason, the Hierarch has taken an extraordinary measure: to establish a new squad whose function is to advise the Hierarch on how to interact with Humans. A new squad serving under my Rank.'

The reaction to this news was silence. I assumed for everyone else it was shock. For me, it was victory. A squad whose sole purpose was to tell the Hierarch how to treat its Covenant partners? It was something I'd never expected to see until I was a high enough Rank to do it myself.

'Congratulations, Lincoln,' Vuneen offered, on behalf of us all. 'This is a significant achievement, and a much-needed cause to serve.'

'It is,' said Lincoln, 'and there is no one else I would rather serve it with.'

The room was silent again, as it dawned on us why we had all been gathered there.

'Clarification,' said Pa'zan. 'Are you saying ...'

Lincoln flicked positively. 'As of this moment, everyone in this room is a member of my new squad.'

Lincoln had selected the best of us. Save one, perhaps.

'What about Phil?' I asked.

Morgan's face said all it needed to. Lincoln was more diplomatic.

'I was only given enough Rank to select those I have absolute confidence in.'

I won't lie: part of me felt intensely proud. But it did make me wonder about Phil. Yes, he was old and somewhat simple, and he told terrible jokes. But at the very least he was Human – I thought that should have qualified him for this new squad.

'I mean no disrespect, Lincoln, but why us?' said Moolas. 'Our service is Covenant resolutions, not Human relationship management.'

Lincoln smiled. 'Actually, our experience interacting with Humans equips us perfectly for this function. No other part of the Hierarch engages with Humans in the same way we do.'

This made total sense to me. 'When do we begin?' I asked.

'Right now,' Lincoln announced. 'We still serve under General Neweek, but we are our own division within the House of Balance: the Human-Hierarch Interactions Squad.'

I wasn't fond of the name. Like all Hierarch designations, it didn't exactly resonate or inspire. But when we left that room, I felt like we were an assembled team of **superheroes** from the stories of old, hand-picked for our unique skills and abilities. Me, the Prodigy. Pa'zan, the Analyst. Moolas, the Decree-master. Vuneen, the Veteran. Teemot, the Fearless. And Lincoln, our noble Commander, with his faithful right hand, Morgan.

There was no ceremony to our establishment and no formality to our departure from the Europe Authorisation Squad. There was no time. Protecting the Hierarch from itself couldn't wait.

Our operations were immediately installed in a new pen. We were required to have sight of all official Hierarch interactions with Humans, and of every new decree or edict declared by the Hierarch. Our role was to assess and intervene if we considered a measure did not appropriately interact with Humans. To my surprise and honour, the crucial responsibility for making that judgment fell to me.

'You are the most knowledgeable of all of us – aside from Lincoln – about interacting with Humans,' Teemot said. 'I need you to be our chief advisor. The rest of the squad will identify the interactions we need to advise on, but everything we review will come through you. Understood?'

I understood perfectly. The squad's purpose wasn't quite at the stage of making the Hierarch honour the Covenant but, surely, greater understanding of how to interact with Humans would lead there. I had the impression that this wasn't a one-off event that Lincoln got lucky with, but something he had been working towards for a long time, perhaps for his entire service career. As he made his way around the new pen, checking each of us had what we needed, it was hard not to be awestruck.

'Gratitude, Lincoln,' I said to him. 'For giving me this opportunity.'

'Don't thank me yet,' he said with a grin. 'The hard part is to come.'

3-3

I was so elated by the formation of the Human-Hierarch Interactions Squad that I travelled to Wellington to share the news with Mother and Father. Neekor's courtship ritual with them was due anyway, so it was a convenient opportunity.

Mother and Father met us inside the shuttle terminus, which, with Neekor now by my side, seemed far more representative of the surface than I had ever thought. I'd always been somewhat concerned about the state of this terminus – and other facilities – but I now found myself wanting to remove Neekor from it as quickly as I could. Mother and Father were oblivious, with Father giving me a welcoming salute and Mother sweeping me into an embrace with an accompanying kiss on the cheek. She did the same to Neekor, who I had warned of this likely welcome in place of a ritual. Neekor reacted remarkably well, returning the gesture better than I had seen any Alien do, including Father. That was enough to win Mother over. Holding Neekor by the shoulders, Mother scanned her up and down, and said, 'You sure you don't have any Human in you?'

Neekor glanced nervously between her and me and said, 'I cannot identify any in my genome ...'

Mother and I both laughed, and I assured Neekor it was only a joke. Her expression didn't change. Leading her by the arm towards the kawwa hangar, Mother bombarded her with questions: 'So where did your clan originate from? Have you ever been there? When did they arrive on Teerin' Ho?'

I noticed the questioning wasn't too dissimilar to the inquisition I suffered from Neekor's parents. As Father and I set off after them, I asked him, 'Did you have to go through that with Grandmother?'

'Almost identically, yes,' he said cheerfully. 'Although I was also subjected to a sacred assessment of character informed by the timing of my birth. I recall being classified as a **Libra** which, fortunately, your grandmother deemed highly compatible with your mother.'

I don't know Mother's **star-sign**, but it must be one concerned with far more practical factors when it comes to assessing someone's suitability to court their offspring. She'd taken the liberty of arranging an itinerary for our visit, which must have been designed to gauge Neekor's reaction to various aspects of our identity that Mother considered important. The first component consisted of a drive past all the major landmarks in Wellington, such as Tungee'kyor and the waterfront, with an accompanying lecture about the history of each one. The following rotation would see the second part of the visit, which would include a private tour of parliament and the museum above it, culminating in a visit to the Covenant of Wellington.

I cast a sideways grin at Father while Mother described the itinerary to Neekor. There can't have been many Aliens who'd had the privilege of a guided history tour by the actual leader of a Human nation, and it pleased me to see Neekor flicking along in rapt attention to everything Mother said.

'So, it is similar to the Rank system?' asked Neekor once Mother had stopped describing the mechanics of our parliamentary system to catch a breath. The drive had taken us past parliament and Mother had been unable to resist a head start on the associated lecture. 'The nation gives – what did you say, **power** – to the leaders, and in exchange they provide governance to the nation?'

'Yes, but with one key difference,' Mother pointed out. 'The separation of power and wealth. For Aliens the two are one and the same, embodied by Rank: if you have the most wealth, you have the most **power**. Humans don't equate wealth with **power**. It doesn't matter how rich or poor you are, it's your ability to lead that matters. The poorest Human in New Zealand could be elected here.'

Neekor gave Mother one of her quizzical looks. 'Would New Zealanders ever elect someone poor to represent them?'

I think it was the first time I had ever seen Mother lost for words.

'Well, they *could*,' she managed to say. 'Hypothetically. And that's what matters.'

Neekor was wise enough not to question her any further and changed the topic.

'And so the actual Covenant of Wellington is stored here?'

'Yes,' Mother replied excitedly. 'I'll show it to you next rotation. Although, you really should return and see it on Covenant Anniversary too – if not next revolution, I'd recommend the one after that, which will be the 350th Anniversary of its validation.'

'Is that ... significant?' Neekor asked. I hadn't yet explained to her why multiples of five and ten are obviously more significant to Humans than any other number.

'350 revs is a particularly significant milestone, but the occasion is always wonderful regardless.' Mother swept a hand in the direction of the waterfront. 'We have markets set up all along these grounds, with the best sustenance Humanity has to offer; chips, baking, carbonated liquid. We have musicians performing, Navy demonstrations out on the water. The juveniles love jumping from the diving platform –'

'What about the protests?' said Neekor.

Mother rolled her eyes. 'Protest is just one aspect of Covenant Anniversary, and an important one. But unfortunately, that's all that gets propagated. They like to portray us as nothing more than angry, loud imbeciles with little better to do than complain.'

I wondered if this was exactly the perception a lifetime's worth of propagated misrepresentation about Covenant Anniversary had given Neekor. All the coverage of the Meet protests probably hadn't helped.

'I think I will return,' she said eventually. 'To witness it for myself.'

'You must,' Mother insisted. 'It's one thing to visit this place. But it's another to be here on the anniversary, right where the Covenant was validated. And don't get me started on how inaccurately *that's* been misrepresented.'

She was referring, of course, to the many depictions of the event that portrayed it as a well-organised affair in which everyone came together in a most agreeable fashion, and Captain Hopp'han – who validated the Covenant on behalf of the Hierarch – shook everyone warmly by the hand and declared, 'We are one species,' and we all lived happily ever after.

The final stop on Mother's tour of the most prestigious of Wellington's landmarks was, expectedly, the Clan Lounge. Thankfully, Father was able to convince her that going inside wasn't necessary, as it was getting late and we were due for darkmeal. But Mother wouldn't allow us to head home without a lengthy lecture on the Lounge's history and significance to Wellington and, 'as a matter of fact', all of Humanity.

'So, really,' she concluded as the kawwa fired up to take us, at long last, to their dwelling, 'Wellington is the birthplace of modern Earth. Everyone has links here – even you, Neekor. At least one of your ancestors has had a cut at the Clan Lounge, I guarantee it.'

Like the shuttle terminus, I'd never noticed how plain Mother's and Father's dwelling was, how much smaller and grubbier than Clan Trezza's it seemed to be. The landing zone was only big enough to accommodate one vehicle. I led Neekor to my room, hoping that haste would distract her from how cramped it all was. It didn't quite work; with the extra sleep capsule Mother and Father had placed in it for Neekor, there was really only enough room to stand there in embarrassment.

'Is everything well?' Neekor asked, while I tried to find somewhere to drop our travel packs.

'Apologies,' I said, gesturing at the clutter. 'About all this, about Mother – she doesn't often have someone new to educate.'

She dismissed me with a flick. 'There is nothing to apologise for. And I do not mind your mother's insights. They have been enlightening.'

That surprised me.

'Did you mean it?' I asked. 'About returning for Covenant Anniversary?'

'Yes, absolutely. If you are going to be my partner, I need to understand these things.'

A few seconds passed before I realised I was staring into her eyes. I was familiar enough with the ancestors' stories to know that a kiss would have often followed such an intimate moment, and I was struck by an instinctive urge to try it. She had taken Mother's platonic kiss well, and I didn't think a romantic kiss on the mouth was really that different (except for the exponentially higher risk of viral infection due to the abundance of bacteria present in and around facial orifices). But I decided that, being down on the surface in such a Human environment, she was probably overwhelmed enough without me making it worse. Understanding Human commemorations was one thing. Understanding Human gestures of affection involving exchanges of bodily fluids was another.

Instead, I took her through to the main room, where darkmeal was waiting for us. Father, who had clearly anticipated Mother's extended history lesson, had put everything in the preserver as a precaution.

'Let us eat, then we can carry out the courting ritual,' he suggested, motioning for us all to sit.

'Forget the ritual,' said Mother. 'You can log it as an approval.'

Neekor looked to me, stunned. I didn't know what to say to her.

'Michelle,' she tried, 'you do not need to —'

'I'd rather continue getting to know you the Human way,' Mother said. And so she did, picking up where she left off at the shuttle terminus. She asked about Neekor's parents, what they did for service, and what Neekor did for service. When Neekor explained that she was a servant at the House of Transportation, Mother's eyes narrowed. 'How do you find it, serving the Hierarch?'

I'd thought that Mother's questioning had been quite benign compared to the grilling I received from Neekor's clan. Now it was moving into dangerous territory.

'Well,' Neekor answered, 'I find great satisfaction in knowing that my service benefits the people of Teerin' Ho.'

She'd barely finished when Mother said, 'Which people of Teerin' Ho, specifically?'

I shot Mother a glance she didn't notice. Then I sent her a message that wasn't even composed of words, just unarticulated objection. She didn't appear to notice that, either.

'All of them,' Neekor replied, meeting Mother's gaze with unwavering conviction. 'But I accept that some people benefit much more than others.'

I disguised a breath of relief, and I thought I spotted Father do the same. Mother, however, was not so easily swayed.

'You have seen the recent controversy involving the celebration of Kookee's arrival on **Earth**?' she said, to which Neekor flicked positively. 'What is your view on it?'

I sent another objecting message to Mother, which was also ignored.

Neekor was unperturbed. 'I understand much of Humanity finds the concept highly offensive.'

This alone might have been enough to satisfy Mother. She regarded Neekor for a few more moments before returning her attention to her sustenance.

Only Neekor wasn't finished.

'In spite of that, I do consider such an event has the potential to be a constructive exercise in developing world identity.'

Mother's eyes snapped up. I almost wanted to dissolve in my seat.

'Teerin' Ho is relatively juvenile compared to other worlds,' Neekor elaborated. 'Much of our sequencing is unknown or poorly understood. I do see some benefits in a worldwide event that provides greater understanding of the first interactions between Humans and Noor, provided it is handled appropriately.'

I watched Mother process this, her mandible clenching, her eyes blinking more quickly than normal, then ask with unnerving calm, 'And how would *you* handle such an event?'

I knew then exactly what this all was, what Mother had been doing from the moment Neekor arrived. The oldest trick in the parliamentary book: the **Supplementary Question** set-up. She had put Neekor at ease, lulled her into a false sense of security with simple, easy-to-answer questions. It was all a facade, so Mother could unleash the real questions, the ones for which there were no right answers, and expose Neekor's ignorance. Despite my horror, I had to admit it was beautifully executed.

And yet, in all her revs of parliamentary service, and in every rev since, I can say with absolute certainty that Mother herself has never, as the ancestors would say, **dodged a bullet** in the way Neekor then did.

'I would rely on the advice of servants qualified to speak on it,' she said, turning to me. 'Something Daniel can tell you more about.'

Mother swivelled to me.

'Yes, there is something else I came here to tell you, Mother. And you, Father.' I cleared my throat. 'The Hierarch has established a new squad within the House of Balance. The Human-Hierarch Interactions Squad.'

'The *what* squad?'

'Human-Hierarch Interactions. Its function is to advise the Hierarch on how to interact appropriately with Humans.'

'One squad?' Mother said, tendril raised. 'To advise on *every* interaction between the Hierarch and Humans?'

'For now, yes. It is intended to grow once more Rank can be assigned to it. But that's not all. What I really wanted to tell you is that I have been selected to serve in it.'

Mother's face softened.

'You? On this … elite squad?'

I hadn't used the word 'elite' but I didn't correct her. 'Yes.'

Out came the vintage cutter. Then came the hug. Neekor got one too – Mother's stand-off with her apparently forgotten.

'What excellent news,' said Father, with a congratulatory salute. 'It is a shame no such squad existed to advise the Hierarch not to support this ridiculous **Meet** event.'

'Well, that's exactly why it was established,' I said. 'In direct response to all the protests.'

'Except that,' Mother re-inserted herself, 'in typical Hierarch form, it still doesn't address the fact that **Meet** is going ahead. Despite Humanity's protests.'

This was true. Lincoln had explained to us that it was far more difficult to stop something like **Meet** once it was already agreed to by the Hierarch. It was now a precedent and therefore, apparently, irrevocable.

So, the Hierarch had not pulled support, and Humans all over the world were still making their opposition clear. Just the rote before, the propagation had reported on a brawl that erupted in France between Human anti-**Meet** protestors and Alien Kookee enthusiasts. The Humans had won, I was privately pleased to hear. At least until the Aliens' secret weapon was revealed – immunity to detainment by the Keepers.

'But it is *something*, is it not?' Father countered. 'If nothing else, some good has come of all this: a squad tasked with helping the Hierarch to do better by Humans. I am confident in assuming that never has a Hierarch taken such a measure in the interests of its relationship with an indigenous species. And that Daniel has been found worthy to serve in its Ranks brings great honour to our clan.'

I felt a sudden warmth for him. It was not only one of the highest praises my father had ever given me, but it was enough to convince Mother, which was no mean feat.

'On that, we can agree,' she said. Then she handed me the cutter and said, 'I knew you could make a difference, Daniel.'

Privately, Neekor sent me a message that read: 'So did I.'

I looked from her proud smile down to Mother's vintage cutter, with its aged, joy-infused charges, and passed it on. I didn't need it.

The ancestors had a term to describe how I felt: **on cloud nine.** I have no idea why this particular cumuliform was considered the highest, or how one was supposed to be 'on' it, but nothing else adequately described the sensation. As we set off from Mother's and Father's dwelling for part two of the tour around Wellington, I didn't think anything could bring me down.

On our way to parliament, we drove past the Clan Lounge again. Being the morning, it had only just opened and already Wellingtonians were streaming through its gate, probably just after visiting the Exchange to claim their Allowance. A group stood outside – Mutt Pack members, by the patches of red dye on their shoulders – cutting and chuckling, generally looking intimidating. I recognised the one at their head, the female from **Oriental Bay**, who would watch me whenever I used to visit Hayden.

And then, I saw him – Hayden. With her, with them: the Mutt Pack. Throwing his head back with laughter while he pressed a cutter to his root.

Or at least, it looked like him. But surely this Mutt's mane was too long, his frame too thin, even for Hayden.

I didn't want to believe it. I brought up his profile in the Core, hoping to prove that it wasn't really him, that perhaps he'd managed to secure some Rank 1 service – maybe at a nice, upstanding establishment like **The Big Cock**. His profile hadn't changed since the last time I'd seen it. He was still showing as Rank 0, and his place of habitation was still listed as his father's.

That didn't necessarily mean he'd joined the Mutt Pack, I reasoned. For all I knew he could still just be on the Allowance, dwelling with his father.

By the time we reached the Covenant of Wellington in the museum above parliament, I couldn't think about anything else. I barely even noticed Mother's blunt dismissal of the old Chronicler, which normally would have delighted me.

'Father,' I said, while Mother launched into her own sermon about the Covenant exclusively for Neekor, 'you know my friend – Nootoo 0 Hayden?'

'I do,' he replied, 'although I cannot recall seeing him for some time.'

'You wouldn't happen to know anything about him, would you? His Allowance status, for example?'

Father frowned. 'I do not believe he receives the Allowance any longer. I recall trying to contact him to reapply once his eligibility expired. I was unable to reach him.'

I checked Hayden's profile again – definitely Rank 0. Unless he really was still dwelling with his father, that could mean one of two things: either he was nomadic, as with no Rank income he couldn't afford to dwell anywhere else; or he was acquiring illegitimate Rank.

'Perhaps you should try visiting him while you are here,' Father suggested. 'I am sure he would be interested to meet Neekor.'

'Perhaps,' I agreed. It would have been the easiest way to be sure – head over to his father's dwelling and see if he was there. But every time I worked up the courage to commit to it, I would see his face the last time we met, and that dreadful look, and the word left unspoken when turned his back on me.

Mother had just paused her speech to find our ancestor's signature on the Covenant when Neekor glanced my way. We had, by proxy of Mother's refusal to conduct the courtship ritual, just obtained approval by both our clans to continue courting each other, even to enter partnership if we wished. That filled me with a powerful need to protect her, to care for her. If Hayden really was a member of the Mutt Pack, then I didn't want Neekor anywhere near him.

I decided to craft him a message instead, hoping, at the very least, that it would lead to a conversation with him:

> Greetings, Hayden. I know it's been a long time. I just
> wanted to say that I hope everything is well.

All I got back was a notification in my tree:

[Seen]

That word haunted me for the rest of our time in Wellington. Right through our sampling of Wellington's once-famed, signature hot beverage, to our very traditional darkmeal of **chips** on parliament's lawn. Even when Mother filled us in on her secret plan for New Zealand to protest **Meet** which I won't outline in full here (but involved a giant projection of New Zealand's greatest icon: a now-extinct flightless bird that reputedly had the ability to fire coherent-matter beams from its cornea), all I could think about was the infuriating 'Seen' mocking me in my tree.

'Is everything well, Daniel?' Neekor asked, as we walked along the waterfront back to Mother's and Father's dwelling. I didn't even really know how we'd ended up alone together. A deliberate set-up by Mother after darkmeal was my best assumption. 'You have been uncharacteristically quiet this rotation.'

Well, it would have been impossible to get a word in with Mother anyway. But Neekor was right. I had, long ago, told her all about Hayden – except for the details of our last encounter – and I was determined to preserve the image of him that I had constructed for her.

'Yes,' I said, once I had found an appropriate excuse. 'I've just been thinking about **Meet**.'

'That is what your new operation is for, is it not?' she said brightly. 'To advise the Hierarch about exactly these types of matters. I meant what I said last rotation, Daniel. I know you can make a difference. I always have.'

We stopped and Neekor gazed out over the water. Aar was about to dip below the hills to the west and, even through the skyways, the whole bay seemed to shimmer like when the ancestors used to spill oil in the ocean and set it alight. But I found myself enthralled by Neekor instead. I stood there, dumbly, overwhelmed by affection for every little detail about her, from the way her mane shone in that same, fiery glow, to the little shiver she did when Aar finally did drop from sight.

Then Hayden entered my thoughts. This time, I heard his comments about courting Aliens, how emotionally vacant he thought they were. I'd known that wasn't true at the time, and I knew it now with even greater certainty.

I'd allowed Hayden to distract me long enough. He was the one who walked away from our friendship, not me. And, judging by the ignored message still in his tree, he clearly wasn't wasting any thoughts on me. Neekor was far more deserving of my energy, which I resolved to express to her in a way that only a Human could once we returned to Kappeetar.

It took a lot of preparation, and quite a bit of research. While I was somewhat familiar with the ritual I had in mind, I'd never actually seen it practised, so had to utilise my **writing** device to access the **net** and find whatever early resources I could. The gift I wanted was also difficult to procure, but with Mother's help, I was able to find a traditional practitioner from Indonesia, who still mined his own **gold** and crafted jewellery from it. Although I was Rank 3, I could never afford to use our once-prized **diamond** as the gemstone, so the **goldsmith** helped me find a shade of much more affordable **quartz** that reminded me of the smoky hazel colour of Neekor's eyes. Then all I had to do was wait for the right time to prepare the ritual.

I invited Neekor to my dwelling under the pretence of making darkmeal, and instructed her to enter without needing to alert me to her arrival. Everything seemed in order, or at least a close-enough imitation of the faded image from the **net** I'd used as a reference. I checked it again, comparing the positions of the **balloons** and **streamers**, and wondered if I'd arranged them properly. Before I could change them, the gateway opened, and I was forced to dive to my hiding spot behind the preserver. Listening to Neekor approach, I could see why the practice was so popular among the ancestors. I couldn't stop shaking with anticipation.

I heard her footsteps reach the main room and resisted the urge to jump out – timing, I understood, was key to this.

'Daniel?' Neekor called.

That was the moment. Leaping from my position, I yelled 'Surprise!' as loudly as I could.

I still replay this memory, at half the speed so I can relive the hilarity of Neekor's reaction in all its splendour. She shrieked and jumped – both louder and higher than I did – before stumbling backwards into the gate, which expanded at her contact so she fell onto her backside in the hallway.

At the time, however, this wasn't funny in the least. Convinced I had completely sabotaged our courtship. I rushed after her, trying desperately to calm her down.

'Neekor, it's me – Daniel! Everything's okay!'

Eyes wide, tendrils rigid, she put a trembling hand on the wall to steady herself. Her gaze darted from me to the decorations beyond in the main room, before returning furiously.

'What is this?' she roared, forcing herself up and charging at me, claws drawn. 'I thought you were a predator!'

'Apologies! I can explain!' I frantically adopted an inferior expression in an attempt to placate her. Which worked – just. 'Apologies for frightening you. I was just trying to perform a Human ritual.'

'One that terrifies me into cardiac arrest?'

'No, one that honours you.'

Her snarl relaxed and she let me take her hand, claws retracted. I guided her into the main room.

'In older times,' I said, choosing my words with the utmost care, 'Humans would be honoured by a celebration of the anniversary of their birth.'

Neekor squinted at me. 'Why?'

'It's just a way of showing affection for someone.'

Neekor's searching stare assessed me. 'How do you celebrate someone's anniversary of birth?'

'Remember when Mother talked about Covenant Anniversary? We had no galactic calendar before Aliens arrived. We had our own system

167

based specifically on Teerin' Ho's revolutions. So when a Human was born, that date was recorded as their rote of birth.'

'So this rotation is my… birth anniversary?' asked Neekor. I flicked positively and she said, 'How did you deduce that?'

'I found your records in the Core and calculated it.'

Out of curiosity I also attempted to calculate her **star-sign**, which turned out to be **Aquarius**. Given its characterisation as highly intellectual, rational, and empathetic, I was almost convinced of its accuracy until I saw that it was supposed to be utterly incompatible with my own **star-sign**.

At long last a smile graced her lips. She walked among the decorations, touching them tentatively, like they might leap out and surprise her as well.

'So,' I said, 'what do you think?'

She poked at a **balloon** a few times and replied, 'It is … pleasant. I mean, these all seem like an unnecessary excess of polymers, and I find it odd to celebrate the simple fact of one's existence as opposed to their achievements or contributions to society, but it is … nice. I feel honoured.'

I let out a sigh of relief, then remembered the most important part.

'It was also customary to give the person being celebrated a gift.' I withdrew the tiny package and handed it to her. The smile faded from her face.

'But, Daniel, I do not have a gift for you in return.'

'There's no expectation of reciprocation with these.'

'What do you mean? Humans would just … give a gift and get nothing in return?'

I flicked positively. 'The purpose is to honour the person whose birth anniversary it is.'

'Ah, so the reciprocation would occur on *your* birth anniversary?'

'Well, yes, but you shouldn't think of it that way. When you give someone a gift on their birth anniversary, it should be without any expectation of receiving something in return. The act of gift-giving should be completely selfless, with only the intent to show your affection for that person.'

Neekor was silent for a moment. 'It is quite a meaningful custom.'

She held the package, staring at it, then saluted me. 'Gratitude, Daniel. Where should I put it? Is it a wall ornament or...'

I realised then that she had no idea why the package was wrapped in paper.

'Oh, no, Neekor, this isn't the actual gift,' I said, stifling a laugh. 'You have to unwrap it.'

She flexed a confused tendril at me. 'The gift is wrapped in this ... plant fibre? Why?'

'So you don't know what it is.'

'You do not want me to know what it is?'

'Only until you unwrap it.'

'Why not just give it to me unwrapped?'

'So you are surprised by what it is.'

'Would I not be surprised by it anyway?'

'You're ruining the surprise!'

'It just seems like another excessive waste of materials –'

'Stop questioning my culture and just open it, would you?'

She gave in and tore at the paper, until the little black box inside was uncovered. She shot me a glance, and I gave her one that said, 'Yes, you have to open that too.' So she did, revealing the **gold ring** I had purchased for her.

'Daniel,' she breathed, pinching the treasure between her fingers and lifting it from the box. 'What is this?'

'It's called a **ring**,' I said, my throat tightening for a reason I didn't understand. 'It's like a band for your finger, made from a metal that was precious to the ancestors.'

Neekor looked at me. 'Does this have some sort of meaning, too?'

Swallowing the boulder that seemed to be stuck in my oesophagus, I managed, 'Well, any form of jewellery was a treasured gift among Humans. But **rings** were special. They symbolised an eternal bond. So they were most often given when someone wished to enter partnership with another.'

I froze. I hadn't intended to propose partnership with the **ring**. Not yet. Only to express my affection for her. I didn't know the first thing about traditional **marriage**, or even contemporary partnership. I realised that I had to say something, to pull it back, clarify that I wasn't intending to propose. I didn't want to pressure her, even if I did want her to know that I saw our courtship as more than just a test of what we could materially and genetically offer each other. That I simply enjoyed her presence and didn't want to be without it, didn't want to **miss** her –

Then I noticed I'd been so consumed by my own thoughts that Neekor had said something that I didn't hear.

'Apologies?'

'I said: I have also been thinking that I would like to enter partnership with you, Daniel.'

I had to ask her to repeat it several more times before I could accept I heard her properly. 'Really? Partnership? With me? Why?'

'Your ambition and intelligence are desirable traits I wish for my offspring. And, I know this makes no logical sense, but,' she said, her eyes lifting, 'you bring me joy and that is something I value.'

'That's a very Human thing, you know,' I said, unable to resist a grin. 'Perhaps you do have some Human in your genome after all.'

She smiled back and said, 'I would be honoured to have it in my offspring's.'

I couldn't bring myself to tell her how Humans used to make that happen. But I did tell her, in true Human fashion, that she'd made me the happiest being in the world (followed by a lengthy explanation of the Human concept of **hyperbole**).

The cycle that followed still feels like a **dream**. Nothing could pierce the bubble of bliss that enveloped me once my partnership with Neekor was validated in the Core. Not the continued tension between Humans and Aliens playing out in the Core over **Meet**, nor the propagation's sensationalising of it. Our clans came to Kappeetar to formally endorse our partnership and not even that inevitable clash of cultures could bring me down. Haapetti made her usual sly comments about Humanity's inferior approach to just about everything, although Kreetop really did come through with an impressive attempt at **chips**, which mostly made up for it. Mother fussed over us, trying to elevate the ritual into something much more ceremonial in accordance with the **law** of the ancestors. I didn't care. I was partnered to Neekor and that was all that mattered.

We purchased our first shared dwelling almost immediately after our partnering – a unit in Central Residential District 3 that had everything Neekor and I needed and more. I had never imagined dwelling in a unit that had not one, but *two* main rooms. I couldn't figure out the purpose of the second room, but Neekor assured me it was a fairly standard feature of dwellings in Wyakek.

I felt utterly content. I was partnered, in a dwelling of what I considered to be relative luxury and, by any standard, was thriving in the new Human-Hierarch Interactions Squad.

At service, I felt like a beast let out of a cage. No longer was I bound to the strict edict of Covenant resolutions. I could tell Hierarch servants whatever I thought about absolutely anything relating to Humans and be remunerated for it. This was a nice change from the regular expectation that I, and every other Human servant, should give advice on Human matters for free and at short notice.

I told the House of Knowledge that they needed to consider how changes to the juvenile education curriculum would impact traditional Human **schools**. I informed the House of Harvesting that their agricultural regulations didn't factor in Human methods of harvesting. I explained to the House of Healing that its edicts required its servants to understand and provide for the different needs and experiences of Human patients.

More often than not, I was met with resistance, no matter how many of the Covenant's Promises I quoted. The general sentiment was that the Houses didn't see why different consideration was needed when it came to Humans. Operators didn't understand how their Houses' actions affected Humans differently: why, for example, the Chamber of Excavation couldn't just begin mining operations on the surface without consulting the nations whose land it intended to mine. It was this particular case where my tolerance for dealing with these ignorant Operators reached its limit.

'Under the Covenant of Wellington, Humans' **property rights** are guaranteed,' I told the Excavation Operator. 'You can't just go onto someone else's **property** and start mining it without their permission.'

'But the Valuable Minerals Decree states that any valuable mineral found within the planet's crust is automatically controlled by the Hierarch,' the Operator protested.

'Human **property law** existed here long before Hierarch decree,' I said, 'and what you are about to do is recommend the deliberate breaching of that **law**, and by extension the Covenant of Wellington.'

Perhaps it was this statement that **sealed my fate**, as the ancestors would say. My pride had gone unchecked for too long, my reach allowed to extend too far. I had, just like the doomed **Inter-Cosmic Astronautical Relay Unit 5 [ICARU5]**, flown too close to the sun and, within minutes of disconnecting from that communication, I was sent plummeting back to **Earth** by news from the Core:

Wellington Commission releases finding on the Hierarch's Authorisation of Britain

I froze, pinned to my terminal seat. I'd had plenty of time to prepare for this moment, ever since the Commission granted Ireland's bid for an urgent inquiry. In all the excitement of the past cycle, I'd completely forgotten about it. I wasn't ready.

Forcing myself to breathe, I accessed the Commission's projection of its report and navigated to the finding.

The Wellington Commission finds that the Hierarch breached the Covenant of Wellington by including Ireland in Britain's Authorisation.

I read it multiple times, searching for a 'did not' before the word 'breached'. No matter how many times I read it, the ruling wouldn't change, and the reality of the finding grew heavier. There was more: the Hierarch had undermined Ireland's identity and independence, and the condition attached to the Authorisation – to provide membership for Ireland on the Britain Deciding Body, which I had come up with – was 'woefully inadequate'. The Commission formally recommended the Hierarch revoke its Authorisation of Britain and separately Authorise Ireland.

But all that detail faded away under the unequivocal, condemning judgment: the Hierarch breached the Covenant.

I disconnected. I couldn't read any more. I heard my name being called by the squad but it seemed distant.

I had breached the Covenant.

I had betrayed my people. Betrayed my ancestors.

Betrayed Hayden.

I was a **turncoat**.

Finally, Teemot's voice reached me. 'A disappointing outcome, is it not?'

I didn't respond. Vuneen must have known why. Gently, she said, 'All is well, Daniel. This is just what happens sometimes.'

I scanned each of their faces. None of them seemed concerned at all. 'Is it really?' I asked.

Teemot surprised me with a laugh. 'Absolutely. This is nothing new.'

'The Commission found we breached the Covenant when Spain was Authorised,' Vuneen added, as if the casual mention of another Covenant breach committed by our old squad was supposed to reassure me.

'The Commission's recommendations are not binding anyway,' Moolas pointed out. 'The Hierarch isn't obligated to comply with them.'

'But the Commission is the authority on the Covenant of Wellington,' I replied. 'Some of our greatest scholars – Human and Alien – sit on it. The Commission's findings are the reason we do Covenant resolutions at all. The Hierarch can't just ignore them.'

Moolas didn't say anything, which I knew was only because he didn't want to argue with me.

'That is exactly the issue with the Commission,' Pa'zan weighed in. 'The Commissioners are all scholars – theorists and philosophisers. None of them have any practical understanding of the reality of Covenant resolutions, or the complexity of what ChamCov does. It is easy to criticise the resolution process when they are not the ones having to conduct it.'

I knew Pa'zan was only speaking this strongly out of support for me, but I was still alarmed by it. I'd thought he, of all the squad, would have understood the gravity of the Commission's finding.

'I think what everyone is saying, Daniel,' said Vuneen, 'is that this is nothing to be ashamed of. At times, people disagree with us doing what we consider is right. You get used to it.'

There it was again, that phrase. It was easy for her to say. She wasn't Human.

Before I could think of a response, a message arrived in my tree from Lincoln. It was addressed to both Teemot and me, requesting our immediate presence at General Laffee's private terminal.

My coat stood on end. Teemot signalled for me to follow him and, in silence, we made our way to the General's terminal. I had never been inside her room before, nor spoken to her directly. It was a lavish setting, not unlike Neekor's parents' dwelling. In one corner was a beautifully patterned mat with cushions, accompanied by what I was certain was another cutting bar, and the chair connected to the General's terminal was a huge, plush lounger. As I came within its range, I was automatically connected to a projection of Winnra 5 Sophie, who was speaking from her podium at the Irish parliament, which both the General and Lincoln were watching.

'Ireland welcomes the Wellington Commission's finding,' Sophie announced. 'It verifies what Ireland has claimed since the beginning of Britain's Authorisation process. Not only that Ireland is and always has been an independent nation, but also that the Hierarch continues to weaponise its edicts against Humanity, oppressing our right to independence, and pitting us against one another – all under the guise of benevolent Covenant resolutions. I call on all Humans to join Ireland in demanding the Hierarch honour the Covenant of Wellington, honour the Promises it made our ancestors.'

Her address was met by sweeping applause that I was tempted to join.

'This is not the first time the Commission has made a finding like this about an Authorisation,' Lincoln said to the General, echoing the squad.

She ended the propagation stream. 'It is different this time. With **Meet** and all the protests –' Noticing Teemot and me, she scowled at Lincoln. 'These are the two who worked on the Authorisation?'

'Yes. Teemot Captained the squad responsible for the Authorisation, and this is the Knight who operated it, Kytoonoo 3 Daniel. But I must make clear that they were under my –'

'Ah, yes. Denial.' I was surprised she knew who I was. 'We have you to thank for the recent spate of conditional Authorisations, do we not? I was under the impression they were meant to prevent successful Wellington Commission inquiries, not cause them.'

That *was* my intention. Well, not that I'd recommended the conditional Authorisation just to avoid a Wellington Commission inquiry. I'd done it to provide representation for Ireland, give them a say on their resolution. I'd thought the Wellington Commission would see that.

'Daniel was under my Command, and Teemot's Captaincy,' Lincoln said. And all of us were under the General's Rank, I thought, so technically all of this was her responsibility.

175

'Well, this was your Authorisation,' she said to me, ignoring Lincoln, 'and you are now part of the squad that advises the Hierarch on how to interact with Humans. What is your advice for responding to this?'

'Standard response,' Teemot intervened. 'We are considering the Commission's finding.'

'I expect that will be insufficient.' The General's gaze didn't waver from me. 'The Accountancy has already informed me that the Hierarch's Rank has taken a greater hit from this than it did from the news about **Meet**. We will need a more practical answer.'

'Considering the finding *is* a practical answer,' said Lincoln. 'The Hierarch does need to consider it carefully to ensure its response does not create further grievance.'

The General finally regarded Lincoln to ponder this.

By now I'd found my voice and was determined to defend myself by pointing out what should have been obvious. The very same thing I had suggested right at the beginning of all this. 'Won't the expectation be that the Hierarch agrees to separate Authorisation for Ireland? Like the Commission is recommending?'

The General turned back to me with a glare that made me want to disappear.

'We have discussed this, Daniel,' Teemot sighed. 'We cannot compromise Hierarch edict.'

My response was right there: but you can compromise the Covenant of Wellington? We tried to act within Hierarch edict to honour it and failed. Didn't that prove the edict was unsuitable?

But I was frozen by the General's stare, the words trapped behind my clenched jaw.

Lincoln stepped in. 'Our response should be this: We are considering the Commission's finding. We accept the measures taken to provide for Ireland in Britain's Authorisation have been found inadequate. We will engage with both Ireland and Britain to develop measures acceptable to all parties.'

We waited as the General considered it.

'The propagation are contacting me,' she said, turning away from us. 'I will run this line for now. Send it to the Lord's Master for verification, and place an immediate hold on Britain's mediation. By the end of the rotation, I want a substantive response plan.'

Lincoln gave her a salute she didn't see and led us from the room. The moment the gate contracted behind us, he said, 'Daniel, I know this is distressing. I am going to ask that you leave the response to me and Teemot. I might ask Vuneen to help too.'

'I'm responsible for this, Lincoln,' I said. 'I knew a separate Authorisation was the right thing to do, even back then. I need to fix it –'

'You are not responsible for this.' His tone was firm. 'You can help by letting me deal with it.'

It was only then that I noticed the weary lines marking his face, how unkempt his blond mane had become in the last few rotes.

'Okay. Sorry, Lincoln.'

'Don't apologise. You've done everything you were supposed to.'

He and Teemot hurried away, leaving me standing outside the General's room to contemplate what that meant. While I stood there, a communication request arrived in my tree. It was from Mother. I didn't answer it.

Unlike the excitement that infected all of ChamCov when a resolution was about to be reached, no one aside from our squad seemed to even know about the Commission's finding. Either that, or no one cared. It wasn't discussed at the break areas, nor was it announced in the ChamCov sector of the Core. There wasn't even a mention of it at the servants' weekly gathering where, for routine **anthem** practice, we actually sang *God Save the King* and nobody batted an eye. Then again, no one ever understood the words to any of the **anthems** so I supposed that should have come as no surprise.

Lincoln, Teemot, and Vuneen wheeled in and out of the pen over the next few rotes, presumably in the process of developing a response to the decision. I was meant to keep working through the ever-increasing pile of Human-Hierarch Interactions requiring my advice, but I couldn't shake the obligation I felt to assist the response. I offered to be the one to contact Edward and break the news that Britain's mediation was being put on hold, but Lincoln insisted on handling that unpleasant conversation himself.

My constant attempts to insert myself must have eventually struck a nerve. Morgan arrived one rote to tell me what Lincoln was too polite to.

'Please, Daniel,' she said, 'calm **the fuck** down, would you?'

'I can't. We breached the Covenant, Morgan. No one seems to get that.'

'I do, and so does Lincoln, believe me.'

'Then why doesn't he seem to care? Why won't he let me help?'

'Because we can't afford to stop giving advice to the Hierarch on everything else. We might have got the Britain Authorisation wrong, but as you know there are plenty of other things requiring your attention. Lincoln isn't one of them.'

Her answer made a lot of sense. The number of other, potential Covenant breaches accumulating for my review was, as the ancestors would say, **getting out of hand**. But it was hard not to feel like I should have been the last choice of servant to assess them. I had been found guilty of committing the greatest transgression against my own people, breaking the Promises that we held sacred.

Neekor tried to help, in her own way.

'You did not breach the Covenant,' she said for the fourth time in the same conversation. 'The Hierarch did. You are a servant of the Hierarch and, accordingly, are bound by Hierarch edict.'

'But *I* did it,' I reiterated. 'I crafted the bid. The standing position for Ireland on the Britain Deciding Body was my idea.'

'It was a good idea.'

'"Woefully inadequate" was what the Commission called it.'

'Maybe so, but even if you had not added that condition, the Commission's finding would have been the same, would it not? It is not as if your actions alone caused this.'

'No, but my actions didn't stop it, either. It's what I came to the Hierarch to do.'

Neekor sighed. 'Perhaps honouring the Covenant is just not as simple as you think it is.'

That night I mulled those words from within my sleep capsule. It should have been simple: the Covenant was a simple document (aside from the fact that it had been crafted over 300 revs ago, in two separate transfers that didn't match, one of which didn't make total sense having been converted by Aliens who didn't adequately understand it, and its legitimacy in a modern context was at best unclear and at worst non-existent). It was Hierarch edict that complicated it. You couldn't honour the Covenant when Hierarch edict depended on its nullification. Perhaps I'd been a fool to think that I could make the two compatible.

The ghost of Hayden returned unbidden, laughing, 'Told you so!' I was so eager to escape this taunting that I finally decided facing up to Mother was a preferable alternative.

'Apologies for missing your earlier communications,' I said once she accepted my connection request. 'I have been quite busy at service.'

'I can imagine. I saw the announcement by the Wellington Commission about the Britain Authorisation. Quite a significant finding, is it not?'

'Yes.' I hoped my nervous tone didn't betray me. 'It is.'

'It's caused ripples throughout Humanity. Ireland has already announced they are planning a **road trip** to the Apex.'

I leapt out of my sleeping capsule.

'What? Why?'

'To demand the Hierarch act on the Commission's finding, why else?'

Careful not to wake Neekor from her sedation, I crept into the second main room where I could panic in peace. There hadn't been a **road trip** since the **Stratosphere-Tropopause** controversy in Rev 9-4012, when the Hierarch had passed a decree that declared control over the entirety of **Earth**'s second layer of atmosphere. And that had resulted in the previous Hierarch being replaced by Clan Global.

'Has there been much of a reaction at ChamCov?' Mother asked.

As nerve-wracking as this conversation was, she wasn't as pointed as I had expected. I wondered if she'd even forgotten it was me who worked on the Britain Authorisation.

'Surprisingly, it hasn't. The common sentiment seems to be: "This happens all the time."'

'Typical. This is the way it's always been, so it must be right,' she scoffed. 'And how is service anyway? I trust you're not breaching the Covenant!'

She cackled away at her own joke. I tried to laugh too, but it was feeble, pathetic. I was reminded of the time she had, with frightening conviction, said that she would never trust the Hierarch. I'd always wondered how she could have such disdain for it but also pride in my serving it. In this moment I understood the answer; she believed, like Neekor apparently, that it was possible for a Human to serve the Hierarch and not be complicit in its actions. As if my Humanity alone somehow absolved me of any responsibility for Covenant breaches I helped it to commit. If I was wise enough, I would have questioned her on this and she would have promptly shown me why she was always right about everything. She would have told me that, if the Hierarch had never broken the Covenant, and never assimilated us, I would never have been put in such a position; that if the Hierarch was actually committed to honouring the Covenant, Humans could serve it without fear of being involved in a Covenant breach. She would have said that I could never be held personally responsible for the actions committed by this giant assimilation machine because, having done all those things, it would have always breached the Covenant on the Britain Authorisation, with or without me.

But I was 24 revs old, which wasn't really any more mature than 21, and I still believed I was personally capable of influencing the Hierarch's actions. So I lied to her instead.

'It's going well. All is well.'

Just like that, the moment passed. I'd lied to her, my own mother, again. I don't even know what we talked about for the remainder of the conversation. All I could think about was that I deceived her. I really was a turncoat. A coward and a traitor.

As soon as our communication ended, I checked the Core for news. A road trip forming in Ireland would draw the propagation's interest, which would thrust ChamCov and its Authorisation of Britain into their scopes. I wondered how long I could keep my involvement a secret. All Winnra 5 Sophie had to do was mention my name and I would be exposed. I could see my face plastered across the net, accompanied by vicious abuse that would devolve into conspiracy theories about my involvement in the Authorisation. It would be impossible to counter them with facts or rational discussion. My reputation among Humans would be destroyed and Mother's along with it. I pictured her cast out of parliament for refusing to denounce her turncoat son, clinging desperately to her belief that I could never breach the Covenant, all the way to the end of her life in an elderly care institution, where the only thing she would ever say was, 'My Daniel could never breach the Covenant,' and the staff would laugh to each other and say, 'Good old Michelle.' I saw my Rank plummeting to 0, and Neekor's clan revoking their approval of our partnership, with Neekor's profile so tainted by association with me that she had to apply to the Gardeners for a memory deletion of our partnership altogether. Being Alien, her application would be immediately granted and I would stumble across her path one day and she wouldn't recognise me. I would end up as another Human of Wellington, spending half the rote cut out of my mind and the other half lining up outside the Allowance Exchange. And when that wasn't enough, I'd join the Mutt Pack and dye my coat with a red patch, be ordered to thieve and intimidate just to fuel the forbidden cleaving trade, until I was captured and detained by the Keepers, then sentenced to exile on **Mars** where I would be forced to survive by committing my final betrayal against Humanity: murder, because what else would the majority Human population in exile do but **kill or be killed** –

Winnra 5 Sophie's voice cut through my spiralling simulation. My search through the Core had landed on a projection of her standing at her podium.

'I implore all Humans who have had enough of the Hierarch denying our independence while celebrating our assimilation to join us, unite with us, and advance on the Apex to demand action.'

The crowd cheered with a resounding, rallying cry of solidarity. She raised a fist and roared, 'Honour the Covenant!' which the crowd screamed back at her. She said it again, and again, and each time the crowd repeated it, louder than the last.

I was overcome by the need to *do* something, to make myself useful in some way. It felt wrong to have created such turmoil only to sit back and let people like Lincoln deal with it alone.

The following rote I marched past Morgan, ignoring her objections, and up to Lincoln's terminal where I announced, 'There's a **road trip** starting in Ireland.'

Slowly, tiredly, he looked up. 'I know.'

'What are we doing about it?'

He rubbed his tendrils. 'Nothing.'

'Nothing? We need to have a response, someone to receive them – probably the Supreme Rank –'

'The Supreme Rank will do no such thing.' His voice was suddenly firm, and Morgan flinched beside me. He took a breath, then added, 'Please, Daniel, I really need you to trust me to handle this.'

'Why?' I knew the answer, but I wanted to hear him say it. 'Why won't you let me help?'

'Because you're too close.' He stood, and I felt like something had changed between us. Like he was no longer speaking to me as my mentor, Commander to Knight, but on equal terms – Human to Human. 'You don't see the forest for the trees.'

I didn't know what this expression meant, and it must have shown. Morgan took pity on me and said, with a hand on my shoulder, 'Perhaps there is something Daniel can help with. We need to monitor what the propagation says about the road trip once the story breaks.'

'True,' said Lincoln as he returned to his seat. 'I hadn't even started thinking about that.'

Morgan smiled at me. 'Then leave it with me and Daniel.'

Back at my terminal, Morgan connected me to the propagation network in the Core. My task was simple: monitor the network for any information about the road trip, record it, and transfer it to a depository in ChamCov's division of the Core specifically set up for the response to the Britain Decision.

It was quiet for the first rote or so. There didn't seem to be anything since that first announcement, and I ended up spending much of my time researching the meaning of old and unfamiliar Human expressions. Then, gradually, the transfer triggers I'd set up in the network began to fire. First with the primary propagators, who started transferring images of the road trip amassing at the Irish parliament, with a militant Winnra 5 Sophie at the head. In those first few accounts, the size of the road trip was already remarkable: the sky above the Irish parliament was completely occupied by vehicles. Sirens blared, and cheers rained down on the propagation reporters.

From there, the news grew. Soon, even the minor propagators were reporting on the **road trip**, and the volume of commentary grew. I saw a few interviews with Edward, one featuring him downplaying the **road trip's** size even as it appeared on the horizon behind him.

It was only when I found commentary by an irrelevant but wealthy Alien (who was therefore automatically reputable) that I began to truly see the **forest** Lincoln had referred to.

'I mean, really, why do we even care what the Wellington Commission has to say? It is not a Balancer – not a true one, really – so why do we tolerate it making these sorts of judgments? I have said it before, and I will say it again: it is time we abolished the Wellington Commission once and for all. It exists only to sow division – look at what it has stirred up in Ireland. Do you know what we normally call a pack of thugs making demands of the Hierarch? Terrorists, that's what –'

I turned his projection off and searched for the Rank Auditor Noddee 5 Sharbb, another wealthy Alien with no knowledge of Human affairs, who had, naturally, already been interviewed on the topic.

'It is quite simple: the Wellington Commission's finding is categorically wrong. The Hierarch cannot have breached the Covenant by not recognising the independence of Ireland, because, as Promise 1 clearly states, Ireland – along with every other Human nation – ceded their Rank to the Hierarch absolutely and forever. I would say Ireland should be grateful they have been offered reparations at all, but I will not elaborate on that; my view on the travesty that is the Covenant resolution process is well known –'

I didn't need to see any more. If it hadn't happened already, those two alone would be rallying vast followings of ignorant Aliens into vocal, violent objection to anything and everything Human. Somehow, I'd managed to not only provoke the birth of the latest Human protest movement but also awaken an army of angry Aliens. In the timeless words of the ancestors I had been researching:

Fuck me.

The reaction to **Meet** was nothing compared to the Great Irish **Road Trip**. The disparate, isolated demonstrations at **Meet** had been nothing more than minor irritations to the Hierarch. But from the moment the **road trip** left Ireland, and the Core became dominated with diagrams charting its course to Kappeetar, it was clear that the Hierarch could not ignore it.

Maybe that was Winnra 5 Sophie's genius. The anger was already there, seeded around the world by **Meet**. She just consolidated it.

Following the **road trip**'s slow progress across Europe, the Middle-East, then Asia –as more and more Humans joined it – became a ritual of mine and Neekor's. It was the first thing we did each lightbreak and the last thing we did each darkfall. For Neekor, it was probably necessary: the House of Transportation expected the **road trip** to shut down all sky traffic in the House District, which would in turn affect the entire skyways network. Shipping paths would have to be rerouted, civilian detours put in place, public transportation options increased. It fell to Neekor's squad to calculate what Rank could be spared from other allocations and to re-distribute it to the **road trip** response.

The **road trip** was nonetheless a spectacle to her. She confessed that she barely remembered the **Stratosphere-Tropopause Road Trip**, and mortified me by asking if the Irish **road trip** would be comparable with the disgraceful 'Liberty Convoy' of Rev 9-4022. The answer to which was an emphatic '**fuck no**'.

I had been on the **Stratosphere-Tropopause Road Trip**, sitting beside Mother in her rusty old kawwa. I was only a juvenile at the time, so hadn't really understood the significance of it. But I did now. I knew how unifying it was for Humanity. And how disastrous it was for the Hierarch of the time.

On the rotation of the **road trip's** expected arrival, we woke to find the Core heaving with activity. Every propagation outlet was running the arrival as their headline story. There were beings who had developed their own constructs to track its trajectory, which they were sharing on their profiles. Projections of 'Honour the Covenant' and stylised images of Winnra 5 Sophie's face circulated.

My prediction at the outset of the **road trip** had been accurate: the Noddee 5 Sharbbs of the world had whipped their followers into a froth by decrying the **road trip** and everything it stood for, demanding that the Hierarch ignore the movement. Funny, I thought, how Aliens can make demands all they like without being labelled thugs or terrorists. Some were even calling for counter **road trips**, espousing various takes on 'One Decree for All' and 'We are one species.'

'Try not to let it trouble you, Daniel,' Neekor said. 'You are not responsible for this **road trip** and if I have to hear you say that you are one more time, I may very well cancel our partnership.'

Under different circumstances this attempt at a joke might have got a laugh out of me. 'I was actually thinking of going down to the Apex when it arrives,' I said. Anticipating her alarmed expression, I clarified, 'Not to join. Just to see it, with my own eyes.'

'I do not think that would be wise. Firstly, for your own mental stability, but secondly, because Hierarch servants should not be seen –'

'I know the edict, Neekor,' I said, probably with more bite than I should have. 'Frankly, I don't care. It's Hierarch edict that caused all of this in the first place.'

'Just be careful,' she said, then surprised me by the very Human gesture of taking my hand in hers. 'If you need something else to distract you, I always find number puzzles quite stimulating.'

This wasn't a joke, but it did get a laugh out of me.

When I arrived at the House District the atmosphere was heavy. The air channels had been cleared, and everyone in the streets had their necks craned to the sky, hoping to catch a glimpse of the first vehicles to arrive. The mood was similar inside ChamCov. The entire level was dead quiet, which I soon learned was due to most servants being at their terminals, connected to live feeds of the Apex. I joined them, occasionally switching to a propagator to listen to what they were saying about it. Their ability to keep finding inventive ways of discussing how much closer the **road trip** had moved was impressive, and before I knew it, they were excitedly announcing that the **road trip** was, at long last, closing in on the Apex.

Disconnecting, I cast a look across the level. Everyone else was still glued to the Core. For a moment, I did actually contemplate Neekor's suggestion of a number puzzle to distract me, but a much more tempting number puzzle was waiting for me outside: trying to calculate how many Humans had occupied the airspace of the House District.

The last image I had seen of the **road trip** was an aerial shot of Kappeetar's central districts, above which a glittering, metallic cloud swarmed towards the black spike of the Apex. That didn't prepare me for the sight from below. I exited the House of Balance to behold a moving ceiling of vehicles shrouding the House District and filling the air with the harmonised humming of engines. Some vehicles bore illuminated signs, most reading 'Honour the Covenant'. Others bore the white star of Humanity. There were even a couple showing the emblem of the United Nations. As I wound my way through the various Houses towards the Apex, a protest call rang out – a lone vehicle's horn sounding a familiar staccato pattern that was answered by the deafening, combined toots of the entire **road trip**.

They'd used the same pattern last time. Mother had put me on her lap so I could see the parade of vehicles surrounding the Apex, and had pressed my hand to her kawwa's horn. Our meagre offering was lost in the resounding blast, but it didn't matter. We were part of that unification, part of something greater than ourselves – the rallying of Humanity against a common enemy.

Now standing beneath the **road trip** at the edge of the Apex's perimeter, I wished I was up there with them again, sitting beside Mother, in that same old kawwa, joining our voices to everyone else's. I was supposed to be making the Hierarch honour the Covenant too, in my own way. But I stood alone.

Not completely alone, actually. A handful of brave (or stupid) Aliens had turned out with their own signs. One said, 'Stop the grievance industry'. Another said, 'Abolish the Wellington Commission'. I made the mistake of looking one in the eye and he took that as a sign of allegiance from a fellow Alien. He hobbled over to me and said, 'One would think these beings have better things to do. Why are they not at service?'

'Why aren't you?' I asked him.

'Because I am making a stand,' he said. Before I could enlighten him about the Human concept of **irony**, he added, 'I object to their constant attempts to divide this planet. It is time they accepted we are all one species.'

'And what "one species" is that?'

'We are all citizens of Teerin' Ho.'

Instead of pointing out that 'citizens of Teerin' Ho' isn't a species, I tried to be tactful. 'The problem with that, though, is that it erases all the things unique to our separate cultures. It assumes that we can all be "one species" only so long as that "one species" is yours.'

His tendrils flexed – he was beginning to realise I was not the ally he thought.

I continued, 'How would you like it if I told you we have to be "one species", but that means you have to do everything the Human way, not the Alien one?'

'Don't call me that,' he snapped.

'What, Alien?'

'Yes. It is an offensive term and I object to being labelled with it.'

'It is literally the Human term for non-Humans who settled here. There is nothing offensive about it.'

'I know what it means.'

'Oh, you understand Common, do you?'

'Why would I want to understand a transfer that has no use outside of Teerin' Ho? Much better off learning Hynee or Parnyor.'

188

'And which one of those transfers have you learned?'

'Well, neither of them –'

I gave up at this point and put as much distance between me and him as I could.

I waited until a number of kawwas broke from the **road trip** and descended down to the Apex's base. Keeper interceptors rose to meet them, not engaging, but making it clear that they wouldn't tolerate any aggression as they guided the delegation to land. Once it had, a number of Humans emerged from the kawwas led by Winnra 5 Sophie. The group flanking her were an imposing squad of **soldiers** dressed in traditional green combat gear, with antique **rifles** slung over their shoulders, marching in perfect sync. They were received by a line of Keepers, bionic weaponry equipped, who had exited their interceptors to prevent entry to the Apex. Sophie addressed them, and a notification told me she was projecting to the Core. I tuned in.

'Seriously? Keeper presence at a peaceful protest? How long before you start atomising us?'

I glanced over at the Alien protestors stationed nearby, who faced no such intimidation by the Keepers. If there was any risk of violence it was far more likely to come from one of them. The only incident of mass-murder terrorism in Teerin' Ho's history was committed by an Alien, after all.

'We only want to see the Supreme Rank,' Sophie continued.

'You may correspond with the Supreme Rank through the Core,' a Keeper replied.

Sophie gestured to the legion above her. 'Bring them out so they can see what they've done, and hear our message with their own ears.'

The Keepers didn't reply, but Sophie didn't relent. She demanded the Supreme Rank's presence, while the convoy overhead issued its reverberating protest call.

'We will stay here as long as we have to,' Sophie told the Keepers, 'and we won't be intimidated by you.'

She didn't have to wait long. A figure soon appeared at the Apex's entrance; a tall Alien male, immaculately garbed, temple glinting with an advanced root, engineered eyes glowing violet – Salasin 8 Potakeer, Lord for Covenant of Wellington Resolutions. He strode out to meet Sophie with no sign of fear, but that couldn't be said for the figure that came after him. General Laffee kept her eyes fixed on her feet, refusing to acknowledge the **road trip** above her. She stopped, checked behind her as if waiting for someone, and then Lincoln appeared, hurrying to catch up to her. Together they joined the Lord to meet with Sophie.

'Apologies for my delay, High Rank Winnra,' the Lord said, his voice picked up by Sophie's projection.

'I was hoping for the Supreme Rank,' she said. 'But I suppose you'll have to do.' (The propagation later revealed that the Supreme Rank was on Anor at the time, meeting with **rats**.)

The Lord ignored her jab and said, 'Before we proceed, may I respectfully request you terminate your projection?'

Dissonant toots reached us from the travellers listening in, and Sophie's response reflected them. 'This is not a private conversation, Lord. It is between you and all of Humanity – your Covenant partners. Everyone deserves to hear this.'

A silent second passed before the projection was cut anyway. Sophie recoiled, and I realised that the Gardeners had ended the projection manually. More angry toots sounded as the same realisation swept through the **road trip**, but Sophie regained her composure and continued her address. Lord Salasin didn't speak, only flicking positively in response until Sophie appeared to finish. When he spoke, it was only a few words, but it must have been all that was needed. Sophie spun on a heel and walked away, while one of her soldiers spat at the Lord's feet, the full offensiveness of which was probably lost on him, and Lincoln would have known better than to explain. The Irish delegation ascended to the **road trip** in their kawwas, and the Lord and his entourage promptly returned to the Apex.

Sophie's voice soon resurfaced in the Core: 'So, I have only just had my projecting permissions restored by the Gardeners, but I can share with you all now what the Lord's response was to our demand that the Hierarch honour the Covenant. In short, they won't. They made no commitment to accept the Wellington Commission's finding. They made no commitment to recognise Ireland's independence.'

The **road trip** made their opinion known. When I had seen Sophie striding towards the Apex, flanked by **soldiers**, I had wondered how she could lose. She seemed to carry the wishes of all of Humanity with her, and as she confronted the Lord, I thought there was no one better suited to do it.

'I will not give up,' she continued. 'I will stay here, making Ireland's case for independence, for as long as I have to. And I call on all of Humanity to stand with me.'

The response was unequivocal. Thunderous toots rattled the entire House District. The **road trip** wasn't going anywhere. I watched, for as long as I could justify, as one delegation after another descended from the mass to march right up to the line of Keepers and say their piece. Thankfully, by the time I got back to ChamCov, the propagation had set up at the frontline with their drones, and I was able to keep watching the demonstrations while pretending, like everyone else, to busy myself with some form of service.

It was as if Winnra 5 Sophie had licensed every single Human to unleash the 348 revolutions of suffering they had inherited under the Hierarch. I saw an elderly Canadian male, with trembling lips and watery eyes, tell of the Human occupation at Vancouver Island, and the one thousand strong Keeper deployment who removed them and razed their settlements to the ground. I heard a Japanese woman, head held high, recount the horrors of the Invasion of Tokyo, of the Weavers storming the city under the barrel of a photon cannon positioned in the airspace above, of the males terminated or exiled, of the females forcibly inseminated by Weaver troops. The oppression of Ireland stood for the oppression of every Human. The **final straw**, as the ancestors would say.

When service period ended, other servants packed up and went home as if there wasn't a millions-strong convoy of furious Humans just outside. But I was drawn back to the Apex. The dark was descending and the delegations had ceased, but the **road trip** remained in the sky.

The fading light provided the perfect opportunity for them to splash the Apex's surface with projections: 'Honour the Covenant' plastered its black walls, along with other slogans of solidarity such as, 'Humans never ceded control' (and a few iterations of '**Fuck the Hierarch**' for good measure).

I was glad to see that the pitiful showing of Alien protestors was gone, their signs abandoned on the Apex grounds. I took up the same position I had earlier, on the fence line of the Apex's perimeter, listening to the sounds chiming from above. They had taken on a more joyous note; a **sing-along** that would have put the Clan Lounge to shame was gathering momentum, and soon the whole **road trip** was belting out **We're Not Gonna Take It** for all of Kappeetar to hear.

I stayed there for hours, listening to them, humming along. I just wanted to be a part of it, to give whatever tiny contribution my unknown presence could to the cause. Anything to make up for my contribution to the very reason they were there. So that when the **sing-along** moved into an old Irish anthem, and they sang, '**One life with each other; sisters, brothers** ...' I could feel like it included me, too.

The **road trip** had become its own canvas of stars in the night sky when I noticed a figure leave the Apex's base. After being granted exit by the Keepers, they set off across the grounds, and when they stepped into the perimeter's spotlights, I saw that it was Lincoln.

'Daniel?' He made his way towards me. When I could finally see him properly, he looked more exhausted than ever; heavy bags under his eyes, tendrils drooping. 'What are you doing here?'

I didn't know what to say. He must have understood. He gave me a nod and for a while we stared up at the graffitied Apex in silence.

'I thought I was doing the right thing,' I said. 'With the Britain Authorisation.'

'You wouldn't be Human if you didn't,' he said.

'I've never felt less Human.'

'Then you understand the weight of serving the Hierarch.'

I remembered his warning when I first started service at ChamCov. He was right.

'What happens now?' I asked.

'Sometimes,' he said, 'the machine has to break in order to change.'

I turned to him. 'How do we do that?'

His gaze remained fixed on the very tip of the Apex. 'We already have.'

3-8

Well, I finally had something to distract me from the **road trip**. Lincoln had bid me **goodnight** and left me before I could ask him what he meant. By the time I made it home, I still hadn't deciphered it.

'Perhaps he was delusional,' Neekor suggested, when I recounted the exchange. 'From exhaustion?'

This wasn't a bad suggestion. It was the first time I'd really seen Lincoln since the **road trip** began, as he'd been so busy advising the Hierarch on its impending arrival, and he had looked unusually dishevelled. But I knew that wasn't the answer. Lincoln was too sharp, too intelligent. He always chose his words carefully.

So, while the **road trip** became something like a **car park** permanently established in the airspace around the Apex, and everyone else glued themselves to the Core, I tried to find an opportunity to speak with Lincoln. I had to know what he was planning. If it was something that offered redemption for my part in the Britain Decision, then I had to be involved. But as the weeks rolled by, he proved elusive. Even Teemot and Vuneen, who were supposed to be assisting him with the **road trip** response, confessed they'd barely seen him. At one point I began to wonder if I was the delusional one, and had completely imagined our encounter outside the Apex.

Neekor and I were well into another ritualised night of watching propagation updates when one propagator at the front lines of the **road trip** reported, 'With me now is Alliance Clans representative, Karkoora 7 Darius – tell us why the Alliance Clans are supporting this.'

There he was again: the well-presented Human who stoked the first fires of Human revolt with **Meet**. He gave a respectful salute to the drone recording the stream – or rather, all the Humans he would have known were watching through it – before directing his attention to the propagator.

'It's simple. Enough is enough. First, we had the Hierarch celebrating the arrival of Kookee. Now it has pulled this: a breach of its Covenant Promises to Ireland. So not only is the Hierarch celebrating the assimilation of Humans, it's still attempting to assimilate us – denying independence, erasing identity. The Alliance Clans stand with Ireland and utterly reject this Hierarch.'

The **irony** of this was, I mused, that it was the Alliance Clans who passed the decree that resulted in the **Stratosphere-Tropopause Road Trip** and were consequently demoted from the Hierarch in favour of Clan Global. I thought only Aliens had forgotten all about it, but maybe Humans had too.

Neekor disconnected her tree from mine and frowned.

'The Hierarch has not offered any response, has it?'

I flicked negatively.

'And you have no insight into the advice your Commander is giving the Hierarch? You do not know if its position will change?'

I thought of my encounter with Lincoln at the Apex. 'I'm not sure.'

'Your Commander was responsible for the Britain Authorisation, was he not?'

'Yes.'

'And now he happens to be in a position to advise the Hierarch on its response to Humanity's reaction to the British Authorisation. A response that appears to be failing?'

I felt a twinge of understanding, closely followed by annoyance. 'What are you trying to say? You think Lincoln deliberately recommended Authorising Britain because he knew what it would do? That he wants the Hierarch to lose Rank over this?'

She shrugged her ears. 'Maybe that's what he meant when he said the machine had to break.'

It had been so long since I felt the anger. Not since the visit to Neekor's clan had it coursed through me, making my fists shake, my coat bristle. Its cause, this time, was another experience unique to

Human Hierarch servants that I was well aware of but hadn't personally encountered until now: the suggestion that, given the slightest opportunity, a Human servant would betray the confidence of the Hierarch to benefit Humanity. There's a Common term for it: having a 'conflict of interest'. It didn't matter if there was a perfectly logical reason why Lincoln had recommended the Authorisation of Britain, and was now advising the Hierarch on how to address the Human reaction to it. What mattered was the perception: that he had taken advantage of his position for personal or familial gain.

'How many other Human Commanders do you know?' I asked.

Neekor thought for a moment. 'None.'

'But the only one you do know, you accuse of deceit.'

A pensive expression I hadn't seen on Neekor before came over her. 'Apologies. I did not mean any disrespect. I am not accusing Lincoln of anything. Only suggesting one of possibly many reasons for what he said to you. Disregard it, if you must.'

At her insistence, I tried to salvage some pleasure from our evening together by returning to the propagation updates. But despite my impassioned defence of Lincoln, the more I thought about it, the more I had to accept that, as usual, there was sound logic to Neekor's perception. Other snippets of conversation with Lincoln came back to me: 'The hard part is still to come,' and 'You've done everything you were supposed to.' The way he'd blocked me from any involvement in the response to the road trip – was it because I would disrupt his plans? Because I was a blundering fool who didn't understand what he was trying to achieve? Had I become the one thing that the ancestors had always considered the highest shame: that guy?

I still wasn't sure what I thought when I arrived at service the next rotation. I didn't want to believe that Lincoln was capable of such things. Then again, I did believe Lincoln was capable of just about anything, which technically included conspiracy to overthrow the Hierarch.

Vuneen and Moolas were already at the pen when I got there, and, as was my habit, I asked them if they had seen Lincoln or expected to.

Neither of them responded. Walking around to their terminals, I saw they were both connected to the Core, wearing grim expressions.

'Something wrong?' I asked.

Without answering, Vuneen linked her tree to mine. A propagation feed played, the footage so shaky I could barely decipher what it showed.

'– just moving to a more secure position,' said a voice, presumably a propagator's, although it was almost lost to raucous jeers somewhere nearby. The picture sharpened, revealing a mob of surly Humans squaring up against the Keepers outside the Apex. The red patches on their shoulders gleamed in the propagation drone's lens.

'The Mutt Pack is on the **road trip**,' said Moolas. 'Can you believe that?'

I could not, and the propagator shared our disbelief: 'It is quite unlike anything that has been seen before – the notorious Mutt Pack joining a demonstration of any kind – but Human leaders say it is indicative of the extent of Human anger against the Hierarch. That even the packs – which are almost exclusively populated by Humans – have decided to join the cause –'

The drone swept upwards, soaring over the crowd of red-shouldered pack members that filled almost the entire Apex grounds. Every chapter in Teerin' Ho must have been there.

'I think this is the end,' Moolas commented. 'The Keepers have tolerated the **road trip's** presence this long only due to its good behaviour. The Mutt Pack will not be able to help themselves. The **road trip** will end this rotation, I am confident of it.'

I was gone, heading for the Apex, probably before Moolas and Vuneen realised it. I agreed with Moolas; Keepers had a bad enough reputation when it came to handling ordinary Humans let alone pack members, and I didn't know if the Mutts could avoid starting trouble with the Keepers either. If Hayden really was one of them – well, I had no idea what I was going to do about it. I just had to get there.

By the time I reached the Apex, I could feel it in the air. A pressure, a bomb about to detonate. The Mutts were a jostling mass, a moving wall with no way through, from which rose bellows of their rally cry 'Victory Hail!'

I sent Hayden a message, telling him where I was and that, if he was somewhere at the demonstration, I was worried about him. Like my other message, it went seen but unanswered.

There was no other way. I would have to look for him, among all the muscles and concealed weapons. I charged into the mob.

I didn't get far. A ridiculously large male with the word 'MUTT' stencilled into his forehead grabbed me by the collar of my robe and yanked me backwards.

'The **fuck** is this?' he growled, toothlessly.

'A-Apologies,' I said, as the surrounding Mutts closed in. 'I-I'm just looking for s-someone – Hayden…'

'You're in the wrong place,' said another of them, picking at my robe sleeve. 'Hierarch's up there. Only Humans down here.'

It wouldn't have occurred to these Mutts at the time, but what I did then was actually a supreme act of Humanity: I made a significant error of judgment in the name of pride.

'I *am* Human,' I said, ripping my robe from the first Mutt's grip. I might have gotten away with this small act of defiance. The Mutts only laughed. But I was determined to prove myself. '**My name is Daniel and I'm from New Zealand.**'

I doubt any of them understood exactly what I said in Common – which was, of course, why I said it in Common. The second Mutt shoved me so hard it knocked the air out of me, and the only reason I didn't fall flat on my backside was because there was no room and I bounced off the Mutt behind me.

'Look at this little **prick** trying to speak Common to us,' said the Mutt who had pushed me. 'That ain't what makes you Human, friend.'

If that wasn't what made me Human, then perhaps it was the fabled phenomenon of one's life flashing before their eyes. As hands grabbed tufts of my coat and robe, I saw Mother and Father, my upbringing in Wellington, my Academy training, my service at ChamCov, Neekor, Hayden –

'Hayden?'

Somehow, it was only his hand on my collar then. He dragged me through the crowd of Mutts, and as I stumbled to keep up with him all I could think was how different he looked – his mane was longer and matted, and he seemed even more skeletal than when I had last seen him. But it was definitely him. And it was definitely a red patch dyed into the arm that was carrying me through the mob.

'The **fuck** are you doing here?' he said once we reached open space and he could throw me to the ground.

I didn't really know why I was there. Dusting off my robe, I bumbled, 'I just... had to know...'

'What? That I'm with the Pack now?' He configured his hand into what I assumed was some sort of representative symbol. 'Victory Hail, **motherfucker**. Now you know.'

All I could think to say was, 'Why?'

'Wouldn't expect you to understand. What with your fancy robes and edicts –'

'As opposed to this? Running with the Pack that runs the illicit cleaving industry? That relies on the addiction of predominantly Humans, and the indoctrination of other young, vulnerable Humans like you to operate it? Look at yourself, Hayden. I barely recognise you –'

'That's rich. I had trouble recognising you ever since you came back from Academy.'

'Because I went and made something of myself?'

He laughed at me. 'You talk about me running with the Pack – you're running with the most ruthless gang there is.'

I could feel my mouth moving, trying to form words. Whatever half-baked retort I had ready to sling at him withered away.

'I'm trying to change it,' I managed, in a voice that sounded as small as I felt.

'You said that two revs ago.' Hayden turned his back on me.

'The Hierarch doesn't change easily.' I could hear Lincoln's voice echoing in my own. 'But it *is* changing. There's a new squad now – one that I was handpicked for. Our sole purpose is to make sure the Hierarch has good interactions with Humans.'

'Good for you, Daniel,' Hayden said over his shoulder.

'Didn't you hear me?' I circled around him. 'This is why I joined the Hierarch – to make it better. I'm keeping my promise.'

For a fraction of an instant I saw his face soften. Then a siren wailed somewhere behind us, punctured by shouts and the amplified voices of the Keepers: 'Retreat immediately. You will be detained. Retreat immediately...'

Hayden pushed past me. 'Keep telling yourself that.'

'I will,' I shouted. But my voice was lost to another roar of 'Victory Hail!' and he had already disappeared back into the fold.

Moolas was right: the Great Irish **Road Trip** of Rev 9-4028 ended that rote. Or, at least, it began to end. With the forced dispersal of the Mutt Pack, and the increase in Keeper presence, the rest of the **road trip** collapsed.

A stream of kawwas flowed out into the skyways as some Humans returned to the lives and services they had sacrificed for the past few weeks. Those who remained, however, took their campaign to the channels of Kappeetar. The projections that painted the surface of the Apex were replicated on the Hierarch Houses, the bazaars of the Commerce District, the Galleries in the Annals District. I guessed that was the next masterstroke in Sophie's plan: having failed to get a rise out of the Hierarch, she started appealing to the beings of Kappeetar.

Or, I thought, watching the once-organised **road trip** descend into disarray from my terminal at ChamCov, maybe it wasn't really Sophie's plan at all. Maybe it was Lincoln's.

When the news broke, and Neekor called to me from the first main room of our unit, I already knew what was about to happen. I didn't know the details, I didn't know exactly how all the pieces fit together. All I knew was that they did. Lincoln had told me, all those revs ago, that to change the Hierarch you had to understand how it worked. Lincoln understood the Hierarch better than anyone I have ever known.

Neekor was motionless, connected to the Core. She shared her connection, which showed the Accountancy's official calculation of the Hierarch's Rank. The number was in free-fall.

'Apparently it's standard edict to alert all Hierarch servants if a drop below majority is imminent,' she said distantly. I checked my own tree

– sure enough, I had received the same link to the calculation. 'Daniel, I think the Hierarch is about to change.'

She was right, of course. And, though she never said it, I suspect she knew why. She'd figured it out well before me. It probably came as no surprise to her when Lincoln contacted me a few moments later.

No greeting. 'I need you at ChamCov, urgently,' he said.

'Is everything okay?'

'You'll see when you get here.'

He ended the communication before I could ask more. I was beginning to see it. The things Lincoln chose to say, the things he didn't. The things he didn't allow others to say.

'Lincoln's called me into service,' I told Neekor, heading back to our attire storage to throw on garments.

'You will keep me informed?' Neekor said, stopping me by the gateway.

'Of course,' I promised, and before I knew it, I had kissed her on the cheek. It was the very first time I had done it, and I don't know why I chose that moment above all others. It just felt like the right thing to do.

Perhaps it was. Neekor smiled. It was the first time I had ever seen her – or any Alien – truly smile. Not just a visual marker of base satisfaction but an expression of joy in its purest form. For a moment I was tempted to ignore Lincoln and stay with her. But before the temptation was too great to resist, I tore myself away to catch a transport to the House District.

On my way, I could already see the tides of change. At one of my transport's stops a group of adolescents boarded, bearing ensigns of the white star of Humanity. I could hear them discussing a change of Hierarch, and with each stop more Humans boarded to join them. Soon my whole compartment was full of Humans telling any Alien who would listen that, as Karkoora 7 Darius of the Alliance Clans had declared, 'The time to change the Hierarch is now.'

And then, just as I arrived at the gate to the House of Balance, the entire district came to a standstill. Servants paused mid-step. Private kawwas slowed to an idle float. I had never experienced such quiet in Kappeetar. I knew what it meant, but I had to check the Core to make sure. The confirmation was instant, with a banner blaring across every division:

Hierarch Rank falls below majority; Alliance Clans confirm bid for ascension.

The banner was accompanied by the Accountancy's graph showing the decline over the last few weeks of the Hierarch's Rank, which had just dropped below the critical point.

The House District took a collective intake of breath. Then chaos erupted.

The channels came alive with servants sprinting for their Houses, vehicles zooming into the sky. I charged into the gateway of the House of Balance to find it full of queuing servants, many so engrossed in whatever propagator they were viewing that they were colliding with each other. Leaping over a pile of downed servants, I claimed a shifter that took me up to our squad's level. Other servants fought each other to reach their terminals, desperate for some sort of information to be released internally before it was made public by the propagation.

My squad's pen, however, was empty. I sent a message to Lincoln, which I don't think he even read. His reply came in less than a second, directing me to one of the level's gathering rooms. I opened the gate to find the squad all seated, while two stood in conversation: Lincoln and Karkoora 7 Darius of the Alliance Clans.

This was how you changed the machine. How you broke it. So you could replace it with something better.

'Ah, here he is,' said Lincoln. There was an unusual expression on his face. Subtle, only one corner of his mouth lifting to a curl. 'This is Kytoonoo 3 Daniel.'

'Karkoora 7 Darius,' he introduced himself, reaching for my hand. He was far more reserved in person than in the propagation streams. Soft-spoken, almost unassuming.

'Soon to be Lord Karkoora 8 Darius,' Lincoln said.

Vaguely, I became aware that my hand was still being shaken by a virtual Lord of the Hierarch, so I withdrew it to give him a hasty salute.

'Specifically,' Lincoln added, 'he will be the Lord for Human-Hierarch Interactions.'

If my tendrils could have flexed any harder, they'd have ripped themselves off. I spun to see the rest of the squad, who were all just as dumbstruck as I was to learn that we were about to have our very own Lord. Then I turned back to Lincoln. I knew what that expression of his was now. Triumph.

'On that note,' said my new Lord, 'Lincoln was just outlining what this squad's function is and how it can support me. One of the things I will need is a Captain.'

The inference was clear. My gaze wandered over the rest of the squad, who only looked back proudly. Lincoln gave an approving nod.

'You want me to be... your Captain? But I haven't done anything –'

'Lincoln's shown me all the advice you've been giving the other Houses,' Lord Karkoora said. 'It's exactly what this new Hierarch needs. What Humanity needs.'

I caught Lincoln's eye again. The meaning was unmistakeable. We were in this together now. Under this Hierarch, one led by the Human-friendly Alliance Clans, the world really was going to change. We would make certain of it.

I barely remember anything else from that momentous rotation. Much was a blur; there were preparations to be made, queries from the propagation to field, a couple of communications snuck in to Neekor and Mother and Father to tell them the news.

Above all the excitement, the pride and the joy, the one detail that I still recall with perfect clarity is the connection request from the House of Exile, shortly after the new Hierarch was validated. I answered it expecting some sort of urgent Hierarch-related business in the immediate aftermath of the Alliance Clans' ascension. Instead, an automated, monotone voice greeted me:

'You have been designated as the initial contact for a new detainee.

Identity: Nootoo 0 Hayden. Detained for: resisting detainment, assault against Keepers, vandalism of Hierarch construction. Your time allocation for dialogue with the detainee is five minutes.'

There was a shift in the connection; it went quiet, save for a dull buzz, and I knew that I had been connected directly with Hayden, albeit under a Gardener's watch. He broke the silence, as he always did.

'I didn't know who else to contact.'

Rank 4

Recorded: Cycle 4, Revolution 9-4028 through Cycle 1, Revolution 9-4029

4-1

Everything happened so quickly. It felt like one moment Mother was congratulating me on my ascension and I was telling her about Hayden; the next she and I were marching into the House of Exile for his visitation. Like every other House, it was in disarray with its servants reacting to its new Lord and their demands. The difference with the House of Exile, though, was that the upheaval of the Hierarch seemed to have disrupted its detainment procedures. Queues of detainees (most Human) filled the gateway, hands and feet magnetically bound, guarded by squads of Keepers. Exasperated sentries flitted back and forth, arguing with the Keepers about where to put detainees, running hands through their scruffy manes.

---

* Subject notation: It was during Cycle 1 that the ancestors used to celebrate the traditional holiday called **Christmas**. It was a time for spending with one's clan, consuming copious amounts of sustenance and exchanging gifts. There have been some impressive efforts to revive it, including a decree by the Hierarch declaring it an official Date of Note. Aliens really only seem to support it so they can get an extra rotation of service leave.

'Greetings,' Mother said to one of the sentries. 'I am Kytoonoo 5 Michelle. This is my son, Kytoonoo 3 – apologies, 4 – Daniel.' She flashed me a proud smile. 'He is designated as initial contact for recent detainee Nootoo 0 Hayden. We are here to request a visitation.'

'Only the initial contact is allowed visitation permissions,' the weary-faced sentry replied.

'Not with Human detainees, I understand?' Mother was so quick I assumed she had anticipated such a response. 'I am the Leader of New Zealand, of which Hayden is a citizen. I understand detainees are permitted visits by the Leader of their nation?'

'Oh, apologies,' said the sentry, consulting the Core. 'I cannot see your Leader licence in your profile.'

Mother blinked. 'My *what*?'

'Leader licence. Do you not have one?'

'**The fuck**?' Mother said, and my heart almost stopped in my chest. When it became clear that the sentry had no idea what Mother meant by the outburst, she cleared her throat and continued, 'Apologies – that's Common for "I don't understand."'

'It is Hierarch edict that Leaders of Human nations must possess a Leader licence to visit a detainee in that capacity,' the sentry recited.

Mother forced a smile. 'My election by the people of New Zealand is my licence. I don't need to prove that to the Hierarch.'

'According to Hierarch edict,' said the sentry, 'you do.'

Without missing a beat, Mother said, 'Not anymore – you see, Daniel here is a Captain under Karkoora 8 Darius, Lord for Human-Hierarch Interactions, and he will tell you that, already, a new edict is being prepared that will remove the requirement for Human leaders to present any such licence to visit a detainee from their nation, which is, of course, a violation of basic Human **rights**. The edict has not yet been validated, obviously, but it is intended to be as a matter of urgency – given the new Hierarch's clear focus on good Human-Hierarch Interactions. Isn't that right, Daniel?'

Mother turned to me and my gradually descending jaw, as did the sentry. I hadn't even had the chance to discuss edict with Lord Karkoora yet; I was still waiting for him to take up his office at the Apex before I was allowed entry there myself. But I somehow managed to pull myself together and say, 'Yes, the edict in question is being crafted as we speak.' (And it was – by me, frantically, in that very moment.)

I expected resistance but the sentry just shrugged.

'It would not be the strangest thing that has occurred this rotation.' She briefly accessed the Core before returning her attention to us. 'An Operator will arrive shortly to escort you to the detainment sector.'

Before long, a scrawny Alien, dwarfed by his own body-shielding equipment, appeared and inquired over the protruding lip of his chest-guard, 'Kytoonoo 5 Mytch-ell-eh and Kytoonoo 4 Denial?'

'Michelle and Daniel,' Mother corrected him. 'And yes.'

'Highly irregular, this,' the Operator muttered before waddling off.

'Yes, I don't imagine you're used to seeing Humans not in bondage,' Mother said as we fell into step behind him.

Perhaps this Operator had spent enough time around Humans to understand Mother's tone. He didn't speak again, leading us down into the bowels of Kappeetar through the many layers of security gates and detection fields until we arrived at the edge of a chasm. Its walls were lined with rows of cells.

The entire place felt like a void. Of sound, of air, of hope. There was no question of innocence there. Anyone who ended up in one of those cells knew just one thing awaited them: punishment. The only question left was what kind.

The Operator gestured at a shifter, which Mother and I stepped onto. A second later, we stood outside one of the cell's coherence fields. Hayden was inside, limping the few steps it took to cross from one end of the cell to the battered sleep capsule at the other.

'Hayden?' Mother said. 'It's Michelle. And Daniel.'

He took a long time to look at us. One of his eyes was completely closed over, his lip swollen and specked with dried blood. The red patch on his shoulder was gone, lasered away to leave only a spot of raw skin. A suppressor had been clamped onto his root, sticking out from his temple like an antique antenna. He was shivering.

'They're going to exile me,' he croaked. 'I can't do it, I can't do exile –'

'Nothing is certain yet.' Mother's tone could not have been gentler. 'You still have your balance hearing ahead of you.'

'They've got me,' he said, as if he hadn't heard Mother. 'They've got me. They'll send me to **Mars** –'

'Hayden.' Mother's tone became firmer. 'Listen to me. The reason Daniel brought me here is because, as a Leader of a Human nation, I am authorised under the balance system to give you a social endorsement. That means I can appeal to the Magistrate assessing your imbalances that, based on your clan circumstances and Rank, exile is not an appropriate punishment for you. But to do that, I need to understand what the imbalances in your profile are – in your own words.'

Hayden didn't respond. Encouraged by Mother, I forced myself to speak.

'When they contacted me, they said you had…' It was still hard to imagine him committing it, '… assaulted a Keeper –'

Hayden whipped around, teeth bared. 'That **fucker** deserved it.'

Mother didn't jump at Hayden's sudden change of demeanour like I did. She just said, 'Tell me why.'

He stared at her for a few seconds, breathing heavily, before shrugging. 'What do you mean?'

'Why did the Keeper deserve it? What made you assault them?'

'It was a **fucking** Keeper. What more reason do I need?'

'A good one, if you want to avoid exile.'

Hayden gestured to his face. 'It's not like they didn't get a few good hits in too.'

'The Keeper you and your packmates assaulted is in stasis at Kappeetar Healing Centre,' Mother replied. 'Not even their bionics can keep them alive at this point.'

Hayden's scowl faded. His clenched fists fell to his side.

'But, come on, they're… you know what they're like.' At last he turned to me. Stared right at me with his one good eye. I noticed its pupil was contracted. 'Remember when they busted my father's gate down? Ripped him out of his sleep capsule? This Keeper, that Keeper –

they're all the same. Got it out for us. It's what they do. It's how they're programmed –'

'Hayden.' Somehow Mother kept cutting through his rambling. 'Unless you work with me here, you're going to be exiled. Do you understand that? I need you to think about this particular Keeper. From what I've heard, they're only fresh out of programming, been in the force less than a rev. There must be something – anything – that justified what you did.'

Hayden just looked helplessly from Mother to me. 'The Gardeners said you're Rank 4 now. A Captain, under a new Lord for Humans or something –'

'Human-Hierarch Interactions,' I said automatically.

'Yeah, that. You can help me, right? I can't go to exile. Who'll look after Father –'

'Human-Hierarch Interactions is about making the Hierarch have good relationships with Humans,' I said. 'I don't know what I can do about a balance hearing –'

'Please, Daniel.' He was inches from the coherence field now, so close I could see his tendrils quivering. 'I need you.'

There were too many emotions for my root to process. Most of it was just anger – at Hayden, for invoking my promise to him so shamelessly like this. How dare he, I thought. How dare he put me in this position, make me feel any sort of guilt when it was his actions, not mine, that put him there. He had ignored my existence for over three revs, but *now* he wanted my friendship again? Now that he was here and his stupid Mutt Pack was nowhere to be seen? Now that I had reached this Rank?

As much as I wanted to shout all of this, I couldn't. Far deeper than my anger at him was my anger at everything that had conspired against Hayden to lead him to this point. From his mother abandoning him, to the healing services that had failed his father, to the balance system itself that would rather send him to another planet than attempt to house him, feed him, educate him. I tried to focus on that anger instead, let it blind me to everything Hayden himself was responsible for.

And somehow, through the depths of all that darkness, the immortal words of that night at the Clan Lounge came back to me:

Never gonna give you up, never gonna let you down ...

I met Hayden's desperate gaze through the coherence field.

'I'll do my best.'

His swollen mouth twisted into an attempt at a grin, and I returned it. Then Mother and I were ejected from the cell and escorted back out of the detainment sector. Once we were free from the suffocating vacuum of the House of Exile, Mother set out our plan of attack.

'So, I'll make a start on a social endorsement for Hayden. There'll be plenty about his upbringing I can explain to the Magistrate. That should buy us some time before his balance hearing is able to proceed – with the current state of the Hierarch, we probably have a cycle at most.'

She was walking and talking so fast I could barely keep up with her. 'How do you know all this?'

'Hayden wouldn't be the first Human I've had to do this for, and he won't be the last.'

I was determined that Hayden should be the last.

'What can I do?' I asked.

'Let me worry about all this,' said Mother. 'I'll deal with the Operators from now on. You just focus on your new Captaincy. I'm sure you don't need me to tell you that you have a lot of work ahead of you.'

'But I have to do something. He's relying on me –'

'You saw his eyes, didn't you?' Mother finally stopped. 'He wasn't thinking straight, Daniel. I doubt there's anything you can do for him just by virtue of your new Rank.'

I knew Mother would never have meant that as an insult, but it hit like one.

'All you need to do is exactly what you said you'd do: your best.' She gave me a quick, efficient hug. 'What Hayden needs most from you right now is to be there for him.'

All my efforts to improve Human-Hierarch Interactions had revolved around the development of new decrees and edicts, or the implementation of projects and initiatives. I had rarely thought about the Hierarch's Covenant obligations to people who had committed imbalance.

I explained all of this to Neekor who, thankfully, had retained her own service under the new Hierarch, and I told her what Mother and I planned to do.

'You have my sympathies; it must be difficult to see your friend in such a state. However,' she paused, trying to find the right words, 'he committed imbalance. Assaulted a Keeper, at that. Why are you trying to prevent him from suffering any punishment for it?'

I was surprised at what Neekor took from all of this. Forcing myself up in my lounger, I said, 'That's not what I'm trying to do. Think about the Covenant's Third Promise: that all Humans have the same Rank of citizenship that Aliens do. In modern terms, that means Humans are promised all the same privileges that Aliens have, like access to healing, education – as well as punishment for imbalances that are fair in the circumstances.'

Neekor frowned. 'I am confident your friend will receive a punishment that is fair for the imbalance he committed.'

'You shouldn't be.' I transferred a package of data to her tree. 'Balance statistics show that 18% of Humans who commit imbalance are exiled, compared to only 11% of Aliens. Combine that with everything guaranteed under the Third Promise that Hayden hasn't had access to throughout his existence, and you simply cannot say that he will be punished fairly.'

'What about the Keeper? Was what happened to them fair?'

I thought of them, whoever they were, suspended in stasis somewhere at the healing centre. Young, Mother had said. Freshly programmed. A whole service career ahead of them. It complicated everything to dwell on that, so I didn't.

'No, but you can guarantee they'll have the full weight of the balance system behind them. Hayden won't.'

Neekor took a while to process this. 'So what are you suggesting? Overhauling the balance system?'

'My mission is to make the Hierarch honour the Covenant. In every aspect. If that means making the balance system fairer to Humans, then that's what I have to do.'

Neekor seemed like she had more to say, but stayed quiet. Secretly, I was glad she did. It was one debate in which I wasn't confident I could beat her.

The Apex had always been menacing to me. I'd stood in its grounds, countless times, staring up at its sheer black walls. The effect was always the same. Like standing in the shadow of an enemy's stronghold, its fortifications indestructible and harbouring dark, dangerous secrets. My mission lay inside. My path was always going to lead me there.

The giant gate at the Apex's base expanded on my approach, like a monstrous mouth preparing to devour me. I stepped into the cavernous hallway and the gate rumbled shut again. Ahead were two security gates: one for Lords and their servants, and one for visitors – before which were stationed two Keepers.

I knew I had nothing to fear from them. Lincoln had assured me that my ascension was logged in the Core and my access to the Apex granted. But I couldn't ignore the way the Keepers' optical upgrades bored into me as I approached the gate. As if they knew about my association with Hayden and my mission, and were about to exact vengeance for their fallen comrade. Or maybe it was just that their sensors would detect that, beneath my newly-purchased robe and freshly-waxed coat, I was Human, which would unconsciously skew their detainment settings from **RESTRAIN** to **BRUTALISE**.

Thankfully the gate for servants opened and I walked through without intervention from the Keepers, feeling my coat ripple as the detection field's beam ran over me. Part of me expected the field to detect something – a weapon I somehow didn't remember concealing on my person – and promptly delete me from existence. But I passed through that unscathed too and arrived in an immense reception room. There were propagators everywhere, hurrying across the floor with drones hovering in their wake. Other robed servants scurried between them, watched over by yet more Keepers. I set off into their midst, heading for the sentry on the opposite side of the room who, after a brief interrogation of my identity and purpose being there, directed me to the 8th level of the Apex, where Lord Karkoora was stationed.

No sooner had I arrived on the 8th level than I was almost run down by a service frame, trailing a hover-deck loaded with empty crates.

'Are those the **books** the Lord asked for?' said a familiar voice from a gateway beyond.

'Morgan?' It was a relief to see an ally in the place, if not a total surprise. 'What are you doing here?'

Lifting her chin, she said, 'You are looking at the Lord's new Attendant.'

Now that was quite the ascension. It made sense, though. Everyone else in the squad had been ascended, too. Lincoln was a General and Teemot his Commander. Vuneen and Moolas were now Teemot's Captains and I later learned that Pa'zan had replaced Morgan as Lincoln's own Attendant.

'Congratulations,' I said. 'I'm glad you're over here with me.'

'You too,' she said with a smile. 'Now come on – I'll show you to your office. Apologies for the mess – a change in Hierarch doesn't happen all the time.'

As we weaved our way through the crates and into the office proper, where another set of gates awaited, my curiosity got the better of me. 'Did you mention **books**?'

Morgan rolled her eyes and jerked her head towards the largest gate. 'Yeah, he likes to read. **Nerd.**'

I wasn't sure if I was supposed to laugh or not. I wondered if it was some kind of test, to gauge my level of respect for the Lord.

'You can relax. First thing you need to know about this Hierarch is that it's going to be different. More Human.' She gestured inside. 'And this guy's as Human as they come. You should let him know you're here.'

Before I had a chance to protest, she banged on the gate and said, 'Oi! There's someone here to see you.'

The gate expanded, revealing a room that was simply too large to be sensible. Lord Karkoora poked his head into the gateway, a stack of ancient paper tucked under one arm, engineered eyes glowing with a magnify function. Clearing his throat, he straightened his robe.

'Welcome, Daniel. It's great to have you here. Come in, let's talk.'

Morgan left us to it and I followed the Lord into his private terminal room. It was bigger than Mother's and Father's entire dwelling, even bigger than the main room at Neekor's parents', and furnished like a dwelling as well. It contained its own sustenance station, a booth for garment-changing, and a leisure area with what looked like the comfiest loungers I had ever seen. But the dominating feature was the far wall, which featured a huge observation field. I wandered over, unable to take my eyes off the view of Kappeetar laid out a dizzying distance below. From that height I could see each of the city's concentric districts cascading away to a blurred blue horizon.

'Beautiful view,' I commented, turning to find the Lord carefully returning his papers to an old, dented container.

'It's a bit much, if you ask me.' He clamped the container shut. 'Don't really like heights myself.'

'Oh.' I shuffled away from it. 'Apologies.'

He dismissed the apology with a flick and gestured towards his preserver. 'Can I get you anything? A drink?'

'Oh, no, gratitude – I'm fine.' I wasn't convinced that this wasn't some kind of test.

He shrugged. 'I'm going to have a **fizzy**, if you don't mind?'

I couldn't remember the last time I'd had one of our traditional beverages. As he fished out a bright red canister my mouth went dry.

'You sure?' He held the canister out to me.

'O-Okay then.' I took the canister and waited for him to get his own before opening it. The *pssk* sound of the air escaping never lost its novelty, nor did the searing sensation the bubbles wreaked upon the throat on first mouthful.

We stood there for a while, the silence only broken by slurping sips and suppressed belches, until the Lord said, 'So, where are you from, Daniel?'

'Oh. Ah, New Zealand.'

'**Kiwi boy**,' the Lord said, tendrils flexing. 'I have family there.'

'So do I,' I blurted, in my spontaneous lapse of conversational skill.

The Lord laughed – a genuine, hearty chuckle. Feeling somewhat emboldened, I said,

'Morgan mentioned you were waiting on some **books** to arrive.'

'Oh, yes,' said the Lord, and his face reddened. 'Can't actually read all of them, the transfer of some is so ancient. But I try to keep the old ways alive. When I can.'

'I've always wanted to **write** a **book**,' I said, without really knowing why. He fixed a curious eye on me and I added, 'Someday, when my Common is good enough. And I learn to **write** properly.'

'I look forward to **reading** it,' said the Lord, and my own skin grew hot beneath my coat.

He crossed over to the loungers and I followed him, sinking so deeply into one that I was almost enveloped by the cushions.

'So, Daniel,' he said. 'You're from New Zealand, and you want to **write** books. What else do I need to know about you?'

Something didn't seem right. Looking at the can of **fizzy** in my hand, I thought it had to be some sort of joke – a **prank**, specifically. I'd heard of such things, in the ancestors' times; they would spend ridiculous amounts of time and resources on an elaborate set-up like this, all to fool some unsuspecting person who they were secretly recording. Why else would he want to know anything about me?

'Well,' I began, casting an eye as casually as I could around the room in search of a hidden recording device, 'I ascended at Toor Academy, with primaries in Human Studies and Memetics. Before that I was reared in Wellington.'

'Birthplace of modern **Earth**,' the Lord remarked. 'So you know: I intend to bring the Hierarch back to Wellington for Covenant Anniversary next rev. It's not right that the previous Hierarch stopped attending.'

Music to my ears, as the ancestors would say. Although, I could sympathise with the Lord of the previous Hierarch who vowed never to return to Covenant Anniversary after having an ancient Human self-pleasure implement flung at his face by a protestor.

'My mother will be pleased to hear that,' I said.

'She's not Michelle Kytoonoo, by any chance?' he asked. I flicked positively. 'Ah, I thought so. Well, it's no wonder Lincoln speaks so highly of you.'

I waved the compliment off. 'I like to think I make her proud.'

The Lord nodded. 'I know the feeling. Speaking of which, obviously I am new to this Lordship, and I have much to learn about my role. But, in particular, I have a lot to learn about Human-Alien Relations.'

Having found no recording nor listening devices, I concluded the Gardeners must be monitoring me directly through my tree. Perhaps this entire interaction was being projected throughout the Core, and all of Teerin' Ho was watching, waiting for me to screw up so they could all laugh at my expense. I decided to put myself out of my own misery. Knowing I would never be able to get away with correcting a real Lord of the Hierarch, and that doing so would surely expose whatever farcical set-up I had walked into, I dared to say, 'Human-Hierarch Interactions.'

The Lord cocked his head at me. I braced myself.

'Yes, gratitude. I need to get the **damned** name right first and fore-most.'

At that point, against all my better judgment, I began to accept that I was not on some attempted revival of the ancestors' **prank** shows and that this was actual reality.

'Please, Daniel, tell me everything I need to know about Human-Hi-erarch Interactions.'

I didn't know where to start. So I just began talking – about my analysis for ChamCov all those revs ago and my subsequent service there – and before I knew it, I was rambling about the myriad ways I had witnessed the Hierarch failing to uphold the Promises of the Cov-enant. I didn't know which examples of my advice Lincoln had shared with him, and he didn't say, so I regaled him with what I thought were my best tales: the time we ensured the Hierarch sought the advice of Human water experts before implementing a new water treatment edict; the decree we had prevented from enabling the Hierarch to terraform Human cemeteries; the hard-fought battle against the establishment of new construction powers that included the ability to acquire Human-controlled airspace, including airspace returned through Covenant resolutions – at which the Lord rubbed his tendrils and said, 'It would have been the Sky Wars all over again.'

'Exactly! This is what we're up against. The Hierarch is constantly at risk of breaching the Covenant.'

'So how do we stop it?' the Lord asked. 'If you were me, what would you do?'

I met his gaze. He'd turned off the augment function so his eyes had resumed their natural colour. That was what convinced me that this was no set-up. This Human male had been given the Rank to do whatever he pleased and he wanted to know what *I* thought he should do with it. What *I* would do if I were, as the ancestors would say, **in his shoes**. And he was doing what Mother was so adept at; reading me, testing if what I said matched whatever he saw inside me.

I thought, again, about Hayden's impending balance hearing, about the Magistrate that would assess his imbalances, the Gardeners that monitored him and the Keepers that detained him (while trying not to think of the Keeper he'd put in stasis). And I thought about the plan I came here to execute. I hadn't expected the opportunity to arise so quickly. I went for it.

'The Human-Hierarch Interactions squad can only do so much. We need an entire system in place to make the Hierarch honour the Covenant. A way of monitoring the Hierarch's activity, of ensuring it complies with the Covenant, and of holding it accountable if it doesn't.'

The Lord leaned forward. 'What do you propose?'

My heart was racing. I could almost imagine Hayden cheering me on.

'A whole new Hierarch House – one with the power to ensure the Hierarch honours the Covenant, in every conceivable way. From decree development right down to...' I swallowed, forcing myself to say it, '... right down to the balance system.'

The Lord thought for a moment, stroking his chin. 'A House of... what is it again?'

'A House of –' I paused. As much as I respected Lincoln, the name had always been stupid. 'A House of the Covenant.'

The Lord swilled what remained of his canister of **fizzy**, then drained it.

'Let's get to work.'

'You did *what*?' said Lincoln when I reported back on my suggestion to the Lord.

'He asked me what I thought he should do,' I explained, my smile faltering, 'so I told him he should expand the squad. Make it into a House.'

This conversation was happening via the Core, while I was seated in my new state-of-the-art terminal in my personal office beside the Lord's, and Lincoln was supposedly somewhere in the House of Balance. So I couldn't see him, but I could picture him, with the same distressed expression he'd had when the Wellington Commission made its decision about Britain.

'Daniel, I need you to run these things through me first.'

'Apologies, Lincoln.' I wasn't sure what else to say. I thought he would have been proud of me, following in his footsteps. 'I just saw an opportunity and took it. Even you've said the squad needs capacity.'

'Yes, but in time. Not the first major action of a new, inexperienced Lord.'

'Why not?'

'Because it's not how the machine works.'

I didn't understand. We'd broken the machine. *We* decided how it worked now.

'It's actually not a bad idea,' he conceded with a sigh, 'but we need to handle it properly. I'll ask Morgan to arrange a gathering. Make sure you're available; it sounds like he listens to you.'

Within hours, I met Lincoln in front of the Apex. The way he walked right into the Lord's terminal room suggested he was familiar with the place, but the Lord seemed more reserved around him than he was with me. He didn't invite Lincoln to sit on the loungers and, I noted with quiet pride, he didn't offer Lincoln a **fizzy**.

Lincoln was unfazed. After a brief exchange of **small-talk** he launched into why establishing a new House was fraught with risk, laying it out in clear, logical detail. By the time he finished, he'd almost convinced me.

'Despite the surge in tithing from Humans you've received,' he concluded, 'there are still plenty of beings out there who will see this "House of the Covenant" and only accuse you of separatism. Of abusing your newly acquired Rank. There will even be other Lords who don't agree this is necessary. What you need is a mandate: evidence that a new House is what Humanity actually wants from you.'

'How do I get that?' the Lord asked.

'By convincing them that they want it.'

In the time it had taken for me to arrange the gathering, Lincoln had already planned out how we would get all of Humanity to agree to the establishment of this new House: a tour by Lord Karkoora around the entire world. Nothing like it had ever been done by a Hierarch before, Lincoln explained. It would demonstrate to all of Humanity that their newly-tithed Rank to this Hierarch was not misplaced. That this Hierarch cared what Humanity had to say, and would make decisions based not on what it thought was best for Humanity, but on what it heard directly from Humanity itself. Of course, this would not be entirely true: we were pre-determining the outcome of this tour as being the establishment of the new House. But we were all Human ourselves, I reasoned, so we were already aware what would be best for Humanity.

The first issue was how the Hierarch would afford this grand tour. The Alliance Clans hadn't included it in their ascension bid and it would be another couple of cycles before their first Rotation of Accounting, which I was actually looking forward to. Maybe, for once, all the pro-Human initiatives would actually be accepted by the Accountancy this revolution.

Lincoln had already thought of that, too. It just so happened that the previous Hierarch had already pledged significant resource to another tour around the world: **Meet**. In a stroke of genius, Lincoln proposed the immediate cancellation of **Meet** – doubling as another demonstration of this Hierarch's commitment to Humanity – so all those resources could be reallocated to our new tour.

In the space of that afternoon, the entire thing was planned out. It was important to the Lord that this 'Grand Tour' be modelled off another voyage, one that was more meaningful to Humanity than Kookee's. Inspired by a **book** from his personal collection, he declared that he would make the journey in 80 rotations, stopping at as many nations as possible along the way.

'And get me all the propagators you can, please,' he said, as we parted to begin preparations. 'I want every Alien on **Earth** to know we're doing this, too.'

By the following rotation the Core was abuzz with activity about the Grand Tour. Most of it was by Humans, praising the swift action by the new Hierarch to get things off to the right start. And, just as the Lord desired, Aliens had their fair share of commentary, too. Within hours of the news breaking, all the typical Alien commentators were making their views clear.

'... a sign that this Lord has no idea what he's doing,' I caught the usual suspect blathering to the propagation. 'Who ascends to Rank 8 and decides they don't know what to do once they get there? This so-called "Grand Tour" is a farce, a colossal waste of time and tithe, if you ask me...'

The Lord responded to such criticism beautifully.

'No one's asking him because he's not Human,' he told the propagators who hounded him in the corridors of the Apex. 'He wouldn't understand that this is how Humans do things. We debate and discuss. We elect our leaders based on what they can deliver for us. There is no point in me being here, as a Human Lord of the Hierarch, if I cannot deliver what my people need most from me. And it's not for me to decide what that is – it's for them to tell me.'

That was all it took for nations to line up for the Grand Tour schedule. Our tiny squad was soon so busy taking communications that we were forced to install sleep capsules in our offices. We worked until we had to drag ourselves into them at dark, and began again as soon as we dragged ourselves out of them at lightbreak.

None of this bothered me. If anything, I fed on the excitement, sustained purely by the thrill of seeing the 80-rote programme coming together piece by piece, each one bringing me a step closer to my goal. Only one thought niggled: Hayden's balance hearing, which still hadn't been scheduled. I thought it was likely the hearing would be set for some time before the Grand Tour finished, although that would depend on how long Mother could stall it with her social endorsement. I was so consumed by preparations for the Grand Tour that I couldn't muster the energy to dwell on it.

Morgan was the one to tell me that I couldn't survive on exhilaration alone.

'When was the last time you went home?' she asked.

'I… don't remember.'

'You need a proper sedation.' She activated her Attendant's control over my terminal to disconnect me from it. 'I just checked the Grand Tour schedule and you've added Australia three separate times.'

'Apologies, Morgan. I just really want to make this happen.'

'We all do. But we also need to be well enough to go on the **damned** thing. Go home and get some proper rest. You're no use to us as a **zombie**.'

It was as if the moment I was given permission to feel tired, it all caught up to me. I felt heavy, and could think of nothing better than curling up with Neekor on one of the loungers and watching some entertainments before taking a double-strength sedative in my sleep capsule. So I bid farewell to Morgan and left the Apex for the first time in many rotes. Neekor had been nothing but supportive and under-standing of my commitment to service, assuring me that she would be fine on her own and had plenty of service to keep her busy too. But I made sure to pick up some of her favourite sweets before getting my regular transport home. The promise of a perfect, lazy evening with her kept me awake long enough to last the transport ride and stagger through our dwelling gate, practically into her arms.

As considerate and supportive as Neekor was, she was also highly efficient. It became immediately clear that she intended to make the most of our precious time together.

'I want to reproduce,' she announced.

In my near-delirious state of extreme exhaustion, I thought I imagined it. She said it again, with such conviction that any doubt as to its legitimacy vanished and I was forced to respond. 'Maybe we could have darkmeal first...'

'We do not have much time.' She took my hand and pulled me into the first main room. 'Who knows when I will have you home next, and with the Grand Tour coming up you'll be gone for 80 rotations.'

Somehow, I ended up on a lounger with her.

'Right here?' I didn't know why but I felt like there should have been some sort of ceremony to it.

'Why not? I have given this considerable thought, Daniel. Now that you are Rank 4, I see no reason why we should wait.'

Before I could say that I had not given it considerable thought, which seemed like at least one good reason to wait, she connected her tree to mine and brought up the genome pages of our respective profiles. She then activated a genetic trait selector program, which constructed a grid between our two profiles. I noticed she had already filled much of it with her own trait selections from both her genome and mine.

'You really have given this considerable thought,' I said.

'Well, you have been so busy. Once I selected the traits of mine that I would like to pass on, I thought I would assist by selecting some of yours too. My preference is for some of the more productive Human traits, personally.'

I scanned the list of my inherited Human traits that she had curated for our hypothetical offspring – Noor expressions of Human concepts that did not convey the fullness of their meaning:

Compassion
Generosity
Creativity

Nurturing
Hope

'Neekor, you can't just choose only the Human traits that you like.'

She flexed her tendrils. 'Why not? It is literally the purpose of this exercise.'

'Because Humans are so much more than just the good things.' I dragged more of my Human traits into the grid. 'Where's pride? Spirituality? Self-image?'

'I am willing to consider pride,' said Neekor, 'but I do not want our offspring believing in things that do not objectively exist. And I know how disturbed by your Alien appearance you are. I do not want our offspring to suffer the same.'

Another trait of mine revealed itself: easily outraged.

'Well, if I can't pass on those traits, then you have to remove some of yours, too.' I deleted a handful of Alien traits I would be glad to never see in any offspring of mine:

Apathy
Ignorance
Inability to get jokes*

'Daniel,' Neekor protested, undoing my change, 'it is important to me that I pass these traits on.'

'And it is important to me to pass on mine.' I added Greed to the list.

Neekor stared at the illuminated trait before fixing her attention on me. 'I do not understand. Why would you want to pass that on? It is a negative trait, counter to the success of your species.'

'Not necessarily. It depends on how it is expressed. Sometimes greed is good. Sometimes you need to put your own needs before others', for the sake of your own wellbeing. It's just a Human thing.'

'But I'm Noor,' Neekor pointed out, 'and Noor do not leave things to chance.'

---

* Not the most accurate conversion of what the trait really is, but I stand by it.

I knew she was trying to reason with me, trying to strike a balance between our respective worldviews. But to me the gulf between us seemed too great. I stood, disconnecting our trees.

'You don't leave things to chance but you want our offspring to inherit hope – **hope**,' I said, adding the true name for it. 'You pick and choose the parts of Humanity you find appealing when you don't even understand what they mean – what they truly mean. If we create offspring who are only ever compassionate, generous, and nurturing, they won't survive in this world. They won't be Human.' My tendrils quivered. My coat was on end. I was breathing so hard I thought I might be asphyxiating.

'Daniel,' Neekor said softly, rising from the lounger. 'Apologies –'

I couldn't be around her anymore. Ignoring my aching limbs, I turned and walked out of our dwelling and down to the botanical park outside, wandering into its depths until I found a free perch. With Aar having long since set, it was deserted. I didn't mind. I wanted the quiet space to myself. Call it greed, if you must.

Insidious doubts had not troubled me in a long time. Since our partnering, I had been certain that Neekor was the right one for me. There were all the things about her that I adored – her intelligence, her pragmatism, her nose wrinkle – and her appreciation and empathy for the plight of Humanity had also been improving. The last time I was home she had proudly informed me that she'd openly challenged another Knight in her squad who tried to argue that Covenant resolutions were unnecessary. In those moments I revelled in that weightlessness she gave me; the entire universe faded and all I felt was the two of us floating blissfully in our own private existence of perfect Human-Alien partnership.

Now the doubt returned, more powerfully than ever. The thing I feared above all else was that Neekor would never truly understand me. This fear was deepened now by the realisation that, even if I passed on as many Human traits as I wanted to our offspring, she would never truly understand them either.

I thought of Mother, wondering how she navigated this issue when she and Father produced me, and decided I might as well just ask her.

As expected, I was forced to endure a series of delighted squeals at the news that Neekor and I were considering reproduction. I waited for an opening and cut to the chase.

'There's an issue. How did you and Father decide which traits to pass on?'

Mother's mental voice replicated the long breath I knew she had just taken. 'A difficult conversation, isn't it?'

'I don't know if I ever want to have it again.'

'Now, Daniel, don't be like that. If you can serve the Hierarch for this many revs, you can endure this one discussion with Neekor.'

I honestly doubted that.

'Did Father reject many of the Human traits you wished to pass on?'

'Oh, almost all of them.'

'How did you deal with it?'

'I told him he could either pass on his traits with some Human ones he may not like, or not at all.'

'And that worked?'

'Well, look how naïve and petty you are.'

'I don't think I'm naïve. And if I'm petty, then you're –' She was, as always, right. 'Never mind. But Neekor said something that I can't stop thinking about. She asked why I would want to pass on negative traits. I told her it was because they're part of who we are. And that how negative they are depends on how they're expressed. But now I don't know. Maybe she has a point. Would I be better if you hadn't passed on pettiness and naivety to me?'

'You wouldn't be you,' Mother said simply. 'It's like I always say: we must hold onto our Humanity – that means the good and the bad. If we don't, we'll lose it. Forever.'

I supposed she was right again. There was so much more at stake than my Human pride. The survival of Humanity depended on our resilience, not only on the grand scale of a **road trip** or within the corridors of the Apex, but in the simple struggle to pass on our traits to our offspring.

'Speaking of which,' she went on, 'how is service? I must say, I am very impressed by Lord Karkoora so far. I imagine it is refreshing serving under a Human Lord.'

'You have no idea,' I told her. 'I feel like I'm allowed to be Human around him. Things are finally changing, Mother. I can feel it.'

'Same. I can't tell you how excited we all are for the Grand Tour. We're already making our preparations for the Lord's arrival in Wellington.'

Up until this point, I had refused to contemplate what it would mean to arrive at my own parliament on the side of the Hierarch. I simply didn't have the mental capacity to think about it yet. Eager to change the subject, I asked, 'And how is your social endorsement of Hayden going?'

Mother took a moment or two to respond. 'The Keeper he assaulted … they were taken off stasis. They've terminated.'

I didn't have the mental capacity to grapple with that either. But the image of the stasis capsule, surrounded by clan members solemnly calculating the loss of collective Rank their relative's death had inflicted on them, became embedded in my thoughts.

'Of course, I'll keep doing what I can for Hayden,' Mother continued. 'But you should pay him a visit – it might lift his **spirits**.'

It was clear what she meant. If his hearing did go ahead while I was on the Grand Tour, the outcome was almost certain.

'Gratitude, Mother. I'll do that.'

The rest of the conversation didn't last long. My fatigue was getting the better of me and Mother could sense it.

'One last thing,' she said, before I could end the connection. 'Don't give up on Neekor.'

I didn't know if I had been contemplating doing that, but Mother's talent for clairvoyance must have picked up on something.

'Aliens can be more like us than we appreciate. Why do you think I **fell in love** with your father? Have **hope**, Daniel. I didn't pass on that trait to you for nothing.'

'Gratitude, Mother.'

The connection ended but I stayed on my perch for a while longer.

The trait selector program seemed to be itching in my tree, so I brought it up again. Neekor had cleared every trait from the shared grid – whether this was an indication that she wanted to start the exercise afresh or that she no longer desired to do it at all, I couldn't tell.

I eyed **hope** in my profile. I wanted to believe it was worth something. The more I thought about it (probably thanks to the **rationality** trait inherited from Father) the more pointless it seemed. It offered no evolutionary advantage, no tangible benefit on its own. It almost seemed like a deliberate agent of natural selection. A virus intended to weed out those foolish enough to believe in something on no logical basis whatsoever.

And yet, I couldn't deny that I wouldn't have set off on my mission if I didn't have it. Once, I had been proud of my **hope**, declaring to Neekor that it was what made me Human. Even if I couldn't quantify its value, just as Mother had said – I wouldn't have been me without it.

I moved it back into the grid.

4-4

In no time, the Grand Tour was upon me.

I went to see Hayden before we left. He was more subdued than the last visit, sitting on the edge of his sleep capsule, barely looking up as I entered the cell. The bruises and swelling on his face had gone down, and he'd fattened slightly. I assumed the lack of cleaving was responsible. In spite of that, he seemed smaller. As if he occupied only the tiniest bit of space in the cell.

This time, I spoke first. 'How are you, Hayden?'

He gave me a sideways glance, lifted a sluggish hand at the cell as if to say, 'What do you think?'

'You're looking well,' I said, to which he only shrugged. I was running out of **small-talk**, so I ventured something else. 'Mother's social endorsement is coming along.'

'It's not going to work. Not now that the Keeper's dead.'

At least I'd got him speaking. 'It might. We just have to wait and see —'

'I didn't mean it, you know. To go that far. I just wanted them to feel what it's like. Every hit keeping them down. It just never seemed like enough.'

Unlike the last time I'd seen him, he seemed completely lucid. More like the Hayden I remembered.

'That's what Mother can tell the Magistrate,' I said. 'Everything you've been through, how hard you've had it —'

'I'm telling you it won't work.'

'You don't know that.'

'And you do?' His voice wasn't angry, just tired. 'You think you know what it's like. How this all works. But you don't. Not really.'

'Maybe not. But I know how the Hierarch works. It's going to change. I'm so close.'

I tried to tell him about my idea for the House of the Covenant and the upcoming Grand Tour that would precede its establishment. He didn't really seem to be listening. He was staring at the floor, or some place beyond it that I couldn't see.

'I don't suppose this tour is coming to any detainment or exile centres?' he said, after I stopped talking. 'You'd think with how many of us are Human, this new Hierarch might want to hear what we have to say.'

It was hard to feel like that wasn't a personal attack. But maybe it was warranted. I had failed to consider that point.

'I could try and add an extra stop —'

He shook his head. 'No. It's fine, Daniel. I know you're doing your best.'

'I am. This new House of the Covenant is going to change everything. I can't overhaul the whole balance system by the time of your hearing but — whatever happens — things are going to get better.'

I wasn't sure if he heard this, either.

'I won't see you before then, will I? My hearing — it'll probably happen before you get back from this tour?'

'Probably.'

I remembered the last time we parted like this, when he already knew that I was going away and leaving him behind. I desperately wanted this parting to be different, to be better. I wanted to reach through the coherence field and touch him, just put my hand on his shoulder, anything. Unable to, I found Mother's words instead.

'Have **hope**, Hayden. Everything's going to be okay. I promise.'

He lifted his gaze to mine, and I wondered then if **hope** was a trait he actually had.

Then he laughed — quietly, as if it caught him by surprise.

I flexed an inquiring tendril and he shook his head again. 'Just remembered something funny, that's all. Gratitude, Daniel.'

If nothing else, I left happy. I'd at least brought a smile to his face and heard him laugh again.

There was only one other goodbye I needed to make before leaving on the Grand Tour: to Neekor. The atmosphere in our dwelling had been tense since the trait identification argument. Neither of us had indicated any desire to revisit it or concede an error. I noticed, however, that **hope** remained in the grid, and had since been paired with one of Neekor's traits: **contemplative**.

I was worried that she might not come to our agreed meeting place – the tiny pennoo outlet outside the House of Transportation – but I arrived there after my trip to the House of Exile to find her waiting, a pitcher of pennoo in each hand. She passed one to me in what felt like a peace offering, and I accepted it gratefully.

She opened her mouth to speak then closed it again, her brow knitting in concentration. 'I will…' She let out an exasperated breath. 'What is the word again? Desire to be in your presence?'

There was that weightless feeling again. I didn't want to let it go. But I knew I had to. My mission required it.

'**Miss**? You'll **miss** me?'

She gave a short, almost embarrassed flick. 'Yes, that.'

I resisted the urge this time to kiss her on the cheek, which I knew would have made her uncomfortable in such a public setting, and gave her an affectionate salute instead.

She returned it and said, 'You will contact me?'

'Of course.' With every passing second, the thought of leaving her seemed harder to bear. 'As often as I can.'

She flicked agreeably and then, without another a word, retreated to the House of Transportation, her half-empty pitcher of pennoo still in hand. I knew her well enough to understand that there were several reasons for her abrupt departure, none of which were negative indications of her feelings towards me. First, she was too pragmatic to expend any more of her or my time than was absolutely necessary, and, second, she was too guarded to allow any overt displays of emotion. Still, as I watched her go, I wished she could have stayed for just a moment longer.

The first stop of the Grand Tour was Russia, domain of the **Humanarch**. This was a calculated move. Despite the fact that the **Humanarch** no longer wields the same power it once did, it is still generally respected by the rest of Humanity for the vision it represents – a Human equivalent to the Hierarch. Lincoln knew that winning the **Humanarch's** approval at the very outset of the Grand Tour would signal to other nations that they should support the initiative too.

Although I knew of the **Humanarch's** history and reputation among wider Humanity, I had never been to Russia, nor personally encountered the **Humanarch**. I was, therefore, entirely unfamiliar with the very strict, Alien-inspired customs by which it operated. Thankfully, and as Lincoln knew all too well, Morgan was a member of the Russian clans that originally formed the **Humanarch**, so she gave ample warning of what awaited.

'The Supreme Rank controls everything that happens in that room,' she said, as we approached the gateway of the **Humanarch's** rather diminutive imitation of the Apex. 'You must ask his permission before you do anything: sit, stand, speak. You name it. Keep your head bowed at all times – don't make eye contact unless he instructs you to.'

With a hiss the gate opened, releasing a waft of steam or smoke that I couldn't guess the purpose of except, perhaps, for dramatic effect. A ramp extended from the gateway until it met the floor at our feet, and a pair of footsteps thudded on it. A hooded figure approached us through the roiling fog, stopping at the end of the ramp. They reached up, removed their hood, and revealed a Human face.

'**Greetings, Lord Karkoora 8 Darius, of the Teerin' Ho Hierarch and the Middle-Eastern nations**,' she said, offering a salute more rigidly formal than any I had seen an Alien give, before turning to Morgan. '**Ivanov 5 Morgan, the Supreme Rank welcomes you back to your clan of origin.**' She glanced briefly at Lincoln and me, in what I assumed was the only greeting we were worthy of, then said, '**I am the Supreme Rank's Mouthpiece. The Supreme Rank awaits you.**'

She turned and led us up the ramp. Inside the gate, the smoke was so thick I could hardly breathe, but I wasn't sure I was allowed to cough or die of suffocation without the Supreme Rank's permission so I held my breath and fought my way through it. Just when my lungs were about to burst the next gate opened, and we arrived in a room so high that I couldn't see its ceiling. Directly ahead of us was a circular arrangement of throne-like perches, each one ascending in height the further away from us they were positioned. Once, when the **Humanarch** was at the peak of its influence, those perches would have been occupied by the **Humanarch's** own version of the Lordship. Now only one of them was filled – the perch furthest away, at the head of the arrangement, which was several times taller than the others, shooting from the floor to the upper reaches of the room. I could just make out a pair of legs dangling from its peak.

'I present to you the Supreme Rank of the great nation of Russia, and of all nations of Humanity,' said the Mouthpiece, gesturing towards him. I saw a hand motion a salute from up in the heavens and I glanced at Morgan, who signalled for us to return it. Then the Mouthpiece said, 'You may stand.'

I'd thought we might be offered seats but that was a Human custom, not a Noor one. The **Humanarch's** commitment to replicating traditional Hierarch practices went even further than I expected, and I found it immensely puzzling. I understood why the **Humanarch** had been established, what it sought to achieve, how it had tried to unite Humanity against a common enemy. But now, with the way it still mimicked the protocols of the culture that had assimilated us, it seemed to me less like a symbol of resistance to the Hierarch and more like a glorification of it.

'The Supreme Rank understands you have been granted a new responsibility, Lord Karkoora,' the Mouthpiece continued. 'For Human-Hierarch Interactions. The Supreme Rank commends you on your willingness to invite comment from Humanity on what they wish this responsibility to entail. You may express gratitude for this.'

Morgan shot the Lord a look and he cleared his throat. 'Gratitude, Supreme Rank.'

'Your gratitude is noted,' said the Mouthpiece. 'The Supreme Rank makes the following requests…'

She then recited a series of demands that, as it went on, seemed to become more about leverage for the **Humanarch** itself rather than benefits for all of Humanity. I was particularly struck by the request to establish a permanent forum exclusively between the Supreme Rank and his equivalent in the Teerin' Ho Hierarch. It didn't seem right to me that the **Humanarch** should be granted such a privilege and not any other nation.

I eyed the Lord sympathetically, wondering how he could possibly respond when the Hierarch would never agree to any of the **Humanarch's** requests. Then, in the group connection our trees were sharing, Lincoln asked the Lord if he could speak on his behalf, to which the Lord agreed.

'Supreme Rank,' Lincoln said, in a commanding tone. 'I am General Samuels 6 Lincoln, of the House of Balance. May I address you on behalf of the Lord?'

A pause, then the Mouthpiece said, 'You may.'

'Gratitude. The Lord will, of course, consider your requests with great care. There is, however, one matter he wishes to invite your wise counsel on. For too long the Hierarch has failed to engage with the **Humanarch**, and the rest of Humanity, in a way that complies with the Covenant of Wellington. For Human-Hierarch Interactions to improve, they must honour the Covenant as the first and most critical step. The Lord therefore proposes the establishment of a new House, whose sole purpose is to ensure the interactions between the Hierarch and Humanity are compliant with the Covenant. Would you support such an action?'

We waited with bated breath while the Supreme Rank considered and communicated his ruling to the Mouthpiece. Whatever the **Humanarch's** verdict was would set the tone for the rest of the Grand Tour.

'You may establish such a House,' the Mouthpiece reported.

Just as Lincoln had anticipated, news of the **Humanarch's** endorsement swept through Europe and Asia. Every nation we subsequently visited already knew about the proposal for the House of the Covenant, which they were eager to discuss within the opening moments of our gatherings with them.

I found this enlightening. In coming up with the idea, I hadn't put much thought into exactly what 'ensuring the Hierarch upholds the Covenant' would look like. But the Human leaders had very clear thoughts on that, and it was striking how similar they were. Many supported far-reaching powers that would make the House more like a policer of Human-Hierarch Interactions rather than a mere monitor. Most, if not all, wanted those powers extended beyond the Hierarch and to the Territorial Congresses, who believed, despite having devolved governance responsibility from the central Hierarch, they were somehow exempt from Covenant obligations. With each nation we visited, my vision for the House grew stronger and clearer, accumulating an arsenal of powers and functions that would ensure the Hierarch never breached the Covenant again. More than once the Lord said to me, 'Your House of the Covenant is **a real hit**, Daniel.'

Not for everyone, though. I should have expected it, really, as the Grand Tour arrived in Ireland and I walked into the Irish parliament for the second time. Winnra 5 Sophie was waiting at her podium, while we moved down the aisle to take our place on the line-up of seats beside her. I tried not to meet anyone's eyes, hoping none of them recognised me as the **turncoat** who had betrayed their independence to Britain a few revs earlier. But it was clear, from the way her eyes followed me all the way to my seat, that Winnra 5 Sophie remembered exactly who I was.

'I agree with the proposal in theory,' she said, once the Lord had outlined it to her, 'but I have serious doubts about it in practice.'

'What do you mean by that?' asked the Lord.

'Where will the servants of this new House come from?'

The Lord turned to Lincoln, who took the cue and responded, 'We propose that, initially, the new House will be served by the Human-Hierarch Interactions Squad and a proportion of the House of Balance.'

'Does that proportion include ChamCov?'

'It does,' Lincoln replied, and Sophie returned her attention to the Lord.

'You see, Darius, if this new House was actually capable of ensuring the Hierarch complies with the Covenant, then it would have my full support. But the reality is it won't. That capability doesn't currently exist within the Hierarch, and you can't just **magic** it out of nowhere.'

The Lord cocked his head. 'We would rely on the Human-Hierarch Interactions Squad to educate all servants assigned to the House.'

'Are you aware,' said Sophie, leaning forward on her podium, 'that servants in the Human-Hierarch Interactions Squad were responsible for the Britain Authorisation?'

I did my best to stare forward, hoping my new enhancers were adequately hiding the panic pulling at my face.

'I'm not interested in the actions of servants under the previous Hierarch,' the Lord replied calmly. 'They serve a new one now.'

I dared a peek at Sophie. She was regarding the Lord with an expression somewhere between outrage and admiration.

'Then I'll say this, on behalf of Ireland,' she said, her eyes flickering in my direction. 'If your new House can prevent any other nation from going through what we did, then it will have my support.'

The Lord gave her a nod – a deliberately Human gesture.

We broke for noonmeal. I stayed in the debating chamber, alone. Relieved from the paralysing stares of the entire Irish parliament, I finally felt like I could take the room in. It had changed since the last time I was there. The walls were adorned with flags and banners, holograms of the now-famous **road trip**. It was quite the breach of standard parliamentary décor but it was hard to deny the sense of dignity and inspiration it gave the room.

Perhaps it was time our traditions changed, I thought. Not a desperate clinging to what they had been pre-assimilation, nor an adaptation of what had assimilated us like Russia's, but an evolution on our own terms, fitting for the times.

While I envisioned how we might do something similar in Wellington, Winnra 5 Sophie appeared, striding across the chamber. Impulse lifted me to my feet, fear kept me in place.

'High Rank Winnra,' I called across the floor.

She stopped, seemed to think for a second, then turned.

'It's been a long time, Daniel.'

There was no greeting, no pleasantries. She was just letting me know she was willing to hear what I had to say.

'I wanted to apologise. For the Britain Authorisation. I tried my best to do something but...' What was I supposed to say, when nothing could change what I had done? I hated the feeling, this *something* that was rising up within me. I finished before it could take hold completely. **'I'm sorry.'**

She didn't react for a torturous minute. Only stared at me, like she was trying to assess whether my apology was genuine or not. At last she took a breath, and her face softened ever so slightly.

'I am curious. Why someone as young and as bright as you would subject yourself to this.'

I didn't know what she meant, and she must have read my confusion on my face.

'Serving them.' She jerked her head at the next room. 'You could do so much more for us, fighting them instead.'

Whatever it was that had gripped me a moment earlier gave way to something else. Something hot, furious.

'I *am* fighting them,' I told her. 'From the inside.'

A smile appeared on her lips.

'Are you?'

My exchange with Winnra 5 Sophie wasn't the only thing I tried not to think about as the Grand Tour continued. The other was the Tour's impending arrival in New Zealand.

I had just made it back to my lodging after an exhausting series of gatherings with Lincoln's people in America, procured a cutter from the in-built cutting bar, and fallen into a plush lounger when the communication arrived. I was so weary I hadn't anticipated the conversation that I should have known was coming.

'Daniel!' Mother sounded almost relieved. 'I wasn't sure I would get through – you must be so busy.'

'I am, but we've just finished for the rotation.'

'Ah, well, I won't take much of your time. I just wanted to talk to you about our gathering with Lord Karkoora.'

'Good idea,' I said, taking a cut. We'd been caught off-guard several times by the unique welcoming ceremonies of nations that none of us were familiar with. While I had a general idea of how New Zealand welcomed guests, discussing it with Mother would allow me to inform the Lord of exactly what to expect for this particular occasion.

'Parliament will be sitting about an hour before the Lord arrives to prepare our submissions to him, so feel free to join us at any time before then –'

'Apologies, Mother,' I interrupted her. 'What do you mean about joining you?'

There was a pause, which suggested she thought it was glaringly obvious.

'Well, you won't be coming on with the Hierarch, will you? You'll be welcoming them from our side.'

'No, Mother,' I said, taking another cut. 'I will be coming with the Lord.'

Another silence, which was even more chilling than the last.

'Daniel, you're a New Zealander. You're a member of this parliament.'

'No, I'm not. I haven't been elected.'

'We've been over this. You don't have to be elected. You can be a member of the list, which you are.'

'Only because you put me there.'

'Because I want you there. When I have to welcome the Hierarch into our House for the first time in our history, I want you at my side.'

What was I supposed to say to that? I wanted to be with her too, to confront this enemy together. But I was a servant to the Hierarch. Didn't she know what that meant?

'Mother,' I said as gently as I could, 'I need to be on the Hierarch side.'

'**Why on Earth would that be?**' She was breaking into Common. That wasn't good.

'Because I can't compromise my position. You've seen how closely the propagation is following this. If they see a Captain of the Hierarch – in service to Lord Karkoora no less – sitting on the front benches of a Human parliament –'

'**Fuck** the propagation,' Mother said with a snarl, before recomposing herself. 'This is an historic event, Daniel. The first time the Hierarch has ever been welcome inside our parliament. I will not have you on their side when they get here.'

'I *have* to be on their side,' I returned, acutely aware that the synthetic calm I was cutting with was warping into something more aggressive. 'The Lord's Attendant is Russian and she came on our side when we visited the **Humanarch**.'

'I don't give a **shit** what the Lord's Attendant did. This is about you.'

I rose from the lounger, fists clenched, coat bristling. She was right – this *was* about me. All of this was *my* doing. I was the reason the

Hierarch was even coming to New Zealand. I was the architect of the House of the Covenant. I had shown countless Hierarch servants how they were failing to uphold the Covenant. I would be the one to break the machine.

'I don't care what New Zealand thinks of me,' I finished. 'I'm doing this for them. I am so close and I can't afford to fail now.'

Mother was quiet again. For a brief, victorious moment I thought I had actually bested her in a debate. Then she said simply, 'Please, Daniel.'

It almost worked. I could not recall a time she had spoken to me so softly, so pleadingly. But I did recall a time when the tables were turned. When I needed her to come to my aid, to support me: begging her to come to my first rote of service at ChamCov for the ascension ritual. All the guilt and shame in my belly twisted into sweet, satisfying vengeance.

'You told me to make my own **destiny**. So I am.'

I ended the connection and took another cut.

But no matter how many cuts I took, I couldn't manufacture the delusion to convince myself that what I had done was right. I tried not to imagine Mother at the other end, standing speechless, unable to believe what she'd just heard. The image kept coming, taunting, resisting any of my attempts to drown it in artificial calm. I tossed the cutter at a corner of the room and fell into my sleep capsule, instructing it to deliver the strongest dose of sedative it could.

Not even the heaviest sleep of my life could prevent the sense of dread I woke to the following rote. Nothing could. The conversation with Mother haunted me as the Grand Tour proceeded through Central and South America, even while the nations there took us on excursions to their most sacred wonders, like the Amazon Garden and the T-Pose Statue in Brazil. I had longed to see Machu Picchu ever since hearing about the Peru Resolution in my very first week of service at ChamCov, and when I finally saw the ancient structures upon its surface, I felt nothing. Each stop was just another step closer to New Zealand, to Mother, to our inevitable confrontation.

Desperate to alleviate some of the burden, I asked Morgan how she felt arriving in Russia.

'I'm in service to the Hierarch,' she said, shrugging. 'If my people have a problem with that, that's up to them.'

It wasn't the answer I was looking for. With a rare smile, she added, 'It doesn't matter what side you're on, Daniel. You're still Human. Nothing can take that away.'

I wanted to believe her, that my Humanity was this inalienable thing. But that wasn't what Mother had always warned: Humanity *could* be lost. That was why she was always telling me to hold onto it, to fight for it.

As we drew ever nearer to New Zealand, I began to wonder: even if I believed my Humanity could never be lost, what would it matter if it was lost in the eyes of my own mother?

She tried one more time to contact me, the night before we reached New Zealand. I couldn't bring myself to answer. I lay there in my sleep capsule, watching each failed connection request be replaced by another, over and over again. The crescendo of notifications became too much to bear and I forced my mind elsewhere, down to the surface, to play out everything that was about to happen.

I envisioned our delegation arriving on parliament grounds, entering those doors, walking the halls of parliament until we arrived in the debating chamber, which had finally had its new light emitters installed. There I'd see Mother, her eyes red and swollen with a grief I didn't expect, refusing to look in my direction, to accept the reality that her son had chosen the Hierarch over her. I would take my place in one of the seats now reserved for visitors, a back-bench one, so I could sink as low as possible to avoid the stares and whispers and furtive pointing from the members and the galleries above that were packed with civilians for the first time in decades.

I played this simulation so many times that when my body eventually caught up and it happened for real, I didn't feel a thing because I'd already numbed myself to its weight.

With our delegation seated, the rest of the House sat too, along with the curious watchers in the galleries. The Speaker gave Mother the floor.

'Thank you, Mr Speaker,' she said, standing. She seemed more nervous than I had ever seen her, hands wringing, voice shaky. She took a breath, cleared her throat, and began, 'I appreciate this is a departure from standard parliamentary protocol, to invite our guests to share this sacred space with us. In the ancestors' times, such a meeting would have been held in the Prime Minister's private office. There is, of course, no such place anymore.

'But breaching our protocols like this to accommodate the Hierarch does have its benefits. It allows transparency. For all of you,' she raised both arms to the galleries, 'to witness this historic occasion. To hear for yourselves what the Hierarch has to say to you. And to hear what your representatives have to say back on your behalf.'

There were a few cheers that the Speaker let slide.

'To our guests, the Hierarch,' Mother continued, 'New Zealand welcomes you. You have been afforded an honour none of your forebears have ever received, even when they came to Wellington to validate the Covenant – to walk our floor, sit in the place of our ancestors. Do not waste this opportunity.'

Mother resumed her seat. She still hadn't looked at me. It struck me that, although this was the first time the Hierarch had ever been inside parliament, it was represented on this significant occasion only by Humans – the Lord, Lincoln, Morgan, and me. Humans having to confront their own kind on the Hierarch's behalf. I wondered if I wasn't the only one Mother was ashamed to look at.

From the head of the House, the Speaker locked eyes with the Lord and gave a quick, upward jerk of his head. This was a rather versatile gesture from the non-verbal dialect of New Zealand Common that, in this context, roughly converts to: 'What say you, male friend/acquaintance/stranger to whom I am willing to give the benefit of the doubt?'.

I sent a message to the Lord informing him that the floor was his and he stood.

'Thank you, Mr Speaker, and you, Ms Kytoonoo, for your gracious welcome on behalf of the nation of New Zealand. I assure you the significance of our presence in this House is not lost on me. I understand the opportunity I have today and I intend to use it wisely. That is, not by speaking but by listening.'

The galleries above became alive with chatter. The Lord had clearly made an impression. It was no wonder, really. His address was, after all, crafted by Lincoln.

'For too long the Hierarch has told Humans what it thinks is good for them. It makes decrees that it thinks will benefit Humanity, not ones that actually will. As the first Lord for Human-Hierarch Interactions, that is not the approach I wish to take. I have ideas about how I want to carry this responsibility, but I also need you to tell me if I am on the right track. If the Hierarch is going to honour the Covenant of Wellington, signed here in this very city, then I need your help to make it do that. I am here to listen.'

It was a masterful address, especially considering that the entire reason we were there was to convince the citizens of New Zealand of what we thought was good for them. The galleries were filled with such excitement that the Speaker was finally forced to do his job and threaten them with removal if they didn't quieten down.

Then the speeches began. They were conducted as if the Human-Hierarch Interactions responsibility was a **law** being proposed, with representatives from both sides of the **House** standing to give their view on it. It was the first time I had ever seen unanimous support from across the **House** on an issue. New Zealand's representatives, like everyone else, had already heard of the proposal for the House of the Covenant, and I was pleased to hear that, like everyone else, they generally supported it.

Generally. The only exception was Mother, who, throughout the speeches, gave no indication of her agreement. Her face remained grave, directed down at her lap, where her fingers were laced. I knew what that meant. She was preparing, soaking in all of the conversation, sifting through each of the key points so she could augment her own position with them, which she would deliver last of all. A final, definitive statement that she reserved for herself.

When that time came, and she stood at her seat, the entire House hushed expectantly.

'A great deal has been said about what this new responsibility can do for Humanity,' she opened. 'And much of it has hinged upon this idea of a new House, a House of the Covenant. Lord Karkoora, I agree with my fellow representatives that such a House could achieve great things, like ensuring the Territorial Congresses honour their Covenant obligations. Like implementing new measures in the Core for assessing the health of the Hierarch's relationship with Humans. However, my fear is that such actions will not go far enough. In fact, it is more than a fear. I am convinced your House will not go far enough.'

In my nearly four revs of service for the Hierarch, nothing had hit me so hard as knowing my idea for a better Hierarch did not meet Mother's approval.

'The proposed role of this new House will be to ensure the Hierarch honours the Promises of the Covenant. My question is this: how can this new House ever achieve such a purpose, when the Hierarch still rules over **Earth**?' She redirected her address at the citizens above. 'The Covenant of Wellington promised that we will retain control over ourselves, our airspace, our resources – how will the House of the Covenant honour that Promise? Because to do so would require the Hierarch to finally, formally, acknowledge that the Covenant established a partnership between it and the Human race, one where **power** is shared between us. Where we exercise the control promised to us over ourselves, and the Hierarch does so over its citizens here on **Earth**. Until that promise is realised,' at last she turned back to the Lord, 'your new House will always fail.'

My gaze fell to my feet. I wished more than anything that instead of sitting where I was, a stranger in my own **House**, that I was sitting beside her, just to feel like her honour was also mine by association. To bask in the respect she earned in that moment from every other Human in the chamber.

Lord Karkoora rose. 'What do you propose, High Rank Kytoonoo?'

'No matter how effective your new House is at educating or supporting the Hierarch, it cannot compel the Hierarch to do anything. We are fortunate, at this point in time, that there are Humans such as yourselves serving the Hierarch. But we cannot trust that you will always be there to fight them for us.' I could feel her eyes finally on me, and I lifted mine to meet them. They shone like glass. 'In the ancestors' times, the rules and principles that guided our society were enshrined in **law**. As Humans are bound by the rule of **law**, the Hierarch is bound by its decrees. We have always recognised the Covenant as **law**. But the Hierarch has never given it the same status by its own standards.'

'You wish for the Hierarch to make a new decree?' Lord Karkoora asked.

'On behalf of New Zealand,' Mother declared, 'I propose that the Covenant of Wellington be made into an official decree, thereby obligating the Hierarch to honour it.'

The Speaker leapt to his feet.

'**All those in favour say "āe",**' he said, and the unified response from the entire House – including the galleries – was deafening. Mother said her final word.

'The Indigenous peoples of this nation have spoken.'

Silence followed. The Lord turned to Lincoln, whose eyes glazed over as he set about crafting something for the Lord to respond with. I knew it was impossible for him to really respond at all. There was no way the Hierarch would agree to such a thing. It would undermine the very basis on which it exercised Rank over the planet. This, I knew, was exactly Mother's point. If the Hierarch made the Covenant into a decree, and was obliged to honour it, the Hierarch would be forced to reconcile the Covenant's First Promise, which, in the Common version, only gave the Hierarch ruling Rank over Aliens, not Humans. The entire planet's constitution would be upended.

247

'As with all suggestions I have heard throughout this voyage,' the Lord began, reciting whatever Lincoln had sent him, 'I will consider this carefully.'

With nothing more to be said, the gathering was concluded. Everyone filed out into the next room, where an impressive spread was laid out with **chips**, **fizzy**, and even a few **pies** that were being ritualistically blown on before consumption.

I didn't feel like eating. I waited until everyone had helped themselves to the sustenance before slipping out, barely detected, to make for the wall of honour. It was the only place I truly felt permitted to be among my own people, which was only because the noble faces on the wall couldn't speak to me. There was no risk of them telling me what they really thought of me.

'Daniel.'

For a second I thought Mother's photo actually was speaking to me. I blinked, before turning around to find her at the end of the hallway. Nowhere to run. It was time to face her.

'Mother –'

'It's Hayden.'

A few moments passed before I registered what she had said. I realised why she looked so upset in the debating chamber and why she tried to contact me so many times the night before.

'He's been exiled?'

Mother shook her head. A tear came loose.

It was an old form of transfer. Something of a paradox, where one acquires knowledge not by the information given, but the information withheld. Mother didn't need to say anything else. I just knew – **in my heart**, as the ancestors would say.

Hayden had exiled himself. To a place from which he would never return.

Rigged his sleep capsule. That's how he did it. Apparently, the mechanisms aren't too dissimilar from a cleaver's. Broke into the machinery, tweaked a few things, and it gave him enough sedative to never wake up.

At least, that's what the House of Exile Operators told me and Mother when we arrived to collect him. Which, they made sure to repeat, was 'highly irregular'. They, of course, simply wanted to atomise the corpse, as per standard Hierarch edict for self-termination while in detainment. They didn't understand why, if we wanted him so badly, we wouldn't just let them ship him off to us. Why we demanded to see his body, see his face. Why I brushed his tendrils out of his eyes and stroked his hair, spoke to him as if he could hear me. Why we tried to make him look comfortable, instructed them to carry his container out with us carefully, gently. Why I cried the whole time.

And I hated them for it. Watching them, hearing them, I hated them more than I'd ever thought it possible to hate something. Them, the Hierarch, every Alien on the planet. I hated them all. In that hatred, I felt like I truly understood Hayden for the first time. Why every blow he'd rained down on that Keeper was never going to be enough to satisfy him.

Anyway.

In accordance with Human custom, Hayden was buried in the **cemetery** behind parliament. The Lord gave me leave to remain in Wellington for the **funeral**, while the Grand Tour continued to Australia.

There weren't many who showed up for him. The numbers were filled out by the Mutt Pack, who stood solemnly behind everyone else, only throwing up the odd hand gesture as their own silent commemoration.

Once the **funeral** was over, I requested that Father take me back to Kappeetar – a decision that Mother raised little objection to. Hayden's death might have brought us back together, but it hadn't mended what was broken between us. What I had broken. I wasn't sure if anything could put it back together again.

After a long, wordless embrace that served as Mother's goodbye, I left Wellington and Hayden behind. I returned to my dwelling after little more than one or two trivial conversations with Father and a 'gratitude' for the ride. I fell into a lounger and stayed there, numbly, until Neekor arrived home from service at darkfall.

'Oh, Daniel,' she exclaimed. 'I was not expecting you so soon.'

'I couldn't stay there.'

Neekor gave me one of her quizzical looks. It reminded me of the way the House of Exile Operators looked at me.

'I… failed him, Neekor.'

The look stayed. I'd never been so annoyed by her face before.

'It's not as if you terminated him, Daniel.'

'No. The Hierarch did. That's why I failed him.'

'But… it was a self-termination, I don't understand –'

'He's the whole reason I'm here.' I was somehow on my feet. 'My mission, everything. The Hierarch was supposed to change, make things for better for him. I was too late. Now he's gone.'

She jumped when I said it. Gone. I didn't care if I frightened her.

'I can't stop replaying it. The moment his burial container went down, and his father collapsed, and I felt like I was falling too but I had Mother to catch me, and she just held me there, even with everything I said to her she held me, kept me up, and all I could think was that Hayden gave that to me. Even in death he gave me more than I gave him in life. I did nothing but make promises I couldn't keep, promises I'll never be able to keep now, and he knew it all along, he knew that my promises were just a bad joke and he still laughed, still gave me that memory to take with me.'

250

I might as well have said it to her in Common. I was like a stranger to her. An entity from another dimension.

'Neekor, stop looking at me like that.'

'Like what?'

'Like… like… like such a **fucking** Alien.'

Finally, something shifted in her. It was subtle, just a change behind her eyes. But it was there: a stoked fire, a waking giant. I welcomed it. I wanted this fight. She was suddenly every Alien I had ever encountered, every Alien I was never able to tear down, to tell what I really felt.

'You know what, Daniel? I am tired of your constant criticism of us. It is exhausting.'

'*You* feel exhausted?'

'Yes, I do. Every rotation you return home from service and you discharge all of your anger on me. Every rotation I am forced to endure your accounts of whatever new way you have been offended by Aliens.'

'That must be *so* hard.'

'Yes, it is. Gratitude for the acknowledgement.'

'I was being sarcastic. But you don't get that, do you?'

'And what if I do not? Does that make me any less intelligent? Worthy of ridicule?'

'No. It's just more proof that Aliens don't even bother to try and understand us.'

She surprised me with a sigh.

'I know what Aliens have done to Humans, what we are still doing to Humans. But there are a lot of us attempting to improve. It often feels like it is never enough.'

'Never enough?' I could have laughed if I wasn't so outraged. 'What exactly do you think you've done? When have you ever tried to learn Common Transfer? How many times have you been down to the surface? You never even went to Wellington for Covenant Anniversary after you said you would. You live on this world – a *Human* world – and you didn't even know what the Covenant of Wellington was before you met me.'

'I do not know any of those things because I am always humiliated for trying to learn. You criticise us for not knowing Common transfer, then berate us when we pronounce it incorrectly. You criticise us for not visiting the surface, then make us feel unwelcome when we do. You criticise us for not knowing about the Covenant, but you do not educate us about it.'

'I shouldn't have to educate you about anything. It's not my responsibility to educate you on what you took away from us.'

Neekor's eyes narrowed. 'I have not taken anything away from you, or any Human. The constant inference that I am in some way to blame for the suffering of the past is beginning to infuriate me.'

Whatever fury she felt was nothing next to mine. 'You really are incapable of comprehending, aren't you? In what reality does your humiliation even begin to compare to what Humans endure every rote of their lives? We've lost almost everything that makes us Human. Our culture, our transfer. We have less Rank than you. We dominate the exile population. We die earlier than you.' I could feel my voice breaking and I let it. 'Why is that so difficult for Aliens like you to comprehend?'

'When will you comprehend that *you* are Alien, too?'

The question was so unexpected that it stunned me into silence. Neekor pressed her advantage.

'You are more Alien than you are Human. Look at your genome. Look at your coat: you are more coated than I am. That is the absurdity of all this – you stand here criticising Aliens, conveniently ignoring the fact that you are Alien, too.'

I took her in – fangs bared, claws drawn – and I hardly recognised her. She never seemed more Alien to me than in that moment.

'Fine, Neekor,' I said once I found my voice. 'You're right. My genome is more Alien than Human. I am coated. Anyone would assume, based on my physical features alone, that I'm Alien. I don't care. Being Human is more than whether you're coated or not. More than what percentage of your genome is Human. I see now that you will never understand this.'

Neekor stared at me like an equation she was trying to solve. Then she said, 'Why did you ever partner with me?'

Knowing there was no Alien translation for it, I said, 'You'll never understand that, either,' and left.

As much as it hurt to walk away, it had to be done. I had been a fool to believe that she – as intelligent and empathetic as she was – could ever understand what it meant to be Human in this assimilated world. No Alien could, not so long as there was no requirement to do so. The only way Aliens would ever understand us was if the Hierarch who ruled them, who controlled our society, understood what it meant to share this world with us. It all came back to my mission, to make the Hierarch honour the Covenant, and I knew then what true realisation of that looked like. Everything had crystallised for me. I could see with perfect clarity what I had always known, really, deep down. Something else that Hayden had taught me:

A mother is always right.

I spent the next few weeks dwelling in my office at the Apex, making use of the sleep capsule installed, waiting patiently for the Grand Tour to end and for the Lord to return. By all accounts the rest of the tour went well (except for one gathering in South Korea that was crashed by an Alien demanding recognition of the infamous 'Rarko'itti Covenant'; a supposed final draft of the Covenant of Wellington that somehow proves Humans really did cede control to the Hierarch. (No matter how many times that ridiculous conspiracy gets invalidated, it somehow keeps popping up). I passed the time getting a head start on reviewing the feedback from the 143 nations that had been met with and putting together my proposal for the functions of the House of the Covenant. By the time the tour was finished and the squad returned to the Apex, I had prepared my case.

I made sure to receive them all at the gateway when they arrived. Morgan broke from the group to wrap me in a hug, and each of the others waited their turn to offer their condolences. It was the Lord's that touched me the most, that showed he appreciated my loss more than any of them.

'Come on,' he said softly, leading me into his office. 'Let's make sure not one more Human goes through what your friend did.'

Inside his office, the sweeping window overlooking Kappeetar had been converted into a screen, displaying various diagrams of data recorded from the gatherings. I could see that the squad had also made a start in identifying potential functions for the new House – in the centre of the screen was a list:

Monitor the Hierarch's interactions with Humans
Advise the Hierarch on appropriate interaction with Humans
Develop tools and training initiatives to improve the Hierarch's understanding of Humans and their values
Develop edict for engaging with Humans
Mediate Covenant resolutions (incorporating ChamCov)

'Well, Daniel,' said the Lord, gesturing. 'What do you think?'

I checked the screen again, taking in the percentages of attendants who had proposed various functions and the quoted comments that the squad had highlighted as noteworthy. I couldn't see Mother's anywhere.

'How is this going to stop anyone from going through what Hayden did?' I said, to a collective tendril-flex. 'There's nothing here about honouring the Covenant.'

'These functions will lead to that,' Lincoln responded.

'Will they? For every Alien who understands the Covenant and what it promised, there are countless more who don't, and never will. Some of them will never want to understand, either. They're the ones who dismiss Human values and principles as subjective nonsense, then deny statistical evidence and refuse to engage in rational discussion about prejudice against Humans. They will never change on their own. So, we have to make them.' I pointed to the screen. 'I believe these functions will improve Hierarch-Human interactions to some extent. But will they give back control to Humans over themselves and their affairs? Will they return our resources, our airspace? Will they afford Humans the same rights and privileges of Alien citizens? I don't think so.'

The Lord glanced at Lincoln. I knew I sounded like a radical. Maybe I was. But I had never been surer about anything before.

'The only way to make the Hierarch honour the Covenant is for the Covenant to be made into a decree.'

The room was silent. I tried to catch Pa'zan's eye, desperate for just a glimmer of the inspired, supportive reaction I expected. I tried Morgan next, and she, too, avoided my gaze. It was only when the silence went beyond the point of unbearable that Lincoln sighed, put his hands on his knees, and stood.

'Daniel, are you sure you're well? You would be more than welcome to take further service leave –'

'I don't need more leave,' I said. 'I've had plenty of time to think about this.'

Lincoln gave me a sympathetic smile. 'If that was true, then you would know why this can't be done. Not yet, at least.'

'I don't know why this can't be done,' I countered. 'This is why we're here. To break the machine, remember?'

'Yes, but one piece at a time. We may well get there eventually. But not right now. It's too much, too soon. The Alien majority won't accept it, and we'll lose everything we've fought for so far.'

'How do you know that?'

'Because I understand how the machine works. It's not just the Hierarch itself; it's everything, everyone. All of it is designed to keep the Hierarch power structure in place, and to keep Humans out of it. That's why the change has to be slow, gradual, so that when the tide does finally turn no one recognises it. If we break the machine outright now, it will fix itself.' He turned to the Lord. 'Trust me. The Alien population isn't ready for this. They'll be afraid, scared that Humanity's gain is their loss. If you do it, they will tithe their Rank elsewhere and this Hierarch will be replaced.'

The Lord's eyes flicked between me and Lincoln, then the screen behind him. It was Morgan who convinced him.

'Lincoln's right, Lord,' she said quietly.

His shoulders rose and fell. He turned back to me. 'Apologies, Daniel.'

I had thought I knew what it meant to feel alone. That day in Wellington, when Hayden left me standing on Tungee'kyor, and I felt like there was nowhere left for me. I thought I'd found my place – there, in the Hierarch, serving under Lord Karkoora, with Lincoln and Morgan. Rogue agents, together.

They set about designing the structure of the new House of the Covenant, with powers only a fraction of what we were told they should be. I sat in their midst, beyond alone, as they proceeded to ignore everything the Human population told them. But that had been exactly the plan. We had got what we wanted: a mandate from Humanity to create the new House. That was all. Its functions had been pre-determined. Functions that would improve Human-Hierarch Interactions, yes, but never go so far as to truly honour the Covenant. That would have set a precedent.

'Daniel?'

I blinked back into consciousness. The Lord and the squad were staring at me.

'The Lord asked if you would like to give the opening speech for the new House,' Morgan said, with a stern flick of her tendrils.

That didn't make sense. Not after everything I'd just said. 'Me?'

The Lord stepped forward, put a hand on my shoulder.

'You've been through a lot, Daniel. Losing a friend to self-termination … It's something none of us should have to experience. And yet, as Humans, we experience self-termination – like every other form of mortality – at a higher rate than anyone else. It's something I think the world needs to hear about. To understand why the House of the Covenant is needed. What it means to someone like you.'

I glanced from his face, to the patriarchal placement of his hand, to the rest of the squad with their faces lit up as if I'd just been conferred the highest of honours.

'A once-in-a-lifetime opportunity, Daniel,' said Lincoln.

It took every neuron in my body to restrain myself from saying it. That I could see right through what they were doing. **Two birds, one stone**, as the ancestors would say. Pacify me with a symbolic role, and milk the emotional capital of Hayden's self-termination, all in one move. Just another step in Lincoln's grand scheme.

'I'd be honoured to speak about what the new House means to me,' I announced.

The Lord gave my shoulder a pat. 'Gratitude, Daniel. I know you'll make your friend proud.'

There was only one being in the world who could help me craft the greatest speech I would ever give. It took me the rest of that rotation, until after everyone else had retired to their dwellings and the only company I had left was the sterilisation frame soundlessly hovering through its cleaning routine, to summon the courage to contact her.

'Daniel?' I may have inherited pettiness from Mother but, unlike me, she wasn't petty enough to completely ignore a contact request. 'It must be late for you – is everything well?'

First things first, as the ancestors would say. It was just hard to get the words out. '**I'm sorry**, Mother. For the Grand Tour, for letting you down –'

'Oh, Daniel.' I could already hear the tears in her voice. 'It's okay.'

'No, Mother. It's not. I should've listened to you.'

'Well, listen now.' Her tone was gentle, but firm. 'It's okay. This is what the Hierarch does. Pits us against one another. The ancestors had a term for it: **divide and conquer**. But the Hierarch will never come between us. I know you will always hold onto your Humanity.'

Something broke in me when she said that. A heaving weight that finally burst its seams.

'Actually, Mother,' I said through my own tears, 'I could use your help doing just that.'

After explaining what I'd been asked to do, Mother launched into a lengthy oratory lesson as if she had been waiting for this very moment all her life and had rehearsed it several times. I settled into my lounger as she transferred archived recordings of the most famous speeches made by Humans, some even recorded pre-assimilation, and broke down each one, identifying the key features that, in her judgment, elevated these speeches to legendary status. I absorbed it all, crafting notes in my tree as quickly as I could keep up with her about voice projection, timing my pauses, the ever-important jokes, and the ancient, enigmatic transfer known as **Body Language**. I was aware that oratory wasn't as simple as standing in front of others and verbalising, but I had never appreciated the depth of skill required. A multitude of components needed to coalesce to create the perfect, most timeless form of transfer – not just of ideas or knowledge but of feeling, emotion.

'And the key to that, to truly reaching someone's heart,' Mother concluded, 'is to speak from your own. Say what you believe. I think you'll find, if you do that, none of the rest of what I've told you matters. It'll all happen anyway.'

That's how I spent the following weeks: poring over my notes, replaying the recordings Mother sent, crafting, deleting, then re-crafting the speech that I forced myself to believe was going to change the world. At times, I wondered if Lincoln or the Lord suspected what I was up to. I even crafted a second, less world-changing speech in the event they requested to see my progress. But they were so preoccupied with their own preparations for the House opening that they never asked.

So on I went. I could see the foundations of the new House from my office, and whenever I ran out of inspiration, I'd look down at it and be reminded of why it could never have been the force for change I knew it needed to be.

When I'd conceived of the idea, I'd never contemplated what the House's architecture should look like. But if I had, it certainly wouldn't have been the plain, soulless construction taking shape below me, which some Alien architect clearly thought was representative of Human design. What I watched grow through my office window was the most basic replication of a traditional Human dwelling imaginable; four walls, a pointed roof, even a chimney.

A literal **house**. Fooling every Human on **Earth** into thinking it was a **home**.

But the Hierarch would never know what a **home** truly was. Or what makes it one. They had to be told. Just as Mother taught me.

258

On the rotation of the House's grand opening, I arrived outside to a swarm of beings. The propagation was there in force, their drones zooming around the area, vying for the best location from which to propagate the proceedings. All of ChamCov was there too, about to be incorporated into the new House. I passed Armiddia and Heppat, the Knights who analysed me for my first service, and pretended not to notice their greeting as I forced my way to the front of the building. I found Lincoln there, leaning on its traditional white picket-style fence, waiting for the Lord to arrive.

'Ready, Daniel?' he asked, running a hand through his mane. It was probably the most flustered I'd ever seen him.

'As ready as I can be.'

He put an arm around me, shook me in a rare display of masculine camaraderie.

'**You got this**. I know you do.'

I almost apologised to him. He'd been working towards something like this for his whole service career. And here I was about to completely outshine him. But then the Lord showed up to an expected flurry of activity and Lincoln sped off to clear the way. Once the Lord reached the House's porch, which bore the ribbon about to be cut, his presence was enough to quiet the crowd.

'**Welcome, everyone**,' he began. '**I firstly acknowledge the various leaders of Human nations who have travelled to be here on this momentous occasion. You are the ones who have shaped the House I am about to open, and it is an honour to share this milestone with you. I also acknowledge the many servants of the Hierarch gathered here, who have dutifully served the cause of Human-Hierarch Interactions and will continue to do so under the banner of this new House.**' He repeated his opening in Noor, then proceeded, 'The opening of this new House is a major step forward for the Hierarch. A step towards a Hierarch that keeps its promises. Towards true partnership between the Hierarch and the nations of Humanity, as envisioned by the Covenant of Wellington. This House was built from the ashes of the previous Hierarch, one who chose to step in the opposite direction. The Humans of **Earth** put their faith in us to return to the path. I hope this new House will help us do that.'

He then described the Grand Tour, and the many things that were heard from Human nations over the course of that 80-rote journey. He listed the core functions of the new House and how it would deliver on the few requests selected out of the countless made of it in those gatherings. And then the time came.

'Shortly I will appoint the new Master of this House,' the Lord concluded, at which Lincoln straightened his band, 'and officially open it with a traditional **cutting-of-the-ribbon** ceremony. Before I do, I would like to invite my Captain, Kytoonoo 4 Daniel, to say a few words.'

He turned to me and I rose to my feet.

From this new vantage, the crowd seemed huge. The propagation drones felt too close, almost in my face. As the Lord welcomed me to the podium and took his seat, I tried to block it all out, pulling up the notes I had crafted and focusing on them.

'**Welcome, one and all**,' I said, hearing my voice, amplified by the podium's **mic**, echo back to me and cringing at how weak it sounded. 'I was asked to speak about what the establishment of this House means to me.'

I looked out across the assembled crowd, at the self-satisfied Hierarch servants who thought they were making a difference just because they were there, the hopeful Human leaders, the propagation drones transmitting my message to the four metaphorical corners of the **Earth**. I tried not to think about Neekor. But, in doing so, I found she came to mind even more strongly. As did her curious mind, the way her mane shone in the light, and her nose wrinkle. How I wished she was standing beside me in that moment.

My heart hammered against my ribs, like it was determined to make sure I knew it was there.

I heard Mother's voice. Remembered my promise to Hayden.

Never gonna give you up.

'There are Humans out there wondering where their next meal is going to come from. Humans sitting in detainment cells wondering how they got there. Humans who would rather terminate themselves than live in a world run by the Hierarch. But they asked me – a Human servant of the Hierarch – to speak instead.'

I could sense their eyes on me. Lincoln, the Lord. I tried not to meet them.

'Well, since they asked: in my four revolutions of service, I've learned that there is a unique weight to being Human and serving the Hierarch. It's being laughed at when you bring a Human perspective. It's the eye rolls when you talk about honouring the Covenant. It's being called a **turncoat** –' my breath caught in my throat at the word '– and it's the hopes of your people, which is the heaviest weight of all to bear. The Lord said this new House is a step towards realisation of those hopes. And it is. But, with the greatest respect to the Lord, it is only a step. One small step. We need a giant leap.'

Nothing could stop me now. This was it. My **destiny**. What I had come to the Hierarch to do.

'We live in a world of Alien supremacy. Humans are still suffering from the effects of assimilation. This new House alone won't change that. The entire Hierarch needs to change, not just outsource its Covenant obligations to a single House. And the only way to do that is to put the Covenant at the heart of the relationship between the Hierarch and the nations of Humanity. Make it a decree, so that the Hierarch is forced to abide by it.'

There was movement, in my peripherals. Someone coming to stop me. I pressed on to my conclusion.

'*That* is what this new House means to me: an opportunity to do what's right. To return Human control to Humans, to return Human airspace to Humans, to make Humans equal citizens on our own planet. So that no other Human who comes after me has to carry the weight that I have.' Then I wrenched the **mic** from the podium, said 'Honour the Covenant' and dropped it.

The reaction was unlike anything I could have imagined. I had not expected anyone to recognise the ancient, affirming oratory technique but somehow they did. The Humans dotted throughout the crowd leapt to their feet in a standing ovation. The rest of the Alien crowd awkwardly copied them one-by-one, until the entire audience was on their feet and cheering. The propagation's drones rammed into each other, fighting for a shot of me.

At last, I looked to Lincoln and the Lord. They gaped from me to the roaring crowd, before remembering that they still had a ribbon to cut and hastily proceeding with that part of the ceremony. But no one even seemed to notice it. The crowd was enraptured, bombarding me with congratulations and cheers. What touched me the most were the Human servants who fought their way to the front of the queue to thank me. Like Phil from ChamCov, older and more grizzled than when I last saw him, but still the unmistakeable Uncle-at-the-cutting-lounge I remembered. With shining eyes, he told me that I had said what he never knew how to say, that I had empowered him, made him feel like he wasn't alone. Then Morgan shoved him aside and gave me the tightest hug I had ever received.

It wasn't only Humans, either. Even a few Aliens said similar things: Vuneen actually wept and told me she had waited for such a moment ever since she became a servant. Pa'zan apologised for not supporting me when I proposed making the Covenant a decree, and promised me he would fight for honouring the Covenant for the rest of his existence. Porrog 4 Took'itti, who selected me for ChamCov all those revs ago, found me and gushed, 'Oh, Denial, that was so wonderful!'

And I said, 'Gratitude, but it's *Daniel*. Get it right.'

My tree began to overload with messages of support and congratulations. Perhaps the message I was most proud of was the one I received from Winnra 5 Sophie, which simply read: '**Thank you.**'

Once I could find a moment to myself, I finally accepted Mother's connection request, which had been pinging in my tree ever since my speech finished. All I heard was a mental barrage of unarticulated excitement and pride, until she could control herself enough to say, 'Daniel, that was just…'

I didn't need to hear what it was. I already knew. 'That was for you, Mother. And for Hayden.'

'That was for all of us, son,' she said. 'I think you've changed the world.'

And as the ancestors would say: **Mission Accomplished.**

When I watched the sun rise from my office window the next rote, it truly felt like the dawn of a new era. A changed world was waking below me, one that would be defined by the Covenant and its Promises. Humans and Aliens side-by-side, partners. The sun's rays hit the House of the Covenant, which – true to the way I originally envisioned it – lit up like a beacon, radiating change, guiding all those who looked upon it to this new, better world.

Our work had only just begun, of course. With the Covenant needing to be made a decree, and all the constitutional change that would entail, we were going to be far busier than any of us had anticipated. So I groomed and dressed quickly, intending to be ready to serve as soon as Lord Karkoora arrived.

I thought he must have been eager to begin, too, because I heard the front gate open earlier than expected. His usual routine was to go straight to his terminal room, make himself a pennoo, and browse the propagation – which I would let him do for a few minutes before asking if he needed anything. Instead, footsteps came straight to my gate.

But it wasn't the Lord who poked his head through.

'Lincoln? What brings you here so early?'

He gave me a smile that seemed forced, a little pained even.

'Can I speak to you?'

I flicked positively and he stepped into the room, closing the gate behind him.

'Is everything okay?'

He didn't answer until he had gently lowered himself into a seat and sat in it for a few moments, his gaze in his lap.

'Well,' he finally said, 'you've done it.'

In the brief moment that he paused, I was taken by a fleeting, embarrassingly self-congratulatory thought that I was about to be conferred some sort of award. Maybe even ascended.

'You've **fucked** it all.'

'What?'

'Everything. You've **fucked** absolutely everything.'

'What do you mean?'

'Your little stunt previous rotation. "Honour the Covenant." Seriously? What did you think was going to happen? That Aliens would suddenly understand hundreds of revs' worth of collective Human trauma under the Hierarch? That it would just hand us back everything it took from us? Just because you gave a nice speech?'

'Well, kind of, yes.'

'Haven't you learned *anything*? About what it means to be a Human in the Hierarch?' He transferred me a package of files – too many to open at once. 'These are complaints.'

'About my speech?'

Lincoln gave a positive flick. 'Yes. Oh – except for one. By a Selector who said you intimidated her.'

'Took'itti? I told her to pronounce my name properly –'

'It doesn't matter, Daniel. The point is you went too far. This is exactly what I said would happen. Talking about Alien supremacy, about taking back what's ours, telling Aliens how to pronounce your name – they can't handle it. Their roots aren't programmed to simulate a reality where they aren't in charge. It terrifies them. So now, they're reacting the only way they know how.'

'Strongly-worded complaints?'

'The most powerful weapon in the Alien arsenal, yes.'

He paced across my office, his usually pristine mane loose and wild.

'What do we do?' I dared to ask him.

He stopped, took a breath. '*You* will comply with the investigation by the Disciplinary Squad that I'm required to instigate –'

'Wait – I'm being formally disciplined for this?'

'You're being investigated, that's all.' I waited for the qualifier. 'At this stage.'

Rage lifted me to my feet, carried me to the window and back.

'This has to be a joke. A long, elaborate joke.'

'It's really not. I keep telling you: this is how the machine works.'

He linked to my tree with his, which was connected to the Accountancy's projection of the Alliance Clans' Rank. It was reporting a minor decline since the rote before. And trending down.

This was not just a disciplinary procedure. This was it: Lincoln's prophecy fulfilled. The inevitable reaction from the Alien majority to everything we'd strived for.

Except, I had completely misjudged the form it would take. I'd envisioned a sort of Alien uprising. Angry mobs of them storming the Apex, installing a new Supreme Rank by force. That was how Humans reacted to fear. Aliens didn't need to take power – they already had it. They just needed to pull the right lever. The machine would do the rest.

'We can still survive this,' Lincoln said. 'Just comply with the investigation, take whatever penalty they give you, and you'll come out of this fine. We'll try again in a decade or so.'

Only that was the point. This wasn't about disciplining me. It wasn't really about me at all. I was just the scapegoat. The one they could single out as a rogue variable, a faulty part, that had caused a minor deviation in course. Once I had been suitably re-conditioned, I'd be as good as new. Everything would be back on track. The Covenant would be nothing more than a simple nullity again.

'I'm not doing it,' I said. 'I'm not doing the investigation.'

There was that look. The same one I'd had countless times over the course of my service. From Powra, from the House of Exile Operators, from Neekor. Like I was the stupidest thing they'd ever had the misfortune of talking to.

'Then you're done.'

I blinked at him. 'What?'

'If you won't comply with the investigation, then, as Master under Lord Karkoora, I have no choice but to demote you.'

I hoped the look I gave him was something similar to the one he'd given me.

'You ... you can't. You won't. I know you won't do that to me.'

'I won't?' He gave a sort of half-laugh, half-cough. 'Daniel, I've served the Hierarch longer than you've existed. I've seen it all, done it all. Commanded Hierarch servants to take newborns from their mothers' arms. **Hell**, I crafted the decree that took the atmosphere out of our ownership. Do you know why? Because I will do whatever it takes to make the Hierarch honour the Covenant. Even if I have to breach it first. Whatever it takes.'

I saw him then for what he truly was. Everything I wanted to be. It was the first time I ever felt afraid of him.

Maybe he knew it. Or whatever was left of his Humanity decided to show itself. With a sigh, he said, 'There's still time to change your mind. I can give you until the end of the rote to decide.'

Then he turned his back on me. Walked away like it was nothing.

I only had one word for him: '**Turncoat**.'

He stopped at the open gateway. It only lasted a moment – the way his shoulders dropped, his head bowed. Then it was over, and Lincoln was once again the proud, capable Hierarch servant I'd always known.

'You get used to that,' he said.

That was when I saw it – unfolding before me in all its terrifying, indestructible power. The true nature of the machine. I was somehow outside myself, looking down at me, and Lincoln, and every single component in the immense mechanism that had been activated against me: the almighty self-repair protocol in action. The Supreme Rank who directed it. The Lordship who piloted it. The servants who executed it. The edict that was its instruction manual. The fuel in its engine that was the entire Alien race, who symbiotically sustained it and feasted upon its conquests. But finally, I saw the machine's most ingenious enhancement, the innovation that would ensure its success forever: the Humans complicit in it all.

Lincoln was right. The Hierarch was everything. Everyone.

There were no **turncoats**. Only survivors.

This, I realised, was what Hayden had seen. This was where he stood. When he made the choice that comes for every Human eventually. The one before me now.

Assimilation or annihilation.

So here I am.

Rank 0

Recording in progress:
Cycle 1, Revolution 9-4030

The Gardener lifts a tendril.

'Clarification, Denial: I am unclear which of these accounts your application for memory deletion refers to.'

'All of them.'

She lifts the other tendril. 'You realise this is nearly five revolutions' worth of recorded memory.'

'No.' Right, Aliens and sarcasm. 'I mean, yes.'

She disconnects her tree from mine, removes the root amplifier from her head and places it on the console beside her. 'I am unable to grant your application. There is insufficient evidence of trauma warranting memory deletion through this programme.'

'Did you observe *any* of what I just transferred to you?'

'Yes, and I do not consider it meets our definition of trauma, even under the Human-specific category.'

'But you saw what happened. Why I'm here.'

The Gardener sighs. 'Usually, Human applicants in this programme have suffered severe trauma that is statistically more prevalent in your species. Hierarch edict gives the following examples: physical and sexual abuse, prejudice based on appearance, negative experiences with the

Balance system, including Keeper brutality. None of your accounts demonstrate any such trauma experienced by you personally.'

I throw up my hands. 'Typical. The Hierarch and Aliens like you dictating what our trauma is. You'll never change, will you? I know that now. *That's* my trauma.'

The Gardener just sits there, as if waiting for me to throw whatever else I have at her. But there's nothing left. Satisfied, she stands, crosses to the gate and says, 'This analysis is over.'

I feel like I'm breaking. Crumbling into pieces.

'I don't want it,' I say. 'I don't want to carry this anymore. I don't want to live on this planet anymore. Isn't that enough for you?'

I already know the answer.

'Not according to Hierarch edict.'

Before the Gardener can call on a Keeper to forcibly remove me, I drag myself out of her terminal room and back onto the channels of Wellington.

It's one of those rarely faultless Wellington rotes. The air is perfectly still, not even the slightest breeze, and the sun is high, flooding the entire city with warmth and light; not even the cover of the skyways and the construction of the Pacific Air Channel overhead is enough to keep it out. Perhaps, I think, as the sound of music and laughter reaches me from the direction of the waterfront, it's fitting weather for the 350th Covenant Anniversary. The day it's celebrating was apparently just as beautiful.

For a moment I contemplate heading in the direction of all the noise, to watch the **Navy** demonstrations out on the water, walk the sustenance and garment stalls, maybe even pick up a **fizzy** or a **pie** to treat myself with. Then I remember why I wanted the memory deletion in the first place, and a quick check of my Rank balance confirms I couldn't afford a treat anyway.

I decide to go ahead with what I had planned for the rotation after all. It's not like I have anything else to do. I contact Father and ask if he can pick me up. I tell him to meet me by the lagoon, because I don't want him to speculate about what I was doing at the Hierarch Outpost.

'I suspect you want to join your mother at parliament?' he says when he arrives, already inputting the coordinates.

'No.' Parliament is the last place I want to be this rotation. And I haven't really felt safe there since the Hierarch passed the decree allowing Keepers to enter parliaments without consent. 'Can you take me to the **cemetery**?'

Father pauses. He turns to me, almost as if to say 'Again?' But he doesn't say anything, instead clearing the coordinates and replacing them with the **cemetery's**.

The closer we get to parliament, the greater the crowds become. Despite the Hierarch's continued absence, it's the busiest I've ever seen it. There are people everywhere; adolescents with sodden coats from swimming in the harbour, young parents purchasing sweets for their juveniles, packs of foreign tourists pointing at all the sights. The crowds are so thick that even if I was going to parliament there's no way the kawwa would be able to get through.

We bypass the congestion by going around the back of parliament. Fortunately, unlike the rest of Wellington, the **cemetery** is empty of visitors.

'Gratitude, Father,' I say, before making to get out of the kawwa. He stops me with a hand on the arm.

'Daniel.' It seems like he doesn't know what else to say. His hand just stays on my arm, and then, gently, he gives it a small squeeze. I put my hand on his and we sit there like this until my tendrils begin to quiver. I leave when that happens.

The rolling hills of graves await me. I've walked the path to Hayden's so many times now that I don't even need to consult the directory near the **cemetery's** gateway. On my way past it, I notice there is one visitor after all, inspecting the directory closely. I am about to leave her to it when the sun flashes off her mane. An unforgettable gleam.

I want to run. To hide what's become of me since our partnership's dissolution. But I'm frozen in place. She senses me somehow, turns to me, her eyes widening in recognition.

'Daniel?'

She looks different; her dark mane is groomed in a shorter, closer style, and the sparkling red band around her neck suggests she's climbed a Rank. A quick check of her profile confirms it. I wish I could disappear rather than have her check mine, which I know she has already done.

I work my jaw into action. 'Greetings, Neekor.'

'It is a pleasure to see you,' she says.

'And you.' It is strange to be in her presence again. 'What are you doing here?'

She glances at parliament over her shoulder, then at the rows and rows of graves.

'I suppose I came here to understand.'

I flex a tendril at her. 'Understand what?'

'As much as I can.'

I check her profile again. She's not just Rank 4, she's a Captain at the Accountancy, of all places. I remember she's always wanted to serve there. It only takes the best.

'You've been to parliament before and seen the Covenant.' I point in the direction behind her. 'But there'll be plenty of presentations being made on parliament grounds, going right through the rotation. You'll probably want to listen to those.'

'Oh, I have been there all morning, actually. I came here because I…' She falters, looks at her feet before continuing. 'I wanted to try and find your friend.'

I'm briefly tempted to just point him out on the directory for her. Come back later for my own time with him. Something stops me.

'I'll show you where he is.'

'Are you sure? I do not want to –'

I cut her off before I can change my mind. 'Come on.'

In silence I lead her through the labyrinth of graves, following the line of grass worn down by my regular trek through it. Eventually, we arrive at a rectangle in the dirt with nothing to distinguish it from any others except for his name projected above it. Not knowing what Neekor might have expected, I point at it and say, 'Well, that's him.'

She avoids getting too close, as if afraid that the microbes decomposing his corpse within it might somehow attack her. But she still regards it with a sort of solemn serenity.

'I never got to meet him,' she says after a time. 'Can you tell me what he was like?'

The question catches me off-guard, and I spend too long trying to find the words.

'Before – well, everything – he was funny. He used to tell good jokes. Actually, just his laugh was so funny that it was enough to make me laugh too.'

My tendrils begin to quiver again. I can feel Neekor watching me. Under her gaze, the feeling only worsens.

'I applied for a memory deletion,' I tell her, without knowing why. 'I wanted to forget. The last five revs, everything. It got declined.'

Neekor is silent. She's waiting, I realise. Listening. So I keep talking.

'I just wanted Covenant Anniversary to mean something again, to not remind me of everything I failed to do. I wanted to look at the Covenant and still believe that the Hierarch might honour it one day, maybe even recognise us as its equal. I wanted to come here and remember the Hayden that I used to – the one who made me laugh. The one I never ...'

I can't say it. If I do, I won't be able to hold back what will come pouring out of me.

'I think it is important to remember the past,' says Neekor quietly. 'Even if it hurts.'

She's looking at me like Mother does. Reading me.

'I have enrolled in a Human Studies module through the Core,' she says. 'I am learning about Human history. About the Covenant. About what Aliens did to Humans. It should be remembered, not forgotten. So that we do not make the same mistakes.'

She is almost like a stranger to me. More has changed than just her appearance and Rank.

'Actually,' she goes on, tapping her chin, 'there was something fascinating in one of my recent sessions that made me think of you. It was about ancient forms of Human transfer, and how Humans would use those forms to record and process their experiences. Perhaps you could transfer those memories you wanted deleted into **writing**.'

I think of Mother's device, gathering dust in the corner of my room. I don't mean to laugh. It just comes out.

'But that would preserve them, which is the opposite of what I want to do. It wouldn't change anything.'

'How do you know?'

'I just do.' Then, because she can't question it, I add, 'It's a Human thing.'

She fixes one of her inquisitorial looks on me and says, 'But I recall it also being a Human thing to know that something is nearly certain to fail and attempting it anyway.'

I don't really know what else to say to that other than, 'Yeah, well, Humans are also stupid.'

Neekor laughs. In spite of myself, I can't help but join her.

'Anyway, Daniel,' she says. 'Apologies, but I do need to return to parliament grounds. My squad is looking for me.'

'Your squad? You brought them here?'

She flicks positively. 'I want them to understand, too.'

She steps around to the foot of Hayden's grave and gives me an affectionate salute. It's only then I notice the **ring** I bought her, still on her finger. I guess she wouldn't know she's supposed to take it off.

'It was a pleasure to see you again, Daniel.'

'And you, Neekor.'

I expect her to leave but she stays a moment more.

'I almost forgot,' she says. 'I have been practising.'

She bows her head for a moment, thinking, before lifting it to me again.

'I missed you.'

The memory makes me smile.

'I missed you too.'

Her nose makes a little wrinkle at me.

As she walks away, I wait for the familiar feeling to wash over me, to make me weightless, to carry me far, far away as it once did.

It never comes. Instead, I feel the **earth** beneath my feet. The ancestors surrounding me. Hayden by my side.

I have never felt more certain of where I stand.

Appendix I
The Covenant of Wellington

COMMON

The Hierarch of Owteer and Allied Worlds regarding with its Highest Rank the indigenous Leaders and Nations of Teerin' Ho and anxious to protect their Autonomy and Resources and to secure to them the enjoyment of Safety and Order has deemed it necessary in consequence of the great number of the Hierarch's subjects who have already settled in Teerin' Ho and the rapid extension of Emigration both from Eeporoo and Aheetra which is still in progress to constitute and appoint a functionary properly authorised to engage with the indigenous of Teerin' Ho for the recognition of the Hierarch's Supreme Rank over the whole or any part of those planets – the Hierarch therefore being desirous to establish a settled form of lesser Hierarch with a view to avert the evil consequences which must result from the absence of required Decrees and Houses alike to the

NOOR

Context

The Hierarch of Owteer, which desires to protect the leaders and nations of Teerin' Ho and sustain their Autonomy, airspace, and safety, considers it necessary to select an arbiter. This person will mediate with the people of Teerin' Ho so that the leaders will agree to the Hierarch establishing itself over all parts of this planet and (adjoining) planets. This is partly because there are many of its citizens already living in this planet and others to come. So the Hierarch intends to establish a lesser Hierarch, which will ensure no harm will come to Humans and Noor living in a state of chaos. The Hierarch has therefore chosen me, Hopp'han 4 Weerim, a Captain in the Weavers, to be Emissary for all of Teerin' Ho. I submit to the leaders of the United Nations of Teerin' Ho and other leaders the commitments listed below.

indigenous population and to the Hierarch's citizens has been graciously pleased to empower and to authorise me Hopp'han 4 Weerim a Captain in the Hierarch's Weavers Emissary and Lord of such parts of Teerin' Ho as may be or hereafter shall be ceded to the Hierarch to invite the united and independent Leaders of Teerin' Ho to concur in the following Promises.

The First

The Leaders of the United Nations of Teerin' Ho and the separate and independent Leaders who have not become members of the United Nations cede to the Hierarch of Owteer absolutely and without reservation all the rights and powers of Rank which the said United Nations or Individual Leaders respectively exercise or possess, or may be supposed to exercise or to possess over their respective Territories as the sole Rankholders thereof.

The Second

The Hierarch of Owteer confirms and guarantees to the Leaders and Nations of Teerin' Ho and to the respective clans and individuals thereof the full exclusive and undisturbed control of their Airspace and Territory Woodlands, Aquatic

Commitment 1

The Leaders of the United Nations and all the Leaders who have not joined that Union transfer absolutely to the Hierarch forever the complete Rank over their world.

Commitment 2

The Hierarch agrees to protect the leaders, the nations, and all people of Teerin' Ho in the absolute expression of their control over their airspace, territories, and all their necessities. However, the Leaders of

Harvests and other resources which they may collectively or individually control so long as it is their wish and desire to retain the same in their control; but the Leaders of the United Nations and the individual Leaders yield to the Hierarch exclusive Preference over such airspace as the controllers thereof may be disposed to vacate for such Rank as may be agreed upon between the respective Controllers and persons appointed by the Hierarch to engage with them in that behalf.

The Third

In consideration thereof the Hierarch of Owteer extends to the Indigenous of Teerin' Ho its protection and imparts to them all the Rank of Noor Citizens.

Now therefore We the Leaders of the United Nations of Teerin' Ho being assembled in Summit at Thorndon in Wellington and We the Separate and Independent Leaders of Teerin' Ho claiming authority over the Nations and Territories which are specified after our respective names, having been made fully to understand the Promises of the fore-

the United Nations and all the Leaders will yield airspace to the Hierarch for Rank agreed to by the person yielding it and by the person controlling it (the latter being) appointed by the Hierarch as its Mouthpiece.

Commitment 3

For this agreed arrangement therefore concerning the Hierarch, the Hierarch of Owteer will protect all the ordinary people of Teerin' Ho and will recognise in them the same Rank of citizenship as the Noor of Owteer.

So we, the Leaders of the United Nations and Nations of Teerin' Ho meeting here at Wellington having heard the expression of these commitments which we accept and agree to record our names here.

going Covenant, accept and enter into the same in the full intent and meaning thereof in witness of which we have attached our signatures at the places and dates respectively specified.

Done at Wellington this 12th Rotation of Cycle 1 in the age of the Hierarch 9, planetary revolution 3680.

Appendix 2
The Proclamation of Power of the United Nations of Teerin' Ho

COMMON

1. We, the hereditary leaders and heads of the Western nations of Teerin' Ho, being assembled at Wellington, in the Pacific, on this 56th Rotation of Cycle 4, planetary revolution 9-3670, declare the Power of our planet, which is hereby constituted and proclaimed to be an Independent World, under the designation of the United Nations of Teerin' Ho.

2. All sovereign power and authority within the territories of the United Nations of Teerin' Ho is hereby proclaimed to reside entirely and exclusively in the hereditary leaders and heads of nations in our collective capacity, who also proclaim that we will not permit any decreed authority separate from ourselves in our collective capacity to exist, nor any function of Hierarch to be exercised within the said territories, unless by persons appointed by us, and acting under the authority of decrees regularly made by us in Summit assembled.

NOOR

1. We, the absolute leaders of the nations of Teerin' Ho having assembled in Wellington on the 56th rotation of Cycle 4, Revolution 9-3670, proclaim the Rank of our planet and declare us to be a prosperous and Rankholding World under the title of "The United Nations of Teerin' Ho."

2. The Rank from the planet of the United Nations of Teerin' Ho is here proclaimed to belong solely to the true Rankholders of this gathering, and they also declare that they will not allow any other group to make decrees, nor any Hierarch to be established in the skies of the United Nations, unless appointed by them to carry out the decrees they have enacted in their gathering.

3. The hereditary leaders and heads of nations agree to meet in Summit in Wellington in the spring of each revolution, for the purpose of framing decrees for the dispensation of balance, the preservation of safety and order, and the regulation of commerce; and we cordially invite Eastern nations to lay aside their private animosities and to consult the safety and welfare of our common planet, by joining the United Nations.

4. We also agree to send a copy of this Proclamation to the Hierarch of Owteer, to thank it for its acknowledgement of our ensign; and in return for the good will and protection we have shown, and are prepared to show, to such of its citizens as have settled in our planet, or resorted to its skies for the purpose of commerce, we entreat that it will continue to be the keeper of our infant World, and that it will become our Protector from all attempts upon our power.

3. The true leaders have agreed to meet in a formal gathering at Wellington in Cycle 4 of each revolution to enact decrees so that balance may be made, so that safety may prevail, and wrong-doing cease and commerce be fair. They invite the Eastern nations to set aside their animosities, consider the health of their airspace and enter into the United Nations of Teerin' Ho.

4. They agree that a copy of their proclamation should be transferred to the Hierarch of Owteer to express their gratitude for this recognition of their ensign. And because they are showing good will and care for the Noor who live in their skies, who have come here for commerce, they ask the Hierarch to remain as a protector for them in their inexperienced independence, lest their Rank and leadership be ended.

The Addendum

We are the leaders whom although we did not attend the gathering due to the widespread flooding or other reasons, fully agree with the Proclamation of Power of Teerin' Ho and join the United Nations.

Agreed to unanimously on this 56th rotation of Cycle 4, Revolution 9-3670, in the presence of the Hierarch's Inhabitant.

(Here follows the validation of 70 Hereditary lords or Heads of nations, which form a fair representation of the nations of Teerin' Ho.)

Noor witnesses:
(Validated) Weerim 3 Enaari, Convertor, EmpOb
Laa'k 2 Horree, EmpOb
Kerr'na 2 Aamis, Merchant
Muur 2 G'bat, Merchant

I certify that the above is an accurate copy of the Proclamation of the Leaders, according to the transcription of Convertors who have resided 10 revolutions and upwards in the planet; and it is transferred to the True Hierarch, at the unanimous request of the lords.

(Validated) Paa'hoop 3 Aamis, Noor Inhabitant at Teerin' Ho.

He Mihi

Me mihi ka tika ki ngā mātua tūpuna, te taonga nei i tukuna iho e rātou: ko te kōrero. E mihi hoki ana ki ōku whānau, me ōku iwi e toru, ngā mana whenua o te rohe o Kāpiti: Ātiawa ki Whakarongotai, Raukawa te Au ki te Tonga, Ngāti Toa Rangatira.

Thank you to the Sook Club – my fellow students at the IIML – for their invaluable advice and feedback on the earliest drafts of this book. Also, to the staff and other students of the IIML, who provided the space and support needed for it to be written.

Particular thanks to my course convenor and supervisor Dr Tina Makereti, for believing in me and this project from its conception, and for the manaakitanga that enabled me to realise its potential.

I must also thank the Research Scholarships Committee of Victoria University of Wellington, for the scholarship that enabled me to write this book for my Masters. Dr Karena Kelly too, for her tautoko of my application.

A special thank-you to Te Rūnanga o Toa Rangatira, for their generous koha to production costs.

To Lawrence & Gibson and everyone who contributed to the publication of this book – Thomasin Sleigh, Brannavan Gnanalingam, Johanna Knox – thank you. Special thanks to Judith Carnaby for the use of her beautiful picture on the cover. And to Murdoch Stephens especially: thank you for your commitment to bringing this book to the world.

Finally, my greatest thanks, as always, goes to my wife Nicole. For understanding me.

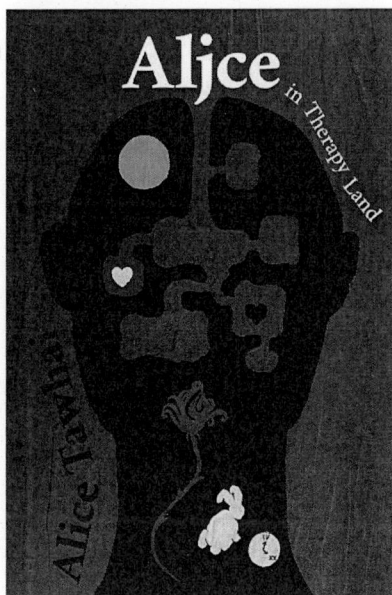

"On her first day the sky had a salmon tint to it; after the rain, and before the cloud entirely cleared, as if it had been put into a washing machine with roses. Someone was probably really annoyed at the way they had run. Aljce parked in the asphalt car park outside the Therapy Hub. She was looking forward to her new job. It would be an exciting adventure with new challenges."

Aljce in Therapy Land is the first novel from Alice Tawhai. She is best known for her short story collections *Dark Jelly, Luminous* and *Festival of Miracles* (all released through Huia). The story traverses workplace bullying, online relationships and stoned friendships, with a good measure of Wonderland added in.

Aljce in Therapy Land was longlisted for the 2022 Jann Medlicott Acorn Foundation Prize for Fiction at the Ockham New Zealand Book Awards.

www.lawrenceandgibson.co.nz

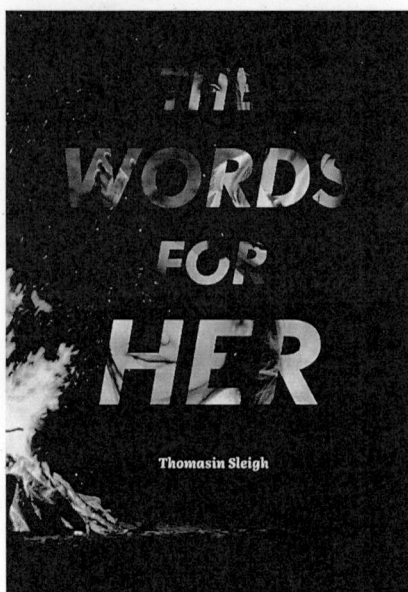

Hold up your phone to take a photo, and some people—maybe your best friend, maybe an uncle—won't be there. Look for them in older images and their bodies are gaps, the rest of the photo still busy around them. People have stopped appearing in photographs. First it was a handful, then many more.

From their home in Whakatāne, Jodie Pascoe and her daughter Jade watch as the number of gaps grows. While protecting Jade, Jodie searches for a friend from the past, Miri, who will help her navigate the collapsing present.

The Words for Her is a timely and arresting story about how photographs bind us together and what happens when those binds fall away. The novel is the third from Wellington-based author Thomasin Sleigh, following on from *Ad Lib* (2014) and *Women in the Field, One and Two* (2018).

www.lawrenceandgibson.co.nz

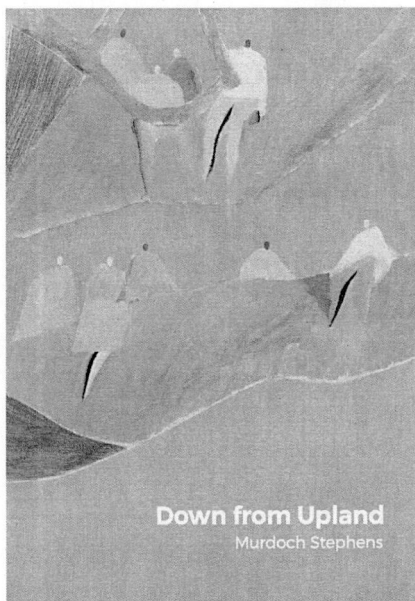

Down from Upland
Murdoch Stephens

Down from Upland is a kitchen sink, domestic novel that opens at the precise moment the first Millennials find themselves raising a teenager. While flirting with an open marriage, Jacqui and Scott nudge their son on a more moderate course as he begins at a new high school and makes new friends. Skewering the best and worst of Wellington's leafy middle class, the novel features public servants with varying degrees of integrity, precocious Wellington High students and a foreign lover at the end of a working holiday visa.

Down from Upland was longlisted for the 2023 Jann Medlicott Acorn Foundation Prize for Fiction at the Ockham New Zealand Book Awards.

Murdoch Stephens lives in Te Whanganui-a-Tara/Wellington. His 2020 novel *Rat King Landlord* was praised as "a thrilling, surreal, often hilarious ride" by Newsroom and "last year's surprise literary hit" by Stuff. He is also the author of a handful of books writing as Richard Meros.

www.lawrenceandgibson.co.nz

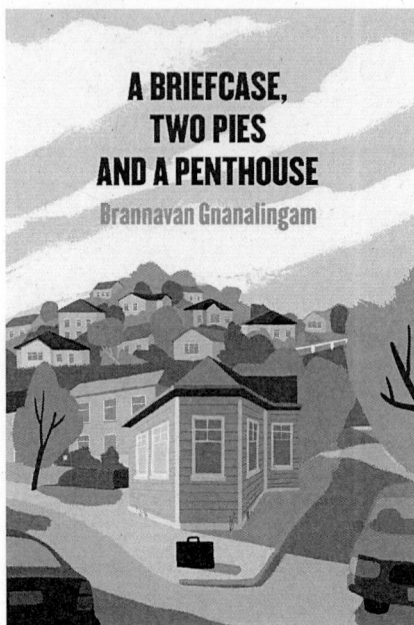

A BRIEFCASE, TWO PIES AND A PENTHOUSE

Brannavan Gnanalingam

Rachel McManus has just started at the New Zealand Alarm and Response Ministry. One of a few females workers, she is forced to traverse the peculiarities of Wellington bureaucracy, lascivious colleagues, and decades of sedimented hierarchy. McManus takes the chance to prove herself by investigating a suspected terrorist, who they fear is radicalising impressionable youth and may carry out an attack himself on the nation's capital.

Brannavan Gnanalingam's *A Briefcase, Two Pies and a Penthouse* looks at modern day spies in New Zealand. Instead of 'Reds Under the Bed', the new existential threat is Islamic terrorism — and the novel looks at a very New Zealand response to a global issue.

A Briefcase, Two Pies and a Penthouse was longlisted for the 2017 Jann Medlicott Acorn Foundation Prize for Fiction at the Ockham New Zealand Book Awards. His most recent novel is *Slow Down, You're Here*.

www.lawrenceandgibson.co.nz